# CASH'S FIGHT

## JAMIE BEGLEY

Cash's Fight

Young Ink Press Publication
YoungInkPress.com

Copyright © 2014 by Jamie Begley
Edited by C&D Editing, and Hot Tree Editing
Cover Art by Young Ink Press

ISBN-13: 978-0692290040
ISBN-10: 0692290044

# PROLOGUE

Cash raised his beer to his lips while pulling the woman next to him closer, notching his cock against her ass. Her indrawn breath had him hardening behind the zipper of his jeans.

"Let's go back to my place, Cash."

A frustrated groan rumbled from his chest. "Give me a minute. I need to take care of a piece of business first. Then we can leave," he promised.

Reva leaned her head back against his chest. "All right, but hurry."

"I will," he assured the woman who had come into the bar to pick someone to scratch the itch she was obviously wanting taken care of.

Moving away from her luscious ass, he walked from the counter, going to the back of the bar. Pulling out a chair, he took a seat at the table.

"Sorry to interrupt your fun."

"You didn't. I just put it on hold for a few minutes," Cash stated, looking across the table at Stud, the president of the Destructors. "What did you need to talk to me about?"

Stud didn't waste time getting to the point of the

meeting. "Three weeks ago, we noticed a new biker club taking up residence in Jamestown. I left several of my men in charge of the Destructors and everything's been cool, except a couple of small confrontations have taken place between the two clubs. Since I'm the president of the Destructors, I'm thinking they're about to challenge me for power of Jamestown. We both know that shithole of a town isn't worth fighting for unless you're running drugs; it's the only back road route to Tennessee and Virginia from Kentucky."

Cash listened, taking another drink of his beer.

"We don't run drugs, so I'm not interested, but what does piss me off is they think they can just push me out of the way."

Cash didn't think anyone was stupid enough to believe they could push Stud.

"What do you need me to do?"

"For now, can you find out what you can about them and what the fuck they are up to? I'll decide what to do after I have the information I need. Sex Piston will kick my ass if another club takes over her town, and those crazy friends of hers might try to become involved."

*There is no* might *about it*, Cash thought.

"I'll check into them in the morning then get back to you as soon as I have something. Any names?"

"Not many, no. One that keeps coming up is Scorpion; another is Vaughn."

"That should be enough to start with. Anything else?"

"That's it. Tell Viper I appreciate his help." Viper, the president of The Last Riders, had developed a tentative friendship with Stud. It was one in which each benefited when help was needed.

"Will do." Cash stood to his feet, his mind returning to the woman he had left alone at the bar.

"Seems like someone already moved in on your action."

Cash glanced back at the bar as Reva stood, flirting

with Tate Porter.

"Yes, it does. Too bad for him I'm taking her back."

"Good luck." Stud's amusement was apparent as he observed Cash's tight-lipped reaction. Cash didn't turn his attention from Reva as Stud left the bar; instead, he swallowed down his anger, determined not to let Tate Porter ruin his night.

Walking back to the bar, he came to stand behind Reva. "Ready to go?"

The provocative brunette looked over her shoulder at him.

Fuck. That wasn't the first time Cash had seen the same expression on a woman's face; she wanted to pit the two men against each other. Cash had been in this position too many times to become involved in a fight over a woman.

Cutting his loss, he was about to turn away when Tate's voice had him pausing.

"Smart move, Cash. Run while you have the chance," Tate goaded.

"I'm not running; I just don't feel like whipping your ass over a cunt I can have next week."

Reva's angry gasp was ignored as Tate straightened from the bar.

"You couldn't whip my ass with six of those pussies you ride with helping you."

Cash's anger rose, his desire to avoid a fight slipping away. "The problem with you and your brothers, Tate, is you brag more than you can actually accomplish with that small dick of yours."

As Tate turned red at Cash's comment, Cash grinned, waiting for the fist to come his way. Surprisingly, Tate only grinned back.

"At least it'll be my dick in her tonight," he said, pulling Reva against him.

Cash gritted his teeth, moving away from the bar. His one consolation was Reva didn't look happy at his withdrawal.

Going outside the bar, he saw Greer sitting on the tailgate of his truck with one of the local women. Cash caught a brief glance at her as he drew nearer. Damn, tonight just wasn't going to be his night.

His slight hope of passing by unnoticed died quickly when the woman turned her head and saw him, a loud squeal passing her lips. "Cash!"

She jumped off the tailgate, throwing herself into his arms, which he kept to his sides. She wound her arms around his neck, her breath strong with the odor of alcohol and whatever she had eaten for dinner, repulsing him. He jerked his head back as far as he could, trying to unsuccessfully move away from her tight grasp.

"Why didn't you call? If I'd have known you were going to be here, I would have met you."

"I was meeting a friend, Diane."

Greer's face was reddening with fury. All of the Porter brothers were hotheads, but Greer's temper was the worst.

Cash tried again to break Diane's hold.

"Let's go inside and get a drink."

"I was leaving," Cash refused her invitation.

She pouted, attempting to pull his head down to hers.

"What the fuck, Diane? You came here with me." When Greer stood up, pulling her away from him, Cash was actually grateful to the asshole for the first time in his life.

"Come on, Greer; loosen up. We could all three have a good time," Diane said suggestively, looking back and forth between the two men.

"That's not going to happen," Greer snapped.

*No, it isn't,* Cash thought while attempting to leave. He was two steps away from his bike, ready to head home to the club. He was going to be a better man and remember the Porter brothers were the ones who had saved Lily's life; the club owed them a favor. However, Greer had to open his mouth.

"Don't be mad, Greer. I was only joking," Diane quickly tried to pacify the man's anger. Cash could have told her it would be a wasted effort.

"If you want to be one of his sluts, why don't you go join the rest of those whores waiting for him? Better yet, why not wait till Friday? I hear they'll all fuck you," Greer snarled, jerking his arm away from Diane's conciliatory touch.

Cash turned on the heels of his boots. "What the fuck did you say?"

"Which part did you miss? The part where I called anyone who fucked you a slut or those women back at your club whores?"

Cash angrily paced back to face him. "Your mouth is shooting out shit that's going to get you hurt if you don't shut up, Greer. The only reason I'm not already beating the shit out of you is because you're drunk as hell, and we owe you for saving Lily."

"Because you pussies can't do anything but fuck," Greer retorted harshly.

"Jealous, Greer? All you and your brothers get are our leftovers." Cash was fed-up with the Porter brothers thinking they could mouth off without repercussions.

"I'm not jealous of you, Cash." Greer laughed mockingly. "There's not a whore of yours I would want."

"No?"

"Fuck no!"

"Cool, then let's go, Diane." Cash took Diane's arm, leading her toward his bike. He was expecting what would happen next.

When Greer pushed him away from Diane with a hard shove against his shoulder, Cash pivoted on his heel, his fist smashing against Greer's cheekbone. Satisfied that Greer would have a black eye staring back at him in the mirror for the next week, he dodged the fist coming back his way.

Cash dropped Diane's arm, stepping away from her so

she wouldn't get hurt, before slamming into Greer and taking him down to the ground. He was so intent on beating some manners into Greer he didn't hear anyone coming out of the bar. The foot that kicked into his ribs, driving the air out of his lungs, had him falling to the side.

Greer took instant advantage and began striking at his body before Cash could stop him. Cash felt the iron taste of blood in his mouth as his lip split. Trying to throw Greer's weight off, he then felt a searing pain in his side; the motherfucker had broken his rib. Forcing himself to ignore the excruciating pain, he hit Greer back as best he could. He brought his hand to his pocket right before it was smashed down under a booted heel.

"This is a fair fight, Cash. Those brass knuckles of yours are going to stay in your pocket."

"You think you butting into our fight is fair?" Cash gasped, bringing his legs up to throw Greer off.

"I call it leveling the playing field," Tate said without remorse.

"Stop it, Tate." Reva's and Diane's screams were drawing the rest of the customers out of Rosie's bar.

Cash managed to strike Greer several times before Mick, the owner of the bar, pulled the two men apart.

"Stop! You three need to go on home." Mick stood between the men, his hand on Greer's chest, keeping him in place.

"That sounds like a good idea. Let's go, Diane." Greer gave him a triumphant look as he helped the woman who had started the fight into his truck. Diane sent him an apologetic glance before sliding in.

"Reva?" Tate asked, holding the door open. With a regretful glance, she slid into the truck, as well. The brothers then gloated as they pulled out of the parking lot by honking their horn.

"Ignore them, Cash. They're both drunk off their asses." Cash gave Mick a skeptical look while holding his ribs, watching as the truck sped off into the night.

The Porter brothers had pissed him off for the last time.

"Come on. I'll buy you a beer and wrap up those ribs for you," Mick offered.

Cash followed him back inside.

The Porter brothers would go home and get laid and forget tonight had ever happened, but Cash was determined to repay them for the insults thrown his way. He never looked for trouble; however, if the opportunity ever presented itself to him, he sure as fuck wouldn't walk away.

# CHAPTER ONE

Rachel dug down into the rich soil, her small hand trowel helping her to remove the Ginseng root she had been cultivating. A smile passed her lips when she saw the size of the root; this one would make her some money.

She never fussed at her brothers for their lucrative business of selling pot, but she made more from her medicinal herbs than they did. If the jackasses would listen to reason, she would be able to triple her revenue with their help.

It wasn't going to happen, though; they refused to listen. Rachel thought they enjoyed the danger and excitement they experienced, growing and selling the illegal crop.

Pushing aside those thoughts, Rachel put the root into the canvas bag she had brought with her then began to delicately dig for another one. The sun was just beginning to rise. She always came out first thing in the morning, after she'd drunk her cup of tea and before the day began to get hot with the summer heat. She had two appointments this morning, and then she was going to volunteer at the church store for a few hours this afternoon.

A sound from behind her had her turning and reaching down for the rifle she kept by her side. Carefully rising to her feet, she pointed the weapon at the man staring nonchalantly back at her.

"What are you doing out here, Cash?"

"Hunting." His terse explanation had her temper rising.

"You're trespassing. You're lucky it's not one of my brothers you walked up on."

"It must be my lucky day."

Cash and her brothers had been having a feud since Cash and Tate had attended high school together. The two men had often found each other in a conflict over a woman. Tate's grudge had begun when Cash had stolen not one but two of his girlfriends.

"If you're hunting, then where's your gun?" Rachel asked suspiciously.

"Never said I was hunting game." His smile quirked to the side as a feminine giggle sounded from the nearby woods.

Rachel rolled her eyes, lowering her rifle. "Play your games on your own property, Cash."

About a half mile up the mountain was a lookout point that was the local Lover's Lane. It wasn't the first time a couple had moved their games to the nearby woods.

"I'll keep that in mind." In other words, he would keep doing what he wanted to do, regardless that he was trespassing.

"Cash!" an impatient voice called.

"Don't keep the lady waiting," Rachel mocked. Ignoring him, she kneeled back down and started delicately digging again.

"You shouldn't be out here by yourself."

Rachel kept digging. She had learned a long time ago it was better for her equilibrium if she didn't stare at him for long periods of time. His dark-blond hair was slightly curly and always ruffled, as if women were constantly running their hands through it, which they probably were. His shoulders were broad, tapering down to a muscular chest. Lean-hipped, his jeans constantly rode low, drawing attention to the considerable bulge that was hard to miss.

She turned back to him, seeing Cash had crossed his arms over his chest. Rachel swallowed hard at his bulging biceps. He was one of the most sexually charismatic men she knew and totally off-limits because of her brothers' hatred for him.

"I'm not." As Rachel blew a faint whistle, a dog lying half-asleep, perched on one of the large rocks, got to his feet, ambling down the mountainside and coming to plop down next to her.

"I can see he's ferocious." Rachel ignored the amusement in his voice, reaching over to scratch Samson's belly.

"Samson and my rifle are the only protection I need." Rachel returned to her digging.

"Samson." When Cash took a step forward, a low growl came from her side.

"I wouldn't come any closer. He doesn't like it when anyone gets near me."

"I can see that," Cash replied, taking a step back. Rachel was glad her back was to him so he couldn't see her smile.

"Cash!" The feminine voice was coming nearer.

Rachel carefully placed another Ginseng root into her canvas bag, brushing a tendril of hair from her cheek. She then carefully replaced the dirt that had been covering the root, smoothing it out before placing small twigs and leaves on top.

"I better go; I don't want to keep the lady waiting. See you around."

Not if she could help it, although she wasn't sure whether she'd imagined the note of promise in his voice or not.

Rachel didn't bother to reply as he strolled into the woods, seemingly in no hurry. She wondered if it was one of the town's women or one of the club's that was waiting to be found. Deciding it was none of her business, she gathered her things to start her hike back up the side of the mountain with Samson following close on her heels.

It took twenty minutes before she reached the cabin she and her brothers shared. Rachel had threatened to move out on numerous occasions, but each time, one of them always managed to talk her into staying.

After her youngest brother had found out he was a father and had moved his young son and surrogate mother into the cabin, it had created an even-tighter fit. Their home was bursting at the seams; however, their solution was to build onto it instead of relinquishing control of their baby sister.

She was twenty-three now and determined to set her foot down in the near future. She was only staying now because Holly still felt uncomfortable being left with the men alone. Her brothers were building her a small cabin next door to theirs, and once it was completed, Rachel planned to move into town, despite her brothers' protests.

Leaving the Ginseng roots outside in the barn, she went into the cabin to get breakfast started. As she started the coffee, her mind went back to Cash.

He had grown up in Treepoint, attending high school with her older brother. The enmity between them had started then. When Cash had left the area after graduating, many had thought he had been killed by someone's jealous boyfriend or lover. However, he had returned years later amongst The Last Riders motorcycle club.

The group stayed to themselves at their clubhouse on the edge of the state line. This didn't stop the women in town from chasing the bikers, many of whom had been taken up on their offers. Four women had even found their husbands among the dangerous men, while others envied them their happiness.

The ones who had been fucked and left hadn't been so happy, wanting more than the men were willing to give.

"What's for breakfast?" Dustin's groggy voice had her reaching for another cup.

Her youngest brother came into the kitchen, taking a seat at the large table. Rachel poured him a cup of coffee before pulling out the eggs from the refrigerator. She started cooking breakfast, knowing the rest of her brothers wouldn't be far behind.

"What dragged you out of bed so early?"

"I haven't been to bed. I was out most of the night, checking the plants. I came in while you were out. Someone's been sneaking onto the property, helping themselves," he grimly stated. "Did you see anything when you were out?"

She set his plate down in front of him before taking a seat for herself. Rachel took a sip of her coffee to give herself time to think. She knew, as soon as she mentioned Cash's name, it would make Dustin furious, despite Cash not being on their property to steal weed. Even if she assured Dustin of this fact, his hatred of the man would have him throwing a fit over Cash being on their property.

Thankfully, Holly came into the kitchen with Logan, diverting Dustin's attention from his question.

Logan climbed onto the chair next to his father. A tender smile came to her lips at the resemblance between the two; both father and son had curly, black hair and grey eyes.

"Morning, Holly, Logan."

"Morning, Rach." Logan gave her his boyish grin.

"What would you like for breakfast, Logan?" Holly asked, ruffling his hair.

"Can I have cereal?"

"No, but you can have oatmeal."

"Why ask if I can't pick anyways?" Logan grumbled.

"You can pick which flavor you want." Holly ignored his protest, making the oatmeal and giving it to him.

Rachel watched as Logan made a face at the bowl in front of him. Dustin winked at him while Holly's back was turned, taking a couple bites of the gooey mess for him.

"I saw that." Holly's frown had them both straightening in their seats.

Rachel couldn't believe how the woman kept both of them in line. She was always firm, managing them with love and care. Rachel had hoped that same love would blossom between Holly and Dustin; instead, only a deep friendship had developed.

Rachel stood up from the table, taking her plate to the sink just as a knock sounded on the door. Going over and opening it, she saw her first appointment of the day.

"I hope I'm not too early."

"Not at all," Rachel answered, opening the door wider for Cheryl.

She led her to the back of the house to a small sunroom their father had added on for her mother's use. A massage table had been set up with clean, white sheets and a small pillow lying on top. Rachel had lit a lavender-scented candle before starting the coffee, and now the relaxing floral scent infused the sunny room.

"Go ahead and lie down," Rachel instructed.

The young woman climbed onto the table, her cheeks flushing red. "I feel silly coming here," Cheryl admitted. "My husband thinks I'm being ridiculous."

"Cheryl, you don't have to stay," Rachel tried to soothe her nervousness.

"I know, but I want to give this a try. Besides, it's better than taking all those hormones the doctor wants to give me. If this doesn't work, then I go that route."

"All right. Let's get started then." Once Cheryl lay down on the table, Rachel zoned everything out of her mind other than the woman lying before her.

Rachael's hands lightly skimmed over her body from her feet to the top of her head then worked her way back down. When she neared her stomach for the second time, Rachel lightly touched it, letting her palms rest there for a minute. Allowing her consciousness to flow through

Cheryl, Rachel searched for something that wasn't there. She frowned, beginning to move her hands away, but Cheryl reached out, pressing her hands down again on her stomach, incorrectly reading Rachel's expression.

"I want a baby, Rachel."

Rachel looked down into the pleading eyes of Cheryl, giving her a brief nod. Cheryl released her desperate grip, allowing Rachel to continue. Once again, Rachel's hands glided over her body several times before stopping.

"You can sit up, Cheryl."

"Well?" Her expectant face stared back at her. The woman was in her late twenties, pretty with long, blond hair and blue eyes. She had married Jared Hicks when she was seventeen, who Rachel despised but Cheryl thought was the reason she existed.

"I can't help you." Rachel always believed in being honest about her skills.

Cheryl's shoulders slumped. Sliding off the table, she reached for her purse. "How much do I owe you?"

"Nothing." Rachel took a step back when, despite her words, Cheryl tried to hand her some cash. When Rachel refused to take it, she put it back in her purse before going for the doorway.

"Cheryl." The woman paused, looking back at her. "Did Jared get checked out to see if the reason you two are having problems conceiving a baby might be on his part?"

Her horrified look answered that question.

*Of course not*, Rachel thought to herself. Everyone always thought it was the woman's fault.

"I couldn't ask him to get checked out."

Her freaking doctor should have mentioned it! "It's something to consider, especially before you take the next step," Rachel advised.

"He'll get mad. He's already angry at me for going to the doctor. He said that, if we get pregnant, it's God's will."

Rachel's hands fisted by her side. The inconsiderate

asshole just didn't want any blame focused on his own possible defects. Jared especially wouldn't want to accept any blame cast on his own masculinity; he was too busy proving it to every woman in Treepoint who would have him. He hadn't been faithful to Cheryl since they came back from their fancy honeymoon in Hawaii.

Honestly, Rachel thought half of Cheryl's desperation to have a baby was to save her failing marriage. Treepoint being such a small town, she was sure Cheryl hadn't escaped the vicious gossip of Jared's affairs.

"Did the doctors say there was a reason you weren't conceiving?"

"No. All my tests are coming back normal, but I made an appointment with a specialist in Lexington."

Rachel sighed. "I don't think the problem is yours, Cheryl. I think you should ask Jared to get checked out before you spend money on more expensive doctors."

She bit her lips. "I'll think about asking him," she finally agreed.

"Good." Rachel took her hand, giving her a reassuring warmth that would lessen her anxiety.

"Thanks, Rachel."

"You're welcome." Rachel was showing her out the door as her new appointment was arriving.

Both women greeted Mrs. Langley. Rachel told Cheryl good-bye before escorting Mrs. Langley to the sunroom, helping the frail woman onto the table. She'd had gallbladder surgery months ago, and the older woman had not recovered her strength yet. Rachel doused the lavender candles and lit her white candles for healing, letting the soothing aroma fill the room as she came to stand over Mrs. Langley with a gentle smile.

"How are you feeling today?"

"Tired. I'm tired all the time now, Rachel." The woman's pale, lined face stared back at her.

"Let me see if I can help with that." Rachel skimmed her hands over Mrs. Langley's body, taking her time to send wave after wave of healing warmth through her. As Rachel worked, she noticed her stiffness gradually became more relaxed.

She worked on her longer than she had anticipated; giving the woman everything she could, hoping it was enough. It was going to take several sessions to ease the toll the surgery had taken on her.

When she finished, Rachel helped Mrs. Langley from the table.

"I feel like I had a long nap."

"You might have dozed off," Rachel prevaricated, handing her purse over without telling her she had slept for over an hour.

"How much do I owe you?" Mrs. Langley opened her purse.

"Nothing, you get the family discount." Rachel smiled, placing her arm around her frail shoulders. "Want to see Logan?"

The bright eagerness in her eyes brought a lump to Rachel's throat as she led her into the living room where Holly and Dustin were sitting, playing a game.

"Grandma!" Logan got up from the floor, running to his great-grandmother, carefully wrapping his arms around her waist, giving her a hug.

"Holly and I are playing a game. Do you want to play?"

"I would love to." While Logan eagerly showed her how to play, Rachel watched for several minutes before going back into the sunroom and removing the sheets, placing them in a hamper she kept in the corner. Blowing the candles out, she went to her room to get changed out of her jeans and t-shirt.

The only time she wore dresses was when she went to church or helped out at the church store which helped the economically disadvantaged in the community.

Pulling on a peach sundress, Rachel brushed her waist-length hair before plaiting it. Her hair was straight as a stick, but it was thick and heavy. The whole process was becoming more and more time-consuming; she needed to cut it off and save herself the trouble.

Sliding her feet into her sandals, she turned back to the mirror. Somehow, even in the pretty dress, she still looked like the tomboy she was. Just once, she wanted to look as sexy and seductive as the women Cash ran after.

Rachel went for her purse, immediately dragging her thoughts from the man she'd had a crush on since she was a little girl. Some things were better left to the imagination, Cash being one of them. She wasn't his type, and her brothers would kill him. On the other hand, a little fantasy never hurt anyone.

# CHAPTER TWO

Rachel straightened the clothes on the shelf as Lily handled their last customer of the day.

"Want to grab some dinner at the diner?" Lily asked after the customer left.

"Yes. Holly volunteered to cook dinner tonight. I love her to death, but she can't cook."

Lily laughed. "You ready?"

"Let me grab my purse."

Rachel curiously studied her friend. Lily was beautiful; she had long, black hair with violet eyes. Today, she had worn a long, maxi skirt with a pretty, white camp shirt. She was feminine and pretty, everything Rachel wasn't.

"Why aren't you eating at the clubhouse tonight?"

"The factory has a big order to get out tonight, and Shade refuses to let me help. Since he's found out I'm pregnant, he hasn't let me lift anything heavier than a book. He's going to order everyone pizza so they can work through dinner, but me and pizza aren't getting along right now." Lily made a face.

"Stomach upset?"

"That's putting it mildly. The doctor said it should pass after I get farther along."

Rachel looked down at the small woman, her morning sickness the only sign she was pregnant. She had told her husband and father last week that she was pregnant at a barbeque celebrating her nephews' Baptism. Rachel had been there and had offered her congratulations to the happy couple. Lily was only a couple of months along, and despite her morning sickness, she was glowing with happiness.

"Try chewing on some crystallized ginger. It will help." Rachel waited as Lily locked the door behind them, then they crossed the street, going inside the diner.

It was slow for a Friday evening, only a couple of customers. Rachel was surprised to see Cash and Stud sitting at one of the tables, quietly talking. Being in two different motorcycle clubs, Rachel would have thought they wouldn't be sharing a meal.

After making their way to a table, Lily waved at the two men while Rachel took a seat, facing away from them. When Lily sat down across from her, they requested their drinks before giving their order.

"Any luck getting your brothers married off yet?" Lily teased.

"No, darn it. I'm beginning to get worried. Tate is getting older; he should be settled down and married," Rachel complained.

"He's got plenty of time. You just want him off your back."

"Yes, I do." Rachel didn't have any problem admitting the truth. "I'm too old for him to be telling me what time to be home or who I can and can't date."

"He actually gave you permission to date someone?" Lily's purple eyes were filled with amusement.

"Payne Macy."

"Oh." Lily shuddered.

"Yeah. He only said it because he knew I wouldn't touch him with a ten-foot pole. It would serve him right if I started dating him."

"You wouldn't."

"I might. They are being big jerks right now."

"Not as big as Payne."

Payne Macy was the town's confirmed bachelor. The gossip-mongers had always tried to find some dirt to dish on him but had been unable to find a speck. He attended church regularly, dated within reason, and never bought weed off her brothers; thus, they considered him the perfect man for her. The big problem for her was that he and anyone who had met him quickly realized he was an asshole. A mean asshole. Rachel was happy she didn't come into contact with him very often.

As their food arrived, they changed the subject, neither wanting to hurt their appetite by discussing the rude man.

Because the restaurant wasn't busy, Rachel heard the low voices of Stud and Cash in the background. Yet, before she could discern what was being discussed, Lily's phone rang just as they finished eating.

"I'll be right out," she said into the phone then explained, "Shade's here to pick me up."

"Go ahead. I'll take care of the ticket," Rachel offered.

"No, I'll pay." She reached for her purse.

"My treat. You can pay next time."

"All right," Lily accepted, getting up from the table. "See you Sunday in church."

Lily left as the waitress brought the ticket. Rachel took it, going to the cash register as she felt the men's eyes on her. Self-conscious, she was glad to escape their scrutiny after paying, leaving through the door as other customers were about to enter.

Jared and one of his friends stopped, blocking the doorway. Rachel knew it wasn't a good sign when, instead of letting her pass to go outside, they backed out of the doorway, keeping her pinned between them.

"I want to talk to you." Rachel stiffened at his harsh voice, unsurprised by his statement.

"What about?"

"Did you tell my wife it was my fault she couldn't have a kid?" Jared was so angry his face was flushed red, and his beady eyes were narrowed, waiting for her answer.

"No, but I did tell her you should be checked out before she spent any more money on expensive doctors," Rachel answered in a calm voice. How some women fell in love with certain men was hard for her to understand. There was nothing nice or attractive about Jared.

"How much money did you con her out of?" Jeeringly, he called into question her motives.

"None." Rachel had dealt with enough. She didn't have to put up with his bullshit; she wasn't the one stupid enough to be married to him.

"Stay the fuck away from my wife and keep your advice to yourself." Jared blocked her path again as she tried to move away from him. "I'll make sure everyone in town knows you're a phony if I catch you near her again."

Rachel wouldn't have been able to call herself a Porter if she allowed the man to continue. Her temper soaring, she reached out, grabbing his arm. Jared tried to pull it out of her reach, but Rachel needed only a minute to find out what she needed to know. When Jared pushed her away from him, Rachel was sickened by what she had found out. His anger had lowered his guard, blasting the knowledge she needed through his consciousness into hers. Rachel was easily able to read what he was hiding.

"You should be ashamed of yourself." Rachel made no effort to hide her disgust, attempting to go around him again.

"What the fuck do you mean by that?" Jared took her arm, propelling her away from the door to the side of the restaurant.

Unwisely, she didn't back down. "I mean, you know you can't have kids, but you haven't told Cheryl, letting her take the blame. Does it make you feel like a big man, Jared, keeping her pinned under your thumb?"

Her rash outburst brought out the ugliness inside of

the overbearing man. "You don't know what the fuck you're talking about."

"Yes, I do. You made sure you couldn't get any of the women you fool around with pregnant, so don't act innocent, Jared."

A sharp smack to her face had her almost falling down. The only reason she didn't was because Jared kept a firm grip on her arm, holding her in place as his hand went back to strike her again. Her face already numb after the initial burst of pain, Rachel braced herself for another strike, but then found herself thrust back against the restaurant wall as a body knocked Jared away from her, throwing him to the ground.

Rachel watched as Cash punched Jared repeatedly in the face. When his friend would have tried to help, Stud held him back. Wisely, the man took a good look at Stud and quit trying to intervene.

"Cash, stop! That's enough!" Rachel reached down, grasping Cash's t-shirt and tugging him away, aware he was releasing Jared only because he was finished.

"Go on home, Rachel," Cash said, getting to his feet.

"I'm going to press charges!" Jared whined from the ground, holding his bleeding nose.

"No, you're not, unless you want me to press charges against you. You hit me first!" Rachel yelled down at him. "Get up and go on home, Jared, before I call my brothers and you leave here in an ambulance."

After Jared managed to get to his feet, he and his buddy took off to their car.

"Are you okay?" Cash asked, staring at her cheek.

"Yes."

"Gotta go, Cash."

"Thanks, Stud," Rachel said before he could leave.

He gave her a nod. "Later."

Rachel began walking to her car, which she had left across the street at the church.

"I don't get a thanks?" Cash asked mockingly, falling in

step beside her.

"Thanks," Rachel said ungratefully as she came to a stop beside her car, staring at it in dismay.

"I guess the restaurant wasn't Jared's first stop."

All four tires of her older than dirt car had been slit. The tires would cost more than the car was worth.

"Dammit." Rachel reached inside her purse for her phone.

"Come on. I'll give you a ride home." Cash took her arm, leading her back across the street to the diner's parking lot.

"I'll call my brothers. One of them will come and get me." She didn't get inside his truck when he opened the door.

"If you call them, then they will go after Jared. You can calm them down if you're home when you tell them."

He was right, but it would be just as bad for them to see her getting out of Cash's truck.

"Get in, Rachel."

"I still think I should—"

Cash lifted her up, placing her on the bench seat in his truck, then slammed the door closed, effectively cutting off her protests. Sliding into the truck, he turned the motor on.

"I can have you home before you make up your mind."

Rachel sat back against the seat, closing her mouth.

"So, why was Jared so pissed off at you?"

Rachel turned sideways in her seat to stare at his profile. "I can't tell you. It's private."

"It quit being private when he assaulted you in public."

Rachel kind of agreed, but she was ultimately respecting Cheryl's privacy, not Jared's.

"I still have to respect his privacy."

Cash threw her a quick glance. "If you can't keep your brothers from going after Jared, it could get messy. Jared has a large family, too. Someone could get hurt." His warning didn't fall on deaf ears. She was well aware of the consequences if her brothers stormed off after Jared.

"I think that's going to happen, regardless." Rachel thought of Cheryl. She didn't think it would be fair not to tell her what she had discovered about her cheating husband.

"How often do you volunteer at the church store?" The abrupt change of subject threw her off-guard.

"Three days a week."

"That's a lot of time to volunteer."

"I enjoy it." Rachel shrugged.

Cash made the turn onto the steep hill that led to her house, the truck bouncing on the rutted lane.

"How in the hell does your little car make it up this hill?"

"I know where all the holes are."

"Jesus. Why won't Tate just pave the road?"

Rachel laughed. "You know Tate; he's a cheapskate."

"Among other things," Cash said grimly.

"I heard that."

"I wasn't trying for you not to. You're his sister; you know he's an ass. They all three are."

"They're not so bad," Rachel defended her brothers.

"When's the last time they let you go out on a date? The last time I remember is last summer when they let you go to a movie with Harvey Green."

His sideways look caught her shudder at the reminder of the disastrous date. It had been a miserable experience from the time he had picked her up at her house, with all three of her brothers casting threatening looks, to the moment Greer had turned the porch light on when Harvey had been about to kiss her goodnight.

Rachel was embarrassed by Cash's knowledge of her lack of social life.

"I don't let my brothers dictate who I go out with."

The truth was Treepoint didn't have a large selection of eligible bachelors she would go out with. They were either jerks or like Cash, only interested in sleeping with someone before moving on to the next available woman.

His snort of disbelief had her temper rising.

"I go out with anyone I want to."

"Prove it." His challenge shocked her.

"How? By going out with you?" Rachel wanted to take back her words as soon as they were out of her mouth. Her face flamed with embarrassment.

"I wasn't thinking of me. I'm too old for you and I don't date." He turned his attention away from the road, brushing her body with his gaze, as if she was lacking what it took to capture his interest.

"I wasn't asking you out on a date," Rachel snapped back at his brush-off.

"That's what it sounded like to me," he said, pulling up in front of her house.

"Well, you were wrong. When I go on a date with someone, I at least have to like them." Rachel opened the truck door, sliding out.

"Keep those brothers of yours under control. A feud between them and the Macys would keep the hospital busy."

"I know how to manage my brothers."

"Good. You can start now." Cash nodded toward a furious Greer, who was heading their way.

"You better go," Rachel responded, slamming the door closed before turning back to her brother.

Hearing Cash's truck deliberately spin gravel on his way out only fueled an already-loaded situation.

"I'm giving you ten seconds to tell me why you were in that shithead's truck."

Rachel thought fast. Cash was right, someone could get seriously hurt in a feud, and she didn't want it to be one of her brothers.

"My car broke down while I was having dinner with Lily. Cash offered me a ride home," she explained.

Greer lost some of his anger. "You should have called. One of us would have come to town to get you."

"Cash drives by here to get home. I didn't think it was a big deal to accept a ride."

"It is. I don't want you anywhere near him."

"It was just a ride, Greer. He was just being nice." Rachel linked her arm through his, walking toward the house.

"Cash isn't a nice guy," Greer warned.

Rachel couldn't argue with that statement. No one in town would use that word to describe Cash, but he had been nice tonight. He had stepped in when Jared could have hurt her then had given her a lift home, despite her lack of gratitude. He had handled the situation much better than her hotheaded brothers would have.

When she was younger, she used to fantasize about Cash. He had always been her knight in shining armor. Now that she was older, the armor was old and rusty, needing to be dusted off. Regardless, Rachel couldn't deny the thrill of watching him beat Jared for slapping her. She guessed she was more like her brothers than she realized.

# CHAPTER THREE

"Throw the ball!" Logan yelled.

Rachel rose higher out of the water, swatting the large beach ball toward Logan. When he hit it back toward her, Rachel used her feet to jump higher out of the water to hit it again.

"You missed." Logan's giggles sounded around the pool with Holly's laughter joining in.

Rachel stuck her tongue out at her nephew as she climbed out of the pool to go get the ball. Her bare feet padded around the concrete pool area to retrieve it. Picking it up, she then threw it back into the pool.

"I need a drink. You're wearing me out." Going to the patio table where she had left a cold pitcher of lemonade, she poured herself a glass as she watched Holly and Logan switch to playing water tag.

Rachel enjoyed the afternoons they spent twice a month at Mrs. Langley's house, playing in the pool. Logan's great-grandmother would spend the mornings interacting with him then, when she watched her afternoon soap opera, Rachel and Holly kept him playing in the pool. Afterward, they would eat a late lunch and then leave.

Sadly, the summer holidays were coming to an end, and Logan would start pre-school in the fall. Rachel would have to find different days for Logan to visit because she didn't want to take away the company Mrs. Langley looked forward to having.

As she took a sip of her drink, she heard the sliding door from the house opening. Thinking it was Mrs. Langley, she looked casually toward the house, almost choking on her drink when she saw Cash and Rider walking outside.

She wanted to pick up her cover-up that was tossed onto the chair but didn't want to show the men she was embarrassed. The ice-blue bikini she wore was nothing to be upset about other than it showed too much freaking skin. At least the bottoms covered her ass, which she was always self-conscious about because it was the largest part of her anatomy. Whenever she gained a pound, it went to her ass. If she tried to work it off, the firmer it became. She had even begun wearing a size up in her clothes to disguise her butt.

Rachel looked toward the pool, seeing Holly's wide-eyed stare; she wasn't any happier than her to see the men. Her large breasts were displayed in all their glory in an emerald-green swimsuit that matched her eyes.

"Well, what have we got going on?" Rider's lascivious stare at Holly's breasts was making the woman turn bright red.

"We're playing ball. Do you want to play?" Logan climbed out of the pool just to jump back in.

"Oh, yeah," Rider said, beginning to take his t-shirt off.

"Rider, quit fooling around. I need your help," Razer said, opening the door from the house. Beth's husband shot the other biker a warning glance, ignoring Rider's angry glare as the two went back inside.

Cash gave a wicked grin. "I guess he doesn't need me." His eyes traced over her body as he took a seat at the patio table, pouring himself a glass of lemonade while Logan and Holly started playing again.

Rachel knew Holly wouldn't get out of the pool as long as Cash was around; the woman was insecure about her figure in the swimsuit. Rachel wasn't any happier.

Casually picking up her cover-up, she pulled it on.

"Don't let me interrupt you're playing." Cash's voice sent tingles down her spine.

"I won't," she snapped. "What are you guys doing here?"

"Beth asked Razer if he would move Mrs. Langley's bedroom furniture downstairs to the back room. She's worried about her going up and down the stairs by herself. Rider and I volunteered." Beth was Mrs. Langley's nurse and Lily's sister.

"You don't seem to be helping much," Rachel admonished.

Cash shrugged, taking another sip. "Most of the things had been moved out before we came outside to investigate the giggles we heard." Cash had raised his voice so Logan could hear, setting off another round of laughter from the little boy.

"Aren't you just becoming Mr. Helpful?" Rachel said snidely.

"I like to think so," he responded, not bothered by her attitude, which caused her to grit her teeth in annoyance. "I saw Lyle yesterday. I asked about your car, and he said you paid cash for it; that you didn't report it to your insurance."

"Obviously I hoped he would keep his mouth closed."

"He will now. I had a talk with him."

"Thanks." Rachel hated to admit it, but Lyle would listen to Cash and not mention the slashed tires to anyone else in town, including her brothers.

"So, you didn't tell your brothers about Jared?"

"He's still breathing, isn't he?"

"Jared bother you anymore?" he questioned, ignoring her sharp reply. Rachel was beginning to feel immature at her snippy responses.

"No, I haven't seen him since that night."

"If he comes near you again, call me."

"I don't need your protection, Cash. I can handle him, and if he tries to touch me again, I'll tell my brothers."

"If he tries to touch you, you won't have to," Cash said grimly.

Rachel decided to ignore his remark when she saw the frantic looks Holly was throwing her.

"Is something wrong with her neck?" His amused expression had Rachel wanting to smack him upside his smug face.

"I think she wants to get out of the water."

"Then tell her to get out." Cash sprawled back lazily in his chair, fixing his avid gaze on Holly.

"Go inside, Cash. She doesn't feel comfortable getting out with you here."

"Pity."

A streak of jealousy curled in Rachel's stomach at his disappointed expression. She hid her reaction by calling for Logan.

"Come on, Logan; it's time to get cleaned up."

Cash set his glass down on the table, lithely standing to his feet. "I discovered something new today."

Rachel wrapped Logan in the towel, drying him off. "What?" she replied, becoming irritable at him for his delay in leaving. She was beginning to feel sorry for Holly, easily understanding her body image issues.

"That you're all grown up."

Rachel's head snapped in his direction, expecting to see the same amused expression he always wore around her, as if he was putting up with a misbehaving child. However, his sleepily seductive gaze was on her butt.

"Kiss my ass, Cash."

"Rachel, believe me, that's one sentence you don't want to use around a man like me." With that, Cash strolled back inside the house, leaving her openmouthed at his comment.

"I didn't think he would ever leave!" Holly grabbed her cover-up from the chair without bothering to dry off.

"I didn't, either. Let's get inside and get changed."

Holding Logan's hand, the women went upstairs to the spare bedroom, taking turns showering and getting dressed.

The smell of food wafted upstairs, causing Holly's stomach to growl.

"I'm hungry, too. I hope they're gone." Rachel's stomach agreed with Holly.

Neither of their wishes was going to come true, though. When they entered the dining room, the three Last Riders were already devouring the food with a happy Mrs. Langley watching them as she sat at the head of the table.

"Sit down. I brought out enough plates for everyone."

"Mrs. Langley, you shouldn't have. I was—" Rachel protested.

"I'm not an invalid yet, Rachel. I don't think carrying a few plates is going to wear me out. The men did the rest."

Rachel sat down at the table next to Rider, letting Holly take the seat at the end of the table, while Logan climbed onto the chair next to Cash. Rachel took a heaping portion of the cheesy lasagna, passing it to Logan, and then made another one for Holly before making her own plate.

Rachel ate, listening to Razer and Mrs. Langley talk. Beth's husband had grown attached to the woman, and his affection was obvious as Razer was asked about his new twin boys.

Cash asked Logan if he was ready to start pre-school, sending the little boy off into a conversation that Rachel could barely keep up with. Cash surprised her at how well he interacted with the child. She'd expected him to be more like Rider, who ignored him to flirt uselessly with Holly. Rachel could have told him he was wasting his time, but she was enjoying watching the man make an ass of himself.

After the meal, Rachel and Holly cleaned the dishes and kitchen for Mrs. Langley, leaving it spotless before going to the room they had turned into her new bedroom. They wanted to make sure all her things had been arranged for her to avoid her having to go up the steps after everyone left.

When they returned to the living room, Mrs. Langley was sitting on the couch while Logan sat on the floor, reading one of his books to her. Rachel sat down next to her, taking her hand in hers as Holly squeezed in at the end, even though Rider had scooted over to make room on the smaller couch for her. Razer and Cash weren't in the room, making Rachel wonder where they had gone before she remembered Mrs. Langley's television upstairs needed to be transferred to her new room.

Rachel's thoughts went to Mrs. Langley, letting her consciousness flow into her. Closing her eyes, she let her strength gather in her hand, allowing it to gradually seep into the older woman. Shifting closer, she infused warmth into her chilled hand.

She had only done this a few times; her grandmother had often warned her against it. When you did, it was hard to gauge exactly how much of yourself you were giving away. If you weren't careful, you could give away too much and have nothing left for yourself.

Carefully, she withdrew, taking her hand away, noticing Mrs. Langley's cheeks were now flushed and her eyes seemed brighter. Rachel felt as if she might lose the dinner she had just eaten, though.

"Logan, tell your grandmother goodnight. You can finish your story the next time we come." Obediently, Logan jumped to his feet, hugging his great-grandmother good-bye.

When Mrs. Langley would have gotten up, Rachel forestalled her. "We'll see ourselves out. Take care."

Rachel shakily got to her feet, feeling a rush of dizziness hit her; however, counting to herself, she managed to regain her equilibrium.

Opening her eyes, she saw Cash standing in the doorway, frowning at her. She had to pass by him as she forced herself to walk steadily to the doorway, and when she did, he reached out to take her arm.

"Are you all right?"

"I'm fine. I must have swam too long."

His eyes searched hers before he slowly released her arm. "Holly, make sure you drive," he ordered, his hard gaze going to Holly.

"I will," she said, taking Logan's hand to lead him out the door.

"I don't know what you did, but—"

Cash's stern expression reminded her of Tate, causing her to cut him off. "I didn't do anything."

"Don't lie to me." His jaw tightened at her obvious lie.

She stiffened. "Let's get one thing straight, Cash. I already have three brothers; I don't need another one." She edged past his hard body that was partially blocking the doorway.

"Rachel." She paused. "The last thing I feel toward you is brotherly. And the next time I'm talking to you and you lie to me, be prepared for me to show you exactly how I do feel."

Her mama hadn't raised an idiot. The advantage to having three brothers was knowing when not to challenge a man of Cash's caliber. It was like a raccoon in front of a coon dog—only one would walk away unscathed.

# CHAPTER FOUR

Cash drove Rider and Razer back to the clubhouse, trying to ignore Rider's description of Holly's tits. Shifting uncomfortably on his seat, he tried to take his mind off Rachel's voluptuous ass.

He pulled into the parking lot of The Last Riders clubhouse, cutting the motor.

"Thanks for helping out," Razer said.

"No problem." Cash slammed his truck door harder than necessary, taking his frustration out on the truck. Climbing the steps to the large house that housed all the brothers, he entered, giving a sigh of relief at putting the woman who was periodically stealing her way into his thoughts behind him.

He grabbed himself a beer from the bar before going to the pool table in the corner. It was still early, but the room was beginning to fill.

"Want a game?" Nickel came up to the table, picking up a cue stick.

"You break." Cash took a step back from the table, letting the brother go first.

Nickel was good; it would be a challenge to beat him, and it would help take his thoughts away from Rachel. She was too young for him, and worse than that, he despised her brothers. He couldn't even remember how many fights he had gotten into with Tate and Greer, not to mention the few he'd had with Dustin. The more he thought of her brothers, the less attracted he felt to Rachel, and by his third beer and second win at pool, he had mellowed out.

Out of the corner of his eye, he saw Bliss sucking off Rider's dick. He was sitting on the couch with the sexy blond leaning over him, her ass in the air. He took his last shot as he heard Rider groan.

Cash lay down the pool stick. "I'm done for the night. You can pay up tomorrow."

"Damn, Cash. I'll have to pay you when I get paid," Nickel complained.

Cash nodded, already forgetting about the large sum of money, his mind only on one thing right now. Striding to the couch, he leaned over, picking Bliss up and tossing her over his shoulder.

"Hey!" Rider complained. "I wasn't done with her yet."

Cash turned back. "Did I say you couldn't join us?"

As Rider grinned, getting to his feet, Cash turned to the stairs, going up them with a giggling Bliss. His stiffened cock was bursting at the seams of his jeans. He was about to go into his room when he noticed Lucky's door open. Looking inside, he saw Raci kneeling on the floor as Lucky pounded his cock into her mouth. Cash went inside the room, tossing Bliss onto the bed.

Jerking off her tight shorts, he spread her thighs, seeing the little dew drops of her passion already clinging to her pussy lips.

Cash took off his jeans then reached into his pocket, pulling out a condom and sliding it on. Notching his cock at the threshold of her pussy, he then adjusted her hips to take him. Bliss's pussy was always tight as hell, and he didn't want to hurt her; he wanted her to enjoy the experience as much as him, instead.

Wrapping her thighs around his hips, he gave the

squirming woman the length of his cock in one hard thrust. She arched under him, grinding her clit against the base of his cock.

"Harder," Bliss moaned.

"Don't talk," Cash moaned, sliding his cock out, only to pound it back inside of her.

It was a relief to have his cock in a warm pussy, driving the need for another woman out of him. He liked his sex dirty and raw, and virginal Rachel would run screaming if he treated her like Bliss.

Picking her up from the mattress, he held her while he lay back against the bed, turning her ass up to Rider who slid his own condom on before sliding into Bliss's ass, tightening her pussy around him even further.

Cash groaned as he reached to grab one of Bliss's tits, squeezing it until the nipple turned a bright, cherry pink. Bliss grabbed his shoulders, digging her nails into him, tearing into his flesh while her mouth went to his neck, sucking on it. His dick lengthened even further in her, forcing a small gasp from her, but Bliss followed directions by not talking.

As Rider began to climax on the other side of her thin wall, Cash felt his own climax build and release into the condom. Then the three lay still, catching their breath on the large bed.

After Rider slid out of Bliss, removing his heavy weight, Cash moved Bliss to his side, removing his condom and throwing it into the trashcan. Then, making himself more comfortable on the bed, he lazily watched Lucky fuck Raci next to him as he played with Bliss's nipple.

"I'm done for the night." Rider zipped his cock back in his jeans before taking off.

Cash's cock began to harden again, watching Raci take Lucky. He loved watching a woman get fucked. Unlike some of the brothers who had married and become monogamous, Cash knew himself well enough to admit to his sexual needs.

He had been in two serious relationships; one before he left Treepoint and one after. Both had ended when he had expected their sexual relationship to not change. The women had enjoyed sharing their bodies before they had become serious, but they couldn't understand his lack of jealousy at watching them be fucked by men of his choosing. Cash had learned to keep his heart to himself and keep the relationships casual.

Lucky stiffened on Raci as the woman screamed her release. She then started to close her eyes and go to sleep.

Lucky rose off her, going into the bathroom, and then came back to stare down at the bed. Raci and Bliss were both almost asleep.

"Should we let them rest for a few minutes?" Lucky asked, grinning at him.

"No, let's give them something to wake up for," Cash answered, reaching for Raci.

\* \* \*

Rachel misted her plants lightly, walking up and down the aisles of her greenhouse. When she finished, she cleared away the dead ones then repotted others that were growing too big for their containers. She hadn't worn her gloves again, so when she began getting hungry, she quickly washed her hands. As she noticed they were becoming rough and cracked, she opened a jar of her hand balm, smoothing it into her hands. She clenched them into fists when she realized she was thinking of The Last Riders' women and the manicured, soft hands they had.

She went into the house, making herself another cup of green tea before starting breakfast. Her oldest brother came to the table, yawning.

"Late night?" Rachel noticed the dark circles under his eyes.

"Yes." He gave her a lopsided smile as he picked up his cup. "But not because of what you're thinking. I spent the night in the fields."

37

"Any luck catching anyone?"

"No, but I set some traps."

"Tate…"

"They have to practically be on top of the pot before they would get caught in one."

"You're asking for trouble," Rachel warned.

"No. Anyone stepping on our property despite all the 'no trespassing' signs is the one asking for trouble."

Rachel fixed him a plate of food. It would do no good to argue with him since his mind was made up. Greer came in looking just as tired.

"It's your turn to watch the field. I'm going to bed. At least I was up all night working," Tate said unsympathetically.

"I was, too. It was hard work to satisfy Diane," Greer boasted.

"You promised to stay away from her, Greer." Rachel glared at her horn-dog brother.

"She's calmed down. She promised she's not seeing anyone but me." Greer avoided her accusing eyes.

"Diane's promised the same thing twice before," Rachel reminded him.

"Well, she means it this time."

Rachel and Tate both shared a glance.

Diane was incapable of being faithful, yet Greer kept giving her chance after chance. He often came across as the meanest of her brothers; however, he was the most softhearted. He wanted to fall in love and have a big family, but the women he chose never had settling down in mind.

"Morning." Holly came in the kitchen, wearing jeans and a yellow top.

Rachel caught the expression on Greer's face before he could hide it. He cared about Holly, but he wouldn't make a move on her because he still held a grudge against her keeping Logan a secret after the boy's mother's death. Rachel, nor the rest of them, blamed her because she was trying to protect the boy, but Greer couldn't let go of the fact that she had nearly left town with Logan. Greer took their family's protection more seriously than his own breathing.

"I'll grab a bite to eat. Then I'll go sit in the deer stand awhile," Greer stated.

"Be careful of the traps I set," Tate warned.

"I will." Greer buttered a piece of toast.

Rachel sat down at the table with her green tea and oatmeal.

"If you would just listen to me, we could bring in more money with Ginseng roots. I could expand the greenhouse to include..." Rachel began her usual speech only to stop as Tate and Greer both shuddered in mock horror.

One of these days, her brothers would have to see that it made more sense to listen than ignore her. She only hoped they weren't behind bars when that time came.

Rachel had no appointments today, so she used the time to clean the house and make Logan's favorite chili in the crock-pot. Afterward, she decided to go back to her greenhouse where she potted several more plants she had taken from the woods that she wanted to experiment with for their medicinal value.

Going to her grandmother's journal to make notations of her own, Rachel ran her hand lovingly over the old book. She was proud of her heritage. Her great-grandmother had been full-blooded Cherokee, a descendent of one who had crossed the Appalachian Mountains during The Trail of Tears. She had passed down her gifts and knowledge to Rachel's grandmother, who had taught them to her as soon as she was able to walk. Rachel would hand down the same knowledge to her daughter someday.

An image of a strawberry-blond little girl flashed through her mind, making her drop her hand tool.

Shakily, Rachel went to the sink to wash her hands. The likeness to Cash in the little girl had been obvious.

Her attraction to Cash had been building over the years to the point her mind was making images of a child in his likeness. She had to put a stop to her wayward fantasies.

Seeing it was getting dark, she headed back to the house. She had spent hours outside, becoming lost in her work. She would back up her notes on the computer before she went to bed, though.

She ate a bowl of chili and was about to take a shower when her cell phone rang. Recognizing Cheryl's number, she answered.

"Hello?

"Rachel, I had a fight with Jared." Cheryl's voice trembled on the other end.

"Are you okay?"

"No. I need to get out for a while. Will you go out for a drink with me?"

"Of course." Rachel couldn't deny Cheryl. The sound of tears in her voice took away any hesitation.

"I'll meet you at the Pink Slipper."

"I'll be there in thirty minutes," Rachel said, disconnecting the call.

"Who was that?" Dustin questioned, looking up from the television with Logan on his lap. The others were listening unashamedly.

"That was Cheryl. She wants to go out for a drink at the Pink Slipper. She and Jared had a fight." Rachel saw no reason not to give them that much information.

"If you have more than one drink, call me and I'll drive in and pick you up," Tate offered.

"All right."

Rachel took a quick shower then pulled on a blue dress that clung to her curves. She had every intention of doing a little man-trolling while she listened to Cheryl cry on her shoulder.

Brushing her hair out, she left it loose to fall to her waist. Stepping back from the mirror, she saw the same tomboy she always saw except dressed up, pretending to be someone else.

She decided to put some light makeup on, giving herself the smoky eyes that everyone said looked sexy on a woman. When she was done, she looked like she had two black eyes. Quickly, she washed it off, simply using a light, natural color and mascara instead.

Feeling more normal, she picked her purse up and headed for the door.

"Why did you get all dressed up?" Tate came out of the kitchen, holding a soda.

"Because I'm meeting her at the Pink Slipper, and I didn't want to stand out like a sore thumb in my jeans." Before her other brothers could chime in, Rachel went out the door, closing it behind her.

She drove into town, pulled into the parking lot, and was surprised to find it empty with a note on the door. Rachel drove closer, reading the large writing from the front seat of the car. Hearing a car pull up next to her, she turned her head and rolled the window down when she saw it was Cheryl.

"A water pipe burst. It's closed until tomorrow." Rachel saw her friend's trembling lips and grabbed her purse. Getting out of her car, she then got into Cheryl's.

"Why don't we go to the diner and get a cup of coffee?" It was really their only other choice at this time of night.

"Because I don't want coffee; I want a drink! This isn't the only bar in town." Cheryl put her car in reverse, pulling out of the parking lot.

"Where are we going?" Cheryl's erratic behavior had Rachel worried.

"Rosie's."

Rachel had never been in the bar on the outskirts of town. Usually, the rougher crowd of Treepoint hung out there. The Last Riders and even her brothers frequented the bar a couple of times a week. Thank God tonight wasn't one of them.

"Cheryl, I don't know what you got in a fight with Jared over, but whatever it was, it's not worth doing something you'll regret."

"Don't worry, Rachel; I don't plan on doing anything I'll regret. Did you know my husband has been fucking around on me for years? Or that he had a freaking vasectomy so he wouldn't get any of them pregnant, me included? He never had any intention of having children with me."

Rachel could only guess at how devastating it had been for Cheryl to learn her childhood sweetheart could be so treacherous.

"Cheryl, you have been married to Jared for a lot of years, too many to throw it away without taking time to think it over."

"I plan to think it over with a couple of drinks inside me."

Rachel wisely remained silent, not wanting her to become further upset while she was driving.

The parking lot at Rosie's was full of trucks and motorcycles. Cheryl got out of the car before Rachel could change her mind.

Following behind her, Rachel felt self-conscious entering the dark bar when all the men's eyes turned to them in the doorway. Cheryl's anger, on the other hand, made her fearless.

Going farther into the bar, she found them an empty table at the back and took a chair. Rachel reluctantly sat down next to her, hoping a quick beer would calm her down enough to get her to leave.

Mick, the bar's owner who attended Rachel's church, came to take their order.

"Two beers," Rachel requested, seeing he wasn't happy she was there, but he didn't say anything. He merely nodded, going to the bar for their drinks.

"How could I not have known?"

Rachel patted her hand, trying to infuse her with

42

calming energy, but Cheryl snatched her hand away, reaching for the beer Mick had just placed in front of her.

Rachel reached into her purse for some money to pay him.

After Mick had walked away, a chair scraped back from the table and a large man Rachel didn't recognize sat down beside Cheryl.

"You seem upset. Anything I can help with?" His obvious leer had Rachel stiffening but drew Cheryl's interest.

"Hello." She took a long drink of her beer. "My name is Cheryl."

Rachel couldn't help rolling her eyes at the falsely seductive note in Cheryl's voice and her obvious flirtation.

This wasn't going to end well. Jared might be an unfaithful bastard, but he would be furious if he knew his wife was flirting with a biker.

However, Rachel could only sit by helplessly as the evening progressed and Cheryl had several more drinks. She had drunk only half of the first one herself and was getting ready to drag Cheryl from the dance floor if she didn't come back to the table soon.

Someone sat down next to her and Rachel turned, ready to blast them with a frigid glare when she saw it was Cash.

"Your brothers know you're here?"

"I don't have to tell my brothers every move I make."

Cash lifted a sardonic brow.

"They think I'm at the Pink Slipper," Rachel confessed.

"How did you end up here?"

Rachel jerked her head in Cheryl's direction. "I'm going to get her to leave when she comes back to the table."

"I don't think Nickel is planning on bringing her back to the table."

Rachel turned, seeing the large biker had his arm around Cheryl and was leading her toward the door.

Rachel jumped to her feet, beating them to the door

and blocking their exit.

"Time to go, Cheryl." Rachel pasted a confident smile onto her lips.

"She's decided to go back to the clubhouse with me. It's Friday night." Nickel placed a possessive arm around her friend's shoulder.

Rachel didn't know what difference the day of the week mattered, but she couldn't let Cheryl leave with him.

"She's my ride home, and I promised her I wouldn't let her leave without me," Rachel tried to reason with the determined man.

The biker looked her over from head to toe. "You're not my type, but I'm sure one of the other brothers will give you a good time." Again, he tried to move around her; Rachel didn't budge, though.

"You're misunderstanding me. She's not going to leave without me."

"You're not understanding me. I'm taking her back to the clubhouse where I'm going to fuck her like she asked me to. Now move."

Rachel paled at his demand.

"Leave her alone, Nickel. Go on to the clubhouse. There are plenty of women there to keep you busy."

"Dammit, Cash."

"Remember that money you owe me? We'll call it even." When the man hesitated then released Cheryl, Rachel hastily moved out of his way to allow him to go out the door.

Cheryl almost fell, but Cash managed to grab her arm, preventing it. Cheryl then transferred her affection to Cash, wrapping her arms around his waist and pressing her breasts against him.

"Where's your car?" Cash asked, making no move to remove Cheryl's arms.

"We drove hers."

Rachel had grabbed both their purses when she left the table. She dug through Cheryl's as she walked toward her car. Pressing the unlock button, she opened the back car door. Cash sat the woman in the backseat, closing the door before she could ask him if she could go home with him again.

"What are you going to do with her?"

"Take her back to my house. I don't think her facing Jared in this condition would help their marriage any."

"I don't know; Jared likes women any way he can get them."

Rachel silently agreed but still wasn't going to take Cheryl back until she sobered up. Looking in the backseat, she saw Cheryl was already passed out. She would wake the whole house up packing her inside.

"I'll ride home with you and carry her in for you," Cash offered.

Rachel bit her lip, not knowing what to do next. If her brothers woke up and saw her with a drunk Cheryl, they would throw a fit. If they woke up and saw Cash, there would be a killing.

"No, thanks. I can handle it," she said firmly.

Cheryl stirred, slamming her hand against the window. "Where did Nickel go?" she yelled.

"Obviously not," Cash retorted, getting into the driver's seat of the car. "Give me the keys." Rachel handed them over after getting in the passenger seat.

"How are you going to get home?" she asked, seeing his truck in the lot.

"I can walk. It's just a mile back to the bar to pick up my truck. I know those woods like the back of my hand."

Rachel was sure he did; he had helped his grandmother bootleg until the county went wet.

"My brothers have traps set up in the woods to catch poachers," she warned.

"Your brothers are morons."

Rachel didn't try to dispute the fact because they usually were.

As Cash turned up the hill to her house, it was a lot

smoother ride than the last time she'd ridden with him.

"I see you're learning where all the biggest potholes are." Rachel smiled at him in the dark.

"That isn't a good thing."

His smart ass answer had her snapping at him. "I didn't ask for your help. You offered."

His hands clenched on the wheel. "Be quiet, Rachel, before I stop the car and get out, leaving you with Sleeping Beauty in the backseat."

Rachel glanced back at Cheryl. Sound asleep with her blond hair and rosy cheeks she did look like Sleeping Beauty. No one could question Jared's taste in women; he had married the prettiest girl in town. Cash had obviously noticed.

Rachel took a deep breath, calming herself. With any luck, she needed his help for the next ten minutes. Then she could send him on his way.

# CHAPTER FIVE

Cash pulled the car close to the house, turning off the lights and motor. It was dark, but the porch light was on. Getting out of the car, Cash lifted Cheryl into his arms while she opened the front door.

Rachel made sure everyone was sleeping before motioning for Cash to bring Cheryl inside. Holly and Logan were spending the night at Mrs. Langley's, so Rachel led him down the hall to Holly's room. Quietly opening the door, she turned on the light to give Cash a view of where the bed was. Rachel turned down the covers then covered her up once he laid her down.

"Thanks, Cash. I appreciate it."

"Stay out of Rosie's, Rachel. You had no business being in there. If I hadn't been there—"

Rachel could tell she was about to get the same speech about being careful from Cash she had to listen to from Tate; therefore, she cut him off. "I don't need a lecture from you, Cash. If I wanted to listen to one, I would have called my brothers. I don't know why you aren't best friends with them; all of you are jerks who think you can order me around."

"I don't know why I fucking try, Rachel. That's what I get for feeling sorry for—"

Rachel reached out and punched him in his stomach. "I don't need you to feel sorry for me."

She thought he would smack her in retaliation. He looked so furious with her that Rachel took a step back, but then found herself caught in his arms before she could make a move.

"Which room is yours?"

"Go to Hell."

"Shh... or you'll wake everyone up. Either tell me which room is yours, or I'll turn you over my knee here and Cheryl might wake up and see."

Rachel felt ashamed of herself. She couldn't understand why she had overreacted in the first place. Maybe because he had compared Cheryl to Sleeping Beauty and all she got was the reproach for protecting a friend.

"The next door on the left."

Cash turned out the light. Then, holding her arm tightly, he dragged her into her bedroom, flipping on the light switch before he closed the door with a quiet snap.

Rachel tried to forestall the fury that she saw had a hold of him. "I'm sorry, Cash. I apologize."

"I'm tired of taking the shit you Porters dish out." Cash sat down on her bed, pulling her over his lap. Rachel gasped, barely able to stop herself from screaming out loud.

His hand lifted her skirt, showing her frilly pink panties.

"I always wondered if you wore panties or boxers." She deserved the sarcasm he was throwing her way, but it still hurt her feelings to be compared to a boy.

When his hand smacked her ass, Rachel jumped, but a hard hand pressed down on the middle of her back, holding her in place as several more hard smacks landed on her butt. She remained quiet, though; determined that, no matter how much it hurt, she wouldn't make a noise. If her brothers ran in here and saw Cash, they would shoot him, and as bad as she hated him right then, she didn't want him dead.

The spanking suddenly stopped.

"What's this?" His finger pressed against the damp crotch of her panties.

"You might not act like a girl, but you have all the responses." His thumb slipped underneath the thin material, finding her clit and swirling around the bud, causing another rush of dampness for his fingers to find.

Rachel felt his cock hardening underneath her belly. She tried to close her thighs, embarrassed by her revealing response, yet Cash simply lifted her up, laying her down on the bed.

The unexpectedness of his move had her thighs splaying open. Before she could close them, Cash had a hand on each thigh, spreading her wider. Rachel felt a blush cover her body when she looked down; her dress was up around her waist and her thighs were held obscenely open with Cash kneeling on the floor beside the bed.

Before she could stop him, he jerked her panties off and buried his face in her crotch.

"Cash!"

"Shh… Do you want one of your brothers to come in and see you like this?"

Frantically, Rachel shook her head against the mattress. That was all the encouragement Cash needed before he lowered his head again, latching his mouth onto her clit.

Rachel shoved her fist in her mouth at the ecstatic pleasure taking over her body as his tongue searched and discovered each and every crevice of her pussy before shoving into her pulsing sheathe. Unable to help herself, Rachel buried her hands in his hair and lifted her hips, pressing herself harder against his mouth.

Rachel had never been able to bear the thought of self-satisfying herself, but that didn't mean her body hadn't felt desire. Now Cash was storming her defenses, rising longing that had been suppressed until she shuddered, wanting him inside her.

As his tongue found her clit and began sucking on it once more, Rachel whimpered.

"You need to come?" He raked his teeth along the inside of her thigh.

Rachel's hands in his hair tried to bring his mouth back to where she needed it most; however, Cash rose from his kneeling position, placing her farther back on the bed before he lay down between her thighs.

Swiftly unbuttoning the front of her dress, he unsnapped her bra, freeing her small breasts. Rachel had always felt like her breasts were nicely sized until she had compared herself to Holly, but Cash didn't seem disappointed when his eyes narrowed in desire. He took the tip of one breast in his mouth, suckling on her roughly while his hand buried itself between her thighs.

"Have you ever been finger fucked before?" Cash asked against her breasts.

"No," Rachel whispered, and one long finger speared her sheathe as soon as the word left her mouth.

Cash moved to her other breast, leaving the one he had been sucking on tender and sensitive. His finger began to move in and out, stroking her into wrapping her thighs around his.

When Rachel began to whimper louder, Cash rose over her and took her mouth with his, using his tongue to trace her lips before plunging into her mouth the way his finger was her pussy.

"I don't know which tastes sweeter, your mouth or your pussy."

Rachel's hands went to his t-shirt, wanting to feel his flesh against hers, bunching the material. Cash raised up long enough to pull his shirt off, and then his mouth covered hers again. His tongue rubbed against hers as his thumb glided across her clit while he plunged another finger inside her.

Rachel tried to turn her hips to adjust, but his weight kept her pinned to the bed. Her hips began to pump against him, giving herself the stimulation she needed to climax and relieve the passion that was becoming an exquisite torture.

"You like having me in your pussy." Cash's statement embarrassed her. She couldn't believe she had let her guard down, yet she nodded, afraid he would stop when she was so close.

"I have something you're going to like a hell of a lot better than my fingers." Cash rose into a kneeling position between her splayed thighs.

After unbuttoning his jeans and working down his zipper, his large cock sprung out, a clear liquid already on the mushroom tip. Rachel kept her eyes on his cock as he reached into his back pocket, pulling out a condom and ripping it with his teeth. His thumb kept playing with her clit while he slid the condom on. Rachel didn't want to think of the expertise required to do it and make it look so simple.

As soon as the condom was on, he took his cock in his hand and placed it at her opening.

"Do you want me to stop? This is going to hurt for a few minutes, but then it's going to feel a hell of a lot better than my fingers."

Rachel stared down at his cock at her entrance while his thumb kept playing with her, making her want to scream for him to make love to her while Cash was just considering this sex. She was trying to gather her control to tell him to stop when he leaned down to take her sensitive nipple in his mouth once more.

"Tell me you want me, Rach. I'll make it good for you, something you'll always remember, sweetheart."

Rachel was afraid he was right, but she couldn't deny the fire consuming her any longer. She had never planned on remaining a virgin until she married. She had kept it longer than most women, but the thing that made her decide to give in was the gentle way his hands glided over her body and the childhood crush she had always carried for him.

"I want you, Cash."

His cock slid inside slowly, slipping into her sheathe with a steady pressure that wasn't going to be stopped by a thin piece of membrane.

"This is going to hurt, but then I'll make it feel better. Okay?"

Rachel nodded, already feeling a burning pain inside her as Cash thrust hard. Tears came to her eyes, which she blinked back. Cash caught her gaze and then leaned down to lick her tears from the corner of her eyes as he continued to move slowly inside her, grinding the base of his cock against her clit, making her wet enough for him to slide more easily inside her.

"Feel better?" He rose up on his arms as he looked down on her, his hips beginning to move harder and faster.

Rachel thought he looked like every woman's wicked fantasy as he claimed her body, not with gentleness, but with a fire that tore through her pussy as he relentlessly used his body to conquer hers.

"Yes," Rachel whispered, wrapping her arms around his shoulders.

"It's going to feel a lot better before I'm done fucking you." As he began thrusting faster inside her, she moved tentatively against him, attempting to match his strokes, but his hands held her still.

"Don't move, or you'll be too sore to walk tomorrow."

"Can you go faster?" Rachel directed, needing more.

"That I can do," he said, moving faster.

Rachel held on, feeling sensation after sensation she had never felt before or knew existed.

"You like fucking?"

Rachel couldn't lie while her body was begging his to

go faster. "Yes."

His mouth went to the side of her breast, sucking the flesh into his mouth and biting down. "Every time you see me, I want you to remember my cock in your pussy." His tongue licked the bruised flesh on the side of her breast. "Every time you touch yourself here, remember I was the first to touch you."

Rachel couldn't hold back a moan at his erotic words as his cock drove higher inside her. She shuddered as she climaxed, her breasts tautening as she arched underneath him.

"That's it, baby. Give that first to me, too," Cash ground out while burying himself to the hilt inside her, his balls against her ass.

He sucked harder on her breast as she felt him climax in the condom. When they both quit trembling, he gave the tip of her breast a final lick before pulling out of her.

"Where's the bathroom?"

After Rachel pointed to a door on the bedroom wall, Cash climbed off the bed, going to the bathroom with his jeans still on. Rachel remembered the rough texture on the inside of her thighs as he'd fucked her.

She covered her body with a blanket on the bottom of her bed just as Cash opened the bathroom door, coming out.

With the heat of passion over, Rachel noticed the hickey on his throat and scratch marks on his shoulders. She had seen enough to know both were a couple of days old; the hickey was fading, not as bright, and the scratch marks were scabbed over.

Cash reached over the bed for his t-shirt, pulling it on.

"I hope whoever left those marks on you won't notice the new ones on your sides."

Cash didn't say anything, pulling on his boots. She didn't even remember him pulling them off.

"Rachel, I did you a favor and everything else kinda got out of hand."

Rachel could sense he was trying to extricate himself from the embarrassing situation.

"It's late, Cash. I'm tired. Are you sure you can make it back to the bar?"

Cash frowned down at her, about to say something, but then he thought better of it. "I'm sure."

Going to her bedroom door, he listened quietly before opening it and leaving.

Rachel sat up in bed. Bringing her knees up, she rested her forehead on them. He hadn't even glanced back as he left.

Of all the men in Treepoint, why had she decided to pick Cash to give up her virginity to right under her family's roof?

Rachel lay back against the bed, ashamed and angry at herself.

Placing an arm over her eyes, she wished she could take back the last hour of her life for a do-over. Hell, she would be content if she could just have the last thirty back. Swiping away a tear, she gathered her composure to go take a shower.

Seeing the condom in the trash, Rachel was relieved there wouldn't be any consequences.

She would place tonight behind her and just be grateful no one other than them would ever know about it. One thing was for sure; she was probably the only woman in Treepoint Cash wouldn't brag about having sex with.

# CHAPTER SIX

"Can we ride it again?" Logan begged.

"No. We've ridden it three times already."

Rachel smiled as Holly refused to let Logan ride the Ferris wheel again. It was already nine o'clock—well past his bed time. Rachel was exhausted herself.

She hadn't slept well the last two weeks since she had made the mistake of going out drinking with Cheryl. Thankfully, Rachel had managed to wake her early the next morning and send her home without anyone realizing she had spent the night. She had dropped her off to pick up her car. Rachel felt as if she had avoided a natural disaster. No one needed to know she had lost her mind and given herself to Cash.

She hadn't seen Cash or Cheryl since that night. Cheryl had called several times for her to go out with her again, telling her she was filing for divorce from Jared. Rachel had refused, though. She had never been the type to hang out in bars, and as much as she liked Cheryl, she couldn't bring herself to now.

Treepoint was small, and it had been hard to avoid the rumors of Cheryl becoming "bffs" with Kaley, a sister of a friend she had graduated with. Cheryl and Kaley were making up for the time they had lost by getting married young. Rachel would walk away when the harsh gossip started. It was none of her business, and she wanted Cheryl to be happy.

"It's time to go home. We don't want to sleep through church tomorrow, do we?"

"Yes," Logan said unhappily.

"Come on, Holly. One more time won't hurt," Dustin said, lifting Logan onto his shoulders.

Holly gave in. "All right. As long as there isn't a huge line."

There wasn't, and Dustin and Logan got on the Ferris wheel. Both women smiled as Logan started squealing as soon as the wheel began to go up. The ride didn't last long, and it satisfied Logan enough for them to head home without further arguments from him. Rachel had her own car because she had worked in the church store that day and had met Dustin and Holly at the fair. They weren't parked far from each other, however.

Rachel listened to Logan tell Holly about his ride on the Ferris wheel as she pulled out her keys from her jeans pockets.

"I'll ride home with you, and Dustin and Logan can drive back home together," Holly offered.

"Sounds good." It wasn't far to their house, but Rachel would be glad for the company. She'd do anything to keep from thinking about Cash.

Dustin reached his truck first.

"I'll follow you home," he said, putting Logan in his car seat.

"Okay." Rachel had learned long ago not to argue with his over-protectiveness.

As she put her key in the door to unlock it and Holly went to the passenger side, a loud giggle drew their attention. On the next row over, Cash was getting out of his truck, holding the door open for a woman to slide out. Rachel's eyes widened when she saw Cheryl taking her time getting out, bracing her hands on Cash's chest. Her hair was a tumbled mess and her top was messed up.

It didn't take a second for Rachel to figure out what had happened in his truck. Rachel felt as if a knife had been stuck in her belly.

"Rachel?" Holly asked, trying to open her still-locked door.

"Sorry." Rachel fumbled with the lock, finally able to unlock the door.

As she opened her own car door, her eyes were briefly caught and held by Cash, who had turned at the sound of Holly's voice. She tore her gaze away, refusing to look at the couple as she got in the car, put her key in the ignition, and reversed out.

"I thought we were supposed to wait for Dustin?" Holly questioned, staring at her curiously.

Rachel's shaking hands gripped the steering wheel, forcing herself to calm down. Finally able to breathe, she stopped at the end of the row long enough for Dustin to come up behind them.

Her hands then clenched the wheel the whole way home as her mind played back the look on Cheryl's face. She had to force herself to focus on driving and not the flushed satisfaction Cash's expression had showed before he had seen her staring at him. Rachel wanted to cry over not being able to keep from revealing her own hurt.

\* \* \*

Cash wanted to slam his truck door closed. Of all the times for Rachel to happen to be standing there, it couldn't have been a more inopportune one.

"Want to go back to my apartment?" Cheryl's voice drew his attention back to her and away from the hurt look on Rachel's face.

He had gone to the fair with several of The Last Riders; however, he and Rider had broken away from them when Rider had run into Kaley and Cheryl. Rider had left not long afterward, headed to the nearby motel with Kaley.

Cheryl had been all over him, so he had brought her to his truck. The lot only had a few vehicles left. Therefore, he had let Cheryl give him the blowjob she had promised, allowing her mouth to give him relief from the torture of wanting Rachel again.

None of the women he had fucked since her had been able to, though, and he didn't know why he expected Cheryl to. Still, her mouth had relieved the fire in his dick enough to keep him from sneaking into Rachel's bedroom, whether she wanted him there or not.

"No. I have something I need to take care of. Where's your car?"

When Cheryl pointed to her car three rows over, Cash walked her to it and waited until she was inside before moving away.

He drove to his meeting spot, pulling into the dark lot of the clubhouse. The bikers gave him curious looks before turning away when they saw him take a seat at their president's table.

"Want a drink?" Stud asked, motioning for Sex Piston to leave the table.

His wife's lips tightened but she got up, going to sit with her crew at another table.

"No, thanks. She's going to make you pay for that." Cash watched as Sex Piston glared at Stud from the circle of her friends.

"What's new?"

Cash had to admire the way Stud handled his wife. There weren't many men who would be able to handle the temperamental redhead. Cash didn't want to think about his own problems with a certain redhead.

Sex Piston and Rachel couldn't be more different. Sex Piston's hair was a reddish gold while Rachel's was deep, burnt red. Stud's wife oozed sex appeal, yet Rachel was quiet and softly feminine. Her appeal was more subtle, grabbing him by his balls and twisting them into knots of desire he couldn't quench, despite the other women he mercilessly fucked.

"Any news?" Stud asked.

"They call themselves Freedom Riders. Scorpion is the leader; Vaughn is vice. They are a large club, mainly anti-government. I thought, at first, they wanted Jamestown to run their drugs or filter money."

"They don't?" Stud's surprise mirrored his own when he'd found out just what plans the Freedom Riders had for Jamestown.

"No, they are in the process of buying a large piece of property that is mainly wooded. Two sides of the property are inaccessible by land or foot, leaving only the front and side open—one by road, the other by boat. It's a nice piece of property; lots of game, trees, even enough to farm with a large house and barn."

"So, why do they want it?"

"To train their anti-government supporters."

"Fuck." Stud ran his hand through his blond hair.

"I figure they think Jamestown isn't big enough to fight them, and they will be left alone, bringing more of their men in once the sale of the property is final," Cash explained.

"Has the sale gone through?" Stud asked sharply.

"Not yet. It's selling for half a million, so whoever is behind them has some big bucks."

"Who owns the property now?"

"Curt Dawkins. He's the football coach in Treepoint." Cash had dug into his past and saw no connection with the group.

"I think we need to set up a meeting with him as soon as possible." Stud's tight voice said he already knew what Cash's next words would be.

"The Destructors are no match for them. I don't think you have enough men even if you add the Blue Horsemen into the mix. They're big, Stud, and deadly," Cash warned.

"I haven't got any other option. When I took over The Destructors for Sex Piston's father, I gave my word I would watch over them and protect them."

"You can't protect anyone if you're six feet under." Cash saw Stud wouldn't back down. "I'll set up a meeting with Viper; that's all I can do. It's up to him if he wants to drag The Last Riders into your war."

"It's not a war yet. I may be able to stop it." Stud's voice was filled with worry.

Cash sympathized with the hard biker. He had a streak of loyalty that was hard to find in many men. Stud also had to be concerned for Sex Piston's safety and his four children.

Cash shook his head. "They are fanatical. Nothing but force will stop them."

Stud nodded. "Set up the meeting with Viper."

"Will do." Cash stood.

"You're welcome to stay."

"No, thanks; I better head back. I want to talk to Viper." Cash stared down at Stud, trying to convey his urgency. The Destructors were on borrowed time until the first strike was made.

"Cash, you have my marker. If you ever need anything…"

Cash stared down at Stud. He respected his desire to pay his debts.

"Get Killyama to back off Train, and we'll call it even."

It took him forty-five minutes to drive back to the clubhouse. Being Friday night, most of the brothers were still up.

Train and Jewell were coming down the steps from upstairs.

"Where's Viper?"

"Upstairs."

Cash went up and saw Viper's bedroom door open. It was rare when the president let others watch; tonight wasn't one of those nights, though. Viper was sitting at his desk in front of the computer with Winter asleep on the bed. Regrettably, he must have missed the show.

"Got a minute?"

"Yeah." Viper leaned back in his chair, giving him his attention.

Cash had already informed Viper of the information he was going to tell Stud that night before the meet. Subsequently, Cash updated him on Stud's reaction and his request.

Viper remained quiet while Cash talked. When he finished, Viper looked at Winter lying on the bed. Cash could see the conflict in his eyes. Viper would want to help Stud out, but he had his own woman and club to watch out for.

"The Freedom Riders aren't going to give a shit about the Destructors, and everyone knows who runs them. They will go after Stud; he's the only thing stopping them from controlling Jamestown. It's going to go down hard on him. It's inevitable unless we add our numbers to his," Cash advised.

"Tell everyone we're having a club meeting tomorrow night. I'll make my decision tonight." Viper stood up, stretching.

"Will do."

"Cash, anything bothering you?" Viper stopped him from leaving the room.

"No. Why?" Cash paused.

Viper powered down his computer, closing it before answering his question. "I don't know; you just seem distracted lately. Now is not the time for distractions."

"My mind is exactly where it needs to be until this is over."

"That's what I want to hear. We have wives and children to protect now."

"I won't let you down," Cash promised.

"If you do, one of them could pay the price."

Viper's grim warning was still on his mind after he'd left the room.

Going downstairs, he passed the word about the

meeting tomorrow night. Then, tired, he decided to go to bed.

He was halfway up the stairs when Raci yelled up at him.

"Want some company?"

Rachel's hurt face flashed through his mind.

"Come on." He held his hand out to her.

With a huge grin, the woman came up the steps and took his hand. He couldn't have Rachel distracting him. If he tried to see her again, her brothers finding out would be inevitable. What's more, The Last Riders needed to have Stud's back, not fighting a feud with three idiots.

Inside his bedroom, Raci quickly removed her skimpy outfit.

"What do you want tonight, Cash?"

"Every fucking thing you've got."

# CHAPTER SEVEN

"What do you want me to do with these?" Evie questioned as she opened the door for the men who were carrying in the furniture she was donating to the church store.

"Bring it to the back of the store." Rachel couldn't believe the amount of furniture Evie was donating. Much of it was expensive and custom-made. "Are you sure you want to donate all of this?"

"I'm sure. I kept what I wanted, and since King and I are living in his house and I'm selling mine, there's no need to keep it. It will make me feel better that it's going to good use. I only used it a few months before King and I got married."

Rachel directed Rider and Train where to put the couch. Not looking at Cash, who was holding the other end of the bed's headboard, she directed Nickel to put it against the back wall. Razer and Viper were busy trying to maneuver the washer through the store.

Rachel kept herself busy, directing the men as the household of furniture was all placed at the back of the store. She ignored Cash as best she could, making small talk with Evie while the men finished and left the store.

"Pastor Merrick will appreciate the donation."

Evie's expression went curiously blank.

Rachel hadn't pried Lily for information on why Evie no longer attended church, but she couldn't help asking for herself. "Why did you switch churches, Evie?"

"I don't exactly get along with his wife."

Rachel didn't care for Brooke Merrick, either. If she hadn't attended the church since she was a little girl, she would have left, too. Truthfully, Rachel didn't see Brooke staying long-term in Treepoint; she snubbed her nose at most of the women in the congregation. Rachel had never met a minister's wife so totally unsuited for her husband's profession.

"That's it," Viper declared.

"Next Friday, we're having a birthday party for Mrs. Langley if any of your club wants to attend," Rachel invited.

Her brothers hadn't been happy about her intention to invite The Last Riders, but they helped the woman out whenever she needed them, and she had a close relationship to Beth, Razer, and Lily. There was no way out of inviting them other than outright snubbing them, and she wasn't going to do that.

"We'll be there," Viper agreed, moving off with his men.

"I hope you and your husband can attend," Rachel teased Evie. "If I couldn't have King, it's nice to see both of you so happy."

"You're lucky I'm not the jealous type, or I would whip your ass for that."

"I think I'm the last woman in Treepoint you have to worry about stealing King from you." Rachel's cheerful voice sounded fake to her own ears. Her simple dress was no comparison to the tight jeans and blouse Evie was wearing.

"I don't know about that. King still talks about your shooting. He asked me if I wanted to get a conceal-and-carry permit. I have no desire to shoot or carry a gun around with me."

"You might change your mind. I think several women in town won't mind he has a wedding ring," Rachel quipped.

Evie laughed. "It might be a good thing Penni sent my gun back ."

"Ready, Evie?" Viper held the door open.

"Coming. See you Friday."

"Bye." Rachel watched them leave; glad she had avoided talking to Cash. She wondered how long it was going to take her to get over being embarrassed whenever she saw him. For once, she wished she could use her powers on herself.

Rachel straightened the things Evie had brought in, trying to organize the heavy furniture as best as she could. She didn't want Lily trying to pull and tug it.

She helped several customers find things they needed before she was able to close for the day. Locking the door, she turned to her car to see Cash leaning against the door.

"What do you want, Cash?"

"I wanted to talk to you to set things straight." Cash ran his hand through his hair, clearly uncomfortable. "Rachel, I don't want you feeling awkward around me."

"I don't feel anything about you at all." Rachel clutched her purse in a tight fist, belying her words.

Cash's jaw tautened.

"Now, if you don't mind moving your ass away from my car, I need to get home and fix dinner."

"Your brothers need to learn to fix their own dinner instead of having you do everything for them."

Rachel wasn't about to let Cash badmouth her brothers. "When was the last time you cooked your own dinner, Cash? Washed your own clothes? Or better yet, when was the last time you worked? As far as I can see, you spend more time being an errand boy for The Last Riders than making an honest living."

"What do the Porters know about making an honest living? Your brothers sell weed and you con people out of money, selling fake medicine and hope."

Rachel's head jerked back at his insults. "I've never made promises to any of my clients, and no one has ever been left unsatisfied."

"I can vouch for that," Cash said crudely.

Rachel's face blanched. "Move."

"Rachel..." Regret showed in his eyes as he stepped away from her car, his hand reaching out to touch her arm.

"Go to Hell." Rachel climbed into her car, slamming the door closed.

Tears escaped as she drove home because she was so angry. She was furious at herself, then at Cash.

By the time she pulled up in front of her home, she had gotten herself back under control.

Surely in a few weeks it would quit hurting so badly. It had to become easier, didn't it? She had only had sex with him the one time. How long was it going to take to forget the feel of his body against hers, to stop wanting him? It was something he had no problem forgetting or moving on from. Rachel was sure he had been with more than Cheryl with a whole clubhouse to choose from.

Cash was totally wrong for her, but the moment he had touched her, it had seemed so right.

\* \* \*

Rachel discovered a therapy for getting Cash off her mind—work. She started her days even earlier, going out into the woods in order to search for new herbs and locations for Ginseng roots. She booked patients every day, further draining herself to the point her eyes became bruised-looking, and she had to wear concealer to hide her tiredness from everyone.

After she worked in the church store for the afternoons, she would come home and change. Once there, she'd head to her greenhouse where she managed to find peace until she went to bed, only to stare at her ceiling, and toss and turn throughout the night until she got up early and started the whole thing again.

On Thursday, she went grocery shopping for Mrs. Langley's birthday party, going up each row to avoid forgetting anything and having to return. She had dropped Holly off at Mrs. Langley's house to begin decorating so all they would have to do the next day was prepare the food.

Rachel went down the frozen food aisle and was reaching in for pastries when Bliss and Jewell came around the ,corner, pushing a buggy. Train and Cash were following along behind them as they shopped. She couldn't catch a freaking break.

As they passed, she was determined to act normally this time.

"Hi, everyone." Rachel smiled at each of them, including Cash.

"Hi, Rachel," Bliss greeted. "Shopping for the party tomorrow night?"

"Yes. I promised Logan I would make his favorite fruit tarts. I told Lily and Evie everyone is invited."

"We wouldn't miss it. We're always up for a party. It gives us a night off from cooking," Jewell joked.

"Good, I'm glad you're coming. See you tomorrow." Rachel waved casually as she pushed her buggy away. She saw Cash look at her, and she didn't try to avoid his gaze.

"Bye, Cash, Train."

She let out a small whoosh of breath as she checked out; relieved she had come through with flying colors. She heard them playing around as she paid but didn't look again.

She was rushing through putting her groceries in the trunk when she heard, "Need any help?"

Rachel jumped; she hadn't even heard him come up behind her.

"Nope, I'm finished. Thanks anyway." Rachel turned to him, giving him a smile before closing her trunk. Train and the girls were all loading their groceries into the back of his truck.

"You seem to be in a better mood since I saw you last," Cash said casually.

"Why wouldn't I be in a good mood? It's a gorgeous day." Rachel sidestepped him, going to her car door and unlocking it.

Before she could open the door, Cash reached out and opened it for her. As he reached forward, his arm brushed against her breasts. She sucked in her breath sharply, bringing his eyes back to hers.

"Yes, it is. I guess I'll see you tomorrow night, then."

Rachel had lost her train of thought but quickly regained her equilibrium. "Bye."

She got into her car, starting the motor. She then gave them a brief wave as she pulled out.

"Shit."

She had never expected Cash to come to Mrs. Langley's party, knowing her three brothers would be there. Surely the four of them could behave long enough for the celebration, though, right?

Butterflies swarmed her already-tense stomach at having them together. She would just have to make sure to keep her brothers under control and Cash separated from them. Her nerves settled down once she had a plan of action.

It would be fine. She had everything under control. She had just proven to Cash and herself she could put that night behind them. What could go wrong?

# CHAPTER EIGHT

"Want to grab us some lunch?" As Lily lay down the paperwork she was working on, Rachel bounced up from the stool.

"I thought you would never ask. I'm starving. What do you want me to bring you back?"

"A hamburger and fries."

Rachel's mouth dropped open. Health conscious since she had become pregnant, Lily was obviously needing a junk food fix.

"Sure thing." Rachel grabbed her purse.

"Stay and have lunch at the diner. It's slow now; take your time and enjoy."

"I might take you up on that." Rachel left the church store, crossing the street to the diner.

Opening the door, she found the restaurant busy. Searching for an empty table, she noticed Willa dropping off some pies to sell. Rachel perked up, going to stand beside her at the counter.

"Hi, Willa."

"Hi, Rachel. Lunchtime?"

"Yes. Have you had lunch yet?"

"No."

"Join me, then. I hate eating alone," Rachel proposed.

"I'm not in a rush, so I can sit awhile."

"Thanks. Let's snatch that table before someone else does." Rachel and Willa sat down at the empty booth, ordering their drinks and food, plus Lily's to-go order.

"What have you been up to?" Rachel asked her shy friend.

"Nothing much." Willa shrugged. "King's restaurant opens next week. We came up with a couple of things for his menu."

"That's all you need is more work." Rachel shook her head at her as the waitress set down their drinks.

"What does that mean?" Willa tilted her head to the side.

"It means you never get out and have any fun," Rachel complained. "Are you coming to Mrs. Langley's party tonight?"

"I'm busy," Willa hedged.

"You can spare an hour. Be there," Rachel ordered. "Lily, Holly, and I will be there, and we are party misfits."

"I don't know."

"Please," Rachel pleaded for her friend's own good.

"All right, but if I'm miserable or make a fool of myself, then I'm never going to talk to you again," Willa threatened.

The waitress put their food down in front of them. Rachel bit into her chicken sandwich, staring at the plain salad Willa was eating.

"Is that any good?" Rachel stared down at the salad made of mostly lettuce.

"No." Willa picked through it, eventually taking a bite.

"I have a big ass," Rachel admitted.

Shocked, Willa looked across the table at her.

"I do. I shove it into Spanx, and if I've had more than one too many fries, it jiggles like Jell-O."

Willa's laughter filled the restaurant and dimples peeked at Rachel.

She motioned for the waitress. "Bring her a grilled chicken breast and some of the asparagus that's on the lunch menu." The waitress moved off.

"I'm tired of dieting all the time," Willa confessed.

"Then don't. You're beautiful; you really are." Rachel reached across the table, laying her hand on hers. Warmth flooded from her into Willa. "I wish I looked like you. You're soft and feminine. I look like a tomboy," Rachel confessed. "I'm twenty-three and look seventeen. When men look at you, they see a beautiful woman, Willa."

When the waitress set the plate down on the table, Rachel pushed it toward Willa. "Cut it up and put it on your salad."

Willa did as told and then took a bite.

"Better?"

"Yes. I was being too strict with myself. Then I get tired of eating boring food and splurge with a cupcake," Willa confessed, beginning to eat her salad.

"If I was surrounded with your cupcakes, my ass would be as big as a barn."

Their laughter drew many appreciative male glances, which brought the color to Willa's cheeks.

A large group of men who had been standing at the doorway approached their booth.

"Mind if we join you? The restaurant is busy, and you have a few extra seats." The men seemed friendly enough, and they were surrounded by familiar faces in the diner, so Rachel slid over. Willa did the same after shooting Rachel a worried glance. Rachel sent her a reassuring look before taking in the men who had sat down with them. She had never seen them in town before.

"Are you traveling through Treepoint?"

"Is it that obvious we're not from here?" The one sitting next to her with blondish-brown hair cut short answered for the group.

"I know everyone in town, so yeah, it is a little obvious," Rachel said, staring at the men sitting around their booth.

"We're new to the area. We've moved to Jamestown and decided to spend the day exploring the nearby towns. If I had seen Treepoint first, I would have picked it over Jamestown." He held out his hand to Rachel. "I'm Scorpion, and the one sitting next to your friend is Vaughn."

"It nice to meet you. Treepoint is smaller, but it's prettier with the mountains," Rachel agreed.

"I was thinking more about the women." He smiled.

Rachel smiled in return, liking his easy attitude. He wasn't coming across as aggressive, just slightly flirtatious. Rachel's confidence received a much needed boost from the appreciation she saw in his eyes.

"My name is Rachel, and this is Willa."

Scorpion reached out his hand, shaking Willa's while introducing his other two friends, Yancy and Scott. The men nodded in acknowledgment as the waitress brought coffee and took their orders.

Rachel was aware Willa felt uncomfortable with the situation and was about to excuse themselves when the door opened and Cash, Shade, Dean, and Rider came in, taking a table. Rachel couldn't have felt more self-conscious with the men's curious eyes on their table.

"So, you're both from Treepoint?" Vaughn asked, staring at Willa.

When she didn't answer, Rachel did. "Homegrown."

She straightened her shoulders. She had nothing to be embarrassed about, sitting at a table of men. Neither she nor Willa belonged to The Last Riders and could do as they wanted.

Yancy had tried to talk to Willa and received only monosyllabic replies, but Scott was more determined, eventually able to pry information out of her about her baking business. When he found out she had brought in pies to the diner, the men all ordered a piece to go with their coffee. The peach pie had the men silent for several seconds as they cleaned their plates.

"I could eat the whole pie by myself," Vaughn complimented Willa, bringing a rosy flush to her cheeks. "Could I have your number? The next time we have a cookout, I'll order a couple."

Willa hesitantly reached into her purse, pulling out a card and handing it to Vaughn. At that point, Rachel felt a chill run down her spine. Instinctively, her gaze went to the table The Last Riders were sitting at; the men seemed furious. Rachel couldn't understand why they were so angry, and she was tempted to sit there longer but decided to put Willa out of her misery.

"I have to get back to work. It was nice meeting you all." Scorpion stood, letting her slide out of the booth while the others stood, letting Willa out. The waitress had already set Lily's take-out food on the table, so Rachel bent down to pick it up with the check, yet found herself forestalled.

"Our treat." Scorpion smiled, taking the ticket.

Rachel started to refuse but was quickly cut off. "For letting us disrupt your lunch and keeping us company."

The gesture was a friendly overture that Rachel saw no need to turn down. "Thanks."

Rachel smiled as she and Willa turned to leave. Unfortunately, they had to pass The Last Riders on the way out and not a single one tried to hide their displeasure. What the hell was up with them? Oblivious to the men's stares, the door was no sooner closed behind them than Willa gave a relieved sigh.

"That bad?" Rachel asked sympathetically.

Willa gave a brief nod. "I become an idiot around men. Just once, I wish I didn't act like a dork."

"You didn't. You're shy, Willa, and there's nothing wrong with that."

"There's a lot wrong with it, Rachel. Just once, I wish I could be more like you. You had those men listening to your every word."

"Willa, you're wrong. Three out of the four were trying to get to know *you*. You're too hard on yourself." There was no middle ground with Willa. Like her salad, she starved herself from both food and male companionship because, to herself, she didn't measure up to this ideal she felt she could never reach. The Barbie syndrome was a bitch to live up to. Rachel felt it herself, which was why she could understand Willa's feelings.

"I'll see you at the party tonight," Rachel reminded her, hoping she wouldn't back out.

"Do you want me to bring anything?" Willa offered.

"No, you're already bringing the birthday cake, and that's enough. The party's in four hours, so just go home and relax."

"All right. Bye, Rachel."

Rachel left Willa, crossing the street to the church store. Lily was still doing paperwork. Handing her the takeout lunch, Rachel began to pull out the donations from the previous day to organize them.

"Was the restaurant busy?" Lily asked, digging into her lunch.

"It was packed. Some men from out of town asked to join Willa and me."

Lily's violet eyes sparkled. "Any of them good-looking?"

"A couple of them were. One managed to get Willa's card from her. I bet he ends up asking her out. I hope so; she needs to get out more."

"You think it's safe? If they aren't from Treepoint, you really can't know anything about them." Lily paused, taking a bite of her hamburger.

"I got their names. I'll ask Tate to check them out if she decides to go out with him."

"Lewis won't be happy," Lily said.

"No, he won't." The recently divorced man had three children of his own and was raising his sister's two after her imprisonment and subsequent death. He was determined to make Willa his, despite her running in the other direction whenever she saw him.

"Shade was at the restaurant, eating with some of his friends."

Lily nodded. "They probably stopped there for lunch, coming back from Jamestown."

"Jamestown?" Rachel separated the toys from the clothes.

"They were meeting someone about buying property there."

Rachel's heart sank. The thought of The Last Riders possibly moving out of town had Rachel about to question her further; instead, she snapped her mouth closed. It was none of her business if they moved to the larger town or not. She had turned over a new leaf; anything to do with Cash was off-limits. With that decided, the women worked steadily the rest of the afternoon.

"If it doesn't get busier soon, you can cut your hours down until it picks up near the holidays. I hate to waste your time when there isn't much to keep you occupied."

"It gives me a chance to get out of the house a few days, Lily. But I may take you up on it next week. I want to get a few more plants I discovered replanted into my greenhouse before the first frost hits."

"I can always help out if she gets busy." Brooke Patterson came into the room from the side that connected to the church. She was dressed expensively in a yellow silk dress that showed her figure in a way no minister's wife should. The low cleavage alone would have the men in the congregation thinking about breaking one of the commandments. She looked overdressed and out of place in the church store.

Lily didn't respond to Brooke's offer. She was always friendly with everyone, thus it was unusual for her to ignore an offer of help.

"Rachel, if you want to leave early to get everything ready for Mrs. Langley's party, I can stay." An internal warning shrilled loudly within Rachel at Brooke's offer.

"I have it handled already. Holly and my brothers are taking care of setting everything up. All I have to do is drive there after work."

"Oh, you're going to wear that?"

Rachel's hand gripped the counter at the subtle insult. She was aware of her shortcomings, but she would be damned if another woman would point them out to her.

"No, my change of clothes is in my car."

"I see. You're just on top of everything." Rachel didn't take her cattiness for a compliment. The woman didn't seriously believe she didn't know when someone was being condescending to her?

The door to the store opened, and Shade came in. The menacing biker took in the women standing at the counter, his mouth tightening into a thin line as he took off his sunglasses. He went behind the counter to place a kiss on his wife's lips.

"Rachel told me she saw you at the diner. I thought you would have already gone home." Lily smiled up at her husband.

"I thought I would stop by and see if you wanted to close the store early and take a nap before the party."

Lily bit her lip. "We haven't had a customer in two hours."

"Go ahead, Lily. I'll stay," Rachel offered, not missing the envious look that was quickly concealed by Brooke.

"Are you sure?"

"Of course. Go. I have to stay in town anyway," Rachel urged.

"All right, then." She gathered her purse.

"Go ahead. I'll be right behind you," Shade said. Lily shot her husband a curious look but left without question.

"Do you mind excusing us, Brooke?" His tone of voice implied he really didn't give a damn if she did. Rachel was shocked at his rudeness; Shade wasn't the friendliest man she knew, but she had never seen him be outright rude to a woman.

Brooke's face blushed bright red. "Not at all." She turned on her high heels, leaving with an expression that made Rachel shiver.

"Anything wrong?" Rachel asked.

"Could be. You tell me."

"What about?" Rachel didn't understand why he was looking so angry.

"The men you had lunch with, how long have you known them?"

"An hour. Willa and I were having lunch, and the restaurant was crowded; they asked if they could sit with us. Is there a problem with that?"

"Those men are bad news, Rachel. Stay away from them," Shade warned.

Rachel felt her anger rising. "Let me get this straight. You're telling me not to talk to them again?"

"Yes."

"Shade, I can talk to anyone I want. I don't even let my brothers tell me what to do anymore," Rachel snapped.

"Listen, Rachel. They aren't someone to get involved with. You've never dealt with men like them before. You're a friend of Lily's, so I'm giving you a heads up."

Rachel swallowed back her anger. "As Lily's friend, I'll take it under consideration. Willa and I shared our booth with them. We ate, we left. It was that simple."

"And Willa gave them her card?"

"They want her to make some desserts for them for their next cookout."

Shade nodded.

"Satisfied?"

"Not really, but I guess it's all I'm going to get. You might drop a word and tell Willa to think twice about going out with one of them. You'll handle it better than me."

"Of that, I have no doubt." Rachel gave him a wry smile. She thought he may be overreacting to the presence of a new group of men in what they considered The Last Riders' territory.

"All right, then; I'll see you tonight."

"Bye, Shade." She watched him leave then walked across the store, going to the front window and looking out. Shade crossed the street back to the diner where The Last Riders were sitting on their motorcycles, waiting for him.

While he talked to them for several minutes, Cash's angry expression was easy to see even from this distance. As Shade got on his bike and they rode out, heading in the direction of their clubhouse, Cash rode out next to Viper in the lead, his body language showing his irritation.

She wondered what had him so pissed off. Surely it wasn't the fact she had shared lunch with those men, was it? She had told Shade there wasn't anything to it, and she was sure he had repeated her words to The Last Riders.

She went back to work, straightening the store until a couple of customers came in, diverting her thoughts.

After they left, she closed the store and drove toward Mrs. Langley's house. She would talk to Willa at the party tonight. The woman would never have met the men if she hadn't let them sit down at the table with them.

Rachel hoped she hadn't set something in motion that was too late to prevent.

# CHAPTER NINE

"Can I have another hotdog, please?"

Rachel ruffled her nephew's hair while reaching onto the platter to hand him another.

"Rachel, it's his third one," Holly reprimanded her.

Rachel could never say no to him; she spoiled him shamelessly.

"Last one, I promise." Rachel winked at Logan, giving Holly a hotdog to pacify her. Holly threw her a mock dirty look, taking the hot dog to go sit at one of the patio tables they had set up around the pool. Her brothers had hung fairy lights around the area, and with all the food and birthday balloons, the area looked very festive.

"What did you get in trouble for this time?" Lily asked, picking up a hotdog for herself.

"Giving Logan too many hotdogs. It's a good thing she hasn't noticed how many cupcakes I've let him sneak."

As Lily laughed, taking a bite of her hotdog, a loud giggle drew Rachel's attention. Greer and Diane were swimming in the pool. Rachel hadn't been happy that he was seeing the woman often, nor that he had invited her to the party.

"I see Greer has a new girlfriend," Lily stated as they

watched the couple play in the pool.

Several of the guests had brought swimsuits, many of them members of The Last Riders. Rachel had been shocked when she had looked up from the grill to see Cash sitting on the edge of the pool next to Rider. She thought he would avoid the party with her brothers present. Bliss, Jewell, Stori, and Nickel were swimming.

Another squeal drew her attention back to Greer and Diane.

"It's the longest he's seen someone." Rachel stared at her brother and the woman whose bikini top was tiny and completely out of place for the occasion. The Last Rider women were in more conservative swimsuits and were acting appropriately while Diane was acting like a drunken slut. To give Greer credit, he was trying unsuccessfully to calm her down.

Rachel reached into the cooler, pulling out a soda for herself.

"Want something to drink?" Rachel offered.

Lily looked into the cooler. "Lemonade would be great."

After Rachel handed her the lemonade, she and Lily took a seat and sat chatting until their conversation was interrupted by raised voices. Rachel winced when she heard Holly's angry voice. She and Greer were at the edge of the pool. Rachel could guess she was giving him hell over his behavior with Diane. Everyone was watching their fight.

"I better go break this up," Rachel excused herself, rising from the table and hurrying to avert a full-scale fight between the two. Holly was constantly on Greer because of his behavior in front of Logan, and Greer would become angry often, saying hurtful things to her.

"I don't need your advice on how to act!"

"Obviously, you do!" Holly argued back.

"If you would get that stick out of your ass, you might have some fun of your own and quit worrying about what

I'm doing," snarled Greer.

"I don't give a darn what you're doing. Just don't do it in front of Logan." Holly had lowered her voice, but it didn't quiet Greer down.

"Don't give me that holier-than-thou attitude. I'm not the one—"

"Greer," Rachel loudly whispered. "Shut up." Rachel wanted to smack her brother at the hurt look on Holly's face.

"You deal with her. I'm done listening to her sanctimonious bullshit." Greer jumped back into the pool, spraying both of them with water.

"He may be your brother, but I hate him." Holly's low voice was filled with tears.

"He's always been a hothead. I'm sorry, Holly; he didn't mean it."

"Yes, he did. He hates me for keeping Logan a secret."

"We all know you did it to protect him," Rachel soothed, reaching out to place her hand on her arm.

The guests were all gathering at the large table set up with the birthday cake. Mrs. Langley was staring in awe at the huge cake. Beth motioned for her.

"I need to go. They're getting ready to cut the cake."

"Go. I'm fine."

Rachel's smile slipped when she heard another argument going on behind her.

"What now?" Confused, she turned to see Cash still sitting by the pool. However, Diane had managed to climb up and sit next to him, pressing her breasts against his arm and placing her hand on his bare thigh, just below his shorts.

Greer's temper was already running hot from his argument with Holly; therefore, seeing his girlfriend plastered against Cash was like pouring gasoline on the flame. Their cutting remarks had Rachel turning pale.

"Greer!" Rachel pleaded.

"Back off, Rachel. He started it."

"How did I start it? I was sitting here, minding my own business," Cash said angrily.

"You never could keep your hands off another man's woman. What is it with you; can't you find one of your own?" Greer climbed out of the pool to glare down at Cash and Diane.

To give Cash credit, he didn't get to his feet; instead, he stared back impassively at Greer's tantrum.

"I know it's hard, Greer, but be smart. Go have a piece of cake and leave me alone."

Tate and Dustin came out from the house. Rachel silently groaned to herself as they came closer to see what had Greer's voice raised loud enough to be heard inside.

"You just can't leave women alone, can you, Cash? Like father, like son."

Rachel sucked in her breath as Cash got to his feet and The Last Riders began to fall in behind him.

"This is a birthday party! Let's go eat some ice cream and cool down." Rachel desperately tried to head off the fight she could see coming.

"Shut up, Rachel," Greer snarled at her attempt.

"Don't talk to her that way," Cash growled.

"I can talk to my sister any way I want to."

"Talk to her that way again and I will—"

"What are you going to do? Rachel is none of your business. She's the only woman in this town of ours you haven't fucked."

"Wanna bet?" Cash grinned. "I fucked her under your own roof," Cash bragged.

Rachel thought she would pass out at Cash's gloating. The horrified looks on her brothers' faces as they turned to her had Rachel taking a step back. When she was unable to deny his statement, all hell broke loose.

"You son of a bitch!" Greer threw himself at Cash, nearly knocking him into the pool, but Rider managed to grab his arm and steady him. Greer's fists flew out, one nailing Cash in the stomach. A free-for-all almost started as her other brothers moved forward, but The Last Riders managed to surround Cash.

Rachel stood with her hand to her mouth as her brothers screamed obscenities at the bikers.

"This is how you repay us for saving Lily's life? You motherfuckers can go to Hell!" Tate tried to go for Shade, who went stiff at his damning insult.

"We are paying you back. We're not beating the shit out of you right now! Back off." Shade's brusque order was ignored.

Rachel made an attempt to stop her brothers one more time, grabbing Tate by his arm when he moved toward Shade. "Tate! Stop. Please!"

"Don't fuckin touch me." Tate shoved her from him, jerking his arm away. Rachel stumbled, but Tate caught her, pulling her to his side, his furious eyes glaring down at her in disgust.

"Get Logan and Holly, Dustin. We're leaving." Tate jerked her toward the patio doors as Dustin and Greer followed.

Rachel started crying, humiliated. Mrs. Langley and half the town had gathered to cut the cake and were now staring at her as her brothers dragged her from the party. They had all heard what Cash had said, and Rachel could read their filthy thoughts as Tate pushed her inside the house where Holly and Logan were inside the kitchen.

"We're leaving," Dustin said, picking Logan up in his arms.

"But we have to help clean up," Holly protested.

"She has plenty of help. Let's go." Tate's harsh expression had Holly hastily closing her mouth.

She didn't say another word, following closely behind the angry group. Rachel tried to break away, but Tate picked her up, tossing her in his truck.

"Greer, bring her car," Tate ordered.

"Where are your keys?" Tate asked her, getting in the truck behind the wheel.

Rachel just wanted to go home. She reached into the pocket of her dress then, angrily rolling the window down, she threw the keys at Greer. As soon as the keys were in Greer's hands, Tate pulled out of the driveway. Rachel expected angry yells all the way home; instead, the freezing silence had her shivering.

As soon as he pulled in front of the house, she jumped out, but she had to stop at the door, realizing her house key was on the key ring she had given Greer.

Tate opened the door and Rachel ran inside, determined to go to her room.

"Is it true?" His harsh voice broke her heart. He had sometimes been stern with her since their parents' deaths, but he had never before used that tone of voice with her.

Rachel stopped, turning back to her brother. The expression on his face froze her in place.

"Yes," she whispered.

"Did he rape you?"

"No." Rachel's back stiffened as she admitted the truth. "I wanted him, Tate."

"Just like the rest of his bitches. Mom and Dad would be ashamed at what happened tonight. You've shamed our whole family. You could have done anyone in town, but you had to do him, knowing how bad we hate him and his family!" Disgust was written plainly on his face.

"I didn't mean for it to happen."

"You said he didn't rape you; that means you could have said no, Rachel. Go to your room and get out of my face." The door opened and Greer, Holly, and Dustin entered, carrying Logan.

Rachel blinked back hurt tears. "Tate—"

"Now, Rachel. So help me God, I can't look at you right now," he growled through gritted teeth. Greer's and Dustin's expressions weren't any more forgiving; their faces were just as condemning.

Rachel turned away to her room.

"Maybe she should go stay with The Last Riders since

they've had her now." Greer threw her car keys against her bedroom door.

Rachel bent to pick them up before going into her bedroom and closing the door. She didn't bother to turn on the light as she went to sit on the side of the bed.

Burying her face in her hands, she let her humiliation free. Silent sobs shook her shoulders as she heard her brothers' angry voices from the other side of the door.

Not only her brothers, but the whole town would know by morning she had given herself to Cash. Everywhere she went, she would be met with the same stares. Her reputation in town was ruined; the townspeople would gossip about her for the next year.

Rachel sat quietly until the house finally settled down. She then silently got to her feet. Kneeling beside her bed, she pulled out her suitcase. It was time she executed the decision she had been putting off. She loved her home and her brothers, but it was past time she stood on her own two feet.

She moved around her room, making sure she made no noise. If they caught her packing, they would lock her in. She chose the few items she didn't want to leave behind. Surprisingly, it didn't take long to pack her lifetime into one suitcase.

Rachel waited another hour to make sure everyone was asleep before she sneaked out of the house. Her hand was shaking as she put the keys in the ignition. Turning on her car without using her headlights, she then drove out of the parking lot, heading down the mountain. She only turned the beams on after the car was away from the house.

She had been trying to gain more freedom from her brothers, but she hadn't really wanted to leave; she loved Treepoint and the mountains. It was like her heart was being ripped out the farther she drove away from home. She had never realized her freedom would come at the cost of losing her family.

\* \* \*

"What have you done?" Winter asked, her stricken gaze watching Rachel and her brothers leave.

Cash ran his hand through his hair. "I lost my temper," he admitted, remorse making his voice come out thick. Clearing his throat, he saw the angry glares of all the women. "I know I fucked up."

"You more than fucked up," Beth said, stepping forward, her voice low and controlled. "You humiliated her in front of the church congregation. The whole town will be gossiping about her, and they won't be kind. You of all people know what kind of damage you just did.

"Now, this is Mrs. Langley's party, and I suggest we get through the next thirty minutes until we can leave." Beth stormed away with the rest of the women following her.

Cash was angry at himself for losing his temper and running his mouth. When Tate had jerked Rachel's arm, Viper had been forced to hold him back, or he would have beaten the shit out of him. Her brothers had confirmed tonight what he already had been saying to himself.

Any relationship between Rachel and him was impossible because of her brothers' hatred of him. He had tried to protect her from him; instead, he had let them goad him into losing his temper.

It was a good thing he had forced himself to stay away from her. From their reactions, it couldn't have been worse if they had discovered she had murdered someone.

Cash ignored the sinking feeling in his gut that he had hurt the very woman he had tried to protect, choosing to believe it would all blow over in a week or two.

# CHAPTER TEN

"Can you hand me the wrench?" Rider asked.

Cash took the device out of the toolbox, handing it to Rider and watching as he tuned up his older than dirt truck. He had shit to do, but he was forcing himself to stay at the clubhouse to avoid inadvertently running into Rachel. He wanted to give her time before she had to face him again. He refused to admit he wasn't anxious to face her after his asinine behavior. He had stayed in all weekend and would give it a couple more days before gradually returning to his routine.

With any other woman, he would have been able to go by her house and privately apologize, yet that wasn't going to happen when she lived with her brothers. They would shoot him if he stepped a foot on their property.

As a car pulled into the lot, Cash looked up to see Lily was back from working at the church store. Cash straightened; neither Lily nor Beth had talked to him all weekend.

Lily got out of her car with a worried frown on her face then shut her car door and walked toward the steps in a rush. When she saw Rider and him, she tightened her lips, ignoring them.

He was going to have to bite the bullet and face her to get the answers he wanted.

"Lily, can I talk to you a minute?"

"I'm in a hurry. I need to talk to Shade."

"He's in the factory," Cash informed her.

At first, he thought she wanted to avoid talking to him, but his discerning gaze could tell she was upset.

After she nodded toward him, going inside the factory, he and Rider shared a glance. Then, without a word, they followed Lily inside. The workers had all left for the day and Shade was in his office, finishing up the day's paperwork. Lily had left his office door open; therefore, Cash quietly shut the factory door so she wouldn't notice their entry. Shade saw them, but Lily's back was to the doorway. Cash unashamedly listened, his jaw tightening when he heard her words.

"You have to find her, Shade!"

"Lily, calm down and start over. What happened?"

Lily took a deep breath, her body shaking. "Pastor Patterson came to the store this morning and told me Rachel had called to tell him she wouldn't be volunteering anymore. I was concerned because I knew Rachel would have a hard time facing everyone, but I thought she would just take a couple of weeks off! I didn't realize until Tate came into the store, looking for Rachel, that no one has seen her since Friday night."

"You said Pastor Patterson told you he had talked to her?" Shade asked.

Lily nodded.

"Then we know she's okay if someone has heard from her." His reasoning calmed his wife.

"Okay."

"What did Tate tell you?"

"He said she was gone the next morning when they woke up. She left them a note, but he didn't tell me what it said. He's worried sick, though. He was going to see Knox when he left the store."

"I'll call and talk to Knox to see if he's found anything out."

"Thank you. I'm so worried about her, Shade. I saw her face, and she was so humiliated. She didn't deserve Cash and her brothers treating her that way. She helps everyone. She gives her skills and usually doesn't even charge people.

"Mary Owen's little girl had something wrong with her stomach and couldn't even hold food down. Rachel gave her a supplement, and she's gained five pounds. Mrs. Willis had the shingles, and when Rachel made a cream for her, she was able to go back to work. Rachel helped me, too, Shade. I don't know what would have happened if she hadn't pulled me out of that nightmare."

Shade got up from behind his desk, taking her into his arms. "Don't worry Lily, I'll find her, but be prepared she may not want to come back to Treepoint."

"You made me come back," Lily argued.

"There's a difference between you and Rachel. You belong to me."

"I didn't then."

"You did. You just didn't know it." Shade smiled down at his wife. "Now, go feed my baby, and I'll call Knox."

"All right." Lily turned, coming to a stop when she saw Cash and Rider. Throwing them an angry glare, she moved between them, leaving the factory.

Shade picked up his phone as soon as she was out the door while both Rider and Cash entered the office.

"Knox, Lily told me Rachel's disappeared. What do you know?" It took several minutes before he disconnected the phone.

"Knox said Rachel left a note that said she was going away and not to look for her. She told them she was sorry for shaming them."

"I'll kill them." Cash turned to find the doorway blocked by Rider.

"Sit down, Cash." Shade's harsh voice had him turning back.

"Don't tell me what the fuck to do. Do you know how badly they must have treated her for her to run off?"

"And that surprises you? You knew Friday night when she left with them what she was facing. I didn't see you running to her defense then."

Cash picked up a chair and threw it against the wall. "*Sit down!*"

Cash forced himself to take a seat.

"How do you want to handle this?" Shade, as always, was a calm bastard.

"I'm going to find her, of course," Cash stated angrily.

"I'm not the enemy, brother."

Cash stood to his feet. "I know," he said running a hand through his hair. "I'm a fucking idiot."

"Piece of advice. Take it or leave it, but I'm going to give it anyway. Figure out why you want to find her before you go looking."

He nodded then left Shade's office, going to the clubhouse and heading upstairs to his bedroom. Taking off his clothes, he took a shower, dressed in fresh clothes then grabbed his bike keys. Once he was back outside and on his bike, he began his search.

It was two in the morning before he returned to his room, no farther along than he had been before he left.

* * *

Cash searched for a week before he had to admit to himself he wasn't going to find her. She hadn't made any contact with any of her friends or the few clients he knew of in Kentucky. Furthermore, he'd found out from Knox she hadn't been in touch with her family or clients from out of state.

On the way back to the clubhouse from Lexington, he had a faint hope she would go to Lily's old boyfriend, Charles, for a place to work, but it was another dead end.

He was about to pass Rosie's when he saw a familiar truck parked outside. Quickly turning into the lot, he parked his bike.

The inside was busy as Cash went to the bar, ordering himself a beer. He searched through the room, looking for a particular face. Finding him at the back of the bar at a table to himself, Cash walked across the floor and took a seat.

Tate glanced up from his drink. "Get the fuck away from me."

"We can talk in here or outside, but we are going to talk."

Tate began to rise from the table.

Cash leaned back in his chair. "You having any luck finding Rachel?" Cash already knew the answer; his haggard face said it all.

Tate sat back down "No, if you know—"

"I don't," Cash cut him off; the last thing he wanted to do was raise his hopes when he didn't have any leads.

"Then we have nothing to say." Again, Tate started to get up from the table.

"We can both keep running around, trying to find her and not coming up with crap, or we can work together to bring her home."

"It's because of you she ran off."

"Was it me or something you said after you dumb-fucks left the party?"

Tate remained silent.

"We all fucked up," Cash admitted. "We can work together or never see her again, which do you want?"

"I want you to stay away from my sister, but I also want to find her, and if it takes your help, then I'll take it. You're the best tracker in the state," Tate gave him the reluctant compliment.

"Where have you searched so far?"

"Everywhere we can think off. Holly has called all her clients in and out of state. We've talked to all her friends, who weren't many—Lily and Willa were basically it. Dustin is watching her bank and credit cards, and they haven't been touched."

How was she surviving without money? Cash had hoped for another avenue to pursue with Tate's help, but he had even less than Cash.

"Any ideas?"

"No." Cash took a drink of his beer. "Email me the client list. I'll go back over it again."

Tate hesitated then nodded.

"If I find anything, I'll let you know." He stood up.

"Cash, when I find my sister, I plan to settle my score with you."

Cash's lips quirked. "I'm surprised you haven't been knocking down my door already."

"Right now, Rachel is more important, and I can't find her when I'm locked up in jail for killing you," Tate warned.

"I deserve an ass-whipping for opening my big mouth at that party, but anything else is between Rachel and me."

"There is nothing and won't ever be anything between you and my sister. I had to watch your father sniff around my mother my whole life, and I'm not going to repeat it with you and my sister.

"I saw how she watched you when she thought no one was looking. Every time your dad would come visiting and bring you, she would sneak and look out the window. I used to tan her hide after they died to get her to quit sneaking off; searching the mountains because she was convinced you were hiding out there. She cried for three days when she found out you fucked her best friend from high school, and she never talked to her again.

"If you want to help find Rachel to alleviate your conscience, you go right ahead. I'd bargain with the devil to get Rachel back, but don't think I'm going to let her become another one of your whores."

Cash jerked Tate up from the table. "Don't ever use the word 'whore' and her name in the same sentence again." Cash had never wanted to hit someone so badly in his entire life.

Choosing to shrug it off, he threw Tate back down onto his chair.

"Send me that list." He reached into his jean pocket, pulling out a card and throwing it down on the table. "My email is on the card."

He slammed out of the bar, his boots crunching on the gravel as he got on his bike, pulling out of the parking lot.

Whenever he had been around Rachel, she had never shown by even a blink of her eye that she was interested in him, while he had basically ignored her existence and fucked his way through the town of women. Regret filled him at the wasted opportunity to get to know the woman he was beginning to learn had been a hidden pearl in their town, from not only Lily's words to Shade, but the other people he had talked to. She had slipped beneath his notice, and now he might not be given a chance to make amends and learn more about the special woman he had fought so hard being attracted to.

He sped his bike home, wanting to get a few hours' sleep before he tackled the list of clients Tate would be sending. He turned the corner at the same time another car was coming from the opposite side of the road. As the car took the curve, Cash had only a moment to realize it was going to hit him.

Trying to get over as much as possible without hitting the gravel on the side of the road, he gunned his motor, attempting to gain enough speed so the car would miss him. He almost made it.

The car hit his back wheel, spinning his bike out. Agony crashed through his body as he hit the pavement, then numbness took over. He didn't feel his spine twist or see the mangled bike that lay only a few feet away. He tried to turn his head when he heard yells, but he could only lie helplessly, staring at the dark sky above.

# CHAPTER ELEVEN

Rachel's hand gripped the bottom rail of the hospital bed as she swallowed hard, trying to catch her breath at the sight of the mangled man lying unconscious.

"Rachel?" She turned at the soft voice from the doorway. "Time's up."

Rachel walked to the doorway. "Thanks for sneaking me in, Tara."

"Everyone is worried about you. You should call your brothers." Her sympathetic voice didn't stir any of Rachel's emotions.

"I don't want to see them; I don't want to see anyone. You promised you wouldn't say anything. You owe me for your little brother. I just wanted to see him."

Tara winced at her words. "Rachel, I appreciate all your help with Toby—it was worth more than sneaking you into a hospital room for five minutes—but I'm concerned about you."

"Don't be." Rachel started to reach out to touch her but pulled her hand back before making contact. "I better go."

"If you give me your number, I'll call you if there is a change."

Rachel told her the number of her new phone with a request. "Please, don't give it to anyone."

"I won't. I'll only call if there's a change," Tara promised.

Rachel took a final look at Cash hooked to the machines. She had attempted to help him, but his injuries were worse than any she had ever dealt with before.

"I better go. His friends will be showing up for the regular visiting hours."

"You can go back out the way you came in—through the employees' entrance."

"Thanks, Tara."

She left unobtrusively. The ICU was small and Tara was the only one on duty; the other nurse was on her thirty-minute break.

Rachel went directly to her car. Before she left Treepoint, she had another stop to make.

Driving aimlessly around town, she finally turned to head up the mountain as the sun rose in the sky. It was just starting to get cold in the mornings, thus she flipped on the heat as she drove over the mountain. Her hands tightened on the cold steering wheel when she passed where Cash had wrecked his bike.

She drove on for another three miles before turning into a private drive. Parking her car, she stepped out, getting her jacket out of the back seat and the wrapped flowers. She made the trek up the path that was kept cleared for those visiting the private cemetery.

The small graveyard held Cash's family that had been born and died in the county since the town had been formed. She passed Knox's first wife's grave and paused long enough to say a small prayer for the young woman who had died overseas. Taking one of the flowers out of her mother's bundle, she lay it down on Sunshine's before moving on to her parents' graves.

"Hi, Mom and Dad." Rachel laid the flowers down on her mother's grave. She stood, looking down at the grass-covered mounds, missing her parents as much as when they had been buried. She stood there a while, knowing it would be some time before she came back.

She wanted her mother so much. She could still remember the smell of her perfume, how soft her hair was, and the feel of her arms holding her close. She hadn't been held since the day her mom had died.

Saying a prayer, she turned from her grave and spotted Cash's father's grave on the opposite side of her mother's. They had been best friends until their deaths. Joe Adams had been over at their house constantly, sometimes even bringing Cash. It was only when she had gotten older and had accidently heard her brothers talking that she had discovered Joe had been in love with her mother.

The path was steep, so going down she had to watch her feet to keep from falling. When she got to the bottom of the hill, she looked up and came to a stop.

"Hi, Rachel."

"Shade." He was leaning against the door of her car with his arms folded across his chest. "What are you doing out here?"

He gave her a mocking smile. "Knox told me you used to come here every weekend. I knew, eventually, you would come by for a visit, so I had the place watched. Old habits die hard."

"Evidently. What do you want?" Rachel knew he wouldn't let her leave until he told her what he wanted.

"I want you to fix Cash." Shade's determined face showed he was serious.

Her mouth dropped open. "I'm not capable of fixing him, Shade. I don't have super powers." She brushed a tendril of hair away from her cheek. "Besides, I already tried."

"Then try again."

"It's not that simple." Rachel didn't know how to explain what she did; she never could. To her, it was simply a part of her, like breathing or blinking. It had always been there when she needed it, but fixing Cash would take more power than she possessed.

"You're just going to leave him lying in that bed without trying?"

"I tried! What don't you understand?"

Shade straightened away from the car. "Rachel, do you feel any better since you left town?"

"No," she admitted.

"Then, if you're going to feel like shit, why not stay in town near Cash? Even if you can help him deal with the pain, then wouldn't it be worth it?"

"I don't owe Cash any favors," she responded stubbornly.

"Don't act like you don't care or you wouldn't have come back to town. No one says you have to move back into your brothers' house."

"Where would I stay?"

"You could stay with Cash's grandmother. No one goes near that old bitch's house."

A slight smile touched her lips. "She's not that bad."

"Yes, she is. Well?"

"All right." Rachel caved in to doing what she wanted to do anyway. Shade had merely made it easier to accept.

"Good. She's expecting you." Rachel rolled her eyes; she hadn't stood a chance against Shade. "I owe you, Rachel."

"That's the same thing you said when you asked me to go to work in the church store to help Lily. I would have helped Lily regardless, but it would have been nice if you would have broken up that fight before Cash opened his big mouth."

Shade climbed on his bike, turning on the motor. "I paid you back when I helped Viper hold Cash back when Tate dragged you away. If he had gotten near Tate, he would have killed him. Welcome back, Rachel."

Rachel watched as he drove away.

"Asshole."

\* \* \*

Rachel sat curled on the chair beside Cash's bed, twisting her hands. The pallor of his normally tanned skin was white, and he was covered in so many abrasions that more of his skin had marks than didn't. He had received spinal and head injuries, but the coma he was in was medically-induced. Rachel was relieved he wasn't experiencing any pain.

When one of The Last Riders came to visit, she would go into the waiting room until they left. She didn't speak to any of his visitors, pretending to read magazines to avoid conversations of why she was there. Cash had no family other than his grandmother, and she had been by several times to visit him in the hospital.

Rachel had moved in with her temporarily. She spent most of her time at the hospital, though, only going to Mag's cabin when she needed to sleep or shower.

Rachel had met her several times before her stroke, and her personality hadn't dimmed since her illness. If anything, she had become even more gregarious.

As the nurse came in to check Cash's machines, Rachel ignored her curious looks, going to stare out the window as his bandages were changed.

After she left, Rachel returned to sitting by the bed. Even unconscious, his virility and masculinity managed to capture you. Her hand reached out to touch his cheek, but hearing a movement at the door, she snatched her hand back to her side.

Dean stood in the doorway.

Rachel looked away, unable to meet his eyes. Stepping away from the bed again, she started to leave the room.

"Stay."

She stopped mid-flight and gave a sharp nod, going to the window.

Rachel heard Dean take a seat by Cash's bed, taking Cash's hand in his own. Rachel watched as Dean spent the next ten minutes talking to Cash as if he could hear what he was saying. It brought a lump to her throat to see a glimpse of the man who had been her pastor for years and whose guidance she had always respected.

Dean bent his head, saying a brief prayer before rising to his feet and coming to stand next to her at the window.

"The nurse tells me there hasn't been any change."

"No."

"Rachel, I may not be your pastor anymore, but I would like to think we're still friends. I'm always here for you to talk to."

"I don't need to talk, and if I did, it wouldn't be with someone who is friends with him." Rachel gave him her back.

"If you're so angry at him, why are you here?"

"I don't know." She shrugged. "Shade thinks I may be able to help him."

"Can you?" Dean leaned casually against the window, blocking her view and forcing her to look him in the eye.

"No. My gift isn't like that. I don't heal; I can't fix what's broken," Rachel tried to explain. She blew out a breath of air. "I'm more of an emotional empath. I can give off warmth and sense things that are out of place. I can transfer my feelings to others, but I am not a healer."

"I don't think Lily would agree with you."

"I didn't heal Lily; Shade did." Rachel believed in giving credit where it was due. Without Shade giving Lily a sense of being protected, she would never have healed or been able to face her demons.

"I see. Have you tried?"

Rachel nodded. "I told you, it's useless. Everyone thinks I'm not helping him because I'm mad at him, though."

"I'm not saying Cash doesn't deserve your anger, merely that your gift comes from love, and hate always stands in the way of love." When Rachel rolled her eyes at his trite words, Dean laughed. "I know it sounds idealistic, but I believe it. Just because I'm no longer a minister, it doesn't mean I don't have faith."

She knew he might be right. Whenever she had felt the warmth in her hands, it had come when she was thinking of how much she wanted to help the person and cared for their happiness.

"I'm not capable of helping him."

"I get pretty mad at Cash sometimes. I wasn't at the party, and he pissed me off."

Rachel blushed.

"The hardest battle I fought as a minister was everyone's view of sex. I don't believe because a woman enjoys her sexuality that makes her a whore. Small towns tend to be judgmental."

"Yes, they do," Rachel agreed.

"Rachel, I don't doubt you're hurt, angry, and embarrassed to have something that was special to you thrown out at a party to humiliate your brothers. You're in love with him, aren't you?"

Rachel looked quickly over her shoulder at Cash, as if he could hear them while in a coma. "I was. I don't even like him now, though," she confessed.

Dean nodded. "If it's any consolation, he felt terrible about what happened. He was trying to find you when he wrecked."

Rachel closed her eyes tightly, not wanting to feel any emotion toward Cash.

"I'm not trying to get you to forgive him. This is about you, Rachel. You are a very giving and kind person who has helped every person in this town at one time or another, yet you didn't give any of us a chance to stand beside you when you needed us. You ran."

"I was so angry at my brothers and Cash. I didn't want to be near them."

"If you keep letting them control you, they will. Learn to stand up for yourself."

"That's easier said than done," Rachel replied.

"I'm willing to bet they're more willing to compromise

since you left. I've seen Tate, and he's in bad shape. Dustin and Greer aren't much better."

Rachel blinked back tears. Her brothers might be idiots, but she missed them. "I'll call them."

Dean's hand squeezed her arm. Standing up straight, he then gave her the smile she had seen on so many Sunday afternoons.

"I've missed having you to talk to. Do you miss the church at all?"

An indiscernible look crossed his face. "I miss talking with and helping the people I grew close to while I was undercover, but getting up early every Sunday? No."

Rachel laughed at his attempted joke.

"If you need to talk, I'm just a phone call away," Dean offered.

"I am, too," Rachel returned the offer as he left then stood, staring sightlessly at Cash on the bed.

Gingerly reaching out her hand, she touched his foot and attempted again to connect with something in him. Nothing.

She sat back down on the chair, waiting.

# CHAPTER TWELVE

Rachel was crossing the parking lot to her car when she saw her brothers walking toward her. She thought about going back inside the ICU where they couldn't go—Shade had put them on the 'do not admit' list to provide her with a safe zone from them—instead, she stopped and waited for their approach.

She refused to feel guilty when she saw how worried they were. Tate's face was haggard, and he had aged at least ten years in a matter of weeks. She braced herself for their harsh words, but was ill-prepared when Tate didn't hesitate to jerk her into his arms, holding her close. When he finally released her, she was enfolded in Greer's then Dustin's embrace.

"I'm going to give you an old-fashioned butt whippin' for scaring the shit out of me, Rach," Tate threatened.

She didn't get angry; she could tell he had taken her disappearance hard.

"I'm not sorry I left, Tate. You needed to cool down. You don't have the right to talk to me that way. And Greer, your behavior humiliated me in front of my friends, and it's not the first time. You need to get your act together. Dustin, you're a father now; you're too old to be picking fights and should be setting an example for your son. You're letting Holly raise your child and set all the limits. Is that how you want to raise Logan? Tate, you told me that Mom and Dad would be ashamed by my behavior, but I don't think my behavior is the one who would be shaming them.

"Not a one of you have tried to do anything but sell weed. Is that the legacy we're going to leave Logan; another generation running from the law, living on the outskirts of society? Until you three get your act together, I don't want to talk to you."

She left her three brothers standing there with their mouths open.

\* \* \*

"We decreased his medication so he's in more of a deep sleep versus a coma."

Rachel stood behind the large group of bikers as they listened to Cash's doctor explain his condition.

"His spinal injury is quite severe, and we're going to begin to wean him off the ventilator." The doctor paused. "I do not anticipate him walking again."

At his proclamation, several of the women began crying. Viper put his arms around Winter, Knox pulled Diamond closer, and Evie turned to King. Everyone there stood stupefied at the doctor's prognosis that the consequences of the wreck would be life-changing for Cash.

The Last Riders began making plans as soon as the doctor left.

"We can put him downstairs. It's accessible with a wheelchair and has the exercise equipment and hot tub," Viper stated.

"I'll call Donna as soon as he's out of the rehab center," Winter said.

Cash was loved by this group of people who he had made his family.

Lily and Beth both came to stand by her side after the

others had left.

"Don't you ever do that to me again." Lily's tearful voice brought a sheen to her own eyes. "You could have at least called me."

"I'm sorry, Lily."

Lily's bright smile appeared, and Rachel was grabbed in a tight hug before she was released and grabbed by Beth.

"Rachel, I understand how you felt. Do you remember how Georgia called me names on Christmas Eve? The men were the ones who made fools of themselves; no one thought badly of you." Lily's words struck home.

"I was just so embarrassed. Then I was angry and wanted to get away."

"I know how you feel. Sometimes, you need to take a step back and let yourself heal before you can face things," Lily said, squeezing her hand. "Next time, please don't go off without telling anyone where you are, though."

"I won't," Rachel promised.

"How are the babies?" she asked Beth, changing the subject.

"Growing big." Beth laughed, showing her pictures on her phone. The twin boys looked just like their father. The chubby babies were both wearing baby Harley t-shirts in the picture.

"Let's go get some lunch in the cafeteria before you come back," Beth said, sliding her arm through hers. Lily slid her arm through the other as they made their way through the hospital.

They sat and talked for over an hour, and it was the most normal she had felt since the party. Then Rachel returned to Cash's room.

She had grown used to the nurses' curious stares, but Shade had gotten the doctor's permission for her to stay in the room with him.

Two days later, the prognosis was looking even grimmer.

Cash was free of the coma-inducing drugs, but he had

yet to wake. Their efforts to wean him from the ventilator had led to two serious crises that Rachel had been afraid he wouldn't pull out of. The latest attempt had been the worst.

The doctor straightened, tired and worn after stabilizing Cash. "You should call his friends and grandmother in to see him. He won't survive if he crashes again."

Rachel could only nod as the doctor and nurses left. She walked closer to his bed, looking down at the man she had loved most of her life, and knew she was going to lose him.

Deep in her heart, she knew why her powers hadn't worked. Lying in this bed for this last week, he had been hers. This was the only way she would ever have Cash—when he was unable to physically leave her. It was sick and twisted, but she had lied to herself each day. If she wasn't honest with herself, she was going to lose him forever.

Rachel shut the door and pulled the curtain across the glass to the observation room before going back beside his bed. Ever since the doctor had told her Cash was no longer in a coma, she had felt his consciousness stirring.

She drew her focus into her hands the way she had been taught by her grandmother. Her gift would be at its full strength since she deliberately hadn't used it, unconsciously building it for this moment.

Relaxing, she touched Cash, letting her mind forget the last time she had seen him, going back to when she was a young girl and had come across him in the woods.

He had been having a picnic with one of the cheerleaders from school, and they had been lying on the blanket sleeping. His hair had glinted in the early morning sun, and she had thought he looked like a male angel. She had stared at him several minutes then run off when he woke, staring at her. They had never mentioned the incident, both pretending it had never happened.

She touched his shoulders, running her hands down his

arms. Moving to his feet, she ran her hands up his legs then touched his waist and chest. She let her energy flow from her fingertips into his body. Gracefully, she slid her hand under his neck and carefully glided her hand under his back, letting her hand rest for several minutes where he was injured the worst before coming to a rest on his lungs.

Praying for her grandmother's and mother's help, she gave what she could, infusing healthy energy into the damaged organs. She made herself stop briefly only because she was covered in sweat and trembling, feeling like she was going to throw up. She took a seat, making herself drink several glasses of water while she regrouped.

She had never worked on anyone this injured, heeding her grandmother's warning that the energy required to heal someone of a critical injury could only come from one source. Rachel prayed for His help as she once again went to Cash, this time placing her fingertips against his temple.

\* \* \*

Cash lay in the darkness, comfortable in the warmth surrounding him. He had tried to get to his feet in the darkness, but every time he tried, the agony overwhelmed him. The darkness wasn't so bad, though; it was a hell of a lot better than the pain.

Somewhere in the void, Cash heard her voice first. She was calling his name.

"Rachel?"

"Cash!" He felt her take his hand in hers.

"What are you doing here? Where am I?"

She didn't answer him, beginning to pull his hands, wanting him to get to his feet.

"Come on, Cash, you have to leave. You can't stay here." She tugged at his hands harder.

Cash attempted to get to his feet, but the sharp pain in his back hurt, forcing him back down.

"Wait. Rachel, it hurts like hell."

"It's going to hurt a lot worse if you don't get up!" Giving in, Cash used what strength he had to get to his feet with her help. As she braced him with her weight, Cash was able to stand—barely—with her support.

"You have to do this, Cash. I can't hold you much longer. Move!"

Cash placed one foot in front of the other, taking one step after another.

"Where are we going?"

"You're going back to the life you've left behind, Cash. All your friends are waiting for you." Rachel kept him walking inexorably forward. "See the sun, Cash? Keep moving in that direction."

With each step, it became easier to walk, but he didn't take his weight away from Rachel, not wanting her to run away again. Suddenly, he felt a threshold, an invisible line he knew he had to cross.

"Hurry, Cash. I can't hold you much longer," she pleaded.

"Are you going to run away again if I go through?"

She remained silent.

"Promise me you'll stay."

"Go, Cash!" Her scream hurt his head, but he refused to let her go. He looked down at her face and realized he was hurting her. Straightening up, he took his weight off her, releasing her. She began to waver and dissipate before his eyes.

"Rachel!"

"Go, Cash. You don't need me anymore." Her sad eyes weren't something he would ever forget.

Cash frantically looked around for her, but she was gone; she had run away from him again. Cash took another step toward the light, hoping she would be on the other side.

He opened his eyes, blinking as he attempted to focus his eyes in the bright room. Carefully, he looked around the blindingly white room. It held no trace that she had ever been there, but Cash knew she had. He still felt the tingles of energy on his skin, and the feel of her palm placed directly over his heart.

# CHAPTER THIRTEEN

"He's coming home today." Rachel didn't look up from watering her plants at Mag's voice.

"That's good." She moved on to the next set of plants, carefully tending the buds just breaking the soil.

"He's walking."

"I'm glad."

"You going to go see him?" Cash's grandmother wasn't going to be ignored.

Rachel put down the watering can. "No. I'm sure he'll have a big enough welcoming committee without me there."

The old woman gave her a harassed look. "You go from spending every day with him when he's in the ICU to not seeing him at all for four months. Why?"

"I only stayed with him while he needed my help. He didn't need me after they moved him to rehab."

"Girl, he needs you. He has for a long time."

Rachel laughed. "Cash doesn't need or want me. I'm just another woman in town who made a fool of herself over him. He's fine now; he's walking. Shade told you the doctors are amazed at his recovery."

"Thanks to you."

Rachel shook her head. "I didn't do anything. The only thing I did was nudge him awake. Cash worked his ass off in physical therapy. He refused to come back to the clubhouse because he didn't want the others to have to help him the way they did Winter. He's done it all on his own."

Mag turned her wheelchair around in a sharp turn. "You're still being pissy because you're mad at him. I went through the same thing with his father; he always had some woman pissed off at him. Cash is just like his father, Rachel."

"I know," she responded, making the old woman suddenly start laughing.

"I'm going to go cook some breakfast. You want anything?"

"No, thanks. If I don't stop eating your breakfasts, I'll be the one in the hospital with a coronary."

"A fried egg never killed anyone."

"It does when you add a half a pack of bacon, biscuits, and gravy. You use enough lard to sink a boat."

"A good breakfast keeps you going all day," she argued.

"Your breakfast will put me in the ER by nine," Rachel told her as Mag wheeled herself out of the sunroom.

Rachel could only shake her head at the woman who refused to listen to the diet restrictions her doctor had given her. How the woman had lived to be eighty-eight, eating the way she did, was a miracle. Rachel understood the woman loved to cook, but there were healthier versions she could fix besides the cholesterol-loaded food she was determined to get Rachel to eat. If her ass got any bigger, she was going to have to buy Cash's grandmother new chairs.

The smell of frying bacon teased her nostrils. Rachel was determined to ignore the tantalizing aroma as she continued to work, though. She heard a knock on the door and Cash's grandmother's voice as she answered it.

Her next-door neighbor came over every morning to

check on her and drink a cup of coffee. Sometimes her son, Jason, would come and check, making sure she didn't need any work done around the house. Mag told her he used to come over once a week, but now it was almost daily. Rachel was glad she had resisted the lure of breakfast; it would keep her from being trapped in his presence for the next hour.

When the door opened and closed again, Rachel decided to grab a piece of fruit on her way into town to work at the church store.

Going through the house, she stopped at the bathroom to get washed and dressed for work, sliding on a dark navy skirt with a pretty, rose-colored sweater.

Deciding she needed caffeine to face Brooke first thing in the morning, she stopped by the kitchen on the way out the door.

She came to an abrupt stop in the doorway when she saw the room filled with The Last Riders. The small table was filled with them eating the coronary-inducing breakfast she had denied herself. She tried to edge out of the room before anyone saw her.

"Rachel, come on in and fix yourself a plate." The darn woman had the entire room's attention on her as she stood in the doorway.

Refusing to make a fool of herself in front of them, she walked farther into the room, going to the coffee pot to pour herself a cup of coffee.

"You going to eat?" Mag demanded.

"Don't have time. I don't want to be late opening the store." Forcing herself to face the man staring her down, she said, "It's good to see you out of the hospital, Cash."

"Thanks, Rachel." His voice had lost none of its rough timber. His appearance was a shock, but she couldn't help noticing how well he looked. The only difference was the amount of weight he had lost and the pallor to his skin.

"I better be going; I don't want to keep the customers waiting." Rachel didn't run from the room, exiting calmly without a backward glance. She was proud of the way she had handled seeing him again. She had proven to herself that any feelings she had held for him had died, and she was more than ready to move on with the plans she had for her life.

The door closing behind her was like a chapter closing in her life and a new one starting.

\* \* \*

"That girl is pissed at you."

Cash made a face at his grandmother's remark. He didn't have to be told; the frostbitten glaze had come across in her eyes well enough to tell him that piece of information.

He had been watching the doorway for her and hadn't expected a tearful reunion, but neither had he been expecting the void of emotion that had been present. He had hoped she would show some emotions when she saw him, yet there had been complete indifference as she'd walked in, just like there had been the last four months of his recovery. It seemed as if she hadn't cared if he lived or died in that accident.

Cash stared down into the inky darkness of his coffee. "Yeah, she is, but Rachel isn't the first and certainly won't the last." His friends cast him commiserating looks at his grandmother's barb.

"You were lucky to seduce that girl once; she's not going to be stupid enough to give you a chance to do it twice." Mag smiled at him pitilessly. "That girl is done with you. I've seen that look too many times on women's faces when they finally decided they're done having their hearts stomped on."

Cash straightened in his chair, wincing at the abrupt movement. "I didn't stomp on her heart. I embarrassed her and hurt her feelings."

"You're sitting in my house, lying, Cash. You're lying to yourself if you think that girl would have slept with you and not cared about you. You've been born and raised in these hills, went to the same church as her. She might not have been expecting a ring from you, but she sure as hell didn't expect what she got."

"I lost my temper."

"That ain't no excuse. Her brothers have been pushing your buttons for years."

He had never been able to win in a battle of words with his grandmother. "I'll try to talk to her."

"Good. You want another piece of bacon?"

\* \* \*

Rachel tiredly got into her car after closing the church store. Her cell phone ringing had her searching through her purse until she found it. Her quick glance told her it was Lily calling.

"Hello?"

"Rachel, hi. I'm sorry to bother you, but I was hoping to ask a favor."

"What's up?"

"I can't find my set of keys to open the store in the morning. I've searched everywhere. I was hoping if I offered you dinner you would run your set out. I could get another set made in the morning before I went into work."

"No problem. I'll be there in ten minutes."

"Thanks." Lily disconnected the call.

Rachel wasn't anxious to go to Lily's house, but at least it was behind the clubhouse and she could avoid Cash as she had the last month. Whenever he had stopped by to see Mag, she'd made an excuse to leave or went to her room.

Several times, he had attempted to talk to her, but she would cut him short, ignoring all his attempts to put the past behind them. She didn't want to forget; remembering what an ass he was kept her from falling for him again.

Ten minutes later, she parked her car in The Last Riders' parking lot.

Going up the sidewalk that led behind the clubhouse, she managed to avoid the members on the trek to Lily's house.

Lily opened the door before she could knock.

"I appreciate you going out of your way."

"I didn't mind. It was no trouble." Lily opened the door wider for Rachel.

From inside the house, she admired what Shade had built for Lily.

"Hungry?" Lily asked, heading toward her kitchen.

"I'm always ready to eat," Rachel joked.

"Good, I have plenty. Shade's working late at the factory. They have a big order to get out. A few of them managed to get finished early and are rubbing it in the others' faces."

The loud music coming from the clubhouse could be heard inside Lily's house.

"Doesn't that noise bother you?" Rachel asked, taking a seat at the table.

"No, I like listening to it." Lily smiled as she placed the chili and cornbread on the table.

Rachel didn't say anything else, feeling Lily's defense of The Last Riders.

They were sitting on the couch, drinking a glass of tea, when Shade came in looking exhausted. His grim face lightened into a smile when Lily got up to give him a kiss that had Rachel catching her breath.

She rose to her feet. "I'd better go. It's almost Mag's bedtime, and I don't want her to lock me out."

"Would she really?" Lily asked in shock.

"No," Rachel laughed. "But she would make me wish she had by the time she quit fussing at me for making her get out of bed." She reached into her pocket and pulled out the keys. "Here you go, I'll stop by the store tomorrow to pick them up."

"All right. Thanks again, Rachel."

"Dinner more than made up for it," Rachel replied, giving her a hug. "Bye, Shade."

He nodded to her while he was making his own bowl

of food.

Rachel smiled, closing the door and going down Lily's steps. It had gotten dark since she had arrived.

As she was passing the backyard of the clubhouse, she heard a woman's moan. Thinking someone had fallen or hurt themselves, she scanned the backyard until she saw a movement in the gazebo. The lights from inside the clubhouse illuminated the couple within, and Rachel easily recognized Cash's tall frame. He had regained most of the weight and muscle tone he had lost since his accident. He seemed to easily hold the woman he had pinned to the side of the gazebo. The woman gave another moan. It was only when her voice impatiently said Cash's name that Rachel recognized her as Bliss.

"Cash, quit teasing me!"

Cash's hand was buried in the opened shorts as Bliss's legs circled his waist.

Rachel stood frozen in place as Cash lowered his head, sucking on a bared breast while she saw Bliss's hands go for his jeans.

"You need something bigger than my finger for that pussy?"

"God, yes!"

Cash's low laugh had Rachel's feet moving again, wishing she had never stopped. The image of them together would be burned forever in her mind. Bliss's pleas and Cash's confidence that he could satisfy the woman took away any doubts of whether they shared a sexual relationship.

Her head lowered, she crashed into a hard chest.

"Oh!" Rachel barely managed to catch herself. If Train hadn't reached out to steady her, she would have fallen.

"What's the rush?"

A small scream had both of their eyes going to the gazebo where Cash's arms were holding Bliss as he thrust into her.

Train's eyes returned to hers. "Come on; I'll walk you

to your car."

Rachel hurriedly followed the path to the parking lot with Train walking casually by her side.

She was about to scramble inside her car when he stopped her.

"You okay to drive home?"

"Of course. Why wouldn't I be?" Rachel shrugged, trying to make light of what she had seen.

"I thought that may have bothered you. I know that you and Cash—"

"Had sex?"

Train hesitantly nodded.

"He doesn't have a problem with getting laid, does he?" Her crudeness made her bite her lip in punishment.

"No, he doesn't."

Rachel flinched at his bluntness.

She didn't think any of The Last Riders had a problem relieving their sexual desires. Train would definitely have no problem finding a woman. His black hair hung down past his neck and was tied back at the nape. His expression was always calm, but Rachel sensed the darkness within him that she had recognized in Shade. He was always the quiet one in the group, yet she felt the undercurrents of his seething sexuality that would be hard for a woman to resist. If she hadn't made an ass of herself a few months ago over Cash, Rachel would have been tempted to find out just what Train was hiding.

"I could give you a ride home on my bike if you're not sure," he offered.

"I'm fine."

"If you're sure." Train reached to her side, brushing her breasts with his arm as he opened the car door. Rachel couldn't hold back the shiver of awareness, hastily climbing in her small car. Train carefully closed her door and then stepped back as she pulled out.

"You going to make a move on her?" Cash asked as he walked out of the shadows.

"Thinking about it. Any reason not to?"

"No. I guess not." Cash started back up the pathway. "Did she see?"

"Yeah."

They walked beside each other in silence until they got to the backdoor.

Train was about to go inside when Cash's voice stopped him.

"Train, I... I…"

"Brother, if you don't want me to touch her, all you have to do is ask."

"I'm asking."

"Cool, I'll leave her to you then."

Cash slung his arm around Train's shoulder, letting him take some of his weight. He had overextended his strength and was tired as shit. Train easily took his weight without saying a word, helping Cash inside and up the stairs to his room.

"Want me to get one of the women for you?"

"Hell, no. You trying to put me back in rehab?" The men laughed.

After Train left, Cash starred at the closed door, still unsure why he had asked Train to back off. It wasn't like he had a shot in hell at Rachel again, but something deep inside him told him that Train wouldn't be a dumb-fuck and screw everything up with Rachel the way he had.

He had heard her voice as he had come inside of Bliss, his dick nearly shriveling in the condom at being seen by her with another woman. He had shoved his dick in his pants and sent Bliss in the house. He had hoped to find Rachel upset, anything to show she cared; instead, he had seen the interest in her eyes for Train. Cash was experienced enough to know what that look on a woman's face meant. His little virgin had been wondering how Train was in bed.

Cash reached over, turning out his bedroom light. He wanted to see that expression on her face when she was staring at him.

* * *

Cash wiped the sweat off his face with the towel Donna handed him.

"You're doing good, Cash. So much better. You don't need me anymore."

Cash lowered the towel in surprise to find her grinning back at him.

"It's true; you don't. You're almost back to full strength. Your workout sessions have really paid off."

Cash threw his towel onto the washer across the room. He had worked out incessantly, attempting to drive Rachel out of his mind. It wasn't working, but his body felt normal again.

"I couldn't have done it without your help."

"I'll call Steve and tell him I'm releasing you." Donna picked up her folder that marked his progress.

"Tell him I said hi." Steve was his physical therapist from the rehab center.

"I will. Of course, he's not going to be happy with me releasing you; he's going to miss Rachel."

Cash stopped stretching, straightening to look at Donna. "Rachel?"

Donna tilted her head quizzically at him. "Yes. She called everyday to check on your progress. Of course, he never gave away any of your medical information, but Shade gave his permission to share your status with her."

"I wasn't aware she called."

Donna nodded, packing her folders into her bag. "I believe she wanted to see if you were progressing. She called several times when you were beginning to walk again."

He had thought she hadn't given a shit, that he hadn't crossed her mind the entire time he had been in therapy. He had been wrong.

Cash hadn't bothered to look at the paperwork Shade had signed for him, trusting his brother implicitly, but there was obviously something he hadn't told him.

He showered and changed before driving to his grandmother's house. Once there, he sat outside several minutes before going in. He had wanted to see her after finding out she had cared enough to keep track of his progress, but he still didn't know how to get past the barricade she had put up against him or why he even wanted to.

He was about to put his truck back in drive when he saw Rachel hand Mag a drink through the front window. The last few months hadn't treated his grandmother well. She looked older and more worn than he had ever seen her.

Rachel bent over and picked up something then moved behind Mag's wheelchair. He realized she was brushing her hair; gently stroking the old woman's hair as they talked.

Not even his mother had been able to get along with Mag. In fact, they had hated each other. Rachel, on the other hand, was developing a close relationship with Mag, and it affected him strangely. He wanted to go in and join them, see what they were talking about. Instead, he drove out of the parking lot, heading back to the clubhouse.

He was concerned over his grandmother's appearance. He needed to spend some time with her and make sure she was fine. Her neighbor was actually paid by him to keep an eye on her and drive her when she wanted to go out, but he would take a few days, assess her health, and see if she needed more care.

Cash refused to acknowledge to himself that it wasn't only his grandmother that he wanted to spend time with. Rachel wouldn't be happy with his presence in the house. However, she would soon realize that he was tired of being ignored.

# CHAPTER FOURTEEN

Rachel was steadily busy during the day. Lily had started taking off one day a week as her pregnancy progressed. Rachel was sure it was to provide her with more hours, even though her friend denied it. She was seven months pregnant, and her beauty had only increased with her pregnancy. Rachel wasn't jealous of her friend's happiness; she more than deserved it from the hell she had survived.

"Are you busy, Rachel?" Brooke's casual question had her rising from the toys she was separating by age.

"No. Is there anything I can help you with?"

"I cleaned out my closet since I bought some new clothes when I went home to Atlanta last month. I also have some bags of clothes that Jeffrey has outgrown. Can you pack them down for me?"

"Of course."

Rachel wondered why she hadn't brought at least one down with her. Although, with the regal attitude Brooke always showed, she shouldn't be surprised. Brooke would have probably thrown the clothes away if not for her husband. She had to know he would ask Rachel or Lily about the clothes.

Rachel followed her through the quiet church into the pastor's house, which was attached to the church by a private hallway. The house had gone through a transformation since Pastor Patterson had taken over for Dean. Rachel, nor any of the congregation, had been invited to Dean's private home, but several times, Rachel had brought food to him and had seen his modest furnishings. Brooke, on the other hand, had decked out the home with expensive furnishings and state-of-the-art electronics. The television alone would have fed two families for two months.

Rachel saw the bags sitting in Brooke's bedroom; it was going to take several trips. Rachel bent and picked two up while Brooke picked up her purse.

"I'm having lunch with Daffney Cole. Just lock the door back to the hallway when you're done."

"All right." Rachel gritted her teeth all the way back to the store.

It took several trips to finish carrying all the bags. By the end, she decided she would go through them tomorrow.

Pastor Patterson came in just as she sat down on a stool to do the day's receipts.

"I see Brooke carried the bags down. I told her I would take care of it, but she never listens. She takes on too much as it is."

Rachel's mouth dropped open at the man's obtuseness toward his wife.

"Are you busy, Rachel?"

She hesitated, dreading packing more bags of clothes. "Not right now. What can I help you with?"

"Brooke has been overworking herself so much lately. I was wondering if you would mind asking your friend Willa if she would bake a cake for Brooke's and my anniversary next month. Every time I ask, Willa doesn't have any openings. Since she's your friend, I was hoping she would be more inclined to make it if you asked."

"I'll give her a call, but I can't make any promises. With King's restaurant having opened, her time is pretty committed."

"That will be fine. Just anything she whips up would be great, but chocolate is her favorite."

"I'll tell her."

His beaming smile made Rachel feel small-minded. She might not personally like Brooke, yet she did like her pastor. He was no Dean; nevertheless, he was a good man.

"Let me know so I can make arrangements if she can't."

"I will."

Rachel got busy. Instead of calling, she decided to stop by Willa's house on the way home. A car was in the driveway when she pulled in. Regretting she hadn't called ahead, Rachel decided to knock anyway.

Willa answered her knock minutes later, right as she had been about to leave.

Her flushed, upset face had Rachel's eyes going over her shoulder to see Lewis.

"I'm sorry to interrupt, Willa, but I wanted to talk to you about a private matter if you have the time."

"Come in, Rachel." Willa's relief was obvious as she opened the door wider for Rachel to enter.

Lewis's expression darkened. "Willa, we were talking—"

"And we're finished talking. I think you should leave." Willa's voice trembled.

"I'll see you later, then." Rachel heard the threat in his voice and saw the shudder Willa couldn't hide.

As soon as the door closed behind him, Rachel turned to Willa. "What was he doing here?"

"He thinks he can bully me into marrying him."

Rachel knew the man had been pestering Willa, but not to that extent.

"Have Knox talk to him, Willa. Don't let him intimidate you."

"I'm not. I told him no. I'm actually proud of myself." The woman couldn't hide her fear.

If she wouldn't talk to Knox, then Rachel would.

"Why did you stop by?"

Rachel told her of Pastor Patterson's request.

"I told him no because Brooke hates my cakes. She tells me so all the time. Give him the bakery in Jamestown's number."

Rachel sighed. "It's an anniversary cake. I think he's planning a surprise party. Her favorite is chocolate."

Willa sighed. "Have him text me the size and how he wants it."

"Okay." Rachel felt guilty for getting her to change her mind, but she knew she would have been the one he asked to drive to Jamestown to pick it up. She was slowly becoming their errand girl.

She stayed and had dinner with Willa, worried Lewis would come back.

She was tired when she finally let herself into Mag's house. Taking a quick shower, she fell into bed exhausted, promising to let herself sleep late in the morning. Lily's day was tomorrow.

Rachel stretched out on the soft mattress, letting her mind go back through her day. She reminded herself to stop by and talk to Knox about Lewis. She didn't trust Lewis around Willa. She underestimated her attractiveness, and he had been one of the worst bullies in town. If Willa couldn't get his ass under control, Rachel would see that someone else did.

# CHAPTER FIFTEEN

Rachel padded barefoot into the kitchen. Yawning, she started the coffee, surprised Mag hadn't already. She pulled a cup from the cabinet.

"Grab one for me." Cash slowly walked into the room.

Rachel screamed, nearly dropping her cup. "What are you doing here?"

"This is my grandmother's house, remember?"

Rachel gritted her teeth at his smartass reply. "I mean, why aren't you at the clubhouse?"

"I've been away from Mag for so long I thought I would stay with her for a few days. I don't know how long I'm going to last on that broken down mattress, though."

Rachel poured her coffee. "I believe it was one of her flea market finds."

Cash grimaced, carefully folding his sore body into a chair at the kitchen table. "Did you forget about mine?"

Stifling the urge to tell him to get it for himself, she got another cup and poured his coffee before setting the cup down in front of him.

She picked her cup up and turned to leave the room.

"You're not going to stay and keep me company?"

"No. Where's Mag?"

"She had a doctor's appointment this morning. Her neighbor took her."

"Oh, she didn't mention it yesterday."

"I guess she forgot."

Rachel left the room, going to the back room of Mag's house that had been given to her to take care of the new clippings she had collected. It didn't have as many windows as the greenhouse at her brothers' house, but it had the advantage of not being at their house.

"Wow, how many plants do you have in here?"

Rachel began watering her plants, rotating from the ones she'd watered yesterday. "Over one hundred twenty-six."

Cash walked farther into the room. "Any weed?" he joked.

"No. If you want that, you'll have to go see Greer."

"No, thanks. He would probably lace it with cyanide," Cash said mockingly.

"No, he wouldn't. He would just lace it with cat shit."

Cash's mouth dropped open. Rachel had to choke back her laughter. She would take a bet The Last Riders would be finding another source for their weed. It would hurt, too, because her brothers might be assholes, but they produced the best-tasting weed in the state.

He reached out a finger to touch a fragile plant. "What's this?"

"Pipewort."

"If you're so interested in plants, how come you didn't go on to college?"

"I did, for two semesters. I didn't like it. I'm taking a few classes online now, though." Rachel didn't tell him how far she had actually progressed with her degree; it wasn't any of his business. She wasn't about to fawn all over him just because he showed a sudden interest in an important part of her life.

She had been gradually moving down the row, watering the plants until she came to him. Rachel looked at his lean body without a shirt, with loose-fitting jeans, and felt absolutely nothing. She lifted her clear eyes, staring him in the face steadily until he moved back, burying his hands in his pockets, so she could continue watering her plants. If he'd thought she was going to see his body and melt in a puddle at his feet, she had just proved him wrong.

She didn't try to make conversation with him, although she did answer his questions with monosyllabic replies.

"Rachel, I want to apologize for the way I acted the night of Mrs. Langley's party."

It took Rachel a second for his apology to set in, then another to get the meaning of what he was saying.

"I'd like us to start over, maybe go to a movie or out to dinner."

She quit watering the plants. "Why?"

Cash cleared his throat. Was he pretending to be unsure of himself? Rachel didn't think Cash had ever felt unsure of himself.

"Why do most people go on dates?"

"I know why most people go on dates, but you don't. You pick the girl up, drive her to one of your spots, have sex with her, and then bring her home. It's the same thing you always do."

"That's not true. I've—" Cash denied.

"Name one woman you've bought a burger for? A steak dinner? You can't, can you?"

Cash's mouth snapped shut.

"I didn't think so. The most you've treated your women to is a picnic lunch Mag packed for you. I don't even know why I called them your women; you've never laid claim to a woman, yet you've taken more than your fair share," she said with a mocking voice.

"You have a really low opinion of me, don't you?" Cash's eyes searched hers.

Rachel gave him her honest answer. "I don't have any opinion of you at all."

He winced at her reply.

Once upon a time, she would have jumped at the thought of dating Cash, thinking she could be the one to change the bad-boy biker. Now, she felt nothing; absolutely nothing.

"I'm not a bad guy."

"No, you're not," Rachel agreed. "You're just not the guy for me."

"How do you know if you don't give me a chance?"

"I don't need to stick my hand in a fire to know it's going to hurt like hell," Rachel replied mockingly.

Cash picked up a tendril of her hair that had escaped her ponytail, pulling it taut. "Sometimes, the best way to fight fire is with fire."

She shivered at the warning in his voice. He was telling her that he couldn't forget them having sex any easier than she could. Her nipples tightened under her t-shirt while she masked her reaction.

"And sometimes, the best thing to do is just pour a bucket of water over it."

\* \* \*

Cash stood, looking down at Rachel, his throat tightening. The young girl who had been in the background of his life for years was gone. Now, in her place, was a beautiful woman who stared at him with revulsion in her eyes. He had fallen off the pedestal she had placed him on, and there was no redeeming himself in her eyes.

She had excused his behavior as sowing his wild oats until he had taken her. Now, she saw herself as another woman he had used. Her witnessing him with Cheryl and Bliss had made her feel as if he had thought of her as one more conquest.

He turned away for a moment, staring down at one of the plants blindly. She had never been obvious about her feelings; she was too cautious for that. It had been the furtive, secret glances that had given her away.

He didn't have to worry about protecting her from the

lifestyle he led; she wouldn't let him touch her now if he was the last man on earth. He had a big hill to get over with her, but he had come to realize she was worth it.

Cash liked that she didn't take any of his shit, that she had a sexy as hell body, and she didn't know it because she was more used to walking through the mountains than onto a dance floor. When he had fucked her, he had felt as if he was burning alive. He had been trying to recapture that same fire with numerous women since then. It was time to face what his body had been telling him all along and get to know the woman who had him by the balls.

He had faced insurmountable problems before. Hadn't the past few months proven that? His doctors had told him he wouldn't walk again, and he had proven them wrong. He would prove her wrong. He was the guy for her.

Rachel set down the watering can before going to the end of the row where she began potting the seedlings, ignoring his presence. He might as well have been invisible for all the notice she took of him. He was used to the shoe being on the other foot. He didn't know which bothered him more: the fact she didn't care he was there, or the disdain in her face when she realized he was.

At a loss, he retreated to his bedroom. He tired easily and needed to be around the exercise equipment at the clubhouse, but he had wanted to spend the night here after coming to his decision. Finding out she hadn't ignored his accident had been a game changer for him.

When he had regained consciousness and Shade had told him Rachel had returned to town, he had been relieved. It had taken away the worry that he would be responsible if she had become hurt. Rachel was a country girl. She'd had a difficult time remaining away from home just to go to college; how would she survive in the real world? Not only had she survived, but she had outsmarted her brothers and him.

Shade hadn't found out where she had been those

weeks, and Cash wanted to know. Wherever it had been was an effective bolt-hole that he wanted beyond her reach. He had never failed tracking anything—animal, man, or woman—yet Rachel had eluded him. He wanted to close that avenue to her to make her less likely to run when he began his pursuit of her.

He had tried to do the gentlemanly thing and leave her alone, but what had it gotten him? Her hatred and a hospital bed.

Beth, Winter, Diamond, and Lily had all adjusted to their men's lifestyle. Rachel could, too, with his care. The Porters believed they were the best hunters in the county, but the fact was, he was going to prove he was the best. He was going to catch a little fox that thought she was over him. She hadn't had the real Cash yet, but she would.

*Rachel will be in my bed before the end of the week,* he thought confidently.

# CHAPTER SIXTEEN

"Would you like another piece of pizza before I leave?"
Cash looked at Rachel balefully as she picked up her purse,
preparing to leave.

"Where are you going?"

Rachel's head tilted to the side, the wispy, red tendrils
giving her a more sophisticated appearance. "Pastor
Patterson is having an anniversary party for his wife. Do
you want the pizza?"

"No, I don't want the pizza," he snapped, sounding
like a whiney, little kid. His hands tightened on the arms of
the chair he was sitting on in the living room. His
grandmother was sitting in her favorite chair, pretending to
watch her favorite game show, but Cash knew damn good
and well she was listening to him make an ass of himself.

"Goodnight, then." Rachel bent over the back of Mag's
chair, giving his grandmother a kiss on her cheek and
treating him to a view of her tits practically pouring out of
the top of her dress. He almost swallowed his tongue and
had to sit lamely by as she glided out the door in her four-
inch heels. When the fuck had she started wearing heels?

"You can put those eyes of yours back in that head.
She's gone."

"Shut up."

Mag's cackle of laughter reminded him of why he didn't stay with her often; a little of her went a long way. Combine that with his lack of sex since the night Rachel had seen him with Bliss, and he wasn't exactly in the best mood.

Mag, being as old as God, sensed his predicament and showed no mercy, flaunting Rachel in front of him like a prized mare. The woman had a truly warped sense of humor.

He was forced to sit and watch television with her for the next several hours, his eyes going to the gigantic wall clock. Mag had told Cash that every minute she lived was a milestone at her age, and she wanted to be able to appreciate them. He thought the clock was the ugliest thing he had ever seen.

At eleven-thirty, his grandmother's bedtime, she gave him an enigmatic smile as she rolled out the door.

Did preachers have parties this late? Cash's fingers drummed on the arm of the chair as he contemplated calling Rachel's cell phone, but then the key turning in the door had him pretending to be interested in the late-night talk show.

"You're still up?" Rachel asked, closing the door.

"I wasn't sleepy."

"You need to get more exercise."

He bit back the retort on the tip of his tongue about exactly what kind of exercise he needed. "I work out enough."

She looked at him curiously at his sharp answer. "Ooookay. Well, I'll leave you to your show. Goodnight."

He hadn't sat there half the night to be blown off the minute she walked into the house. "How was the party?"

"It was fun. There are several new people who have moved into town that have started going to church. It was nice getting to know them. Beth brought the babies. They are so cute—"

"Any new men?" Cash interrupted her.

Rachel had been walking across the room, talking to him like he was one of her fucking brothers after being out.

"Yes, two. King hired them. One's a chef and the other his manager."

"Single?"

Rachel's face lost her friendly expression. "I believe so, yes."

"You going to chase after them like the rest of the women in town?"

"I'm thinking about it." She narrowed her eyes on him, turning to face him fully.

"I wouldn't if I were you, unless you want them to leave town before they have a chance to unpack." He was tired of pussyfooting around her, trying to make amends for being a jackass. If he wasn't careful, she would be in someone else's bed while he was still trying to gain her forgiveness.

"You son of a bitch! You can go to Hell. You think you can sleep with me then have any woman you want, flaunting them in my face. Your attitude toward women sucks. I want a man who wants marriage and children. I want a house and four kids. I want a husband who, when he walks out that front door, I'm never going to doubt he's mine. And I sure as shit don't want you. I not only hate you, I despise you."

She angrily reached into her purse, pulling out her cell phone. "If you want to relive old memories, call Sleeping Beauty; maybe she hasn't woken up and discovered you're an asshole." She tossed him her phone.

Cash barely managed to catch the phone she threw at him. He felt each word slap him in his face, her hatred blasting at him from across the room as she left him with a look of total disgust.

Damn, he had forgotten calling Cheryl 'Sleeping Beauty.' Rachel was obviously not happy with his choice of nicknames. He had been a stupid prick fucking around with Cheryl. Damn.

He had forgotten the only piece of advice his father had ever given him, downplaying its importance as he had moved from one woman's bed to another, not believing its value.

When he had been sixteen, he had broken his first girlfriend's heart. It hadn't bothered him, just made him impatient because she kept calling him. He had learned after that he didn't have to say he was in love to fuck them.

His father had seen him hang up the phone, shaking his head.

"She won't quit calling," Cash had told his dad.

"She will."

"Not soon enough," Cash had said without pity.

"Son, make sure you want her to quit calling because a woman has a breaking point. She'll stand by you if you kill someone, but when she finally reaches her breaking point, she's done with you. There's no getting her heart twice."

"It's not her heart I want." His young, arrogant voice still sounded in his ears after all these years.

A sad look had come over his father's face. "Make sure, Cash, or you'll spend the rest of your life wanting something you can't have."

# CHAPTER SEVENTEEN

Rachel was sitting on her bed, making notes on her computer when a knock sounded on her door.

"Come in."

She thought Mag would open her door; instead, Cash stood leaning on her door frame.

"Busy?"

The pinched look on his face showed he hadn't fully recovered from his accident.

"No, do you need something?"

A brief silence met her question before he answered. "There's a swap meet going on in Jamestown. Feel like giving me a ride? I want to look for a new bike."

Rachel started to mouth off and ask why he didn't ask Bliss; instead, she slid off the bed and put on her shoes. He probably didn't want any of his women seeing him when he wasn't able to hold himself up much less them. Rachel blocked the image of him holding Bliss from her mind. She had been right; it wasn't an image she had been able to forget.

In her car, Cash slid the seat back as far as it would go then leaned his head back on the headrest.

"Did you take anything for pain?" Rachel asked as she

drove toward Jamestown.

"No. I would have smoked some weed, but I was too scared of what your brother put in it."

Rachel stifled her laughter.

"I didn't take you for a coward," she teased.

"I'm not. I just don't want to smoke cat shit."

Not able to hold back, her laughter filled the car.

"You're not going to tell me you were kidding around?"

Rachel took her eyes briefly off the road to see his head turned toward her. "Sorry, Tate and Greer are both vindictive a-holes."

"Tell me something I don't know. Tate's still mad over a girl dumping him in high school because he thinks she dumped him for me."

"She did. He had saved his money to rent a limo to take them to prom. He hadn't slept with her. He had planned a big night only to find out you had beat him to sleeping with her."

"She told me he had broken up with her."

"She lied," Rachel informed him.

Cash remained silent the rest of the drive.

When Rachel glanced over again he was sleeping. His vitality was so overwhelming it was easy to look over the fact he was still healing from an almost fatal accident. Instinctively, she reached out to touch his arm but then drew back. She didn't want to wake him needlessly.

Her hands gripped the steering wheel. The powers that had helped save his life were gone. She had prayed they would come back to no avail. She had used everything she had to bring him back. However, it was a decision she didn't regret; she only wished she had it now so she could help with the pain he attempted to keep hidden from everyone.

Cash took his loss of strength as a weakness while she saw it a completely different way. Even without her help, he would have lived. Cash was a survivor who didn't give up easily; his recuperation was a testament to that fact. He had proven the doctors wrong about his walking. Now he forced himself not to limp in front of others, but when he thought no one was observing him, he moved slower and with a slight limp. Rachel knew he wouldn't stop until nothing other than the scars from his accident remained to remind him of his brush with death.

Cash woke as she parked at the packed motorcycle swap meet.

"Looks like every biker in three states is here," he remarked, stretching as he closed the car door.

Rachel gazed at the rough looking crowd of men and women walking around, examining the motorcycles on display. Several were for sale and some were just being shown off by their owners.

She moved closer to Cash's side as they walked through the heavy crowd.

"Nervous?"

"I really don't know what to think," Rachel admitted, coming to a stop next to him as he paused in front of one bike. Its gleaming chrome and appearance attracted Rachel, and she didn't know a thing about bikes. Cash, on the other hand, moved along to other motorcycles.

"Are you just browsing or looking for one in particular?" Rachel asked.

"I have a couple I've been thinking about, but I haven't made my mind up yet." He stopped at one black monster that was huge to Rachel, but when he sat on it, he took the machine over. It suited him.

He climbed off and then took a step back, looking it over. "Sit on it."

"What?" Rachel cleared her voice.

"Sit on the bike," Cash repeated.

Rachel tentatively climbed on the back of the bike, sitting there self-consciously as he took out his phone and took a picture. She climbed off.

"Why did you take a picture?" she snapped.

"So I would have something to remember the day I bought my bike," he said, taking several more before putting his phone back in his pocket.

Rachel watched as he bought the bike. She noticed the surprise of the seller when Cash paid him in full for it.

"You're not going to test drive it?" Rachel asked.

"No, I drove it yesterday when I was here with the brothers but couldn't make up my mind. I just needed to see one more thing before I decided to buy it."

"What?"

"You on the back of it," Cash stated.

He set up the delivery and then moved her to where a large crowd was standing, watching several motorcycles racing. On the opposite side of the track, Rachel saw Sex Piston and her crew cheering.

The motorcycles were flying by so fast Rachel couldn't see the riders' faces. However, after the race, Rachel saw Stud take his trophy while moving away from the woman in a short red dress, who was trying to give him a bottle of champagne.

"What's he doing? He's going to fall off the stage if he isn't careful."

"I have no idea," Cash answered as the woman finally managed to hand the bottle to the runner up.

"Want a hot dog?"

"Yes." Rachel's mouth watered as they drew closer to the hot dog stand.

Cash bought them each one and a bottled water. They walked and ate as they looked over the different types of bikes. Rachel had never been interested in motorcycles before, but she listened as Cash showed her the different brands.

As they walked, whenever they neared Sex Piston and her friends, he managed to nudge her in another direction.

"You don't want to congratulate Stud?"

"Not if it means having to talk to those bitches."

"They're not that bad."

"Yes they are," Cash countered.

The biker women certainly made a statement with their large entourage and biker clothes. Rachel didn't think a bottle of oil would let her get in those leather pants that Sex Piston was wearing.

It was dark when they returned to her car. Back in the close confines of her car, she fell back into silence. She had enjoyed the day and had felt some of the antagonism toward him slipping away.

"When I get my bike, you'll have to go for a ride with me," he said casually.

"No, thanks. I'm sure the women at the club will all be lining up for that privilege." The harsh words passed her lips before she could stop them.

Cash's grim face turned away from her, staring out the window for the remainder of the ride.

She put on the blinker to turn into Mag's house when he stopped her.

"Take me to the clubhouse."

Rachel kept driving, refusing to say anything. She drove the extra miles to the clubhouse with the tension boiling in the car.

When she came to a stop, he turned to her. "How long are you going to make me pay for giving you a ride you'd been wanting for a while?"

Rachel's hand swung out, aiming for his face. "You bastard!"

"Hell, no. That's not going to happen." His hand caught her, placing it directly on his jean covered cock, forcing her fingers to tighten on him. "Even if I am a bastard, we had a good time today whether you want to admit it or not. We could have had an even better time tonight, but you're too worried about proving to yourself and the town that you're the good girl sitting in church every Sunday to have any fun. When you decide to get off your high horse, you might realize we could have a good thing." He released her hand and got out of the car, slamming the door behind him.

Rachel swallowed hard, her hands trembling on the wheel as she felt her body's response to touching him. She wanted to stop him from getting out of the car, to unzip his jeans and find the release she had only had found once with him. Her pride had held her back, which wasn't much of a consolation prize as she drove to Mag's home alone.

* * *

Cash stood, looking down at his wrecked bike. It was irreparable. He was amazed he had lived through the wreck that destroyed it.

"What do you think about it?" His brothers had gathered to watch it be unloaded from the delivery truck. He couldn't have picked better.

The brothers slapped him on his back.

"Ready for a ride?" Viper's hard-eyed stare watched for his reaction.

"Hell, yeah!"

The large group of bikers mounted their bikes, pulling onto the road in rows of two. They rode down the mountain, through the town, obeying the speed limit until they hit the county line. Cash rode next to Viper, who flung him a shit-eating grin before accelerating his speed, taking his bike wide-fucking-open down the road. Cash felt a twinge of nervousness as he sped up to keep pace. Then his love of the ride kicked in, and he felt nothing except the bike underneath him.

They rode until they reached Jamestown, pulling into a half-empty local bar. Give it another hour and it would begin to fill as the working stiffs rolled in at the end of the day.

Cash ordered everyone a round of beers and had just sat at the bar to drink his when the door opened and the men who had sat with Rachel and Willa all those months ago walked in. He could immediately tell there was going to be trouble.

"Fuck," he muttered to Viper, who had stiffened beside

him.

The group of ten men took up the remaining tables.

"Hey, hot stuff." A pretty blond sat her perky ass down on a stool next to him. "I haven't seen you in here before."

"Been out of commission for a while. Decided to go for a ride tonight," Cash explained, taking another sip of his beer.

"Want another one?" She slid her hand up his arm, tracing over one of his tats. Cash felt his skin crawl at her touch. Once upon a time, he would have taken her out back and banged her then returned to finish his beer without another thought.

Cash moved his arm away from the woman's reach. "No."

"You married?"

"No," he said abruptly.

"Gay?"

"No."

"Then why not?" She leaned forward, sliding her hand up his thigh. "Baby, I can suck your dick like it's never been sucked before."

Cash began to get angry at her refusal to accept his rejection, jerking her hand away again. As she leaned forward, swiping her tongue against his neck, her overpowering musky scent had Cash's head jerking away.

"I doubt that," Cash said, amused. "Listen to me: I'm not interested." Cash started to get really rude then thought better of it. "I've got a deal for you."

He spent the next few minutes telling her what he did want from her then slid a hundred dollar bill toward her with Viper blocking anyone else in the bar from seeing what he was doing. With a wink, she sauntered off to another man, but not before giving Viper a once-over. Viper raised his hand, showing his wedding ring and sending the disappointed woman on her way.

"Think she'll be useful?"

"Who knows?" He shrugged. "At least I got her hand

away from my dick. That was worth the Benjamin."

"Motherfucker, you better back off." Rider stood to his feet, his chair falling to the floor as the one who had taken Willa's card came to his feet.

"You're the one who needs to fuck off." A fist flew out, which Rider dodged while his own nailed the man in the jaw.

Viper cocked a brow at Cash. "You up for this?"

"Hell, yeah." He had been dying to blow off some steam, and this was the perfect opportunity. "The one in the red shirt is mine." He slipped his brass knuckles out of his pocket.

When the bar became engulfed in fighting, Cash made sure he was the one to take on the guy who had come on to Rachel, using the brute force he had been steadily regaining during the months of rehab. He managed to beat the asshole so that his own mother wouldn't recognize him. His body was weak, drenched in sweat and he was shaking when the cops came through the door. Cash didn't put up a fight as he was handcuffed, but he did manage to land a last solid kick against the ribs of the man lying on the floor.

They were taken to jail. Cash, Viper, Lucky, and Train were in one cell while the three other cells were filled with the remaining Last Riders.

"Notice anything funny?" Viper's voice was muffled by the t-shirt he had removed to stem the blood flowing from his nose.

"We're the only ones arrested," Cash confirmed.

"We wanted to know how far they had taken over this town; our question just got answered."

"Stud's not going to be happy."

"I'm not, either. I think they were scouting Treepoint to see how easy it would be to take over." Viper lowered the now-bloody shirt.

"They'll control the main road through the mountain," Cash surmised.

Viper nodded. "And all the side roads that lead through both towns."

"Fuck, Viper. If they pulled something really big, it would take an army to get to them."

"I think that's what they're planning on."

The men stared at each other grimly.

Cash got sick to his stomach. To want a getaway of this magnitude, they were planning on doing a job that would have massive fatalities, and then even more lives would be lost trying to get them off the land that provided them plenty of cover from attack.

"I'll make some calls." Cash was already thinking of several buddies in Homeland Security.

"I will, too," Lucky chimed in, flexing his hand with the bruised knuckles. "But I'm not becoming a minister again."

"How about a nun?" Cash joked.

"Fuck you." Lucky leaned his head back against the grey wall.

The men started coming up with ideas for Lucky's next undercover assignment, but when Train's idea landed him face down on the floor, they quit laughing. Lucky, satisfied he had shut everyone down, sat back down.

"Motherfuckers, if you don't shut up, I'll tell the women those yahoos beat your asses."

The cell went quiet. Lucky never made promises he didn't keep.

* * *

Cash let himself in his grandmother's house. It was two in the morning before Diamond had been able to get them out of jail. He was tired while at the same time wired. He knew his brothers were going back to the clubhouse with beds that would have women waiting for them while the one waiting here for him was cold and empty.

He stumbled over a table leg as he walked through the living room. "Shit!"

His grandmother was constantly getting new furniture

from flea markets. How she maneuvered her wheelchair through the cramped space boggled his mind; he couldn't walk through it without constantly bumping into something.

"Who's there?" a feminine voice sounded from the hallway along with the unmistakable sound of a gun being cocked.

"Who the fuck do you think it is?" Cash grunted, bumping into a chair.

"Cash?"

He was standing in front of her, seeing the gun in her hand.

"Put the gun up, Rachel."

"What are you doing coming in so late?"

Cash could see her in the dim light coming from her opened bedroom door. She was wearing a thin nightgown that came to the tops of her thighs, the low neckline showing the pale flesh of her breasts.

"I went for a ride."

"So I smell." She wrinkled her nose, taking a step away from him. "It's so late I'm surprised you didn't stay the night at the clubhouse or at least take a shower."

Cash couldn't help but grin, not missing the dart she threw at him for staying last night at the clubhouse.

"I wasn't out fucking. The brothers and I took a ride to Jamestown." He reached out, running a finger across the tops of her breasts. The gun, which she had lowered, rose again, pointing at his chest.

"You don't have permission to touch me. Do it again, and I'll blow your left nut off," Rachel threatened.

Cash lost his grin. "I don't like having a gun pointed at me, and I sure as shit don't like you threatening to blow off my dick."

"I didn't threaten to blow off your dick, just one of those balls you're so proud of. I'm a good shot; I wouldn't miss."

"My hand isn't going to miss if you don't cut back on

143

some of that sass you've been throwing in my direction."

"What's the matter, Cash? Can't take a woman who doesn't want to drop her panties when she sees you?"

"That wouldn't be you; you dropped yours fast enough the first time I tried. Don't put yourself on a nonexistent pedestal. Your sweet pussy was one of the best I've ever had."

When Rachel reached out to hit him with the gun, Cash jerked it out of her hand while maneuvering her backwards into her bedroom, shutting the door with his foot. He laid the rifle down on the dresser.

"I warned you last night that, if you want to hit out at me, you better be prepared for what comes back at you."

"You're the biggest ass I know." Rachel struggled against him. "Let me go, you goon, or I'll scream loud enough to wake up Mag."

"You do, and I'll tell her you're coming on my dick and to go back to bed," Cash said, enjoying the feel of her body against him.

He pinned her against the bedroom wall with one of his legs between hers as she hit at his chest with her fists. When he pressed his knee against her pussy, she quit struggling, stiffening against him.

"Get out, Cash." Her cold voice had his arms dropping away from her as he took a step back. She took a shuddering breath, and Cash angrily narrowed his eyes on her.

"Don't act like I was going to rape you, Rachel." Her face paled. "I don't play like that. Never have, never will. Don't twist it around in your head; you wanted me to fuck you that night."

Rachel's shoulders stiffened. "I didn't suggest you did. It might not have been my proudest moment, but I accept full responsibility for being an idiot."

Cash tilted his head to the side, studying her expression. "Why were you an idiot?"

"Because I shouldn't have wanted you. I know what

kind of man you are, and I still let myself have you."

Cash gave a sensuous smile. Stepping closer, he braced his hand on the wall next to her head. "You don't know what kind of man I am, Rachel. You couldn't possibly know. If you did, you wouldn't keep insulting me." His voice turned seductive. "I'm not my father. When I want something, I take it."

"Shut up, Cash." Rachel started to push off the wall but was pressed back against it.

"What? I'm not allowed to talk about it? We all know your mother and my father were in love. If my father hadn't fucked up and cheated on her, then she would never have married your father."

"She loved my father," Rachel said forcefully.

Cash shook his head. "She loved *my* father and turned to his best friend when she found out dear old Dad had knocked up the town whore. Both of them regretted their mistakes for the rest of their lives. When Dad realized he wasn't getting your mom back, he married my mother. Together, they became sanctimonious idiots every Sunday while I had to watch. I, on the other hand, don't plan on regretting the best mistake of my life."

Her expression became confused. "The best mistake of your life?"

"You were the best mistake of my life," he confirmed. "I've been attracted to you for a long time, but to tell you the truth, your brothers didn't make you worth the effort, and I sure as fuck wasn't anxious to follow in my father's footsteps to try to romance you."

"You wouldn't know romance if it came up behind you and bit you on the ass."

Cash burst out laughing. "I know romance, and I can prove it."

"There's no need. I'm not interested."

"I think you're the one who has trouble dealing with romance, not me," he mocked her frightened expression.

"You think romance is wham, bam, and telling

everyone in town you fucked the girl." Her tart reply had him laughing again.

"No, that was stupidity. I let your brothers piss me off into opening my big mouth. I'm not sorry, though." Cash saw the wounded look in her eyes and continued, "It was a hard way for your brothers to find out about us, like ripping a band-aid off, but now they know." He shrugged.

"There isn't an us!"

"There will be. Right now, you're still mad, but I can wait until you cool down. At least a little longer," he qualified his words.

"You're the most egotistical man to ever exist."

"Not really, just confident. If I can get in your panties once, I can do it again." Cash stared down into her eyes.

Her face flushed red, and her bottom lip trembled as she shook her head at him.

Cash softened his voice. "You're mad as hell at me, but you still want me."

"No, I don't," she denied.

"Yes, you do. I can prove it." As his lips swooped down on hers, Rachel pressed her hands against his chest. Cash's tongue licked her lips, but didn't try to enter her mouth; instead, he learned the contours of her lips as his other hand reached out to slide against her neck to hold her in place. His thumb traced the delicate lines of her face as he gradually increased the pressure against her lips, sliding his tongue inside to explore the warmth of her mouth. He went from seductive to demanding, breaching the defenses she had built against him, trying to turn the fire of her hatred to one of passion.

He skillfully waited for her body to soften against his before he pressed her harder against the wall as he lured her into responding to him. His hand went to her gown, tugging it downward so his fingers could find a nipple, brushing it with the tips of his fingers, teasing it with soft touches.

A tell-tale soft whimper passed her lips, and his mouth

left hers to trace the line of her jaw until he felt her abruptly stiffen as she pushed herself away from him.

"Don't try to freakin' seduce me when you smell like another woman."

"If I was trying to seduce you, you would be lying on the bed, and I would be fucking you by now," Cash snapped back.

"Get out!"

"I'm going. I think I made my point."

"The only point you made is that you're good at playing with a woman's body. You should be; you have enough experience," she bitterly remarked.

"Experience I plan to use until you're underneath me again. I'm giving you fair warning, Rachel; I'm done trying to make up for embarrassing you. It's time to move on. I've got a news flash for you: most of those people sitting in church next to you do engage in sexual activities." His voice dropped to a seductive whisper. "They may even enjoy fucking as much as I do."

While she gaped at him, Cash couldn't resist smiling at her expression. "Don't worry. I'll take it easy on you until you can accept we're together."

"We'll be together over my dead body. My brothers will kick your ass."

Cash had a sudden idea that could save him a lot of aggravation. It wasn't the brightest idea he had ever had, but he was willing to do anything to reach the stubborn woman staring up at him defiantly.

"If I can get your brothers' permission to date you, will you go out with me?"

She laughed in his face. "If you can get my brothers' permission for me to go out with you, then yes, I'll go out with you." She kept laughing at him unwisely. "Hell, Cash, I'll even give you a blowjob to top the night off."

"Really?" Cash gave her a sinister smile, which she failed to recognize.

"Really," she mocked.

"Goodnight, then. If I'm going to be dealing with your brothers, I'm going to need my rest."

"If you're going to be dealing with my brothers, you're going to be needing a bulletproof vest."

Cash opened the door, pausing before he left. "Don't forget, I was in the military. I've dealt with terrorists, sneak attacks, and snipers. I have all the skills I need to deal with your brothers."

"If you've got a death wish, I can't stop you."

"I've handled worse. They'll be a piece of cake." Cash went out the bedroom door, laughing softly when it slammed behind him. He loved riling her temper.

He whistled all the way to his bedroom, stripping off his clothes before stepping naked into the shower, washing the bar whore's scent off his skin. Drying off, he lay down naked on his bed.

Rachel thought he was joking. She would find out just how serious he was when she was planting her ass on the back of his bike. He was willing to put up with her brothers long enough to get their permission. Hell, her promise was enough to put up with a lot of shit. How bad could it be?

# CHAPTER EIGHTEEN

It was bad, really bad. Cash wanted to kick the Porters' asses so bad he was ready to do a stint in the jailhouse just for the pleasure of doing it.

The brothers had been sitting in Rosie's, having a beer, when he had gone in with Shade. He had psyched himself up to walk over to their table to greet them. Their hate-filled expressions and lack of response had him gritting his teeth, though. He felt the silent amusement of Shade by his side.

"Mind if we join you?" Silence met Shade's request.

They didn't wait for acquiescence, both of them taking a seat at the table. The brothers might hate Cash, but Shade was a regular customer and he would be harder to piss off.

The men looked like the beer in their stomachs was turning sour as Cash and Shade both ordered their drinks.

"What do you want, Cash?" Tate didn't hesitate to bring out in the open why Cash would be willing to sit down at the table with them.

He decided to be honest with the Porters. He wanted a relationship with Rachel, and to accomplish that goal, he was going to have to get along with these three yahoos.

"We need to come to an understanding and cut out this bullshit between us."

"Why? It works for us." An evil grin came to Tate's face. "This has to do with Rachel, doesn't it?"

The smug bastard was going to be picking his teeth up off the floor if he wasn't careful.

"Why does his talking to us have anything to do with Rachel?" Dustin confirmed Cash's opinion that he was the slowest of the group. His two older brothers rolled their eyes at the question. Realization slowly hit Rachel's youngest brother. "Hell, no." Dustin's reaction mirrored his brothers'.

"We can keep fighting between us and we'll all lose Rachel, or we can pretend to get along and keep Rachel in Treepoint; it's up to you. I'm willing to tolerate you three for Rachel."

Without another word, the three brothers got up from the table, leaving him and Shade staring at their backs as they left the bar.

"That went well," Cash said drily.

"Did you expect any different? You four have spent years pissing each other off. It's going to take more than a meet to change that."

Cash studied Shade speculatively. "I gave Lily my vote for your marker."

Shade's amusement died. "Yes, you did. So?"

"I want your help to bring those assholes around," Cash laid out his terms.

"I promised you my marker, not a fucking miracle."

"Shade, you're the most manipulative bastard I know. If anyone can get those assholes to tolerate me, it's you. Can you think of a bigger challenge for your skills?"

"Actually, no."

* * *

Rachel opened the door to Pastor Patterson and his wife.

"Good morning, Rachel." Pastor Merrick led Brooke

inside the small house. Rachel closed the door behind them; she had dreaded this day.

Once a month, the pastor visited Mag. He ritualistically visited all his homebound parishioners to talk and pray with them.

Rachel led them into the kitchen where she had already prepared sandwiches and ice tea for them.

"Afternoon, Pastor." Mag's jovial greeting lightened the atmosphere as Brooke's superior gaze lit on the simple food.

"Good afternoon, Mag. How are you feeling?"

"Right as I can be."

Rachel had to keep her temper under control at Brooke's slight wince.

They sat at the table, the pastor graciously eating a few of the sandwiches while Brooke refused. To give Mag credit, she ignored the cold reception of Brooke, concentrating her attention on the pastor.

"May I use the restroom?" Brooke interrupted the conversation.

"It's around the corner. The door's open," Mag directed her.

Brooke rose from the table and the conversation resumed. Rachel enjoyed listening to Pastor Merrick discuss the Bible so much she became lost in the conversation. It took several minutes for her to realize that Brooke had not returned to the table. She was about to go check on her when she returned, retaking her seat.

Rachel took another sandwich and had just taken a bite of the roasted chicken salad when the front door opened and Cash walked into the kitchen. He was shirtless and his jeans clung low on his lean hips. Why was he showing so much flesh when the weather outside was frigid?

While Rachel almost choked on her sandwich at his appearance, Brooke's veiled eyes did little to hide her appreciation of his masculine appeal.

Mag introduced the Pastor and Brooke.

"Want to join us?" Mag invited.

Rachel expected him to refuse and had to hide her surprise when he accepted.

"Let me get cleaned up; I've been working on my truck."

Cash left, returning within minutes, freshly showered and having changed his clothes. He sat down next to her, grabbing several sandwiches and pouring himself a glass of tea.

"You don't attend church, Cash?" Brooke spoke for the first time, actually trying to participate in the conversation.

"Afraid not. It's still standing, isn't it? I would hate for the pastor to have to rebuild just because I walked through the door," Cash joked.

"You can't be that bad." Brooke's voice lowered with innuendo.

As Cash's hand paused halfway to his mouth, Rachel's stomach churned at his recognition of Brooke's interest in him.

"My wife has a true calling to get new members into our church." The pastor patted his wife's hand affectionately.

Seriously? Surely the pastor couldn't be as dense as he seemed not to recognize his wife was coming on to Cash in front of him. The woman had unfortunately underestimated Mag, however.

"She's calling for something that's going to get her an ass-whooping if she doesn't stop."

Rachel's mouth dropped open at her sarcastic remark, and Cash broke into laughter.

"What she means, Pastor, is that people around here take church seriously, and I happen to be one of Treepoint's citizens who isn't very well liked," Cash tried to explain his grandmother's lack of manners. Rachel, personally, thought Mag was the only one in town who had the nerve to call Brooke out.

"*'We're all God's children in the search for salvation,'*" Pastor Merrick quoted.

"Some need salvation more than others," Mag agreed.

Rachel wanted to slide under the table, praying Brooke would be wise enough not to set Mag off again. Luckily, Cash changed the subject to fishing, which was one of the pastor's favorite topics. Rachel was able to relax until the Pattersons rose to leave.

At the door, Cash shook the pastor's hand as he went out.

"It was nice meeting you, Cash." Brooke waited until her husband stepped out the door, blatantly ignoring the two women also by the door, taking Cash's hand in hers. "If you need any help getting caught up in your Bible studies, give me a call." She then released his hand, following her husband out the door.

Rachel had to grab onto the handlebars of Mag's wheelchair to hold her back.

"Let my chair go, Rachel. That good man needs to know what kind of woman he's married to."

Cash quickly closed the door, standing in front of it with his arms crossed in front of his chest. "Calm down, Mag. You'll give yourself another stroke."

"That's okay. The good Lord will reward me for shining a light on that bitch's behavior. No Christian woman would behave like that."

Rachel rolled Mag into the living room before getting her some tea. It took several minutes for the old woman to calm down. She sat down next to her until the anger passed and Mag decided to go take a nap.

"Don't forget to pray," Cash said as she rolled herself out of the room. Mag turned to face him, pointing a long, bony finger at him.

"You stay away from that skinny bitch; she's trouble. That God-fearing man has no idea what he got himself tied to."

"I'll stay away," Cash said solemnly with twinkling eyes.

Rachel had learned that Cash liked to rile his grandmother and couldn't help her own lips twitching in amusement at Mag's anger.

"You should be ashamed of yourself. If she had a stroke, it would be your fault," Rachel accused as soon as Mag left.

Cash leaned back against the couch, putting his booted feet up onto the coffee table. "I couldn't help it. When she gets like that, it reminds me of when she was younger and she was like that all the time. I'll never forget when two drunks got in a fight in her back room on moonshine. She broke them up by beating them half to death with a mop handle. Even drunk, they didn't want to hit a woman, and she took advantage of it. She's got a mean streak a mile wide. Don't let her fool you."

"I won't. I remember her before she had her stroke, too. My brothers are scared to death of her. They broke her window out one time when Dad took them to her house, and she wore them out with a switch. They never went with Dad again; they were too scared of her."

Cash laughed until he couldn't breathe at the idea of his grandmother spanking Rachel's brothers. Mag had been the biggest bootlegger in the county for decades until the county went wet. Shortly thereafter, she'd had a stroke. She had barely survived, only to be left in a wheelchair, but her fighting spirit had accepted it and had adjusted.

Rachel went into the kitchen and began cleaning up the table, washing the dishes before putting them away. Cash watched television as she worked, aware she was trying to ignore him, but occasionally, he felt her eyes on him.

"You done?" he asked when he saw her put the last dish away.

"Yes."

"You want to go for a ride on my bike?" He saw the refusal on her face. "You scared to ride with me since I wrecked?"

"No, everyone in town knows that the wreck wasn't

your fault. The driver crossed the center lane. Knox said anyone else less experienced would have died on impact."

Cash shrugged. "Been in a couple of them. That one was the worst."

"Why do you keep riding, then?" She came farther into the room, taking a seat in one of the chairs.

"Because there's nothing else like it on earth. It gets in your blood; the freedom of movement, how it feels when you ride it. It's hard to explain. Go for a ride with me and you'll see," Cash prodded.

"All right. Do I need to get changed?"

"No, your jeans are fine. Grab a jacket, though."

Before she could change her mind, he led her outside to his bike. Handing her his helmet, he climbed on.

"What about you?"

"Woman, you trying to insult me? I usually don't ride with one. The only reason it's on my bike was because I was hoping you would take a ride with me." He saw it was the wrong thing to say. She was about to change her mind. "Get on, Rachel. We won't be gone long," he lied. He planned to keep her out as long as he could.

Gingerly, she climbed on his bike. As soon as she wrapped her arms around him, he turned on the motor, going slow until he felt her begin to relax. They rode through the mountain roads. It was still winter, and the massive pine trees hung over the road creating a canopy, shading them from the bright sun.

He drove until he came to his old homestead, pulling in to stop by the fire pit.

"Come on; I want to show you something." Cash got off the bike, holding out his hand to help her off.

Rachel climbed off, removing the helmet. The trail was opposite the one she took to her parents' graves, winding deep into the woods. Both of them walked steadily until they reached a small stream.

"It's beautiful."

"It was my grandfather's favorite place to fish." Cash

squatted down to pick up a small stone before tossing it across the water.

"You're pretty good at that."

"He taught me, like he did most everything." Cash's voice wasn't bitter, merely matter of fact. He had made peace with his lack of a relationship with his father years ago.

"Your father and you didn't get along?" Her tentative question brought a wry smile to his lips.

"No, I couldn't understand a grown man standing back and watching what went on in that church while he called himself a Christian."

She didn't question what he was talking about. She had attended the same church he had. Her parents had left the church, she returned only when Dean had taken over as Pastor.

"Mag quit going, your parents stopped attending. Only the self-righteous idiots like my parents kept going."

Rachel reached out, touching his arm. "You stopped it, Cash."

"I didn't stop anything. I left town and sent someone in to do what I didn't."

"But your conscious didn't let you forget. Ultimately, you showed your Christianity more than they ever did."

"I'm no Christian; I've committed every sin in the Bible and then some." Cash looked at her and wanted to lower her to the grassy bank and show her exactly how pleasurable sinning could be. However, being here had brought back bad memories of his mother's and father's disapproval of Mag's life.

They had cut her out of their lives and had attempted to cut him out of it. He had learned early to use the mountains to run to his grandmother and grandfather, despite their attempts to keep him away.

"Let's go." He walked away, forcing himself to slow so she could keep up.

As soon as she got on the bike behind him, he drove

back onto the road and headed to where he knew he could find the answers he needed.

He drove until he came to the turnoff to the lake. Slowing down, he turned into the spot where The Last Riders often went swimming. Some of them were there now. The January weather was cool, but for the last couple of days, the weather had been unseasonably warm. A large cooler was placed on the picnic table and several of the members were enjoying their Saturday off from work.

When he turned the bike off, he felt Rachel stiffen at his back.

"What are you doing? I don't want to stay."

"Come on, Rachel; I'm thirsty. One drink, and then we'll leave if you want to."

He felt her hesitation before she climbed off the bike. They walked to the picnic table where Stori, Raci, and Jewell were sitting while Nickel, Train, and a couple of the other brothers were lying on a blanket with Ember.

Cash pulled a cold beer out of the cooler. "Get a drink. There's different ones inside."

As Rachel opened the cooler and pulled out a bottled water, Cash sat down at the picnic table and began talking to Nickel.

"Was that your first ride?" Raci asked her.

"Yes."

"I remember my first ride."

"I bet you don't," Jewell said sarcastically.

Cash threw Jewell a warning look, which she returned with one of her one. He wanted Rachel to get used to the women, not get run off by them. Cash had a suspicion the women wouldn't be as friendly with even more new additions to the club, what with the most popular of them getting married and becoming monogamous.

He hadn't participated in any of the club parties since Rachel' had caught him with Bliss, and he knew several of the women weren't happy with it. Hell, he wasn't happy with it. It had been a long time since he had felt his dick buried in a warm pussy, but he was determined the next one would be the one he wanted.

"Do you want to dance?" Cash asked as Nickel turned on the music.

She quickly shook her head.

"You don't know what your missing out on," Jewell advised.

"No, thanks."

"Suit yourself." Jewell rose to her feet, stretching and showing off her body, running to the bonfire that had been made. The others got up to join in. Soon, the area was filled with the sounds of laughing and voices rose as they began to dance to the music.

"Sure you don't want to join in?"

"I'm sure."

Cash raised his brow at her response. "Since when did you become a prude? They're just having a good time."

And they were. He wanted to join, too. He missed the carefree days of taking a timeout just to play. It was why he hadn't wanted to become involved with her. She didn't fit in with his lifestyle, and the way she was acting was making it blatantly obvious she never would. He had been right to bring her here and see for himself that the sanctimonious side of her which wanted to change her brothers would want to change him, as well.

# CHAPTER NINETEEN

Rachel let herself back into Mag's house, trying not to watch as Cash drove off down the driveway. She didn't have to be told he was going back to party.

Closing the door behind her, she went to her room, taking a long shower. She leaned her head against the shower wall, breathing deeply, getting her emotions back under control.

She had frozen when surrounded by the women in their sexy outfits, too self-conscious of her own tomboyish body to join in the fun. She had been raised with three overprotective brothers, who had never let her experience the typical girly experiences other woman were used to.

She dried off after her shower, dressing in a pair of faded denim cutoffs and a tank top. Trying to shake off the feeling she had let an important moment slip through her fingers, she went to work with her plants. They never failed to give her peace when she was upset.

She had several seedlings she wanted to organize. She was using her grandmother's notebook to make notes.

There was one plant in particular she was interested in. She had been researching its genus but hadn't been able to locate it. She had found a couple that were close, though.

She took a picture of it on her cell phone, determined to ask a friend, who was a botanist, if he recognized the species.

When she was finished, she put the plant up, frowning when she saw a couple of the cuttings were missing. Rachel carefully looked around where the plant had been sitting and on the floor to make sure she hadn't dropped them. She only had three cuttings of the plant left and she always took five.

She searched until she was sure they weren't in the room then saw the broom by the door. Relieved, she believed Mag must have accidently knocked it over with her wheelchair in the tiny space and cleaned it up. Mystery solved, Rachel finished straightening her plants.

When she heard Mag in the kitchen fixing dinner, Rachel went out to help her. They ate the pot roast she'd fixed and watched television for the rest of the night, but Cash didn't return. Rachel made herself go to bed when Mag did, although it took a long time to fall asleep.

When she dragged herself out of bed in the morning, Cash's bedroom door remained open, his bed un-slept in.

She went into the kitchen, uncertain as to why she was disappointed he hadn't come home the night before. It was why she had refused to go out with him on a date. His wanting to be with her had lasted a whole day. His record was four days with Missy Vines, his junior year in high school.

"I see Cash didn't make it home last night." Rachel poured Mag a cup of coffee to avoid her angry gaze.

"I guess I better go get ready for church." Rachel set her cup down in the sink.

She donned a new dress she had bought. The pretty yellow highlighted the reddish sheen of her hair and set off the faint tan of her skin. It felt like spring, and she felt it in the dress. Rachel, for once, didn't braid her hair back or put it in a ponytail, leaving it loose down her back.

The church was filled to capacity. After the service,

Rachel was one of the first out of church, not in the mood to be forced to talk to Brooke as she stood at the door by her husband as the parishioners left. She never brought her son to church, telling the other women in the congregation the sound of a baby crying grated on her nerves. Rachel smiled as Razer and Beth brought their sons every Sunday.

Outside, Rachel went next door to the Sheriff's department.

"Can I speak to the sheriff?"

"Sure can. He's with someone right now, but when he's done, I'll tell him you're here." The older woman sitting behind the desk was wearing a leopard-print dress and at least a dozen bangles. Rachel was tempted to ask her where she'd bought it. It was a sad day when a sixty-year-old was more attractive than her.

Rachel took one of only four seats in the small lobby and stared out the plate-glass windows at the motorcycles lined up outside the diner. She wondered which table and women Cash was sitting with.

When the sheriff's office finally opened, Knox walked out with Cash.

"Sheriff, Rachel is here to see you."

The idea of blending into the woodwork vanished when both men turned to look at her.

"Rachel, you can come into my office."

She slowly got to her feet, moving forward into Knox's office while avoiding looking directly at Cash.

When she glanced over her shoulder as Knox closed the door, Cash was inside, also.

"I'd like to talk to you alone," Rachel told Knox.

"Are you going to need me to do any investigating?" he asked, taking a seat behind his big desk.

Rachel frowned. "I don't know exactly. Maybe. I suppose so."

"Then he needs to be in here. He's my investigator." Knox leaned back in his chair, crossing his hands over his muscular stomach.

"He is?" Rachel's confused eyes met Cash's amused ones.

"Yep, I use him when my deputies are busy. Last night, he had to track down a stolen tow truck. Lyle left his keys in the ignition and a bunch of high schoolers took a joy ride."

He hadn't spent the night with the women at the clubhouse? Rachel's thoughts whirled, but Knox quickly reminded her of why she had stopped by his office.

"So, what did you want to talk to me about?"

"Willa. I'm concerned that Lewis is harassing her."

"What do you want me to do about it?" Knox raised a brow.

"I want you to make it stop. I think she's afraid of him and is too embarrassed to ask anyone for help." She didn't try to keep the anger out of her voice.

"I've already talked to Willa back in the summer. Evie had the same concerns and came to talk to me about them. She also had Shade talk to Lewis."

"Well, it hasn't worked. The other day, I stopped by her house and he was there. She was frightened, Knox," Rachel insisted.

"I'll stop by her house again and have another talk with her. But if she doesn't want me to help her, there's not a lot I can do," Knox explained.

"You obviously don't know Willa; she will not ask for your help. Never mind, I'll get my brothers to handle it."

She angrily turned to the door, only to find Cash blocking it.

"Just a damn minute, Rachel. I said I would talk to her. If you set your crazy-ass brothers off on Lewis, it's the Porters who are going to be arrested." Knox lost his relaxed appearance, straightening in his chair.

Rachel placed her hands on his desk, leaning toward him. "If she were one of The Last Riders' women, you wouldn't be talking to her; you would be talking to Lewis. You wouldn't give a shit about protocol. I'm not going to let that jerk make her scared one more day!"

This time, when she turned to leave, she moved toward the door.

"Move!" she ordered Cash.

"Rachel, calm down." Cash's voice tried to soothe her temper, which she wasn't in the mood for, but he took her arm, leading her to the chair in front of Knox's desk.

"Knox isn't saying he won't do anything, but he has to talk to Willa first. Give us a couple of days. I'll keep an eye on Willa, and if I see Lewis doing anything to make Willa uncomfortable, we'll get a restraining order and put a watch on her. If you go off and set your brothers on him, you could be escalating an already bad situation."

Rachel took a deep, steadying breath. "Willa was a senior when I was a freshman. Even then, I saw Georgia tormenting her." Rachel looked down at her work-roughened hands. "Georgia tried to pick on me a couple of times, but she wasn't really brave enough to do anything with Dustin always watching out for me. Georgia didn't get any nicer as she got older, though. Everyone, including Willa, learned the best way to deal with her was to stay away from her.

"You know the funny thing about it? Lily was the only one who ever had enough guts to actually confront Georgia." Rachel ran her sweaty hands down the sides of her dress. "I stood by then, but I'm not going to ignore it anymore. I know he's going to hurt her." Every time she was near Willa, she felt the fear and terror the woman was dealing with on her own.

"I'll make sure we all keep an eye on her," Knox promised.

Rachel nodded. Getting to her feet, she went to the door. This time, Cash opened it for her and then followed her outside.

"Have you had breakfast yet?" Cash asked as she walked to her car.

"No, why?" Rachel answered absently, her mind still on

Willa.

"Let's get some, and you can tell me more about Willa."

She couldn't refuse if he was going to help with Willa; therefore, she gave in, crossing the street with him.

Inside, the diner was busy with the church members; however, The Last Riders had their usual large table. When she saw Lily, Beth, and Winter, she smiled, relaxing as she followed him toward the table.

She sat down at an empty chair beside Beth, whose twin boys were both sitting in highchairs, nibbling on finger foods Beth had placed in front of them.

They were beautiful, chubby baby boys.

"They're gorgeous, Beth." They had inherited their father's dark hair and complexion.

"Thank you." Beth smiled, handing one of the boys a toy he had dropped.

The waitress came and took their order. Rachel enjoyed playing with the babies while she and Lily argued over which one was the cutest.

"They're identical," Cash's voice interrupted their good-natured argument. "Only a few people seem to be able to tell them apart."

"I don't know why." Rachel wasn't aware the large table had quieted as everyone listened. "Noah is larger than Chance." There was only a slight difference in the weight, Rachel thought, but Noah's cheeks were fuller as well as his chubby little thighs. "Chance's hair is slightly darker, and he looks a little bit more like Razer." Chance wasn't as loud or playful as Noah, either. His beautiful eyes stared back at her solemnly as he sucked on the teething giraffe he had nabbed from his brother. "Besides that, Beth brushes their hair in opposite directions," Rachel finished.

"I do?" Beth studied her children. "I didn't even realize it. Noah's hair is thicker and lies better that way."

The waitress brought their food.

"I've been trying to figure out which was which for the last month. They look more and more alike every day. You're very observant," Cash stated.

"Yes, I am," Rachel said. "That's why I'm so concerned for Willa."

Cash nodded. "I'll take care of it."

"You better, or I will," she promised.

"I get the message," Cash said ruefully, studying her stubborn expression.

She was determined to take up for a friend, and she had noticed something about Razer's kids he hadn't. His parents would never have stuck up for another person, nor would they have paid attention to someone else's children enough to notice the smallest detail of where their mother parted their hair. His little vixen had a heart. She might be a prude, but she didn't place herself on a moral shelf that no one could reach.

The door to the restaurant opened, and two teenage boys and an older man came into the restaurant. Rachel observed them coming in, trying to decide if she wanted to make her presence known to her cousin. The decision was taken out of her hands when he was about to sit down and noticed her at the table with The Last Riders. He said something to the two boys.

Rachel set down her orange juice glass as she saw him approach, preparing herself for his disdain at sitting with the group. Although, Drake was much more laid back than her brothers. He didn't share the same enmity for Cash since he was older and had never, to her knowledge, come into conflict with him over women. She was closer to Drake than he was to her brothers because of their refusal to get a regular job. Drake had tried to convince them, to no avail, to quit dealing their weed.

"Rachel, I'm glad to see you're back in town."

"Thank you. It's good to see you, too. How are you and Jace doing?"

"Fine, other than I had to bail him and his sidekick out

of jail just now for joyriding in one of Lyle's vehicles."

Rachel looked at Cash in surprise that he hadn't mentioned it was her cousin he had tracked down.

"Jace's taking after my side of the family?" Rachel couldn't help the small dig at her wealthy cousin. He owned a large chunk of the properties in and around Treepoint. He was the one who had sold the property of The Last Riders to Viper's brother Gavin. When it came out that Phillip Langley was behind his murder, Rachel had worried Drake had been involved. However, the subsequent investigation had cleared him of any wrongdoing. He had sold the property to the investment group, and that had been the end of his part.

"Seems so." Rachel noticed he kept looking toward Bliss, who was ignoring the conversation and talking to Train. "I've been letting Jace go hunting with your brothers so much I think they're starting to rub off on him. He looks up to them, so when he hears about their exploits, it puts ideas in his head."

Rachel blushed, remembering Dustin's own joy rides he had gotten in trouble for.

"I'll talk to them," Rachel offered.

"Me and you both," he said grimly, turning his gaze to Cash.

"Hello, Cash." Drake reached out to shake hands. "I appreciate you driving the boys into town instead of calling Knox. Knox told me you talked Lyle into not pressing charges. I owe you one."

"I hope my getting them off won't lead to them trying it again."

"It won't. I plan to sell his favorite rifle to pay for the damages to Lyle's truck."

Rachel winced. To a country boy, guns were prized possessions. Given a choice, Jace would have probably picked jail time versus having his gun sold.

Cash's lips twitched. "A fate worse than death."

"He'll survive," Drake said without remorse.

"Would you like to join us?"

Rachel saw his eyes go to Bliss again before answering Cash's question. "No, thanks. It would make those boys' day to sit here. They were admiring all the motorcycles when we came in. It will hurt like hell when I tell them you invited us to sit with you."

"You don't let him drive your bike?" Rachel teased.

"No. He lost that privilege when he got thrown out of high school and started going to the alternative school. I was going to buy him one when he graduated, but that's not looking so good."

Winter sent him a hopeful look. "He's doing much better."

Drake gave her a wry smile. "Not good enough to get that bike he's wanting, especially not with this latest stunt. I better get back to the table. Again, it's good to see you back, Rachel. Call me next time those asses give you a hard time." His glance at Cash indicated that he grouped Cash in among the asses that had given her a hard time.

Cash's lips tightened at the silent message, showing it had been received.

"I will, Drake." Rachel smiled.

Cash wasn't going to be winning any of her family's hearts anytime soon.

She sent him a victorious look. He wouldn't be cashing in on that bet she had made him. If Drake was warning him about her, then he stood a snowball's chance in Hell of getting her brothers to agree to her going on a date with him.

# CHAPTER TWENTY

"What are we doing here?" Cash questioned why Shade had them sitting outside the movie theater.

"Trying to pay you back."

Before he could say anything else, the movie let out and the moviegoers came through the doors. Cash observed the people leaving, wondering which one Shade was looking for. His question was soon answered.

"You sneaky son of a bitch." Cash's admiration of Shade's skill grew. He wanted to kick his own ass for not thinking of it first. He could have held on to the favor Shade had owed him. He was going to have to find another way to get his vote for Rachel, and he hated owing Shade favors; he could be a bastard when he wanted his repayment.

The two boys drew closer to the bikers, sitting on their bikes. Their gazes were all for the bikes. Cash had to hide his grin, remembering when all he could think about was wanting a bike.

"Hi, Shade, Cash." Jace and his friend came to a stop at the bikes.

"Hey, Jace, Cal."

Cash was surprised Jace and Cal were friends. Cal came

from one of the poorest families in town while Jace was from the wealthiest. It was a mismatched pair, but the two had been firm friends since preschool.

"Can we talk?" Shade's expression made it seem important.

"Sure." The boy's chest puffed up that someone like Shade had deliberately sought him out while Cal's expression became impassive and watchful.

"Your dad will be here any minute."

Cash had to admire the kid for trying to watch out for his friend.

"This won't take long. I have a favor to ask. Cash here wants to make friends with those cousins of yours. I was hoping you could hook him up with a helping hand. Of course, I could help you out with something you're wanting real badly, too. I have an extra bike I don't need any more. You would have to get your dad's permission and get your motorcycle license, but it would be yours, free of charge."

Of course the boy was a Porter, and he was suspicious of their motives, despite the gleam in his eyes when the motorcycle had been mentioned. "Why do you want to become friends with them? They hate your guts."

Cash winced at his blunt question. "I was hoping you could help me out with that problem. I'm going to be straight with you: I don't give a shit about your cousins, but Rachel won't go out with me without their permission."

As the two boys looked at each other and burst into laughter, Cash shifted uncomfortably on his bike.

"You have a whole clubhouse of chicks, and Rach is giving you trouble?"

At Cash's silence, their laughter continued.

"Do we have a deal?" Thank God Shade intervened because he was about to kick another Porter's ass and doom any hope he had of getting Rachel.

"Yeah, I'll help. But let's be clear, if he hurts my cousin

again, I'll tell my dad, and believe me, if you think Rachel's brothers are a pain to deal with, he will become your own personal nightmare."

"I have no intention of hurting Rachel," Cash said through clenched teeth. He was going to have to take a couple of Valiums just to steady his nerves when he was around anyone with the last name Porter.

"Cool, it's settled then," Shade intervened once again, seeing Cash's temper wearing thin.

"I'm going hunting with them this weekend. We've been dying to hunt on your private land. We could stay the night at your cabin. That would win some brownie points with them."

Cash wasn't anxious for them to be anywhere near him with loaded weapons, but Jace was right. That property was marked no trespassing, and everyone in the county knew it held a large number of game.

"All right. Set it up. I'll pick you guys up Saturday morning at five a.m."

"We better go," Shade warned.

Cash looked up the street and spotted the cherry-colored Porsche at the red light, ready to pull into the theater's parking lot.

"Later," Cash said, starting his motor.

While both men rode out as Drake pulled in, Cash lifted his hand in acknowledgment. It couldn't have gone better.

Cash enjoyed the ride back to Mag's house, already anticipating the feel of Rachel's lips on his dick.

* * *

Cash stood in the doorway, watching Rachel work with her plants. Her gentle hands worked with them like they were precious jewels instead of seedlings in clumps of dirt.

"Where's Mag?"

Rachel jumped at the sound of his voice.

"She went to bed a few minutes ago." She looked at him through the veil of her lashes. "I didn't cook any extra for dinner. I didn't expect you back tonight."

Cash frowned. "Why not?" He had already eaten at the diner with Shade, but it still pissed him off for some reason.

As she turned bright red, Cash couldn't keep the smug grin from his face.

"Don't tell me you thought I spent the night at the clubhouse last night and was going to do it again tonight."

"What you do is none of my business." She kept fiddling with her plants.

"I didn't go there when I left here last night. I went to Rosie's, where I had a meeting. That's when I got the call from Knox and spent the night chasing after that cousin of yours."

"Oh." Rachel shrugged. "Like I said, it's none of my business. I could make you something if you're hungry, though."

Cash was tempted, just to have her do something for him, but he saw she was busy and he was still full. "That's okay. I'm not really hungry."

Cash saw no reason to alleviate the guilty expression on her face. He was a self-admitted bastard, and he planned to use the opportunity to gain something he wanted.

"You could give me your cell phone number, and the next time I'm late, I could give you a call or you could call me."

Rachel bit her lip. "All right."

Cash felt he had won a minor victory. He already had her cell phone number, but he wanted to establish a more intimate bond between them under her radar. Her defenses were so raised against him he had to insert himself into her life by small degrees.

He pretended to key her number into his phone. When he was done, he walked around the transformed room, which had remained empty as long as he could remember. Mag used to say that, if the good Lord had meant for you to sit your ass in the sun, he wouldn't have created shade.

Now, every time he entered the room, he saw more and more plants.

A machine bubbling in the corner drew his interest. He walked closer and saw it was a large fish tank, but he had never seen one set up this way. He had seen several tanks set up for survivalists to make purified drinking water, yet he had never seen anything like this one.

"This is amazing. You did this?"

"Yes. I've been working on it for a while. I have another set up at my home, but I wanted to see if it worked as well with larger tanks."

"Does it?"

"Yes."

"Damn, Rachel. I'm really impressed. Now I see why you're spending so much time back here. I was wondering why you don't see your clients anymore. Several of the customers coming into the church store have been asking Lily why you're not taking their calls anymore," Cash asked curiously.

When she turned, going back to spraying the plants, Cash looked at her stiff back, guilt hitting him. "Rachel, your clients aren't going to say anything about me opening my big mouth."

"It's getting late. I need to get to bed. Night, Cash."

He watched her leave the room. Hearing the closing of her bedroom door, he turned the lights off in the room and went into the kitchen to get himself a beer. Every time he took a step forward with Rachel, he ended up taking two steps backward. He felt like he was never going to be able to reach her.

"Got one for me?" Mag asked as she rolled herself into the kitchen.

"Yeah." Cash reached into the refrigerator, pulling her out a beer.

Some people might think it was strange drinking a beer with their eighty-eight-year-old grandmother, but Cash didn't. She had never done a proper thing in her life. When she was sixteen, she had run off with a carnie worker and married him. After three years on the road, she had returned to Treepoint with him in tow and two babies. Her husband had become hurt and could no longer do the rigorous work of putting the tents up and down.

Her parents had given her hell but had opened their doors to the family. Everyone had expected her husband—Cash had privately believed there wasn't a marriage certificate—to not be able to support his family, but he had proven them wrong, working in the mill yard and saving enough money to buy a piece of property. It was the same property he had built the original log home on with his own two hands, managing to buy the scrap lumber for it. They had been married fifty-six years when he had died, and Cash still remembered that day along with his grandmother's face as they had become concerned when he hadn't returned from a fishing trip. They had found him peacefully lying on the bank; he had passed away while doing what he loved.

For the first time, his strong-as-a-rock grandmother had broken, begging God to undo what they had found. Losing a man he had admired and loved had been heart-rending for Cash, as well.

She now sat in a wheelchair, studying him as she drank her beer.

"I used to go to your football games and watch you make play after play. The harder the game, the harder you played, Cash."

"I got knocked around plenty." He took a drink of his beer.

"Yes, you did. Remember when we played Jamestown and we were losing? Everyone had given up. The crowd wasn't even yelling; people were leaving. It was raining and freezing. Parents were standing by metal trashcans, lighting fires to stay warm. Most miserable night of my fucking life, but the proudest I'd ever been of you. The more defeated those other boys became, the more determined you were.

You made those touchdowns that won the game. You never quit, and you don't know how to lose gracefully. Don't start now when you could lose the biggest prize of your life. She's worth the fight."

Cash set his beer down on the counter. "I know she is, but she hates me. I fucked up, Gram."

"I know you did. A woman don't get that look in her eye unless she's been hurt past what her heart can bear, but I have faith in you. Seduce her. You've had to have learned a thing or two after all I've heard about you."

Cash arched his brow at his grandmother.

"I'm old, not senile." His grandmother finished her beer. "I'm giving you the same advice I gave your father, but he was too arrogant to listen. Court, seduce, or better yet, knock her up. I'd like to see my great-grandchild before I die, but don't let that girl get away from you. She's a good woman, Cash."

"I know she is," Cash said softly.

"Good. Now I'm going to bed." The old woman turned her wheelchair around to leave.

"Mag, which one of those worked for Granddad?"

"I was three months pregnant when I ran off with him."

# CHAPTER TWENTY-ONE

"Shh…" Dustin threw Cash a silencing look as they made their way through the woods.

By this point, Cash didn't know how he had restrained himself from raising his gun at Dustin. Only the knowledge the man had a child at home had saved his life.

They finally reached a screen Cash had set up years ago. It was small, but because Rider and Train liked to hunt, it was big enough for the Porters, Jace, and him. They hunkered down to sit, waiting for the game to appear. It was a long, tedious process, but Cash was determined to be affable toward the men. While Jace's easy nature made it more comfortable, Cash kept trying to talk to the Porters, receiving only brief replies.

"How old were you when you went in the Navy?"

"Eighteen," Cash answered in a low voice.

"Did you kill anyone?" Jace's eager questions were beginning to wear on his nerves.

"A few."

"I want to go in the service, but my dad told me no."

"The thing about being eighteen is you don't have to have anyone's permission to do whatever you want," Cash answered then backtracked at seeing the Porters' glares.

"Of course, you want your dad to approve. He may know what suits you better," Cash ended lamely.

The suddenly mature expression on Jace's face showed he had only heard the first half of his answer.

"It's not fun and games, Jace. If you don't like your dad telling you what to do, then you're not going to like having people ranked higher than you doing it all day long. It's hard work. It means getting your ass out of bed early every morning, working hard all day, just to be told when to go to bed. They won't put up with an attitude; you have to be respectful at all times. It means giving a commitment to a way of life that means something to you, to help and serve others enough to give your life at any time."

"Wow. I'll think about everything you said."

"Why don't you do that and shut the fuck up before you scare all the game away," snarled Greer.

Both Cash and Jace stopped talking. It was twenty minutes before Cash saw a movement at the beginning of the clearing from a red fox and her little kits entering it.

Tate edged closer to the opening, placing the barrel of his gun through the blind opening while Greer positioned his own rifle.

"I'll take the mama. Greer, you take the first two little kits, and Cash, you're such a good shot, you take the last three kits."

His eyes went to the small family sniffing the air for intruders. He nodded.

Moving forward, his foot jarred the side of the blind, making a loud rustling noise. The family darted from the clearing as if their lives depended on it, which they did.

The men stared at him in anger. Even Jace looked disappointed in him.

"What the fuck?" Tate snarled.

"Sorry, I tripped," Cash explained without remorse.

"You have been hunting before, right?" Jace looked at him pathetically.

"Yes, Jace, I've been hunting before."

"Often?"

"Shut up!" Tate's frustrated voice had them both snapping their mouths closed.

It was an hour before another animal came into the clearing. *I can't catch a fucking break today*, Cash thought as a small fawn came farther into the clearing with its mother walking not far behind.

Cash could just hear Rachel's reaction if he let Bambi die. Thinking quickly, Cash had a sneezing fit that had the deer fleeing.

"Motherfucker, did you bring us out here just to bug the piss out of us?" Dustin's harsh voice had Cash shrugging apologetically.

"I can't help it if I'm allergic to Jace's cologne."

Jace glared at him but took the brunt of the brothers' anger. The boy wanted the promised motorcycle enough to become the patsy.

"You wore cologne?" Dustin sniffed toward his cousin.

"I didn't want to shower," Jace mumbled.

"How about we just go on to the cabin and fix some breakfast. We can get an early start on fishing." Cash stood as best he could in the small confines of the blind, going outside the small structure.

"I guess we haven't got a choice with Jace polluting the air," Greer grumbled as all the men came out.

They hiked the two miles to his cabin. When he opened the door, the Porters from oldest to youngest whistled.

"Now this is what I call a cabin," Jace said admiringly.

"Put your backpacks up. I'll fix breakfast." It didn't take long for him to fry bacon and eggs and make a strong pot of coffee. The men all dug in, eating as soon as he put the food on the table.

They spent the rest of the day outside fishing, getting along because they remained quiet. Jace had quieted down, too, throwing him hurt looks every so often. Cash felt like he had stepped on a rambunctious puppy's tail.

However, everyone's mood improved as soon as the

fish started to be caught. The size of them had them all trying to outdo the others to catch the biggest one.

As Cash's line pulled taut, he drew the pole back, and he could tell by the strength of the tugging it was a big fish. Unobtrusively, he released the line, letting the fish go.

Reeling in his line, they taunted him for losing the fish.

"You don't fish any better than you can shoot," Greer taunted.

Cash remained quiet.

After another hour, he stood and stretched. "How about I go back to the cabin and clean a few for dinner?"

"Sounds good. It's not like you're catching anything anyway." Dustin laughed. "You might as well play bitch and cook." Dustin laughed again, throwing his line back in the water.

"You sure you don't want to stay and let us give you a few pointers?" Greer added, throwing the fish he had just caught into the cooler.

"We'll save that for another day," Cash replied, picking up the cooler and leaving Jace to pack Cash's pole back when he returned with his cousins.

It took Cash a good hour to walk off his anger when he got back to the cabin. If he hadn't wanted their approval for Rachel, he would have thrown them into the water and driven back to town alone.

After his walk, he burned off any anger he had left by gutting the fish and getting them ready to fry. The gas stove was old but had cooked many good meals. He remembered several of the ones he and his father had shared in the cabin that had been built by his grandfather and dad. There used to be an old, dirt road that led from his grandparents' cabin to this one, but it had long ago grown over.

His father had passed away when he was in the service, and by the time he had returned to Treepoint, Mag had moved and he had liked the remoteness of the cabin. Only he, The Last Riders, and the Porters even knew the cabin was back this far in the woods. It was off the grid with two generators as back-up, well water, and propane for the stove and water heater. It had two bedrooms and a loft that held several bunk beds.

Cash was flipping the fish over when the Porters returned. After everyone washed up, they ate. The night dragged on while they played game after game of poker, which he lost.

Tate leaned forward to pull the last of his money toward him.

"I guess that's it for me tonight." Cash threw the cards down onto the table.

Greer smirked while Tate stared at him. "Sure you don't want to play another game?" Tate asked, dealing out the cards.

"I'm sure. I'll do the dishes."

Greer opened his mouth, but Tate shot him a quelling look.

"I was beginning to wonder how long you were going to let us take your money."

Cash hesitated in getting up. "What?"

"You heard me." Tate didn't look down at his cards; instead, he stared directly into his eyes. "Is five hundred all you think my sister's worth?"

"No, but it's all I brought with me." Cash's hands clenched into fists.

Tate's lips quirked. "Smart answer."

"Jace told you?"

"Of course. He may want a motorcycle, but he's our blood. Blood always comes first; you should have known better."

"If you knew, then why did you come?" Cash stiffened in his seat. This could go really badly. He didn't want to have to hurt any of the assholes to protect himself, but he sure as fuck couldn't be with Rachel if he was six-feet under.

"Relax, Cash." Dustin laughed, going to the refrigerator

to get more beers, which he set on the table with a thump. Everyone reached out for a beer, the sound of the tops popping starting the negotiations.

"We've all come up with certain concessions before we give you our vote of approval to court Rachel," Tate said, laying down his cards, literally and figuratively.

This didn't sound good, but he was willing to see how far the bastards expected him to cave for Rachel.

"It's just five simple rules. You should be able to live with them with no problems."

"It depends on just what the five rules are, now, doesn't it?" Cash said. Nothing was ever simple with the Porters.

"Yes, it does. Rule number one: no fucking around on Rachel. That means no women in town or those women you got stashed at that clubhouse of yours," Tate began their demands.

"Rule number two: you can't lay a hand on her when you're mad. She can get a man's temper riled, but you're not allowed to ever hurt my sister.

"Rule number three: she gets to keep working with her plants and clients. They're a pain in the ass—you can't go to the fucking bathroom without having something disgusting growing on the shelf—but they're important to her.

"Rule number four: you have to start going to church with her. We watched our parents fight about that for years. Rachel wants a man who will sit next to her in church on Christmas Eve." Tate's voice was much too chirpy when he voiced this rule. Everyone in town knew Cash's feelings on attending church.

"Rule five, and it's the most important to us: if you have kids, you have to let us be involved in their lives. I don't give a fuck how much you hate us, but you won't show our nieces or nephews that you do. We keep this personal bullshit between us. Deal?"

Cash didn't hesitate. "Deal, but this doesn't mean we

have to become best friends, does it?"

"God, no," Greer shuddered.

"I have a demand of my own. When Rachel and I get in a fight, you keep your noses out of it."

Dustin looked at his brothers. "Agreed."

"Unless you break any of our rules," Greer clarified.

"I can live with that," Cash agreed. "So, you already knew you were going to agree to me seeing Rachel before we started this morning?" He narrowed his eyes on their unrepentant expressions.

"Yep. We decided we were going to have some fun making you squirm, though. I don't know which I enjoyed the most: you scaring off those foxes or throwing away that big-ass fish you caught." Tate grinned.

"I do. Him letting me call him a bitch." Greer slapped Cash on the shoulder, almost knocking his beer out of his hand.

"Jace, it's bedtime. Cash, you got anything harder than beer?" Tate asked, picking the cards up again.

"Yes."

"Then bring it out. Let's play a few more hands, and this time, you can play like a man instead of a pussy."

Cash looked around the table at the Porters. It was going to be a long night.

# CHAPTER TWENTY-TWO

Rachel parked her car in front of Mag's house. She had gone to the store after church to pick up a few things they needed. She was struggling to carry the three bags of groceries and the beer that Cash and Mag liked when Cash's truck pulled into the driveway. She had the beer juggled on her hip as she tried to open the front door.

As Cash opened his truck door and got out, she was shocked at his exhausted appearance; even with the sunglasses on, he looked like shit. His jeans and t-shirt were rumpled, his long hair was tousled, and his face was white as a sheet.

"Need some help?" Cash's jovial voice set her temper off.

"Yes, you can carry your own beer. From now own, you can get it your own self, too. It doesn't seem like you have any trouble getting liquor."

Cash reached out, taking the beer with one hand before opening the door with the other. "Mag home?"

"No, she's next door." Rachel nodded to where Mag was sitting on her neighbor's porch, talking.

Rachel went in the house, packing the grocery bags and

setting them down on the counter.

"I bought them, so you can put them up," she snapped. "I'm going to get changed." She turned around after setting the groceries down and barreled into Cash's chest. She'd thought he had moved away after setting down the beer.

"Careful, Rachel," Cash warned. "I'm not in the best mood. I just spent yesterday with your brothers and Jace, and I spent the night at my cabin with them trying to give me alcohol poisoning with that moonshine they've been making."

"You went hunting and drinking with my brothers?" she asked, stunned.

"Yes," Cash gritted out, his head about to explode.

"Are they still alive?"

Cash bit back his laughter at the worry in her voice. "For now. I'm not making any promises, though. It depends on if I have to go to the hospital to get my stomach pumped."

"Why would you...?"

"You know why." Cash glared at her, lifting his sunglasses to his head.

At his look, Rachel took a step toward her bedroom. Cash leaned a hand out, bracing it on the wall, and blocked her escape.

"N-No."

"Because I happen to have their approval for us to date."

Rachel shook her head. "No way. They wouldn't—"

"They did. Call them if you don't believe me."

Rachel didn't have to; she saw the truth on his face. "That doesn't mean shit. I'm not going to go out with you."

"You going back on your word?"

Rachel's eyes widened in shock. "I was freaking mouthing off. You know that!"

"Well, your mouth is going to be plenty busy Friday

night. You've got a week to get used to the idea, or I'll spread it all over town that a Porter's word isn't worth shit."

"You better go on to the hospital because obviously my brothers' moonshine has done some brain damage."

Cash dropped his hand, letting her pass. "Friday, Rachel."

She pushed past him, going to her bedroom and slamming the door shut. Pacing angrily around the small room, she was so mad she was tempted to throw something. Instead, she jerked her phone out of her pocket, pushing down on the familiar number.

"Hello?" Tate's cautious voice answered his phone.

"What the hell, Tate?" Furiously, she laid into him.

"Rach—"

"How could you?" she stormed, ignoring his interruption.

"Rach—"

"I can't believe my brothers stabbed me in the back!"

"Rach—"

"You called me every name in the book when you found out I slept with him!" she screamed into the phone.

"Rachel!"

She went quiet, recognizing that tone of voice from her childhood.

"Listen to me for a minute. You've been mooning over him since you were a kid. You're the one who slept with him and ran away when you couldn't stand seeing him with other women."

"I left town because you all humiliated me."

"Rachel, we've embarrassed you your whole life; that was nothing new. You ran because you didn't know how to deal. You still don't."

"I don't want to go out with him," Rachel said stubbornly.

Tate's voice softened. "Then don't. We gave him our permission to date you. You do have the option to say no.

The choice is still yours."

Rachel went silent. She was conflicted; she couldn't have her heart broken by Cash anymore.

"Sister, ask him about the rules."

"What rules?"

"The rules he promised to keep if you started seeing each other. He agreed. He didn't even put up a fuss. Have I ever not looked out for you?" he reasoned.

She remained silent.

"Rachel?"

"The night of the party... you really hurt me, Tate."

"I know." He didn't apologize, but his voice was filled with remorse. "Give him another chance, Rachel. Give both of us another chance."

Rachel sighed. "Okay."

"That's the sister I know and love." He teased a smile out of her before she disconnected the call.

Changing out of her church clothes, she put on her jeans and t-shirt. As she braided her hair back, she felt much calmer than she had before entering the room. Pulling out her computer, she backed up her notes on her plants. She was very meticulous on keeping up-to-date with the progress of the seedlings.

Afterward, she cooked dinner. Cash didn't emerge from his room for the rest of the night. Aware of how strong her brothers' hooch was, she would be amazed if he was able to get out of bed for a couple of days.

Her brothers might have given their approval, but they had made him pay for it.

\* \* \*

"What are you doing?" Rachel came up behind Lily, seeing her trying to slide a chair to the corner.

"I was just trying to make some more room," Lily explained.

"Shade would be furious if he saw you doing that."

"Then it's a good thing he's not here, isn't it? You're not a tattletale, are you?" Lily wrinkled her nose at her.

185

"Let me catch you moving any more of this heavy furniture, and I'll call him," Rachel threatened.

"Okay, okay, you win. I just feel silly asking you to do things that I'm perfectly capable of doing myself."

"I don't mind." Rachel slid the rest of the furniture closer to the wall.

"Lily?" They both jumped when they heard Brooke's voice behind them.

"Hi, Brooke. What can I help you with?" Lily asked politely.

Rachel walked to the side, moving a headboard casually while listening to their conversation as she worked.

"I'm doing a church Bible group tomorrow, and Willa has several of the texts that we use. Would it be possible for you to pick them up on your way home? The pastor and I are having a dinner tonight with several of the deacons. If you can't, I suppose…"

"No problem. I don't mind at all. I'll enjoy visiting Willa." Lily smiled.

*Willa will be relieved*, Rachel thought. The woman would be a nervous wreck waiting for Brooke to arrive.

"Fine, then. That's a relief. I was nervous about leaving my roast in the oven when I ran out." Brooke gave them both a practiced smile. "I'm afraid cooking is not where my talents lie."

"I'm sure you're an excellent cook," Lily complimented.

Rachel turned her back so Brooke couldn't read her expression.

"Thank you, Lily. I better get back to my dinner. I'm making a cobbler for dessert. I've never made one before, but it's Merrick's favorite, so I thought I would give it a try."

"I'm sure it will be delicious. I'll drop the texts off in Pastor Merrick's office in the morning."

"Thanks, again. Goodnight, Lily, Rachel."

The girls both told her goodbye, watching her leave in

her expensive dress and high heels.

"You just saved Willa's ass," Rachel told her, coming to stand next to her.

"I know. I knew Willa would prefer me picking the books up. I'm supposed to meet Beth after work to go shopping, though. I'll have to call her and tell her I'll be late."

"I could do it for you. I'm not doing anything. You could even leave early if you want," Rachel offered.

"I may take you up on that. Beth will be waiting with the twins."

"It all works out perfect, then."

\* \* \*

Three hours later, Rachel closed the church store. Her car was steaming hot, so she took off the lightweight jacket she had put over her dress. The church and the store always remained uncomfortably cool since Merrick had taken over. The mornings were the worst when she opened the store, the frigid air hitting her as she entered. She had mentioned it hesitatingly to the pastor, and he had told her he kept the air on the same setting as always, but he'd agreed it was cold also. He had promised to get Brooke to call the repairman, but that had been over a week ago. Rachel promised herself, if it wasn't repaired soon, she would call the repairman on her own.

She made a left onto Willa's street and saw Lewis's car. When she had called earlier to tell her she was stopping by, she hadn't mentioned Lewis would be there. Looking at her watch, she realized he must have just gotten off work.

Rachel parked her car next to his vehicle, careful not to block him in. Willa would probably thank her for stopping by and getting rid of the overbearing man.

As she drew closer to the door, she heard a scream from inside. Not bothering to knock, she flung the door open. Rachel let out a scream of her own when she saw Lewis had his belt off and was whipping Willa with it. Fury soared through her.

She ran toward him as he lifted the belt to strike Willa again, and without thinking, she pushed him away from Willa.

"Don't you dare touch her again!" she screamed at him.

Lewis stared angrily at Rachel. "Get the fuck out!" He came toward her with the belt raised and Rachel froze. She wasn't going to let him scare her.

"Willa, get up and go call Knox now."

When Lewis swung back toward Willa, Rachel's words stopped him cold. "If you lay another hand on her or me, my brothers will kill you. I'm going to be real fair to you, Lewis, and tell you that you have three days to get out of town before I tell my brothers what happened here."

"I'm not afraid of your fucked-up brothers," Lewis snarled.

"Then it's your life to kiss goodbye. Because I'm telling you, when Greer hears what you were doing in here, he's going to kill you for thinking you could raise a belt to me and get away with it."

Willa tried to shuffle to the side, but Lewis bent down and jerked her to her feet by her blond hair.

"You stupid cunt. Go sit down on the couch until I'm ready to deal with you."

"Stop it, Lewis. Rachel can leave, and we can sit down and talk."

Lewis's hand flung out, backhanding Willa across the cheek, knocking her down to the floor. His foot then kicked her sharply in the stomach.

"You fat-ass bitch! I don't know why I want you anyway," he snarled.

Rachel lost control of her temper.

"You son of a bitch." She flung herself at him when he drew his foot back to kick Willa again. Rachel pummeled him with her fists wherever she could strike. When he tried to grab her hands, she raked her nails down his face before he could get a tight grip. Her legs kicked at him, desperately trying to nail him in his groin.

However, as his fist came out, striking her in the stomach, her breath left her in a rush as she fell to her knees. She tried to gasp for breath but couldn't get it back. Lewis's hand struck her cheek, knocking her to the floor. Before she could get her breath back, he was on top of her. His face was filled with fury, all control lost.

His hands went to her throat, tightening into a grip that took what little oxygen she had left. Black dots filled her vision as his triumphant face loomed over her.

A sudden, loud pop had Lewis falling to the side, blood gushing from his chest.

It took several seconds before Rachel could get her breath back enough to rise up on her elbow.

Willa was standing in her kitchen doorway, holding a gun in her hand. Rachel turned her head to the side, seeing Lewis's blank stare at the ceiling.

Rachel heard Willa's frightened whimper and forced herself to sit the rest of the way up. Managing to get to her knees, she crawled toward Willa, who had blood coming out of her nose and a swollen cheek.

"Willa, it's okay." Rachel gingerly reached out to take the weapon from her, placing it carefully on the floor next to her.

"I killed him." Her horrified whisper broke Rachel's heart.

"If you hadn't, he would have killed me," Rachel soothed her. "What set him off?"

"I don't know. He came banging on my door. I had forgotten to lock it after my last delivery, and he came in before I could stop him. He was in a rage when he got here."

Tears were pouring down her cheeks as she began trembling. Rachel knew shock was setting in.

"Where's your phone? I'll call Knox."

Willa looked wildly around before managing to point to her purse. Rachel got to her feet, feeling every sore muscle in her body. Opening Willa's purse, she called the Sheriff's office, explaining what had happened. She disconnected the call when the dispatcher said Knox was in route.

Rachel went back to Willa, sitting down next to her on the floor, placing her arm around her trembling shoulders.

"I'm going to burn in Hell for killing a man." Willa covered her hands with her face.

"The only one who's going to Hell is Lewis."

# CHAPTER TWENTY-THREE

Rachel sat in Knox's office as he questioned Willa in the interrogation room. She hoped he didn't traumatize the woman any further than she was.

She looked up expectantly when the door opened to see Cash come in.

"You all right?" His concerned gaze had her nodding. Somehow, she couldn't bring herself to be upset that Lewis was dead.

Her brothers came in the door behind him. Unlike Cash, they were furious.

"It's a good thing he's dead—"

"Greer, calm down. It's all over, and I'm not hurt. The best thing is that he's not going to hurt Willa anymore."

Tate pulled her out of the chair and into his arms. "I'm happy that you were there for Willa, but I lost ten years off my life when Knox called and told me what happened."

"I'm fine, Tate." She circled his waist.

She lifted her head from Tate's chest when Knox came into the room with Willa. Rachel immediately went to her side.

"You can come home with me tonight, Willa."

Willa shook her head. "If I don't go back to my home

tonight, I never will."

"I can stay the night with you," Rachel offered.

"That's all right. I'm just going to go home and go to bed." Willa turned her bruised face to Cash then Knox. "I want to apologize. If I hadn't lied and said Lewis wasn't harassing me, then maybe he would still be alive. I honestly believed it would make him even more violent if he knew I had told or pressed charges against him."

"I knew you weren't telling the truth. I had a talk with him Friday. I thought he would back off after I threatened him with a social services investigation toward his kids," Knox said.

Willa went even whiter. "What's going to happen to the kids?"

"A foster home will be found for them. Don't worry, I'll make sure they find a good home," Knox said, picking up his phone on the desk.

"Please, I would never forgive myself if they were hurt because of my actions."

"Willa, none of this was your fault. Lewis had real problems. You are the victim here," Knox reassured her.

Willa didn't seem convinced, but she nodded.

"Come on, Willa. We'll give you a ride home. Let's go, Rachel; you're coming home with us," Tate said while they left Knox's office as he talked on the phone.

"No, I'm not. I'm going to Mag's. You can drop me off to pick up my car." Rachel wasn't about to place herself back under her brothers' thumbs. She still hadn't forgiven them for how they had talked to her at the party.

"How long are you going to hold a grudge?" Greer spoke up. "You almost got yourself killed because we weren't keeping a watch over you."

"I almost got killed because I was at the wrong place at the wrong time."

"I forgot about the texts. I'll get them for you when we get to my house," Willa offered.

"What texts?" Cash asked, frowning.

"Brooke asked Lily if she would pick up some books from Willa. She was busy, so I offered," Rachel explained.

Cash's face turned even more forbidding. "I need to talk to Knox before I leave. I'll see you back at the house tonight."

"Okay." Rachel left the Sheriff's office, her curiosity aroused by the look on Cash's face. It was plain something was going on that he was keeping from her.

Rachel got into Tate's truck next to Willa. She had no choice other than to wait until tonight to question him. She took Willa's hand in hers, trying to help her in the only way she could.

\* \* \*

Cash pulled out his cell phone as he headed to his bike. "Crash?"

"Yeah, what you need?"

"I want all the information you can pull up on Lewis. He just tried to kill Willa and Rachel. Something sent him over the edge and I want to know what it was. The timing said he went to Willa's house after work; check out the factory and see if any of the other workers picked up on anything going on with the motherfucker. Text me his address from the employee files, too. I'm going to go check his place out."

"Will do. I'll call when I have what you want." Crash disconnected the call.

Cash started his bike. A minute later, the address he wanted came to his cell. He was going to search Lewis's home and find out exactly what had sent him over the edge, hoping that he was wrong in what he suspected. No man went that ape shit crazy unless something or someone had pulled his trigger.

\* \* \*

She had to wait to question Cash since he didn't return to Mag's house until Friday morning. When he came in looking tired and worn, she was tempted to ask him where he had been, but he didn't give her the opportunity.

193

"I'm tired, hungry, and I need a shower. I have just driven over a hundred miles. I would have stopped for the night, but I kept riding to get back here. I expect you to be standing by that door at seven tonight. We made a bet, and you're keeping it."

Rachel started to open her mouth to argue but closed it at the anticipatory gleam in his eyes.

"Okay," Rachel agreed.

He gave her a sharp nod before going down the hall to his bedroom.

"Don't make me come looking for you. You know I enjoy chasing my women down."

That hard-ass had read her mind; she had intended to go visit Logan tonight at Mrs. Langley's. She had spent too many Friday nights there for him not to be able to find her, though.

Mag was sitting in the living room, reading the paper. Rachel had forgotten she was there. Rachel threw her a quelling look when she would have opened her mouth.

"I wasn't going to say a thing," Mag denied.

"I bet." Rachel left the house to go to work at the church store. Fridays were always pretty busy, so Rachel liked to make sure she got there early.

As she opened the door, surprised Lily was running late, the frigid air hit her in a blast and Rachel shivered, pulling on the sweater she had taken from the car. She had meant to call the repairman a couple of days ago and had forgotten. This was beyond ridiculous. She couldn't understand why Pastor Patterson hadn't seen to it. His family couldn't be comfortable living in what felt like an igloo.

Rachel went to the back of the store and put some water in the coffeepot to heat for tea and had just decided to raise one of the rear windows to let in some warm air when she heard the front door open. She went back to the front of the store and didn't see anyone. A chill ran up her back that didn't have anything to do with the cold air.

No one had come into the store, which meant someone had gone out. Whoever it was had been in the store when she had come in.

Rachel started going through the store carefully. None of the things there were expensive, all the items second-hand. With an observant eye, Rachel began to itemize the missing items: a few cans of food and some clothes. Several of the books on the shelf were out of order, and she had straightened them just before she had left to go home yesterday.

Going back behind the desk, she called the pastor's office. He answered on the first ring, and when she explained what she had found, he came immediately to the store.

"Were you able to see anyone?"

"No, I would have never known anyone was here if I hadn't heard the bell over the door ring. I was out back, opening a window, when I thought someone had come in."

Pastor Merrick frowned at her. "Why were you opening the window?"

"Because I was freezing. I was trying to let in some warm air."

"The air conditioner still isn't fixed in here? The repairman fixed the other unit for the church and house last week. I assumed he had fixed this one also."

"No, it's still freezing in here. I've been leaving the windows open in the back to let in warm air."

"I'm sorry, Rachel. I'll call him immediately," he apologized.

"I should have mentioned it before now." She should have told him she had mentioned it to Brooke several times.

"Do you want me to call Knox?"

Rachel thought of the items missing. Whoever had been in the store had been hungry and needing clothes. "No, that's all right. I'm sure, whoever it was, they were just hungry. They were probably frightened off when I came in early," Rachel speculated.

"If you're sure…"

"Yes." The door opened and Lily came in with a bright smile.

"All right, then. I'll go call the repairman."

"What has the both of you looking so serious this morning?" Lily questioned as she stashed her purse under the counter.

"How the repairman hasn't fixed the air conditioner yet. I'm on my way to give him a call. I'll talk to you both later." The pastor excused himself.

"I hope he fixes it soon. It's like Alaska in here," Lily admitted.

"I'm freezing," Rachel shivered.

She fixed Lily and herself both tea as the customers began coming in. The intruder and the customers kept her thoughts too busy to worry about her date with Cash tonight. She wanted to call it off, and she certainly had no intentions of going through with her promise of a blowjob, but her pride kept her from bowing out of the rest of the bet. Besides, she knew Cash would be able to track her down wherever she hid out.

"What are you doing tonight?" Rachel asked.

"Babysitting for Beth and Razer. They haven't had a date night since she's had the babies. How about you?"

"I'm going out on a date with Cash."

Lily threw her a startled look as she arranged clothes on a rack. "I didn't know you were seeing him."

"I'm not; this is our first date." Rachel blushed, aware of how this made her sound when everyone in the freaking town knew she had lost her virginity to him.

"Where are you going?" Lily asked with a worried frown.

"I figured we would go to a movie or dinner." Rachel paused in hanging clothes at Lily's reaction.

"That sounds like fun." Lily's overly enthusiastic voice

had her raising a brow in question. "I mean, that's better than sitting at home on a Friday night, isn't it?"

"Depends," Rachel replied.

"On what?"

"I've never really dated anyone, Lily. He's used to being around sexy women who can keep up with him. I'm not even in the same league as the other women." Rachel hated how unsure of herself she sounded.

Lily bit her lip. "No, you're definitely not that," she agreed.

Hurt, Rachel picked up their empty tea cups, packing them to the back room.

"Rachel?" Lily's soft voice from the doorway had her turning back to her. "I didn't mean that the way it sounded. What I meant is that you are a sweet, warm-hearted woman who wants a husband and kids. Family is very important to you, and he doesn't get along with your brothers."

"He got their approval to go out with me," she confessed.

Lily burst out in laughter. "I wish I could have seen that."

"Me, too." Rachel laughed along with Lily.

The two women spent a busy afternoon, which passed much too quickly for Rachel's nervous stomach.

"Have fun," Lily said mischievously as she pulled her car out of the lot.

All the way home, Rachel thought about what she would wear, not coming to a decision until she was standing in front of her closet, choosing a black skirt and a sapphire-colored blouse with tiny buttons up the front. It looked both casual and dressy, but she still felt uncertain whether she was overdressed. She brushed out her hair, letting it fall down her back in a mass.

As she checked her watch, she saw that she had only a few minutes to spare. Hurriedly, she went out of her bedroom to see Cash was waiting by the doorway.

Rachel's feet slowed as she approached him. She had never seen him looking so handsome in his dark jeans and casual button down shirt. His sensual mouth was curved in a seductive smile as his eyes traveled her body, over the curves of her hips to linger on the firm thrust of her breasts.

"You look pretty all dressed up. Ready?" Cash asked.

"Yes. Where are we going?" Blushing, Rachel picked up her purse.

"I thought we would check out King's new restaurant."

"That sounds good. I haven't been there yet." Suddenly, she was more at ease; she was eager to see King's new place.

"Me, either." Cash opened the truck door for her.

Rachel wasn't used to seeing the courtly side of Cash, and it was making her nerves pick back up worse than ever. She stared out the window as he climbed behind the wheel and started the motor.

"Rachel?"

"Yes?"

"Relax." He gave her a cocky grin as he pulled out onto the mountain road. "It isn't like it's your last meal."

"It feels like it."

Cash reached across the seat, taking her hand and rubbing his thumb over her calloused palms. Embarrassed, Rachel pulled her hand away.

Out of the corner of her eye, she caught his frown.

"What's wrong?" she asked.

"Your hand. I just noticed something was different."

Self-consciously, she rubbed her palms against her skirt. "I should wear gloves more often. I get caught up—"

"I don't give a shit about a few calluses; it's just that something's different."

"What?" Curiously, she looked over at him in the dim interior of the truck.

"They aren't warm like they used to be. Whenever I touched them before, they were abnormally warm; now they're cold."

Rachel turned back to stare out the window again, avoiding his probing gaze.

"I guess the old saying is true: cold hands, cold heart," she replied ironically.

Sadly, Rachel thought it was his hands that should have been as cold as ice.

# CHAPTER TWENTY-FOUR

Cash wondered about Rachel's calm façade. The only hint she was uncomfortable with the conversation was the way she was twisting her hands on her lap.

The parking lot to King's restaurant and lounge was filled, although Cash found a parking space toward the back of the lot. Opening the door, he was going around to open Rachel's when he saw she was already sliding out.

"I was going to open it for you."

"Why? I can open my own."

Cash shut the truck door. The date wasn't exactly getting started the way he'd wanted. Every time he was making a gesture, she seemed to want to keep a distance between them.

Sighing, he took her arm, leading her into the restaurant.

After a bit of a wait, King's hostess seated them at a booth. Cash had intended to sit down next to Rachel, but she didn't slide over far enough, and he didn't want to make an issue of it while the customers from the nearby tables were staring at them with curiosity.

Once the waitress took their drink order, leaving them alone, Cash noticed Rachel's hands tremble as she opened the menu.

"Why are you so nervous?" Cash questioned.

"I'm not. I'm just not used to everyone staring at me."

He had felt the stares but hadn't let them bother him. He had long ago grown used to being a topic of gossip in Treepoint.

"Are you ashamed to be seen out in public with me?" His curt voice startled her into dropping her menu.

"What?" Her confused eyes met his.

Cash relaxed, sensing that wasn't the reason. "Never mind. They'll quit staring in a minute. I think they're surprised to see a Porter and an Adams sitting at the same table."

The waitress returned with their drinks, taking their food orders.

Cash's eyes met a pair of violet ones staring at him from a stool at the bar. He nodded at King—the owner of the restaurant who had married a member of The Last Riders last summer. His rugged face and sophisticated air had been transferred to the restaurant, creating a hit in the small town. The big-city feel was popular with the younger crowd while scaring the more conservative sect who were leery of embracing anything new.

The food was good, and Cash smiled when he saw the tension finally ease as Rachel enjoyed the steak she had ordered.

"I noticed your plants in the tank are growing larger."

Rachel looked up from her plate in surprise. "You noticed?"

"Of course. I would be blind as a bat to miss them."

"My brothers never did. They used to gripe about the money I wasted on the tanks."

A thought struck Cash. He knew for a fact the job she did at the church store didn't pay because he and other members of the club pitched in to give Lily her salary. He didn't think her brothers were giving her money since they wanted her to move home, so how was she supporting herself? She had given Mag rent money for sharing the house, even though he had heard Mag arguing about it. She also bought her own groceries and supplies. So, where was she getting her money from?

He didn't think she had started her own weed business, or had she? There was no doubt she had a green thumb. He started to ask, but foreseeing that she would tell him to mind his own business, he decided to find out for himself. It shouldn't take much to do so; Cash was a master on the computer. He would be able to see where her money was coming from and if it was legal. If there was no trail, then he would have his question answered.

"Are you growing the plants to be a new food source?" Cash joked.

"No." Her serious expression had his smile disappearing at the determination in her expression. "To purify it. With all the mining, a lot of the wells that most of the people still use are tainted; the plants can purify it and make it clean drinking water again. I'm also seeing how they do with water that's been polluted with oil spills."

Cash was impressed with her explanation.

Holy fuck. She was attempting to do what scientists with doctorate degrees had been attempting to do for years. The last big oil spill had resulted in booming business for those who had developed cutting-edge techniques to remove the oil. The possibilities were endless. Developing countries with contaminated water supplies would also benefit. However, the chance of a mountain girl with only a high school education of finding such a discovery was almost nil.

"I can tell you don't think I can do it." When he opened his mouth, she raised her hand in the air. "Don't deny it. I can see it on your face." She looked down at her plate, hiding her expression. "I went away to college for a couple of semesters. One of the first classes I took was aquaculture. It opened my eyes to how many lives are affected by polluted water. Even Treepoint isn't exempt. Most people in the mountains still depend on well water that's contaminated or have streams that are."

"Shit."

"So, even though everyone thinks it's a waste of my time, it's mine to waste." Her eyes stared into his with determination.

Cash put his fork down. "I wasn't being snide. I can tell you have a deep interest in what you're doing." Whichever way he turned, he felt like he was taking a step farther away from the woman he was becoming more and more intrigued by.

Seeing she was finished eating, he tried to save the date he was sure she was anxious to get over. He felt like he was bombing the only chance he had with her.

"Let's go into the lounge for a drink." Cash paid their ticket before they moved into the lounge area where King had made the atmosphere more intimate with a bar and dance floor. The booths were more romantic and the lights more subtle.

This time, when Rachel slid in the booth, he slid in beside her, leaving her no choice except to move over to allow him to sit next to her. She cast him a startled look as she scooted as far away as the seat would allow.

Cash ordered them both beers as they sat, listening to the music. He was about to ask her to dance when a familiar voice waylaid him.

"May I join you?" King sat down across from them without waiting for their reply. While his darkly amused gaze studied them, Cash threw him a quelling look.

"Hello, Rachel. It's good to see you again."

"It's nice to see you again, King." Rachel's blush showed her embarrassment. "How are you liking Treepoint?"

King's harsh face softened. "Unexpectedly well. I'm enjoying being married and looking forward to my first grandchild. The restaurant is doing well; it keeps me out of Evie's hair."

"She hasn't managed to get you on a bike yet?"

"Occasionally. I won't let her ride with me until I get more experienced." Cash and Shade had both been riding with King to teach him the skills needed to be a safe. He was proving to be a good rider; his reflexes and strength were making him a natural.

"I don't imagine there isn't much you can't accomplish." Rachel's compliment had Cash's hand tightening on his beer bottle.

"Evie wouldn't agree with that statement," he said wryly. "She thinks I'm a clutz around the house."

Rachel's laughter bubbled over at his expression; Cash couldn't remember the last time she had laughed in his presence. This date was going even further down the crapper with King's appearance.

"Evie is in the kitchen. If you want to go say hi, it's just through that door," King directed.

"I think I will. Lily said she went over to Willa's to check up on her last night. She hasn't been answering my calls."

After Cash stood up, letting her out of the booth, he resumed his seat, throwing King a disgruntled look.

"Don't look at me that way. I don't know what you're doing, but that poor girl seems miserable."

Cash's shoulders slumped. "I agree." He ran his hand through his hair, messing up the neat appearance. "I don't know where I'm fucking up."

"Perhaps because you're not being yourself, so she can't be," King advised.

Cash went quiet, thinking about his words.

"Listen, I don't know what's going on between you two, but I do know that isn't the same woman who I met flirting with me at the diner, nor is she the woman I saw saving my ass when Lily and I were trapped by Digger."

"I hurt her with my big mouth. I don't think she can

get over it. She's so mad at her brothers she hasn't moved back home."

"I don't believe you're going to change her mind by pretending to be someone else. She's going to sense your insincerity," King stated as they both saw Rachel's approach. "Each woman is different. Evie got over being mad at me after a couple of months, other women don't ever forgive. What you have to decide is how much you actually give a shit."

King changed the subject as Rachel reached the table. "Find out what you needed to know?"

"Yes, thank you. I'm going to stop by tomorrow and see how she's doing myself," Rachel answered, sliding in on the other side of the booth that King had vacated, even though Cash had risen to his feet to let her back in. Clenching his teeth, he sat back down.

She was thwarting every attempt he was making to draw closer to her. Cash studied her worried eyes as she took a sip of her beer.

"Something wrong?" he questioned her.

"I'm just worried about Willa. Evie said she was acting strange when she was there yesterday. I'll feel better once I've had a chance to talk to her."

"Let's dance. That will take your mind off her." Cash got to his feet, taking her hand and ignoring her faint murmur of protest as he led her to the dance floor. He had deliberately waited until a slow song was played.

Circling her small waist, he pulled her close to his body. Her hands went to his chest, trying to keep a small amount of room between them.

"I'm not a very good dancer."

"That's okay. Just relax and move to the music." It took several minutes, but gradually, Cash felt her body relax against his. His hand pressed her tighter against him, her arms sliding up around his shoulders.

Cash had to think hard to control the erection she was beginning to arouse. He wanted a fresh start with her, to take it slow and court her the way she deserved. Shade had done it with Lily; he could do the same with Rachel.

They danced to another couple of songs together before they returned to the table. As they passed a table, a group of women caught his attention. The women were familiar; he had partied with them a few times with Rider.

His hope that they would let him pass by without acknowledging him was doomed just as the thought entered his mind.

"Cash!" a loud squeal drew several eyes, including Rachel's, who was walking in front of him. The woman got out of her chair, grabbing his hand. "Thank, God. I thought it was going to be a boring night."

"Hi, Lynn, ladies." Cash put his hands around Rachel's waist to keep her moving, but her feet had come to a sudden stop.

*Fuck! I'm screwed,* he thought.

"Come on, Cash. There's no one here who can dance as good as you. Dance with us."

"Sorry, Lynn, not tonight. I'm with someone."

"When has that stopped you?" The giggles from the table grated on his nerves

Rachel was rooted to the spot. Cash's hands on her waist exerted pressure to move her forward, but she refused to budge.

"The more, the merrier, you always say. She might as well get used to sharing you now. We all did." Lynn's eyes went to Rachel and her mouth drooped. "I don't know how much fun she'll be, but we'll be gentle."

Cash didn't have to try to get Rachel to move again; she took off like a shot. The night had gone from bad to worse. Cash followed, trying to keep up with Rachel as she fled the restaurant. She had to wait for him to unlock the truck door to slide in. Her stiff posture as he climbed into the truck showed she didn't want to hear anything he had to say. Cash's experience with women made him wise enough to know at least that much.

"Take me home." Her order had his own anger rising. Hell, she knew he wasn't a fucking virgin. He might have resolved to be patient with her, but her stony silence had him rethinking his own wisdom of whether this was the right time for them. She was younger than him, had a terrible temper, and was jealous-natured. All three qualities were ones he didn't like in a woman.

"Rachel—"

"I think you need to take me home, Cash." He expected anger in her voice, not the resignation he heard. "You can come back and meet them after you drop me off."

"You're overreacting." He narrowed his eyes on her cold expression before starting the truck, driving back to Mag's house.

"My last name is Porter. You know my family and what kind of person I am. Do you really think I would ever share anything that was mine?"

"I'm not asking you to share, but Treepoint is a small town and we're not going to be able to avoid women I've been with. Are you going to ride my case every time?"

"No, because I'm not going to put myself in this position again." Cash brought the truck to a stop in front of Mag's house. "Go back to those women; they can show you a better time than I will."

"You're telling me to go fuck someone else?"

"I'm telling you, I don't care."

"If you want to test me, write it down. Don't tell me you don't care about me and to go fuck another woman. I'll fail, Rachel, every time."

# CHAPTER TWENTY-FIVE

Rachel stood on the porch, watching the taillights of Cash's truck disappear. She had let her mouth get away from her again. She refused to let herself regret what she had done, however.

She could tell from the onset of the night that she wasn't Cash's type; she never would be. You couldn't fit a square peg into a round hole no matter how hard you worked at it. The truth was, she was a country bumpkin while Cash played games that were more experienced than she was capable of handling. They would end up fighting over her possessiveness and hating each other. She couldn't go through another heartbreak over Cash; she had already spent too many wasted years mooning over him.

She went into the house, changed into her nightgown, and climbed into her bed. She desperately needed the warmth of her mother's arms, yearning for the reassurance she had done the right thing.

Rachel spent the rest of the night wondering if he had gone back to King's place or to the clubhouse. She didn't know why it mattered; each held his choice of women.

* * *

Cash sat at the bar of The Last Riders' clubhouse,

nursing his drink while watching Train play with Bliss's nipple. Her lace vest left nothing to the imagination; you could see her daisy-chain tat on her bared breast.

"I need to go talk to Nickel for a minute. When I come back, you going to suck my dick for me?" Train questioned, pinching her nipple even tighter.

"I'll be waiting." Bliss ran her hand over Train's dick before he slid from the stool. "Hurry back."

"Give me five." Train patted her butt before moving away.

When he left, Bliss leaned forward, running her tongue over Cash's bottom lip. Her hands curled into his t-shirt, pulling him closer.

"What about you, Cash? Want me to suck your dick, or do you want to fuck me while I suck him off?" Her tongue laved his bottom lip suggestively.

Cash saw the greedy excitement in her eyes; Bliss loved doing two men at once.

"No, thanks. I'm good." Cash tilted his head to the side, taking his mouth away from hers only to see Lily's furious eyes as she came into the room from the kitchen, Shade hot on her tail.

Lily stormed up to him, ignoring Bliss. The fire shooting out of her purple eyes showed exactly why Shade had fallen for her.

"Beth told me you were over here when she came home. I can't believe you took Rachel out then came back here to get... get..."

"Laid?" Shade said helpfully. His wife threw him a quelling look, which he responded to with a raised brow. Lily took a step away from Shade, giving him her back.

"After everything she did for you, I thought you were smarter." Lily suddenly lost her fury, her expression changing to something Cash couldn't explain. "Beth and I owe a debt of gratitude to you, Cash. If you hadn't sent Shade's father here to Treepoint, then we may never have met Razer and Shade. You showed compassion and concern for Beth when you saw she was being mistreated at church. I just don't understand how the same man could treat Rachel the way you have."

"Lily, I wasn't—" Cash began.

"She sat beside your bedside from the moment she heard you were hurt. Did you even know that?"

"No." Cash got to his feet, something telling him he needed to brace himself for what he was about to hear.

"Well, she did," Lily said empathically. "The doctors didn't think you were going to make it. She had already tried to help you the way she does her clients, but it hadn't worked. She told Shade her gift wasn't powerful enough to help you. I think whatever she does comes from inside her. I can't explain it. The times she helped me, it's like a part of her went inside of me to give me strength. When she touches you, you feel the strength of her love and caring. I think, when you and her brothers hurt her at the party, it damaged that part of her. After the doctor told us all that you weren't going to make it, I went back to your room to talk to her because I could tell she was upset by what the doctor had told us."

Lily paused, taking a shuddering breath. "She didn't even know I was in the room. God, I don't even know what I witnessed, Cash. What I saw was a man dying, but then she touched you. When she started touching your body, I could feel a presence in the room. I saw you gradually begin to move, and then she passed out.

"I ran to get a nurse, and when we came back, she was sitting in the chair and you were coming to. The nurse started helping you while I took her to Mag's house. She was in bad shape; she was shaking and freezing. I stayed with her and saw what she suffered through for helping your ungrateful ass!"

Lily waved her hand at Bliss. "She certainly doesn't deserve for you to be two-timing her. She was so nervous about going out with you tonight. She does everything for everyone and doesn't ask for anything in return."

"Why didn't anyone tell me she had been in my hospital room?" Cash asked hoarsely, remembering the cold hand he had tried to hold, mistaking her nervousness as coldness. He was ashamed of himself for not seeing through her façade.

He was the one who had all the experience, thinking he was too old for her, while he had been the one to act immature when she didn't fawn all over him like other women.

"Rachel asked us not to; that was her price for helping you," Shade answered, pulling Lily back against his chest.

"Do you know where she was when she disappeared?" Cash's suspicions were aroused. Lily had drawn closer to Rachel than he had realized.

Lily remained mutinously silent.

"I wasn't going to touch Bliss or any of the other women. I was pissed off, but I cooled down before I got here."

"I promised I wouldn't tell." Her bravado was wavering at his explanation.

"Please, Lily. I need to know." Cash played on Lily's soft heart.

"I can't break my promise, but if you figure it out for yourself, that's not my fault, is it?"

"No." Cash's lips twitched in amusement.

"Rachel was in high school, but wasn't in high school," she hinted.

"I don't understand—" Cash began.

"I do," Winter broke in. She laid down the cards she had been playing in the game against Viper and Crash. "Rachel took accelerated courses in high school. By her sophomore year, she was taking college classes. She stayed at the high school because Tate had worked it out with me so she could still stay with her own age group.

"By the time the students her age were graduating, she had a Bachelor's in Biology. I believe, for the last four years, she's gotten her Master's and is now almost finished writing her thesis for her doctorate in Aquaculture. I'm willing to bet she was able to find housing in the dorms at the university." She shrugged at Lily's accusing look. "I didn't promise her. I figured it out."

"So, both you and Lily knew where she was?" Viper carefully laid his own cards down on the table.

"We talked about it. It wasn't rocket science for anyone who knew her." Winter's snide tone had Viper, Cash, and Shade all turning red.

"Then why didn't Tate know?"

"Because she didn't tell him she was working on her doctorate. Seems that was why Greer had gotten busted selling weed to that undercover cop; they were trying to sell extra to pay for her tuition. She'd told them she had dropped out; she didn't want them to go to jail to pay for her education," Winter answered.

"So, how's she been paying for it?" Viper questioned.

"Her parents left each of them a plot of land. She sold hers," Diamond spoke up from Knox's lap on the couch. "I handled the paperwork. After the clients left, she went to the restroom, and I heard her crying. She told me that property had been in her family for generations."

"It has. Who bought it?" Cash asked.

"Drake Hall," Diamond answered.

"So, let me get this straight. While we were all looking for her and her brothers were worried sick, none of you told?" Viper glared at his wife, then each of his men's insubordinate wives.

"It took us a while to figure it out. We didn't think they deserved to know," Winter explained cautiously, seeing the furious look Viper was sending her. The women began to sense the undercurrent of their husbands' angers.

"Do you have my tat on you?" Viper growled out through gritted teeth.

"Yes, but women should stick together." Winter tried to soothe her husband with her explanation; she failed.

"So should Last Riders," Viper snapped. "Did Beth

know, too?"

Winter snapped her mouth shut.

"I'll take that as a yes. All four of you will be pulling from the punishment bag next week." The women wisely remained silent, staring at their husbands in trepidation.

"And I'll deal with you upstairs." His eyes on Winter were promising retribution.

Cash struggled to contain his emotions at what he had found out. He wanted to rush back to his grandmother's house, but he knew Rachel needed time for her emotions to settle. *Come tomorrow, she isn't going to know what hit her,* he promised himself.

"Thanks, Lily." He reached out to cup her cheek. "I sent Shade's dad here, not only because of Beth, but you, too. I lost every bit of faith I had because of Saul Cornett. He might have adopted you, but he was a sick son of a bitch. It was only a matter of time before he hurt you, and I couldn't stomach watching Beth be hurt one more time."

Lily grasped his wrist. "You changed our lives. Thank you."

His eyes went over her shoulder to Shade's closed expression.

"You're welcome." Bending down, he brushed his lips against her cheek. "Now, go on home. I promise Rachel won't know you talked to me."

"Okay," Lily said happily.

"I'll be there in a minute. Don't go to sleep; we need to have a little chat before you do." Shade's deep voice wiped the smile from her face.

"I'm tired. I have to get up early for church," Lily said evasively.

"You can go to the evening service," Shade countered amicably.

Lily flounced angrily out of the room.

"Ten to one she's calling Beth as soon as she gets home." Cash grinned.

Shade grinned back, taking his phone out of his pocket,

quickly texting a message to Razer before putting the phone back in his pocket.

"Lily's going to be furious at you for telling on Beth," Cash warned.

"I'm counting on it," Shade said with an anticipatory grin.

# CHAPTER TWENTY-SIX

Rachel knocked firmly on Willa's door, determined this time not to be rebuffed. She had worried during church about her reclusive behavior. She had stopped answering her phone, and Evie had called Rachel that morning to tell her Willa had missed her last delivery of desserts. Evie was just as worried as her; therefore, Rachel had promised to check on Willa as soon as church was over.

Maybe she was overreacting and Willa was simply ill. Several members had been absent from church that morning—Lily, Winter, Beth, and Diamond rarely missed, yet none of them had showed. Maybe a virus was going around and Willa was sick.

Rachel froze in shock at the little boy answering the door.

"What do you want?" The belligerent boy, who judging from his size was around eight, had Rachel's mouth dropping open in shock.

"Is Willa here?"

Had the woman moved and not told anyone?

Her eyes moved over the child's shoulder, seeing another, smaller girl behind him, staring at her with baleful eyes.

"Charlie, what did I tell you about opening the door?" Willa came rushing toward the door, wiping her hands on a dish towel.

"I'm sorry, Rachel. I was cleaning up some broken glass."

"Uh, okay." Rachel took a step into the house, colliding with the small body of a little girl who reached out with grubby hands to grab hers.

"Move back, Chrissy." Willa gently pried the small hands away from her.

Rachel closed the door, staring at the three children. Her eyes lifted to Willa, recognizing the children staring up at her.

"Willa…"

"Charlie, take Chrissy and Caroline to their room and put a movie on for them."

"Why?" Stubbornly, the boy stared back at her.

"Because I asked you to," Willa pleaded. "It won't take long, and then I'll fix lunch. All right?"

"Grilled cheese?"

"Yes," Willa agreed.

The three children went up the stairs, leaving Willa trying to smooth back her hair.

She lifted her hand at Rachel. "I already know what you're going to say," she said before Rachel could open her mouth. "They were all going to be separated. I couldn't let that happen when I was the one responsible for their father getting killed."

"You had no choice, Willa. He had gone off the deep end. He would have killed me if you hadn't shot him."

A movement behind Willa had Rachel regretting her loud words when she saw the teenager listening to every word. Willa turned to stare at the teen girl.

"Sissy…"

"I finished cleaning up the milk and glass. Can I go to my friend's house now?"

"I don't know. How long were you planning on

staying?"

"I'll call and let you know." The girl passed Rachel, going out the door without waiting for Willa's reply.

"Want a glass of tea?" Willa offered.

"Yes, thanks." Rachel went into the kitchen, stepping over the toys lying on the floor. Willa's usually immaculate home was a mess with toys everywhere and dirty dishes on the table.

"I'm sorry about the mess. I didn't realize taking care of children could keep you so busy. Leanne, could you check on the kids upstairs for me?"

"Okay." A pretty girl around fifteen got up from the table, closing her book. Georgia's daughter gave Rachel a smile as she passed. The sweet girl didn't take after her mother, who everyone in town would agree hadn't had a sweet bone in her body. Her older sister seemed to have inherited that particular gene in spades, though.

As soon as the girl disappeared from the room, Willa faced her with a resigned expression. "Okay, you can let me have it now."

Rachel looked at her friend, who had been tormented by Georgia and then abused by Lewis. "You are the kindest person I know. Is there anything I can do to help?"

Deep in her heart, she didn't blame Willa. It was a terrible responsibility, taking someone's life.

Willa gave a relieved laugh. "Don't tempt me. I'm behind on my orders and the house is wrecked."

Rachel rolled up the sleeves of her dress. "I'll do the dishes then clean while you bake."

"I can't ask—" Willa began

"You're not asking; I'm volunteering. If I can donate my time to strangers, why wouldn't I give it to a friend?"

"You consider yourself my friend?" Willa's eyes filled with tears.

Rachel reached out, taking Willa into her arms, wishing she could give her the warmth of her touch the woman desperately needed. Instead, she tried to give it to her with words.

"You have a lot of friends that would help if you let us. Lily, Beth, and Evie—we all consider ourselves your friends."

Willa brushed her tears away with a hand, giving a small laugh. "I always assumed I was pushing myself on you guys."

"Willa, you couldn't be pushy if you tried. Now, get busy while I take care of this mess." Rachel sensed her being uncomfortable with the conversation, so she busied herself cleaning the kitchen around Willa, doing the dishes behind her, leaving her free to bake.

When she had the kitchen spotless, she worked throughout the house, picking up the toys and placing them in an empty laundry basket, making a mental note that would make Willa's life easier. It came in useful that she had learned by living with Logan just how hard it was to entertain little ones.

She went upstairs, cleaning the bedrooms. The bathrooms were a mess of towels and a full laundry hamper. Rachel started a load while she cleaned the bathrooms, then dried that one when she'd finished and started another.

The children ignored her as she cleaned around them while Leanne flushed, looking away when she met Rachel's recriminating gaze. Leanne and Sissy were both old enough to help out with the housework. Willa had literally been thrown into the deep end of the ocean without any help.

She folded the clothes and put them away, starting the last load before going back downstairs. It was beginning to get dark, so Rachel pulled out her phone, ordering three pizzas. Satisfied, she went into the kitchen to see Willa making roses to place on top of a cake while two other cakes were sitting on the counter as well as three pies.

"I can't thank you enough, Rachel. I'll call King and ask if someone can stop by and pick up his order."

"I'll drop it off on my way home. Which ones go?" Willa boxed up one of the cakes and all the pies. "His orders are getting larger each week. The money is really helping out with the extra expenses," Willa said, closing the last box.

Rachel packed the boxes out to her car. She had closed the door when the pizza delivery truck pulled up. Rachel paid the driver then turned to take the pizzas inside before hesitating, turning back to the driver. Carl was a member of her church, working part-time at the pizza restaurant after being laid off from the coal mine.

"Do you have any more deliveries to make?"

"Nope, I'm headed back to the store." The pizza joint was next door to King's restaurant.

Going to her car, she pulled out her purse and took out another twenty. "Would you mind dropping these desserts off at King's for me?"

"No problem. Mike won't mind; it's slow tonight." He carried the desserts to his car.

"Willa has to make several deliveries a week." Rachel took out a pen and paper and wrote down Willa's number. "Why don't you give her a call tomorrow? Maybe you two can work out something."

Carl's face brightened; Rachel guessed he was eager for additional income.

"I can't promise, but I'll mention it to her."

"That would be great. Thanks, Rachel."

"I hope it works out," she said, picking up the pizzas and saying goodbye.

Willa's eyes widened when she saw the food. "You shouldn't have."

"I thought I would invite myself to dinner," she said, taking out the plates.

Rachel explained that she had asked Carl to deliver the desserts and had told him to call Willa about a possible job.

"That's a great idea. I can't offer him a lot of hours, but

it would take a load off my shoulders. I have to bundle everyone into my car plus the desserts to make a delivery now. Hiring him for a few hours a week would make it much easier," Willa said, enthused by the idea.

"I think he will be happy with whatever hours you offer."

Between the two of them, they fed the kids, and Rachel stayed and played with them while Willa gave the three younger ones their baths. Leanne had gone upstairs to her room.

Willa came downstairs after putting the kids to bed.

"Sissy's still not back?" Rachel questioned.

"No." Willa sank down on the couch next to her, clearly exhausted. "She comes in usually around ten and goes to bed. I'm not managing her very well."

Rachel didn't think she was managing any of the children very well. They all were dominating a soft Willa into exhaustion.

"I'll stop by Tuesday. If you need me before then, just call." Willa opened her mouth, but Rachel forestalled her. "I'm going to help regardless of what you say, so just deal with it."

"I wasn't going to refuse; I was going to say thank you. School will start back next week, then I can get better organized and do my cooking while they are in school." The local school was on a year-long calendar. Unfortunately, they had the last week off and the one following.

"Sounds like a plan." Rachel hid her worry over the older two girls' behaviors, saying goodnight. It was going to take a firm hand to get those children under control, and Willa, bless her heart, was too soft to provide that discipline.

Rachel drove back to Mag's house, deep in thought. She should have expected Willa to do something regarding Lewis's children. However, the responsibility of caring for the five of them was going to be more than she was able to handle. Rachel was afraid for her. Willa set an impossible goal of perfection for herself that would be difficult for anyone to live up to.

Rachel pulled into the driveway, seeing Cash walking angrily toward his motorcycle, although he came to an abrupt stop when he saw her pulling in. Rachel parked, wondering why he looked so furious. Worried something had happened to Mag, she got out of her car.

"Where in the fuck have you been all day?"

Stunned at his anger, it took her a couple of seconds to reply. "Is something wrong?"

"Yes. Next time, answer your damn phone. Where's it at?"

Rachel reached back into her car, picking up her purse. Pulling it out, she took out her phone and saw several missed calls from Cash. "Has something happened? I stopped by Willa's and spent the day there."

Relief crossed his face before hardening once again. "Next time, tell me where you're at so I won't worry that you've taken another hair up your ass to take off again."

Rachel put her hands on her hips. "It's none of your business where I go!"

Cash angrily stalked toward her, and Rachel found herself pressed against the door of her car.

"Listen to me carefully, Rachel. I'm pissed off right now, so I'm not going to be nice about this. You and me are going to happen. So, when I tell you I want to know where your ass is, you need to make sure I know."

"You're joking, right? Have you been smoking Greer's green?" Rachel sniffed him, not detecting the scent of weed.

"I'm not high, I'm furious. I had planned to spend the day with you."

"You planned to spend the day with me without asking me first? Then you're dumber than my brothers." She tried to push him away from him, only to find him immovable.

"Is that so?"

Rachel ignored the glint of warning in his eyes. He'd actually thought she would be sitting around waiting for him after their disaster of a date?

"Why would I want to spend the day with you?" she mocked. "I get to spend time with you between all the other women in town. Big freaking deal! You've lost your ever-loving, crazy-assed mind."

Cash's mouth twitched in humor at her words. "Sweetheart, if you spend time with me between two people, it won't be women."

His vulgarity had her blood boiling.

"You're crude."

"No, I'm telling you like it is." His hand burrowed into her hair, tilting her head back to force her to stare into his eyes. "I'm done pretending. I'm not kind or sweet, and I sure as fuck am not a gentleman. I'm not going to court you the way you and your brothers want because that's not working for us. We've already fucked, and as much as you want to pretend it didn't happen, it did."

Rachel squeezed her eyes closed, unable to look at him any longer.

"I watched my father become a shell of the man he was, devoting his life to a church and wife he didn't care about to replace your mother. I wasn't going to let a Porter woman steal my soul, so I stayed away until I realized when you disappeared it was already too late.

"We both know that you care about me." Rachel opened her mouth to deny his assertion. "If you deny it, I will carry you to your bedroom and prove it." He paused, waiting for her response.

Rachel wisely remained silent, glaring at him; she wasn't stupid. Cash was an experienced lover. In the battle between bodies, she would lose, hands down. She might be furious at his arrogance, but the man had a body no woman in her right mind would want to resist.

"So, I'm giving you notice to prepare yourself. I will not have you throwing it out to me later that I swept you off your feet, that you weren't experienced enough to handle me, or you didn't know what you were getting yourself involved with. You're going to be in my life as my woman from now on." His thumb brushed against her nipple over her shirt. "Some things you're going to enjoy and others are going to piss you off. But either way, you're going to be mine." His ruthless words excited something deep within her.

Cash released her, stepping back to get on his bike.

She started to argue with him, but the obnoxious man couldn't hear her over the roar of his bike as he rode away. He had said what he wanted to say and left before she could tell him to jump in the lake. Rachel stood staring at his dust with her hands on her hips.

He thought he could order her to be his woman? Did he not know her at all?

Rachel stomped angrily into the house.

Their next date wouldn't go any better than their last. Maybe then he would realize it was useless to keep pestering her.

She went into the house, locking the door behind her, wishing she could lock her feelings away as easily. The feel of his body pressed against hers had aroused emotions she had thought his hurtful behavior had erased. Her traitorous body wanted him again, any way she could get him, while her mind screamed to tell him to get lost. She was a smart, intelligent woman; she would be able to keep herself under control.

She needed a backup plan that would prevent her from losing to Cash again.

* * *

Rachel nervously waited for her date to show up. This plan may not have been one of her brightest, but she was determined to go through with it. King's restaurant was just as busy tonight as when she had gone out with Cash.

"Hi, Rachel."

"Hi, Evie." She had been watching the door so closely

she hadn't noticed Evie approaching her table. King's wife and a member of The Last Riders was someone she didn't know well yet had gradually become acquainted with because of Beth and Lily.

"You here alone?"

"Not exactly," Rachel prevaricated.

"Cash meeting you?"

"No," she said out of time, her date walking across the busy restaurant toward her.

"Hi, Rachel." Scorpion smiled down at her then looked inquiringly toward Evie.

"Um… Scorpion, this is Evie. Her husband owns this restaurant."

"It's nice to meet you." He held out his hand which Evie ignored, her gaze going to Rachel.

"I need to get back to the kitchen." Rachel nodded her head as Evie left and Scorpion sat down.

"I was surprised you called and invited me to dinner," Scorpion commented, ordering a glass of tea from the waitress who had come to take their order.

"I told you I would think about it when I saw you again at Pastor Patterson's anniversary party."

"I knew that something good would come out of me starting church again."

Rachel smiled at his compliment.

"Why did you decide to start going to church in Treepoint instead of Jamestown?"

"Have you met the pastor in Jamestown?"

"No."

"I don't like to be told I'm going to Hell if I indulge in a beer."

"Hell and brimstone?" Rachel laughed.

"That and the headaches he was giving me from the yelling."

Rachel had suffered through too many of Saul Cornett's sermons not to sympathize with him.

They ate their dinner and Rachel was pleasantly

surprised at how well they got along.

"So, you work in the church store?"

Rachel nodded, leaning back in her seat. "I also study plants." She found herself telling him everything about her schooling.

"I have a friend that works at the university."

"Really. Who?"

"Dr. Alden."

"He's the advisor for my dissertation."

"That's cool. I'm buying some property. You're welcome to look it over if you want."

"I'd like that," Rachel said enthusiastically.

After dinner, she was glad she had decided to meet him at the restaurant as they said their goodbyes in the parking lot; it took away the pressure of being alone with him.

"I'll give you a call when the sale goes through," Scorpion promised.

"Do that. I enjoyed dinner," Rachel said and meant it.

There was no chemistry that had set her on edge, but she could see herself and Scorpion becoming friends.

He watched as she drove out of the lot.

She was sure Evie would tell Cash she had seen her with a date. As a back-up plan, it wasn't the greatest, but Scorpion was just the first. She had every intention of beginning to date and put herself out there to find the type of man she was searching for.

# CHAPTER TWENTY-SEVEN

Cash walked into the factory, seeing Shade talking to Jewell and Bliss as they filled their orders. Nodding his head toward Shade's office, Cash went inside and waited.

"What did you find out?"

"Nothing concrete. I talked to Jewell; she said that Lewis received a phone call about twenty minutes before he got off work, and he finished his order and left. You talked to her?"

"Yes, she told me the same thing."

"I checked his phone records; it came from a pay as you go phone. I couldn't find out who bought it," Cash said grimly.

"Find anything at his house?"

"He was fucking someone. He had a bag filled with sex toys and condoms."

"Willa?"

"I don't know. If so, she wasn't giving it to him; he was taking it. She hated him, but I don't think it was her."

"Why not?"

"Because he had an underwear set in the bag and I'm pretty sure it wouldn't have fit Willa. I checked the local hotel, then Jamestown's. No one recognized his picture."

"Go further. Start with the towns closest to the Virginia border. If you don't get a hit, try the Tennessee border," Shade ordered.

"He wouldn't be able to drive far. With the kids, he would've needed to stay close," Cash reasoned.

"Unless he had a sitter."

"Thought of that. Beth is going to ask around church and see if any of the women there were babysitting for him."

"That it?" Shade asked.

"Pretty much. If I find out anything, you'll be the first to know." Cash went to open the door.

"Cash, while you're flashing around Lewis's picture, show them one of Brooke. She may be the more memorable of the two."

"Will do." Cash closed the door behind him.

Going back to his bike, he started it before heading back out on his search, turning in the direction of the Virginia border. He wouldn't stop until he found what he was searching for. If there was a connection between Brooke and Lewis, he would find it and give the information to Shade. What he did with it from there was his call.

* * *

*For a man who's promised to storm my defenses, it's anticlimactic to not see him for three days*, Rachel thought glumly.

It had taken two more dates, one with King's cook and the other with Lily's old boyfriend, for her to realize that finding the chemistry she shared with Cash wasn't going to be easy to find with another man.

"Do you want something to drink?" Rachel asked Mag as the television show they were watching went off.

"No, thanks. It's my bedtime."

Rachel smiled warmly at the woman as she laid down her crocheting. It was a mess, but she kept doing it. She said it kept her fingers limber.

Rachel blinked back tears. The old woman's health was

declining. She would have moved back with her brothers weeks ago, but Rachel couldn't bring herself to leave the woman's side. She had missed her gift more and more each day as she wished she could have eased the woman the last few months. Mag had lived a full life, but a hard one. Rachel would have liked to help with the pain of her passing.

Rachel got off the couch, brushing a kiss against the woman's cheek. "Goodnight, Mag."

"Night, Rachel."

As she was about to wheel herself from the room, Cash came in with a tired expression.

"What are you two up to?" he asked, staring between the two women.

"Nothing. I was just telling Rachel goodnight. I'm going to bed. From the looks of you, a good night's sleep would do you some good."

"I'll get plenty of sleep when I'm dead."

Rachel winced at his choice of words, reaching down to pick up the tea glasses and leaving the two to talk.

She was finishing the dishes when Cash came in, leaning against the counter.

"She looks tired tonight." Cash frowned. "She's always so full of energy; I forget how old she is sometimes."

Rachel didn't make a remark to his observation. Cash and his grandmother had a strong bond; she didn't need to tell him what he already sensed was near.

"Mag is in bed."

"Yeah, so?" Rachel paused in wiping the table.

"So, go put on your shoes; we're going out."

"I am not."

Cash stalked toward her, and Rachel dropped the dishcloth onto the table, backing out of the kitchen into the living room. Once her ass landed on the couch, Cash squatted down in front of her, sliding her tennis shoes on and tying them for her. Rachel could only stare at him in stupefaction.

"Mag's neighbor is going to stay with her for a few hours while we go out."

"I don't want to go out with you again, Cash."

"Rachel, go out with me this last time. If you don't want to go out after that, I won't bother you again."

Rachel's gaze narrowed on him, listening to the nuances of his voice. "You're lying."

Cash shrugged. "I am, but I'm willing to bet none of the men you've been out with this week makes you feel like I can." His hand took hers, lifting her from the couch. "Come on, Rachel. Your brothers are the wildest men in town; don't you have a little bit of that in you?"

Rachel looked away. None of the men she had gone out with had her wanting to touch them the way her body craved Cash's. What's more, she had always felt that same wildness he'd spoken of, controlling it by working and studying hard. Her mother had begged her brothers not to take after their father, who had stolen her mother's heart away from Cash's father, and hadn't let it go until the day they'd died together. After their deaths, Rachel had wanted to make her mother proud, and subsequently, she had smothered the inherited wild streak burning in her blood.

Giving in, she followed him outside.

"You brought your bike?"

"I figured you need to get used to being on the back." Cash grinned, handing her a helmet. Rachel climbed on behind him, wrapping her arms around his waist.

"I've seen plenty of women on the back of your bike, Cash; it's not exactly a privilege when a hundred other women have shared the experience." Rachel wasn't going to let him lead her to believe she was special.

He shot her a look that had her closing her mouth. She was pushing it with him again, and from that look, she was treading on dangerous ground. She held on tighter as he drove out onto the roadway. She'd thought he would head into town; instead, he headed in the opposite direction. As they passed Rosie's bar, she wondered if he was taking her to his clubhouse.

When he passed it, she assumed he was simply taking her for a ride. She took a deep breath of the brisk, night air. There was nothing like the fresh, mountain air.

The throbbing bike underneath gave her a sense of freedom she had never experienced before. She could understand the lure of the motorcycle club; it was the tie that grounded them. If not, it would be easy to just keep riding without the responsibilities of life holding you back.

Cash slowed the bike, turning into the lake where he had brought her before. When he pulled in, she saw several of his friends were already there. She stiffened, fearing this time wouldn't be any different than the last.

She had been around them enough with Beth and Lily to recognize several of them. She wasn't the type to be made nervous, but she didn't know how to interact with them. She felt self-conscious around the women, who were completely feminine. The small blond with the spiked hair was dressed in a small, red bikini with a thong bottom. Next to her was Raci, a pretty brunette with a bright-pink bikini that was even smaller, the top barely covering her nipples and the bottoms barely covering a small patch.

Rachel swallowed hard, uncertain of how to deal with the uncomfortable situation. The weather was unseasonably warm, and the women were taking complete advantage by showing they hadn't gained an ounce during the winter while her own ass had grown from Mag's comfort food.

"Hi, Rachel." Lily's soft voice had her releasing a relieved sigh when she saw her friend sitting beside Shade. Beth was sitting on the other side of her, next to her husband, Razer.

"Hi." She walked closer to the blanket they were sitting on.

Lily scooted closer to her husband, giving her enough room to sit down next to her. Beth then edged closer to Razer on the opposite side, giving enough room for Cash to sit down next to Rachel.

"It's beautiful out here at night, isn't it?" Lily smiled, handing her a soda out of the cooler. "Rider came out earlier to set out the torches."

"It's nice here. Holly and I bring Logan." Rachel looked at Beth cuddled up to her husband's side. "Who's keeping the babies for you?"

"Evie and King. I think she would keep them if we let her," Beth said wryly.

Rachel agreed with her. She had seen Evie with the children, and her attachment to them was obvious.

Winter came out of the water with Viper's arm wrapped around her waist. The tats on him and the others caught her eyes. They all had similar ones on different parts of their bodies. The center was a Navy seal insignia with a snake wrapped around it from the bottom up, leaving the face of the snake glaring back. Objects surrounded the insignia: two revolvers with a metal chain wrapped around the barrels of the gun, linking them together; brass knuckles; a hand of cards; and a razor knife. The whole tattoo had a layer of shadows, giving it a eerie effect. Rachel's mind began playing with the thought of where Cash's tattoo was. He had one on each of his biceps, but she hadn't noticed a similar one on his chest.

Winter sank down on the blanket across from her while Viper reached into the cooler, pulling out two beers and giving one to his wife.

"I'm surprised you're out on a school night, Winter," Rachel teased, never imagining in a million years the woman, who had been her high school principal, would be sitting across from her in a bikini, drinking a beer. She had thought her staid and boring. She had been a mentor, and Rachel hadn't thought of her as a flesh-and-blood woman.

"I usually don't. I hate being tired first thing in the morning, but we all punish ourselves sometimes for a good cause." Rachel didn't understand the sidelong glance Winter threw her husband, which he ignored, lifting the beer to his lips.

A sudden squeal had Rachel jumping until she saw Rider throw Bliss into the water, going in after her and pulling her into a passionate kiss, gradually edging her over to the darker side of the water. Rachel lowered her gaze, embarrassed and unaccustomed to seeing couples make out in front of her.

"Let's go for a swim." Razer helped Beth to her feet.

Rachel watched as all the couples except Lily and Winter went into the water. The air rang out with splashing and laughter.

"I'll open the store tomorrow. I need to organize a few things for Willa," Lily said. "Lewis's younger children need a few things, and I thought I would make a couple of bags for them and deliver them when you come in."

"I'm sure she's going to need several things. I picked them up some games to keep them occupied."

"I offered to take them to the Saturday matinee to give her a break." Winter's husky voice was due to her husband kissing her neck.

Rachel looked away from the affectionate couple, only to see Lily's mouth captured by Shade's, his hand on the back of Lily's neck holding her in place.

"Let's go for a swim." Cash rose to his feet, holding out his hand. Rachel took it, standing up.

"I don't have a suit," she protested.

"Lily brought you one. You can go into the trees and get changed." Cash went to his saddle bags, pulling out a swimsuit then handing it to her.

She really didn't want to swim, showing her body, but all the women wore suits. Rachel was sure Lily's suit wouldn't be too brief. Looking at it, she saw it was a one-piece. She could do this.

Hesitantly, she went into the trees as Cash pulled off his t-shirt and began unbuttoning his jeans. Her mouth dropped open when he changed into a pair of blue shorts he pulled out of his bags, changing in front of everyone.

He didn't have on underwear, his semi-hard cock visible to everyone sitting around. Lily and Winter were not even paying attention, though.

She went into a copse of trees, gingerly changing into the one-piece. Nervously, she came back out, but no one looked in her direction as she walked into the cold water. Cash was already in, waiting for her.

"That wasn't so bad, was it?"

"I'm a private person," Rachel defended herself. "It's freezing."

"You're shy," Cash corrected. "But Lily is, too, and she manages to go swimming with us. You'll warm up in a few minutes when you get used to it."

Rachel treaded water as he talked, not noticing he was gradually maneuvering her toward the part of the water that was shaded from view by the bank from the overhanging trees. She stopped following him, but Cash swam back to her, sliding his arm around her waist and bringing her slick body toward his.

"Need my help warming up?"

She placed her hands on his muscular chest, her eyes going to the tats on his bulging muscles. "Do you have a tattoo like the rest of the men?"

Cash raised a brow, letting her turn his back to her. It was on the back of his shoulder. She looked closely at the separate symbols, a laugh escaping her.

"Each symbol represents a member, doesn't it?"

"Yes." He turned back to face her. "Guess which one is mine."

"I don't have to, I know. Greer and Tate have come home busted up too many times from those brass knuckles of yours."

As they talked, their bodies drifted into the deeper, shaded water. Cash's arm slipped around her waist, pulling her close once more, at the same time Rachel turned toward the shore. Someone had turned on some music, and she could hear the soft sounds from the bank.

"Your friends like to party, don't they?" she mused.

"They work hard and play hard." His mouth brushed the side of her neck.

Rachel turned her head away, placing her hands on his chest. "Stop, Cash. I'm going back to shore." Cash's hand tangled in her fiery hair.

"When do you play, Rachel? I never see you around town, just having a good time. Don't you want to let loose and have fun?"

"I lost control one time with you, Cash, and look what happened." Her voice tightened as his mouth traced to the base of her throat, his tongue licking the droplets of water pooled there.

"Was it so bad, Rachel?" he murmured, his mouth going to the curve of her breasts exposed by the modest swimsuit.

When her hands moved to his shoulders, trying to push him away, Cash tangled his legs with hers, forcing her to hold onto him to keep from slipping under the water.

"Not until you opened your mouth to the whole town."

Cash lifted his head. "If I hadn't said anything, would you have ever told your brothers?"

"Of course not."

"So it worked out, didn't it?" Cash's smug face had realization dawning on Rachel.

She began hitting his chest. "You bastard. You deliberately humiliated me in front of everyone in town," she yelled.

Cash grabbed her hands, twisting them behind her back and holding her in place with his strength. "What I did was force you to admit you were attracted to me. Even if we had started seeing each other, you would have dreaded telling them and put it off, worrying about their reactions. I took that pressure away from you, like pulling a band-aid off a sore."

"Did you see how they freaked out? Tate said some hateful things to me."

Cash's face tightened. "What did he say to you?"

"Never mind," Rachel said haughtily. "You threw me under the bus then weren't there to protect me from the consequences. Thanks for nothing, Cash. Can we go back to shore now?"

He didn't release her. "They are your crazy-ass brothers, Rachel. If I had planned to keep you away from them, then I would have handled it differently. I knew you would want to maintain your relationship with them, though, so only you could handle them, and you did. They're afraid, if they say anything to you now, you'll run off again."

She bit her lip. He was right. If he hadn't interfered, it would have driven a wedge between her and her brothers. This way, they had learned she could stand on her own two feet without them.

"Of course, if I never saw them again, it wouldn't break my heart." His mouth returned to her breasts, tugging down the top of the swimsuit before nuzzling her.

She felt a rush of warmth between her legs as she began to get aroused, her hips unconsciously pressing against his. The feel of his hardened cock against her stomach had reality storming back as his hand released hers, going between her thighs and slipping under the material to rub her clitoris.

"I'm not going to do this again, Cash... never again...never ever again..." While her head shook back and forth, tendrils of her damp hair clinging to her cheeks, his finger began stroking her. "Do that again," she begged.

His mouth covered hers, sliding his tongue into her mouth, taking control of her mind and body in one motion as he began to manipulate her body toward an orgasm.

"Cash, there are people around." Rachel tried to clamp down on the rising tide of arousal that was threatening to gain control.

"No one's paying attention."

She arched as a finger entered her, thrusting in firm

strokes that had her breath deepening and her body twisting closer to his. The cold water enveloping her no longer seemed so frigid.

Cash's hand cupped her ass, pulling her closer to him as his finger thrust harder and his thumb swirled in the wetness of the bud of her clit. A sudden pleasure had her screaming into his mouth as she felt her pussy spasm, coming on his hand.

When she finished, Cash kissed her mouth again, dragging the tip of his tongue over her bottom lip. Rachel was embarrassed, uncertain of how to act.

Cash didn't release her, still rubbing her bud and extending her orgasm. She felt his hand at her waist as he lifted her slightly out of the water before lowering her back down. She felt the brush of his cock at her opening.

"Wait, you're not wearing a condom."

"You can't get pregnant if you fuck in the water," Cash stated, thrusting inside her.

Rachel shuddered at his hard thrust, giving herself over to his demands. His hands on her ass lifted her higher so his mouth could latch onto a beaded nipple. She could only hold on to his hard body, afraid if she let go, she would drown in more ways than one. The water surrounding them muted the sound of his body slamming into hers, driving her to another climax.

This time, when she came, she felt Cash groan as he joined her, crushing her mouth underneath his as he jerked inside her, arousing primitive emotions Rachel had no idea she could experience.

"Are you all right?" Cash's hand slid to her jaw, raising her eyes to his scrutiny.

"Yes." Her strangled reply brought a tender smile to his face, which had her pulling away from his controlling touch.

When he let her go, she could tell he was adjusting himself back into his shorts. She was relieved the dark shadows hid her embarrassment at losing control to him twice.

"Rachel…"

"Don't worry, Cash." Her voice was unintentionally harsh. "I'm not going to make more out of it than there was, so you can spare me that speech. Can I go home now?" While Rachel was unaware of the hurt her words provided, Cash swam by her side as she headed back to the bank.

As soon as her feet touched the grass, she picked up her clothes and went into the trees to change. When she came out, she was startled to see that The Last Riders were all mounted on their bikes.

Cash was sitting grim-faced on his bike. Something about his expression sent a warning signal through her body.

As she drew closer, he handed her the helmet. Rachel scanned The Last Riders. None of them wore helmets, even the women members, but Winter and Beth were sitting with them on their heads. A spark of warmth began to bloom in her chest, which she ruthlessly smothered as she climbed on behind him.

Viper started his bike and Cash moved his forward, going directly behind him. Rachel's heart pumped hard as they all pulled out onto the road in twos. The bikes flew through the night in a roar of noise and excitement, even if they were just driving down the dark road.

Rachel could only guess at the adrenaline rush of actually driving the machine. Maybe she would learn to drive one. The thought of buying such an expensive motorcycle disappeared. She didn't think she would achieve the same thrill of sitting behind Cash, gripping his waist, and leaving the skill to handle the monster between their legs to him.

Lily waved when she turned to look behind her. She was sitting next to Shade, who was driving Rider's truck. Razer rode with Beth behind him at the end of the pack. He looked fierce with his hair pulled back with a do-rag and his leather jacket.

Her attention was jerked forward as they rounded a sharp curve, coming to a straightaway. The Last Riders' compound was ahead. As the men cut their speed, pulling into the parking lot, Rachel expected Cash to keep going. Instead, he pulled in alongside Viper, turning off his machine.

Rachel stared at the clubhouse sitting on the hill with the large flight of steps leading up. She had been inside a couple of times: once to help Lily during one of her panic attacks and another to celebrate the baptism of Beth's sons. Tonight, it looked different, as if a den of inequity was just waiting for her to step inside.

The question remained, was she brave enough to take that step?

# CHAPTER TWENTY-EIGHT

"Why are we stopping here?"

Cash climbed off his bike, staring down at Rachel. He reached out, taking off her helmet. "I thought I would show you my bedroom."

He deliberately let his eyes run over her shirt where the damp material showed the outline of her breasts. He wasn't surprised when she stiffened, gripping his bike with her thighs and refusing to get off the machine.

"I'm ready to go home. I'm working the church store in the morning."

"Lily is going to open for you," Cash stated casually, leaning down to lift her, despite her attempts to smack him away.

"But it's my turn," Rachel argued.

"Lily is paying back a punishment; she's opening for the next week." He took her hand, leading her up the steps. Rachel didn't try to jerk away; in spite of herself, she wanted to spend more time with him before returning to reality. She damn sure didn't want him to come to the realization he could make her want him despite herself.

The others watched in amusement as they came in the door. Before she could utter further protest, he ushered her up another flight of stairs. She had never been upstairs in the clubhouse. He led her down a long hallway, stopping at the next to the last door. This place was huge with the amount of rooms it had available.

Cash opened the door and pushed her inside, turning on the bedroom light and closing the door. Startled, she jumped at the loud sound.

Before she could gather her defenses, Cash went to her, winding her hair around his fist, using his body to back her toward his bed.

"Cash, I want to go home."

Her vulnerable eyes almost swayed him, but if he relented, he would have to start over with her tomorrow. He was sick of waiting for her to realize he cared about her. The best way for her to realize she was his was to show the stubborn woman.

"I'll take you back in the morning. After we eat breakfast, and I fuck you again." His hand went to her top, peeling it off. Her bra was harder to remove because it was wet and she was struggling against him.

"And what if I say no?" Rachel objected to his high-handed treatment.

Cash stopped momentarily, becoming angry. "I'd stop when I heard it. I haven't heard it yet, though. Do you really want to tell me no, or are you worried about what that good girl inside of you is trying to tell you? Tell her to fuck off. You owe me a blowjob, and you're going to pay up. If you're good, I'm certainly willing to return the favor."

His hand went between her thighs, grinding the palm of his hand against the inseam of her jeans. She had come twice in the lake with him; it should be impossible to become aroused again so soon, yet she was burning for him. His dirty talk and commanding her had her getting hotter, stroking that part of her which had always fantasized about Cash.

Why not have some fun with him? She had never

planned to cling to her virginity; it was gone anyway, already lost to the desire she had carried for him. She wasn't in love with him anymore, and unlike the other women he'd slept with; she knew it would only be temporary. Maybe giving in and playing out her desire for him was the only way to move on.

Cash pulled off his t-shirt, showing his muscular chest. He had regained all the weight he had lost during his convalescence, and his blond hair was longer, brushing the back of his shoulders.

He took off his jeans and boots before going to the snap of her jeans. He sat down on the end of the bed, his cock hard and ready.

"You ever suck dick before?"

Rachel shook her head. She had been involved with her books more than she had boys, and she was beginning to realize just what she had missed, staring down at Cash. His sensual body made her want to discover every ridge and muscle displayed before her avid gaze.

Instinctively, she went to her knees between his thighs, gently reaching out to touch his cock.

"You're not going to hurt me; I like it rough."

Rachel's eyes briefly lifted to his. Desire was etched on his handsome face, giving him a menacing appearance, which she sought to appease.

Her mouth lowered to the tip of his cock, sucking the head into her warm mouth. Her hand went to the length and began sliding up and down. A groan had her smiling against him as she sucked him farther into her mouth.

Cash's hand went to her hair, guiding her down even farther. "You're going to learn to take every inch of me and give it to me the way I want." His hand went to her breast, taking a nipple between his fingers. "I like dirty, raunchy sex, and that's what I'm going to teach you to enjoy. You're going to be mine any way I want, when I want."

Rachel stiffened. "I'm not going to be your personal

sex slave!"

"Yes, you are, and I'm going to be yours. Anytime you want my cock, all you have to do is ask. And, baby, I'm going to give it to you in ways you never dreamed possible."

Rachel didn't doubt he would.

Pushing the argument aside, she went back to her task, and he stroked his cock in and out of her mouth, going deeper with each thrust. His fingers tightened on her nipple as she felt his cock getting harder and his balls tightening under her stroking fingers. She licked him as he held her steady, thrusting out his climax in her mouth. When he was finished, he used her hair to raise her head.

"You did good for a amateur."

Rachel brushed his knee with her cheek, lowering her guard for a brief second. Being here with him had played out one of her fantasies. Maybe she could handle this. If he wanted to keep pretending he wanted more from her, who was it going to hurt?

"I think you're just easy to please," she teased.

"No, I'm not." He lifted her onto the bed beside him. "I'm hard to please, and you're going to spend the night doing it until you get it perfect."

"I'm a quick learner," Rachel teasingly boasted.

"Not quick enough." He laid her back on the bed, spreading her thighs wide. His mouth brushed her belly button before kissing his way down her thighs. His tongue then slid between the lips of her pussy, laving the tiny bud until she lifted her hips, trying to press harder against his mouth. The sensations were way beyond anything she had imagined as he stroked her with his tongue before using his teeth to tease her.

His fingers pulled and tugged at her already sore nipples until she didn't know which part of her body to concentrate on. His hand left her nipple, sliding underneath her to grab her ass and lift her higher against his mouth. Whimpers began escaping her as she bit her lip, trying to prevent them from escaping. She didn't want him to know how his touch was breaking down her barriers.

Her body twisted underneath him as she experienced one sensation after another, the desire building to a painful pitch that had her grasping the sheets in her hands before going to his hair, trying to jerk away from him while at the same time force him to let her come.

"Cash, I can't take anymore," she wailed.

"Baby, I'm just getting started." His hand on her ass started exploring her, his thumb sliding between the globes of her butt.

Nervously, she tried to twist away while keeping his mouth exactly where she wanted it.

His thumb pressed against her rosebud, the sounds escaping her now escalating because of it.

"Relax..." he growled against her.

Rachel wasn't sure she liked the uncomfortable feeling he was provoking. She'd thought she was hot before, but he had ratcheted the flames into more than she had thought possible.

"Easy." His tongue was flicking her clit, and then he sucked it into his mouth.

She let out a small scream as he filled her with his finger. She lost all touch with reality as he tormented her body. She climaxed, but instead of coming down, it only made her want more. She didn't recognize the woman she'd become as her hands grabbed his shoulders, losing all control over her wild movements.

He removed his thumb when she began begging him, flipping her onto her stomach. After he jerked her hips back toward him, she wasn't given any warning before he pounded his cock deep within her, satisfying the ache she hadn't been aware he was building in her. Every time she thought she had felt all the sensations involved with having sex, he showed her she hadn't begun to see what he could teach her.

"Oh, God," Rachel moaned as she thrust back against

him. The feel of his flesh inside her, rubbing against her walls, had her burying her face in the soft sheets.

"Wait, Cash! You need to put on a condom." She tried to wiggle her hips away from him, but a hard smack on her butt had her freezing in place.

He bent over her back, his cock burrowing deeper within her grasping pussy. "You can't get pregnant unless you're on your back."

"*What?* That's ridiculous."

Another hard smack landed against her butt. His mouth lowered to her shoulder, placing soothing kisses as he pistoned inside her. She felt every ridge of his cock as he ruthlessly took her pussy, as if laying claim.

"I'm not joking, Cash. I'm not on any birth control." She tried to remember exactly why she was fussing at him. His bare cock felt so good inside her.

"Don't worry; I'll take care of it."

"You're not doing a great job of it so far," she moaned.

"I'm not?" he mocked. "Let me fix that." His hand slid from her hip to the front of her pussy. His fingers then rubbed against her, sending her back into a hazy cloud of desire where nothing mattered except the climax he was building. When he pinched the sensitive bundle of nerves, she screamed at the small pain as she came, almost blinded by the pleasure that ended only when he released her from his possession.

When she collapsed against the sheets, unable to stop herself from trembling, Cash pulled up a sheet to cover her butt, leaving her back bare. He lay down next to her, his large hand smoothing over her back.

"You got a tat while you were gone." His statement had her burying her face in the pillow. His finger traced over the dream catcher tattoo that was on the back of her shoulder. Rachel had given the picture to the artist who had inked her. "I didn't take you for a tattoo girl."

"You don't know anything about me, Cash. You never took the time to get to know me." Her voice was even, without a shred of the emotion she had once felt for this man.

"That's not true. I might not know everything, but I know you, Rachel." Cash's sincerity failed to impress her. She was just one of many women with whom he'd had sex, nothing more or less.

She didn't answer, pretending to be asleep. She was exhausted, but she was far from sleepy, her mind in turmoil at what she had let happen. She had no willpower where he was concerned. She was like an addict when faced with their drug of choice, swearing not to indulge again, but when it was within reach, giving in to the temptation.

She felt Cash scoot in closer to her, and then he pulled the sheet up over both of them. Rachel lay silently by his side for over an hour until she was sure he had fallen asleep before quietly sliding out of the bed and getting dressed.

She didn't look back at the bed before leaving the bedroom, too afraid she would change her mind. *Maybe I should start a twelve-step program for getting over Cash,* she thought wryly.

The downstairs of the clubhouse was quiet as she let herself out the front door. It was over a mile walk to Mag's house. She should call one of her brothers to come get her, but couldn't bring herself to. The look in their eyes, that she had become another one of Cash Adams's whores, would put an irreparable rift between them. Instead, she started walking. She had never been afraid of the dark. She was much more afraid of what waited for her in Cash's bed if she stayed.

\* \* \*

Rachel ignored Lily's curious stare when she came into the church store to already find her there. It took her the better part of the morning to relax around her. Lily never questioned her, though. She was not the type to pry, and Rachel appreciated that about her.

"Lily?" Rachel smoothed out the t-shirt she was folding.

"Hmm?" Lily looked up from the paperwork she was filling out.

"Are the rumors true about the clubhouse?" Rachel asked the question that had been drilling a hole through her heart for the last several months.

Lily looked back down at her paperwork, fiddling with her pen. "I think that is a question you should ask Cash."

"I don't have the right to ask; he's made me no promises. Hell, I don't even know what's going on between us," she admitted.

"You may not know what he's feeling, but you know your own. Shade, Razer, Viper, and Knox all belong to The Last Riders and they are faithful to us. You can't judge Cash, thinking he won't remain faithful if he is committed to you."

"Cash will never be faithful to a woman. He isn't capable of it."

"You can't be sure of that," Lily protested.

Rachel gave her a wry look. "We've both watched Cash chase after women since we were young. He chases them until he gets them, then he dumps them. The only women I think he's been with regularly are the ones in the club, and they don't expect anything from him." Rachel folded another shirt. "Doesn't it bother you to be around those women, knowing Shade's been with them all?"

Rachel looked up to see the hurt look on Lily's face.

"I'm sorry, Lily. I didn't mean it like that. It's just..." Rachel's frustration at herself reached a boiling point. "I don't want to be attracted to Cash. He's a horny hound dog who is going to make my life miserable."

"Or he's a horny hound dog who is going to keep you very satisfied."

Rachel gaped at Lily's blunt comeback. She seemed surprised by herself, blushing bright red.

"That's one way of looking at it," Rachel laughed. "So,

what's the big secret about Friday nights?"

# CHAPTER TWENTY-NINE

Rachel was bagging a customer's purchase of clothes when the door to the church store opened. She looked toward it to meet Cash's furious gaze. As he stalked toward her, she paled.

Birdie Jacobs, her current customer, was the biggest gossip in town; anything Cash said would be repeated and spread around town within minutes.

"I'll be with you in a minute," Rachel tried to forestall the confrontation she saw coming.

He ignored her silent request. "What the fuck, Rachel? What time did you sneak out of my bed last night?" He crossed his arms over his chest, giving her a malicious smile at Birdie's avid interest.

When Lily and another customer stopped talking to listen, Rachel silently pled for her help and received an eye roll for her effort; both women knew there was no stopping Cash.

Pasting an injured look on his face, Cash played to his audience. Rachel gritted her teeth, preparing herself for the show.

"What kind of woman takes advantage of a man then leaves him? I feel so used."

Birdie's mouth softened in commiseration.

"I thought we had something special, then I woke up, and you were gone."

"We'll talk about this later." She handed Birdie her bag, but the nosey woman made no effort to leave.

"We need to talk about this now. Lily can watch the store for you, can't you?"

Lily walked behind the counter. "Of course. I can see you two have a lot to talk about."

Rachel threw a glare at her friend, who gave a negligent shrug in response. "It's almost quitting time anyway," Lily reminded her.

Giving in only because she didn't want Birdie to witness her murdering Cash, Rachel reached under the counter to pull out her purse, angrily leaving the store with a farewell to her traitorous friend.

She ignored Cash once she was outside, going to her car and opening the door. Cash's anger hadn't evaporated; he grabbed her arm, keeping her from getting in.

"Get on my bike." His order grated on her already-sensitive nerves.

"Go to Hell. You're ruining my life, Cash." Rachel angrily swung back around to face him.

Before she could utter another word, she found herself marched to his motorcycle where a Cash she didn't recognize stared down at her.

"I'm ruining *your* life? I wake up and find out you're gone. How did I know what happened to you? How did you get home? I fucking doubt you called one of your brothers to come and get you. And you can't get a cab in Treepoint after twelve a.m. because that's when it closes. So, how did you get home?"

"I walked," Rachel admitted reluctantly.

"In the fucking dark? Someone driving on the road wouldn't be able to see you." His hand on her arm tightened.

"I didn't walk in the road; I walked through the

woods," she snapped unwisely. She admitted it might not have been so smart when he literally shook her.

"Are you trying to get yourself killed? If you had fallen and hurt yourself, it would have taken us days to find you. You didn't even have your cell phone on you." He reached into his pocket, pulling out her phone before handing it to her.

"Thank you." She thought she had lost it in the woods. She was relieved to have it back.

Cash looked at her as if she had lost her mind. "Get. On. The. Fucking. Bike!"

"Okay!" Rachel yelled back at him before angrily climbing on.

Cash stared down at her, his face ridged. "You're lucky we're not somewhere private, or I would set that fine ass of yours on fire." He got on the bike, handing her the helmet.

When he started the bike, pulling out onto the road, Rachel expected him to drive recklessly, to take his anger out on the road, but instead he drove carefully. Rachel wanted to go back to Mag's, but he drove past her house, despite her yells at him to stop. He simply kept driving toward his clubhouse. Rachel didn't want to return there but was given no choice as he pulled into the parking lot, cutting the motor.

"I wanted to go back to Mag's." She refused to get off the bike after he did.

"You can go back later. We need to talk."

"We can talk there," she repeated stubbornly.

"No, we can't."

"Why?" Rachel couldn't understand his insistence they talk here.

"Because I can't fuck you when we're done talking."

Rachel had a fierce temper when roused, and this man was lighting her short fuse. "I'm not going to have sex with you anymore. It's counterproductive."

"It's what?" Cash's confusion brought a vindictive

smile to her lips. Rachel thought it was past time Cash got a taste of his own medicine. Cash Adams wasn't the only man in Treepoint.

"It means I don't get any benefits from having sex with you when I'm looking for a serious relationship with a man who will eventually be my husband," she explained.

"It seems to me you benefited from me fucking you last night when you came on my dick."

Rachel waved her hand airily, dismissing his boast. "The man I pick will be just as able to provide me with sexual satisfaction."

"No, he won't."

"Yes, he will. You're not the only man who can give a woman an orgasm."

"I'm telling you he won't because I'll kill any motherfucker who lays a hand on you without my permission."

Cash's expression gave Rachel pause, but her temper didn't heed her internal warning. "So, it's all right for another man to touch me as long as he has your permission?" Rachel screeched.

She started walking toward the road, only to find herself thrown over Cash's shoulder.

"What are you doing?" She hit at his back with her fists as he packed her up the long flight of steps.

"Quit! Do you want to make me drop you?"

"Yes." Rachel hit at him harder, not stopping when he carried her in the front door and continued upstairs. She lifted her head to see Bliss, Train, and Rider staring up at her from the living room.

"I'm going to kill you!" Rachel threatened.

Cash didn't answer, remaining silent until he packed her into his bedroom and tossed her harshly down on his bed. Rachel bounced to her knees, ready to fight him tooth and nails if he so much as laid a finger on her.

"Will you calm down so we can talk reasonably?" Cash suggested unsuccessfully.

"You practically kidnap me from work, bring me here without my permission, act like a freaking caveman, and you want me to be reasonable?"

Cash's amusement at her tirade had her losing what control she had left. Reaching toward his nightstand, she picked his alarm clock up and threw it at him. When he dodged it and she had no further ammunition, she threw herself at him. While Cash tried to catch her flailing hands, her knee made contact with his nuts, giving her a burst of satisfaction that was short-lived as she found her feet swept out from underneath her and she fell backwards onto the bed.

Cash jerked her legs apart, his hands going underneath the side of her panties, burying his finger in her in one swift stroke. Rachel moaned, wrapping her legs around his waist as Cash's mouth went to her neck underneath her ear. The bastard had learned her most erotic spot, sucking the flesh into his mouth and nipping it with his teeth.

"Is every Porter a hothead?" he grunted, raising his body off her long enough to unzip his jeans and pull out his cock.

The argument forgotten, Rachel turned her head toward him, seeking his mouth with hers. Cash let her have his mouth at the same time he ripped off her underwear then plunged his hard cock into the tight warmth of her pussy, pounding his length into her.

Rachel groaned at the pleasure of being pinned underneath him as his body took control of hers, bringing a clenching need to feel him deep inside that had her hips lifting to his with each of his strokes so he could slide further inside her.

"Harder, Cash," Rachel demanded. She didn't feel defeated by succumbing to him; hell, the man could make any woman give it up.

He tore at the front of her dress, exposing her bra. Then he pulled out of her long enough to pull off her dress and bra before pressing her back down into the mattress.

"Cash, you need to get a condom."

"Don't worry, you won't get pregnant. I'll use the rhythm method." His cock filled her slowly, his movements gradually building until the bed was shaking from the power of his thrusts. Just as she was about to come, he slowed, bringing her budding climax to a low simmer.

"I…" Rachel licked her lips. "I don't think this can be considered…" He began thrusting harder once again, building her climax until it was within her grasp and making her forget what she had been about to say.

When she ran her hands up his sides, bunching up his t-shirt, Cash let her pull it off him. She tossed it to the side as her mouth found one of his nipples, biting it softly before exploring his chest with her tongue, liking the salty taste of him.

Cash's fingers found one of her nipples, pinching it until a stinging sensation had her gripping his hips harder with her thighs.

"Like that?"

Rachel's only answer was a soft moan, which gradually rose as his touch became more erotic while his hard cock slid in and out of her.

"Cash…" As he released her nipple, the sting as the blood rushed back to the tip had her screaming her climax.

"Your nipples are so sensitive." His tongue laved the still-tender tip as he stroked out his own climax while Rachel's teeth found his nipple, biting down.

She was rewarded when his hands went under her ass as he fucked her with a strength and wildness he hadn't shown her before. Rachel could feel his loss of control as she widened her legs, letting him have what he needed. She watched his taut expression, fulfilling a need she had been unaware of.

Afterward, he lay on top of her, pressing her into the bed, and Rachel smoothed her hands across his back, giving him the softness she had kept carefully hidden.

He moved to her side, splaying his hand on her firm stomach, his thumb playing in her fiery curls at the apex of her thighs. It didn't last long; his pleased expression sent warning signals off.

"Satisfied?" Rachel turned her face away.

"What do you mean by that?" Cash's hand on her jaw forced her eyes back to his.

"Another woman bites the dust. You win, Cash. You've proven that I can't resist you. Are you happy now?" Rachel couldn't prevent the bitterness from entering her voice.

"What the hell does that mean?"

"Don't play games, Cash; you know exactly what I mean. Remember Lisa Finley? How long did it take you to get her in your bed? Two or three weeks? Tanya Estes? A month? Robin Wagner? Four weeks? Sola Brown? A year? I sure as hell didn't break any of your records, did I?"

She tried to slide out of the bed yet found herself pinned under his heavy weight with his serious face gazing down at her.

"You broke all the records, Rachel." His soft voice gave her hope that something more was there. "You're the youngest girl I've ever looked at and wanted. I had to leave town to make sure I didn't go to jail over you. You're the woman I've wanted the longest. I've wanted you ever since I saw you standing on the porch when Lily was lost. You're the first woman I fucked that I couldn't walk away and forget with another." He ignored her hurt gasp at being reminded of Cheryl and Bliss and God knew how many others.

"I live a life I don't know if you can accept. That's going to be up to you. I tried to stay away because I like living the life I lead. Razer, Viper, Knox, and Shade have shown it can be done, but that doesn't mean it's going to work for us. I'm willing to try if you'll quit busting my balls over my past."

Rachel didn't know what to say or do. She couldn't

imagine living her life within a motorcycle club, yet she knew her friends were happy. Beth had children, Lily was expecting, and Knox and Diamond were part of the club but didn't live within its walls. Each couple had found a way to make it work for them. Rachel wasn't a coward; she was a fighter. Hell, she had a body count to her credit when she had helped rescue Lily.

She pushed against Cash's chest until he fell back against the bed, then she raised herself over him, looking down into his handsome face. "If we're going to try this, there are going to be some rules," Rachel stated.

Cash made a face up at her. "More rules?"

Rachel smiled down at him. "What are the ones my brothers gave you?"

Cash recited them to her amusement. "No fucking around on you. I can't beat you when you piss me off. You get to keep growing weird shit in my bathroom, and have strangers come by. I have to drag my ass out of bed on Sunday mornings to go to church with you, and let them turn my kids against me."

"No fucking around on me is the one that's most important to me." The tips of her breasts grazed his chest as she swung a thigh over him, raising herself until she was sitting on his waist, waiting for his answer.

"I can do that. Are you going to be on my ass about trusting me here with the women?"

Rachel shook her head. "No, I'll believe you until I catch you cheating. Then I'll just shoot your ass."

Cash's chest rumbled with laughter. "Is that any way to begin a relationship, threatening to shoot me?"

"Yes, it works for me. Now, since I'm thinking about you courting me, will you answer a question for me?"

Cash didn't want to spoil the moment by telling her they had been courting since he had gone fishing with her brothers, so he merely nodded.

"What happens on Friday nights?"

"Why don't I just show you instead?"

# CHAPTER THIRTY

Rachel both looked forward to and dreaded the rest of the week. Whenever she questioned Cash further, she received a predatory look, which had her both nervous and excited. When she broached the subject with Lily, a worried frown was her only response, leading her to believe she might be better off not knowing.

Friday morning wasn't starting off great. She had woken late, forcing her to skip her morning tea. Then she had almost fallen and broken her kneecap when she had tripped over a new end table Mag had purchased at a flea market with her neighbor, Janet. Rachel was seriously thinking of threatening Janet with bodily harm if she pulled over for another flea market.

She had finally managed to make it to her car, only to run into a ditch halfway down the mountain when she had swerved to miss a deer. Shaken, she had called Lyle, the tow driver, and was sitting, waiting for his truck, hoping he hadn't gone on another binge and would actually show up.

Seeing the tow truck pull up behind her, Rachel got expectantly out of her car. She was shocked to see Jo, Lyle's daughter, climb out of the big truck.

"When did you get back in town?" Rachel asked,

coming to stand beside her, looking at the damage to her car.

"A week ago. Dad's laid up with a broken leg, so I'm pitching in until he's better."

Rachel stared at the pretty brunette woman wearing overalls smeared with dirt and oil. The oversized overalls did little to hide the curvy body underneath. Jo had been born and raised in Treepoint until her mother had dealt with enough when Jo was a sophomore in high school. Being the daughter of the town drunk had made Jo the brunt of many jokes and the prey of the less scrupulous. Her mother had divorced Lyle and left town after a popular senior had tried to rape Jo following a football game.

She and Rachel had been friends since birth. The backwoods had been their playground and four wheelers their toys. She had missed her after she had left.

"Let's go out to dinner tomorrow night and catch up," Rachel said.

"Sounds good. Let's get your car out."

Jo climbed back into the truck, doing a u-turn and backing up to the car, briefly blocking the road as she made the maneuver. As she worked, Rachel heard the familiar sounds of a group of motorcycles headed down the mountain. She turned bright red when The Last Riders turned the curve and she saw them. Her hope that they would pass by was dashed as they pulled over.

Cash and Rider got off their bikes, watching the truck expertly drive.

"Why didn't you call me? We could have gotten your car out," Cash said.

"Because I don't need you or my brothers to handle things I can do myself. As you can see, I have everything under control."

Jo climbed out of the tow truck, going to the back and getting the heavy chains. The men stood there gaping as the woman hooked the car up and then pressed a button that slowly started pulling the car out of the ditch. When the car was once again on firm pavement, she unhooked the chains, placing them back in the truck.

Jo went to her truck and grabbed her clipboard before coming back to Rachel.

"That'll be sixty, Rachel."

Rachel started to reach inside the car for her purse, but Cash had already pulled out his wallet. He handed Jo a hundred.

"Just a second and I'll get your change."

"That's okay, keep the change." Cash smiled.

Rachel watched him suspiciously, yet she saw no interest for the woman on his face.

"Sweet. Thanks." She slid the hundred into the top pocket of her overall. "See you tomorrow night for dinner, Rachel."

"Can I come?" Rider quipped. "I know all the best places."

Jo's friendly gaze turned frosty as she surveyed Rider from head to toe. "As there are only five places to eat in the whole town, I think we can manage on our own."

"You don't know what you're missing out on."

Rachel enjoyed the show of Rider making an ass of himself. Jo was no Holly, to become easily embarrassed or overwhelmed by Rider's flirtatious behavior.

"Oh, I'm pretty sure I do. Bye, Rachel."

"Bye, Jo."

Jo ignored the men's presence, turning on her heel, climbing back into the tow truck, and driving away.

Rider stood frowning as she pulled away. "She's not very friendly, is she?" he complained.

"Depends," Rachel said, getting back in her car and rolling her window down.

"On what?"

"On whether you're a man or woman."

"That explains it. All the good-looking women are always lesbians," he said, turning on his heel in disappointment before going back to his bike.

"Is he really that big of an ass?"

"Yes," Cash admitted, leaning in her window. "You sneaked out again last night."

Rachel looked down at her hands on the steering wheel. "I wanted to get home to Mag."

"Then I'll make sure I get someone to spend the night with her tonight."

Rachel started to argue but was cut off when his mouth covered hers. "I'll pick you up at eight." He walked away without another word.

"I bet being an asshole is a prerequisite to being a Last Rider," Rachel said to herself as she put her car in drive.

When she finally made it to work without another catastrophe happening, she unlocked the door to the store, coming to a stop; she sensed someone was inside. Swallowing back her fear, she closed the door behind her.

Carefully, she surveyed the room and saw a tiny movement to her left. Sensing fear, she closed the door.

"I know you're there. Come out, and I won't call the sheriff."

Several moments passed before a figure stepped out of hiding behind a rack of clothing. Cal Harris stared at her with both fear and bravado.

"What are you doing in here, Cal?"

She could see the desire to lie to her, but she guessed his pride didn't outweigh his needs.

"I'm sorry for breaking in. I've only been taking what we need. My mom and dad have been laid off and haven't found jobs yet. They won't ask for any help..." His voice trailed off in embarrassment.

Rachel blinked back tears. The proud, young man needed help, not her pity. It was for families like his they had opened the church store.

"You're the one who has been breaking in?"

Cal nodded. "I kept messing with the air conditioner so you would leave the back window unlocked. I would climb in after everyone left."

"All you had to do was ask," Rachel gently reprimanded.

"Dad says we can't take any handouts," he replied proudly, clearly mimicking his father's words.

"What did he say about stealing or destroying someone else's property?"

His red face answered her question.

"Are you going to call Knox?" His bravado hid his discernible fear.

"No, I'm not going to call Knox, on one condition."

"What?"

"That you take a few items I've been trying to get rid of." Rachel bustled around the room, picking several items she knew Cal's little sister could use with the warmer weather approaching. She had seen her the other day with her mother.

Picking out some dresses and t-shirts, she made a large bag full of clothes, hoping she was gauging the right size. She critically surveyed Cal, placing several jeans and t-shirts in another bag for him. When she finished that task, she got a large box and began putting grocery staples into it until it was packed to the top. Setting the two bags of clothes on top, she pushed the box on the counter toward Cal.

"Here you go."

Cal looked like he was going to refuse, so Rachel picked up the telephone with a raised brow. When he picked up the box, she lowered the phone.

"What am I going to tell my parents?"

"Tell them you helped clean the store for me, and I paid you in merchandise."

He looked relieved at her excuse, obviously wanting to take the items. "Thank you, Rachel. I'm sorry I broke in... I..."

"Come back next Friday, and I'll have another box ready for you."

Cal nodded, hesitating, about to say something when the door opened and Lily came in. His expression shuttered and he closed his mouth, leaving.

"I didn't know his family had applied for aid," Lily said as she came behind the counter.

"They didn't." Rachel told her what had happened, and that she had given him the items from the store.

"You did the right thing. I know his family won't like it if we offer any help." Lily bit her lip.

Rachel sat, thinking for a moment, before a solution finally occurred to her. Picking up the phone, she called her cousin; he picked up on the third ring.

"Drake, did you know Cal's parents both lost their jobs?"

"Jace mentioned it."

Rachel bit back her anger; Drake required deft handling. "I thought, since Cal was the one to pull Jace out of the lake last summer when he almost drowned, and he was also the one that kept him from getting his ass whipped by half the football team, and he also—"

"Rachel, I get your point. I'll see what I can do."

"I'm glad to hear it, cousin. We Porters always pay our debts."

Drake's laughter sounded over the phone. "I almost feel sorry for Cash. I'll take care of it today. Satisfied?"

"Yes, but be discreet," she clarified.

"Okay. Anything else?" he inquired mockingly.

"Nope. Thanks, Drake." Rachel hung up, happy her cousin would help out Cal's family.

Lily smiled at her. "I was going to ask Shade to help them out, but this works out better."

"Why?" Rachel asked curiously.

"That way I can save it for the next time I need a favor." Lily's happiness was almost tangible as she talked about her husband. Her confidence that he could solve any problem was heartwarming.

The sound of Brooke's heels on the tiles in the hallway

warned of her approach. Rachel braced herself for her presence; she was really beginning to dislike the woman. There wasn't a day she didn't come by to ask for help with some task she needed done. She was passing off her duties of being a minister's wife to both Rachel and Lily while she took all the credit from her husband and the congregation.

"Hello, girls, how are you both doing today?" The false sweetness in her voice had Rachel wanting to heave. "I'm having a small dinner for the wives of the deacons. Would it be possible for you to do the grocery shopping for me, Rachel? I would do it, but Jeffrey is teething and running a small fever." As she held out a list, Rachel reached out and took it. It would take over an hour to do the shopping for the large list.

"I'll do it during my lunch hour."

"Perfect. I knew I could count on you."

Rachel thought she would leave since her purpose had been achieved; instead, she lingered, leaning casually against the counter.

"Lily, I have several maternity outfits that I no longer need. If you'd like, I could give them to you. I noticed yours are getting tight." A long, manicured nail tapped the counter. "You may want to watch your weight. Baby weight isn't easy to get rid of."

Rachel couldn't believe the bitchy remark. Lily was smaller at eight months pregnant than Brooke was now.

"I bought my maternity clothes in Atlanta. They aren't as tacky as the ones you'll buy in Treepoint."

Rachel almost smacked Brooke when Lily self-consciously ran her hand over her blue-jean maternity dress that she looked gorgeous wearing.

"I don't think it's the clothes that make a person pretty, but the person wearing them," Rachel told Brooke sharply, moving protectively closer to Lily, who was sitting on a stool behind the counter.

Brooke's eyes lowered to Rachel's simple, blue dress, letting her distaste show. "I'm going home to Atlanta next week. I could pick up a few things for you, Rachel."

"No, thanks. Clothes are clothes to me. I don't place much importance on them. You can turn shit into fertilizer, but it still smells like shit." Rachel had dealt with enough of Brooke's snide comments, and she wasn't going to tolerate her attitude any longer. She wanted to give her the grocery list back and tell her where to shove it, but she was afraid she would get Lily to do it instead.

"If you change your mind, let me know." Brooke didn't let her comment bother her. The plastic expression on her face didn't change. "I need to be getting back to Jeffrey."

"I'm really starting to hate that woman," Rachel stated once she had left.

"I don't think she likes us very much, either," Lily said unhappily.

Rachel fumed. "She's really going to dislike me when I shove my foot up her ass."

\* \* \*

The rest of the day didn't get much better. The grocery shopping took longer than expected, and when she returned to the church store, it was crowded. It took over an hour to see that the customers were waited on.

When she and Lily were able to catch their breath, Rachel went to the diner to get them a late lunch and came out to pouring rain. Lily was unable to keep from laughing at her disheveled appearance.

"I'm really starting to question our friendship." Rachel dried herself off with a towel.

"I'm sorry." Lily straightened her face, taking the sandwich Rachel handed her.

"You can make it up to me. Tell me what I should wear tonight so I don't look like a dork."

"As little as possible."

When Rachel choked on her sandwich, Lily had to hit her on the back several times before she could catch her breath.

She stared at her through watery eyes. "Are you

serious?"

"Well, the women like to show some skin."

"It can't be any worse than their swimsuits." Rachel thought about what was in her closet. "I have a cream-colored halter sundress. It's a little early for it, but I could wear a shrug over it. Will that do?"

"Ah... maybe. Has Cash told you about Friday nights yet?" Lily asked tentatively, wrapping up the remains of her sandwich. Rachel wondered why she had lost her appetite.

"Not really, just that it's the night you don't have to belong to the club to party there if you've been invited. I'm not really worried about it. You, Beth, and Winter will all be there."

"Shade and I haven't been to a Friday night party since he found out we're pregnant. He became very possessive. Beth and Razer usually stay home with the boys..." Lily gave her a bright smile. "You're right; you don't have to be nervous. We will all be there. Diamond, too. I'll give her a call." Lily patted her hand. "You don't have to worry about a thing; we'll all have your back."

Rachel almost called Cash and said she was too sick to go out tonight. Lily's words had sounded like a battle plan. She lost her own appetite, throwing away her half-eaten sandwich. The only reason she didn't cancel was because it was past time she found out what really happened on Friday nights. It couldn't be as bad as she was beginning to stress out about, could it?

\* \* \*

She was a nervous wreck by the time Cash picked her up.

When she came out of her bedroom in the cream halter dress with the navy shrug, he raised a brow. "Aren't you going to be hot in that?"

She was disappointed he hadn't complimented her on her appearance. "It's a halter underneath. I can take the shrug off if I get hot."

His eyes went to the top of the dress covered by the shrug. "That works then. You ready?"

"Yes." Rachel went to Mag, who was pretending to watch a game show, and gave her a quick kiss on her wrinkled cheek. "Goodnight."

"Night, Rachel. Have some fun."

"I will." Rachel gave her neighbor Janet a smile, glad she was staying the night with Mag. Her kind gaze reassured her that Mag was settled for the night.

Cash had driven his truck to pick her up. Rachel climbed inside when he held the door open, settling comfortably on the seat. Hopefully, the night would be a lot of fun and she could put the terrible day she'd had behind her.

# CHAPTER THIRTY-ONE

Rachel sat on one of the couches, drinking the beer Cash had given her. She stared around the room, amazed she had been so naïve. She swallowed hard when Jewell began dancing suggestively in front of Nickel and Train came up behind her, pressing into her from behind, his hand sliding down the front of her tiny, black skirt. The top had already been taken off by Nickel and laid on the floor.

Rachel moved her eyes away from the tableau, but everywhere she looked in the crowded room was more of the same. Half-naked women, some she was familiar with that belonged to the club and others she knew from town. All of them here for the men and the sex that took place out in the open.

She stuck out in her clothes like a nun in a nudist colony.

She turned to Cash, who was sitting next to her, watching her reaction.

"Where's Lily, Beth, Winter, and Diamond?" Her voice was emotionless as she saw Bliss unzip Rider's jeans as he sat sprawled out on a chair. In one motion, she pulled out his cock and went down on him.

"They won't be here tonight," Cash drawled.

"Why not?" Rachel squeaked as Nickel turned away from the show Train and Jewel were putting on to snag Raci as she passed with Crash. She was wearing a dark-purple short set. The top wrapped around and tied at the waist, leaving a deep vee of naked flesh between her breasts. Every time she moved, the slinky material showed her bare breasts. Rachel had to admit the woman was sexy and could see why every man's eyes were on her as Crash pushed her over the arm of a chair, unzipped his jeans, and entered her from behind.

"Because they earned a punishment this week. They didn't tell me where you were when you disappeared, even though they had figured it out." Her eyes darted to his, seeing the visible anger at her not telling him about her studies. "To make matters even worse, Shade overheard Lily trying to rally the women into behaving tonight in front of you."

"What was wrong with that?" She winced when Raci started screaming with her climax.

"Because I didn't want to hide this from you any longer. It was just a matter of time before you found out."

The door to the kitchen opened and Cheryl came out with Ember and Stori. She was dressed in a black leather mini-skirt and wasn't wearing a top. Ember and Stori only had on t-shirts.

Rider reached out and grabbed Cheryl's hand, tugging her down on his lap. Bliss, who had climbed onto his lap after finishing his blowjob, reached out and lifted one of Cheryl's breasts to Rider's mouth where he sucked a bared nipple.

"I don't think Cheryl's missing Jared," she remarked impassively.

"No."

"You've participated in these parties?"

"Yes. Fridays, we let the women from town in, but unless they are going to become members, they don't come out during the week."

"How do they become members?"

Cash was silent for a moment. "There are eight original members. The women have to get six out of eight votes. They get the vote by having sex with the member—or they used to. Now, the ones who are married give their vote to another of the men to vote, usually Crash and Nickel."

"You're an original member?"

"Yes."

"Have you given Cheryl your vote?"

"Yes." She could hear no emotion in his voice. "She only needs one more vote to become a member. Lucky hasn't given her his vote yet."

Rachel paled; she had forgotten Dean, her former pastor...

"Lucky does not participate in the club activities where Lily can see, nor would he in front of you."

"Thank God." The irony of the situation brought a hysterical laugh to her lips. She put her hand on her mouth to stifle the sound.

"Rachel?"

She gathered her failing reserve, removing her hand to her side before getting to her feet. He reached out, taking her hand, but she jerked it from his grasp.

"You bastard. You're surrounded with a freaking smorgasbord of women." She gave a bitter laugh. "I wondered which ones you had been with. I never thought you had been with them all. That you shared them all!"

Her hand swung out, slamming into the side of his face. "You fucked me with no condom!"

"You're the only one I haven't used a condom with; it's a hard rule here. We also have regular blood work done. We're not irresponsible." Cash's face hardened as he rose to his feet.

Rachel backed away from him, refusing to cry. She wasn't hurt; she didn't care about him anymore. This had merely confirmed everything she'd already known—they had no chance together.

When Cheryl paled and sat up straight on Rider's lap, she realized she had been screaming at Cash.

"Did you get a laugh when you saw how I was dressed tonight? How lame I was? I hate you..." A broken sob escaped her.

Humiliated, she ran from the room before Cash could stop her, running down the long flight of steps and nearly falling in her heels before she tore them off and threw them at Cash as he chased after her. He almost caught up with her, but she darted between the bikers standing at the bottom of the steps, running into the woods before he could stop her.

"Rachel! Come back. I'll take you home."

Rachel ignored his yells, running through the forest as if a monster from Hell was after her.

* * *

Cash squatted down, reading the tracks on the ground. She wasn't heading back to Mag's house; she was heading home. He followed behind her as quick as he could, furious at himself that he hadn't handled telling her the truth about the women better. Lily had warned him when Shade had told her the women's punishment included not attending the party.

He had known Rachel would be furious. He had even figured that she would be hurt, but what he had witnessed had gone beyond what he had thought her reaction would be. He should have guarded the doors where she couldn't get out. Now she was heading for her brothers' home and would have an arsenal at her disposal.

He followed her trail until he found her not far from home. She was sitting under a tree, crying into the neck of her huge-ass dog. A loud growl alerted her to his presence.

"Go away, Cash. Please, just go away."

Cash remained still. "I can't, Rachel." Slowly, despite the dog's growl, he moved toward her, kneeling down in front of her then brushing her damp hair away from her cheek.

"I'm sorry that I'm an ass. I thought it would be easier for you to deal with if you saw it like it was."

"Ripping a band-aid off?" she asked sarcastically.

Cash winced. "Yeah. I'm not going to lie and pretend I don't like the life I lead, or that I live it because I'm fucked-up. I'm not. I like to fuck, and I like to fuck a lot. I like sex, the raunchier the better. I could have hidden it from you, pretended that part of my life never happened, but the truth would have eventually come out."

Rachel buried her face back in the dog's fur.

His hand slid to the back of her neck, lifting her face to his. "I haven't fucked another woman since you saw me with Bliss."

Her suspicious gaze didn't shy away from his.

"It's the truth. I haven't really wanted anyone since I was with you at your house. I wasn't ready to accept that you got under my skin, though. I like to say that your brothers are slow. The truth is, I was slow in admitting that it was more than just sex with you, Rachel. I didn't plan on falling in love with you. I didn't care if you wore a trench coat tonight, only that you were there, with me."

"Go back." She moved away from his touch. "I couldn't ever do the things I saw there tonight. I wouldn't want to."

"I didn't show you so that you would participate; I showed you because I didn't want any secrets between us. I like the Friday parties, but if you don't want to go, that's cool." Cash tried to make her see she had all the choices.

She raised her face from the neck of her dog. "Do Lily and Beth and the others?"

He wanted to respect their privacy, but he needed to tell Rachel the truth. "Yes. They found the part that they enjoy and leave the part they don't alone. Tell the truth, Rachel. Be honest to both of us. Did you find the whole thing upsetting? There wasn't *one* thing you found arousing?"

"No."

Cash took hope that she sounded unsure. It was her first experience with their lifestyle. None of his brothers' wives had taken it any better when they had found out.

"That's okay," he assured her, moving closer to her side and placing his arm around her shoulders. She still clung to her dog, but she sank against him, letting him hold her. He sat holding her quietly, letting her absorb everything she had learned.

"I don't know," her voice was quiet in the darkness, "if I can get over the fact you've had sex with all my friends."

"I haven't had sex with any of your friends," he denied. "Cheryl isn't your friend. I haven't fucked Lily, Beth, Diamond, or Winter."

"Willa?" He caught a faint trace of amusement in her voice.

"Nope."

"Melody Ward?"

"Who?"

"My best friend in high school."

"Her, I fucked, but she doesn't count," Cash stated, refusing to let her pull away.

"Why in the hell doesn't she count? She was my best friend!"

"Because I didn't know I was going to be courting with you then! I've fucked around, okay?" Cash said, frustrated, raking his hands through his long hair. "If I knew I was going to be with you, then I could have done things differently, but back then, she was just another girl."

"You don't remember her?"

"No!"

She looked at him suspiciously. "Does it count if you don't remember them?"

Cash thought she was talking to herself and kept his mouth shut. He wasn't touching that question with a ten-foot pole.

She must have answered it for herself because she laid

her head on his shoulder. While the dog gave him an unhappy look, he brushed his mouth over her still-damp cheeks, smiling to himself. They sat there quietly in the dark, holding hands with the dog lying beside them.

After a while, a shadow moved from behind a tree not too far from them, heading toward Rachel's home. Cash recognized Tate as he left them in the darkness. He wondered how long he had been listening and why he hadn't tried to keep him from Rachel when it had been plainly obvious she had been running from him.

"How are we going to get back?" Rachel asked sleepily.

Cash pulled out his cell phone. "Rider, sorry to interrupt, but could you pick us up at the bottom of the Porters' driveway?" He hung up when Rider said he would be there in ten minutes.

Stiffly getting to his feet, he helped Rachel up.

"Go home, Sampson. Go!" The dog trotted off toward the Porters' home.

"Whose dog is it?" Cash asked.

Rachel sighed. "It's technically Tate's dog."

Cash hid his relief. He didn't dislike dogs; he just thought they should be dog-size, not horse-size.

Rider was waiting for them at the bottom of the driveway.

"Where to?" Rider asked.

Cash let Rachel decide. "The clubhouse."

As Rider pulled out, driving back to the clubhouse, Cash squeezed Rachel's hand in his. He had been afraid she would want to go back to Mag's. He'd wanted her to make the decision to spend the night with him and was relieved when she did.

When they arrived back at the clubhouse, Cash pulled her upstairs to his room before she could become upset again. Closing the door behind them, he started tugging off her clothes.

"Cash, slow down."

He didn't slow down; instead, he tore off his clothes

before pushing her down on the bed. Wedging himself between her thighs, he took her pussy in one hard stroke.

"Cash!"

Now that he was in her, he slowed down, lowering his mouth to give her his. She stared up at him with heat and a trace of uncertainty. It was the indecision he planned to fuck out of her. By morning, she wouldn't be able to sneak out of his bed because she was going to be too tired.

"Are you always going to run off when you get mad?" Cash brushed his mouth against one of her nipples.

"Probably. I hate fighting."

Cash laughed so hard Rachel hit his chest.

"What's so funny?"

"You don't know yourself at all, do you?"

"Better than you do," she smarted off. "If you don't shut up, I'm not staying." She rolled over in a huff.

She was here, but she wasn't. Rachel was still keeping a part of herself away from him, and it was pissing him off. He rolled her back over to face him. Her hands clutched his shoulders as he lifted her hips so his cock was notched at the opening of her tight pussy.

Taking her hands in one of his, he pulled them over her head, stretching her taut underneath him, under his control.

His mouth moved to her ear. "You want my cock?"

"Yes…" she moaned.

"Where do you want it?"

Rachel moaned arching her hips, but Cash kept himself from sliding in her moist warmth.

"Where do you want it?" He gritted his teeth, expertly rubbing her clit.

"Inside me."

"Say it. Say, Cash, I want your cock in my pussy." His fingers left her clit, going to her nipple and wiping her juices on the tight bud before lowering his mouth to taste her.

He felt her become wetter against his cock at his crude

273

words. His little vixen was going to learn hard and fast that she was his woman, and the days of her walking away from him were over.

"I want your cock in my pussy."

Cash let the head of his cock slid inside of her before stopping.

His tongue licked her lips. "This is going to be rough this time. I'm going to give it to you the way I like to take it."

"Oh…"

Cash pounded his cock inside of her until he was balls deep. He had always consciously gone easy on her, aware of her tenderness and newness at being in an intimate relationship; however, the only way he was going to tame his vixen was to give her something she wasn't going to forget when she sneaked out of his bed despite his best attempts to keep her there. Every time she would move, the aching awareness between her thighs would bring him to her mind. He was going to become her addiction, as she had become his.

He fucked her harder, sucking her nipple harder to torment her. He played with her body until she called his name out over and over. In the past, he had always preferred women to be silent when he had sex with them. Her whimpers of arousal almost made him come, but he controlled his climax with an iron will.

"You are mine and no one else's. Stay away from Scorpion, Patrick, and Charles."

He still saw the light of battle in her eyes, but this time, he also saw the beginning of her capitulation.

"All right!" she gasped as he sucked her other nipple into his mouth.

It was enough for tonight.

Sliding his hand down, he slid a finger between the fleshy lips, brushing across her clit, giving the stimulation she needed.

"Cash!" When she screamed his name as she came, he

let his own control go, pumping inside her until his own release stormed her body.

He had every intention of keeping her by any means. Fair or foul, his little vixen was going to find herself trapped.

\* \* \*

Rachel sneaked cautiously down the hallway. She really didn't want to be confronted with another pair having sex. She had to work hard to keep the erotic images she had participated in herself that night from entering her mind.

She went down the steps quietly, she saw the club room was almost empty. Going to the front door, she was about to open it when she glanced back and saw Dean sitting on a large chair with his back to the door.

Cheryl approached him, sitting down on the arm of the chair and leaning over to glide her hand across his chest toward his thigh. She almost went out the door, not wanting to see her former pastor engage in sex with Cheryl.

Dean's words had her pausing with her hand on the door.

"Stop, Cheryl. I'm going to save you the effort and tell you now: you won't be getting my vote."

"But... why? I can make you come." Her suggestive voice lowered as her mouth bent toward his neck.

"No, you can't." Dean took Cheryl's hands in his, moving them away from his body. "I'm not attracted to you, Cheryl. You're not here for the men or sex. Payback against Jared isn't going to be a good enough reason for me to believe you want to belong to The Last Riders."

"I do, and I can prove it." Cheryl slid off the arm of the chair, kneeling before Dean.

His casual air disappeared in a flash at her refusal to listen to him.

"I'm trying to be nice without having your ass thrown out of this club. I told you no."

Rachel had never seen the expression on Dean's face

that she saw on his profile now. Goose bumps rose on her arms and even Cheryl's blatant behavior died and fear replaced it when she saw his face.

She hastily rose to her feet, but she wasn't fast enough to escape Dean's hand that reached out. He grabbed her by the back of her neck, forcing her back to her knees in front of him.

"I'm not your pastor anymore, but I'm going to give you some guidance. When I say no, I mean No! Now, you can fuck any brother you want here—I don't give a shit—but stay away from me. You got me?"

Frantically, Cheryl nodded her head. Dean released her and she shakily got to her feet before running to the front door where Rachel was frozen in place.

Rachel barely managed to open it before Cheryl flew through it. Rachel's eyes met Dean's before she went out the door behind her. Rachel followed Cheryl through the front door and down the dark steps, hoping that neither of them fell. Cheryl made it to her car and was opening the door when she saw Rachel.

"You saw?" she asked tearfully.

Rachel had been about to pass her without a word but stopped. "It was kinda hard to miss."

"Did it make you happy?" Cheryl's caustic question had Rachel wanting to smack her.

"I would have been a hell of a lot happier if that had been Cash's answer, but it wasn't, was it?"

Cheryl's bravado disappeared.

"No, it wasn't. I'm sorry, Rachel." Cheryl ran her hand through her tumbled hair.

Rachel unwillingly felt the turmoil she was going through. Sometimes, her gift wasn't a gift. She didn't want to feel sorry for her.

"Cheryl, it was only last year that you were asking Dean's spiritual guidance on why you weren't getting pregnant. He probably felt wrong in taking advantage of your breakup."

"Why are you trying to make me feel better? If Cash offered me another turn at him, I wouldn't turn him down."

*At least she's honest*, Rachel thought.

"Not many would turn him down," Rachel acknowledged. "Is that what you want for yourself, Cheryl? To be just another woman to those men?"

"Why not? That's all I was to Jared." Cheryl leaned against the side of her car, tears sliding down her cheeks.

"I don't think so, Cheryl. He married you. He had affairs, but he always came home to you. He may have been an idiot, but to him, you were special."

She wiped the tears away from her cheeks, staring at her hopefully. "You think so?"

"Yes, I do."

"He's pretty mad at me. He's fighting the divorce," Cheryl admitted.

"Make him pay for cheating on you, just don't lose yourself in the process."

Cheryl nodded her head before getting into her car.

"Need a ride?"

"Thanks." Her and Cheryl would never be friends, but Rachel might as well get used to tolerating her presence just like the rest of the women at the club. Heaven help her, she knew it wasn't going to be her last visit to the clubhouse.

# CHAPTER THIRTY-TWO

"What's taking so long?" Mag's impatience had Rachel hurrying to her side.

"I had to park the car," she explained.

The whole town must be at the festival; she'd had to park at the end of the parking lot.

She took the handles of Mag's wheelchair, pushing it along the busy street filled with townspeople and tourists. Rachel didn't know why anyone would waste the time to come to the annual Arts and Crafts Festival, but it drew a huge crowd every year. She was finally able to make it to the church parking lot, which had been set up with different booths showing the artisans of the area and various foods. She pushed Mag to one of the tables.

"I'll grab us something to eat."

"Hurry up; I'm starving," Mag demanded.

Rachel looked down into her tired eyes, realizing her blustering behavior was because she wasn't feeling well.

"I'll be right back," she promised.

She found a booth, getting Mag a plate and drink before taking it back to her. Rachel wasn't hungry, so she sat and talked to Mag as she ate, sipping on her iced tea.

"Hi, Rachel!" Rachel waved as Lily, with the rest of The

Last Riders following, approached the table.

Cash took a seat next to her, his expression telling her he wasn't happy with her leaving him during the night again.

"Hi, Lily." She ignored Cash's tight-lipped anger to greet her friend.

"You're not eating?" Lily asked.

"I'm afraid to. There's enough fatback in those dishes to take down a horse." Rachel had managed to find a few things for Mag that weren't swimming in grease.

"I'm starved. I'll be back in a minute." Lily left while the bikers remained clustered around the table.

"Exactly when did you sneak out?" Cash asked, breaking his silence.

"Around two. Don't worry, I didn't walk home; Cheryl gave me a ride."

Cash didn't look any happier with her answer. Rachel shrugged, not letting his injured masculine pride ruin her day.

Beth gave her a wink, listening to the conversation.

"You're not hungry?" Rachel asked her.

"I'm with you. Thank God I'm not pregnant anymore and don't get the cravings Lily does."

Rachel watched as Lily went from booth to booth, getting samples of everyone's food.

"When did Brooke learn to cook beans and greens?" Rachel was surprised she would participate in the festival.

"I have no idea," Beth said then added, "You going to try it?"

"No, it would be too depressing if she can cook as good as she looks." No self-respecting country girl could stand for her cooking to be upstaged by a city girl.

Lily came back to the table with a huge plate, sitting down between her and Mag.

"Aren't you going to eat?" Rachel asked Cash.

"Later." His eyes were on a large group of men, sitting at a nearby table.

"You don't like them, do you?"

"No."

"Why? They seem friendly enough."

"So was Ted Bundy."

Shocked at the comparison, she saw that the rest of The Last Riders weren't happy to see Scorpion and his friends. Viper had a frown, and Shade's eyes had turned deadly. Something was going on that made these men nervous. Rachel was smart enough to realize that if they were worried, she should be also. Furthermore, she didn't think it was a good thing Cash had compared them to a serial murderer.

"I can't eat anymore." Lily pushed her plate away, looking queasy.

"You only ate a biscuit." Rachel looked down at Lily's practically untouched plate.

"I guess it's not agreeing with the baby." Lily turned green, getting up from the table with Shade's help. Seconds later, she darted to the nearest restroom inside the church.

"No need wasting food." Mag reached out, pulling the plate toward her.

Rachel didn't say anything. Compared to the plate she had fixed her, Lily's looked like a banquet.

"I heard that things didn't go well last night," Beth broached the subject tentatively.

Rachel made a face. "That's putting it mildly."

"I was shocked the first time I went, too. I ended up leaving." Beth's face was red from embarrassment. "Lily ran back to college."

"I tried to run, but Viper wouldn't let me," Winter gently butted into the conversation. "It was after my attack. Believe me, if I'd had use of my legs, he wouldn't have been able to catch me, either."

"I would have caught you," Viper stated. Rachel believed him. With his hard, muscular body and long legs, Winter wouldn't have gotten far.

Beth's scream and her chair falling back as she rose terrified Rachel as she looked to see what was happening.

"No!" Rachel's own scream parted her lips as Beth yelled for someone to call nine-one-one.

Mag had turned deathly pale and had passed out, her head falling back over the wheelchair. The men quickly pushed it back from the table, laying her on the ground. Rachel watched as Beth frantically took her pulse. Shade moved Lily back as she came out of the restroom, turning her so she couldn't see what was going on. Cash knelt by his grandmother, holding her hand.

"Her heart is racing," Beth told Cash.

Rachel stared down at Mag, crying. She fell to her knees beside Mag, laying her hand on her heart. After she had touched Cash, she'd had nothing left. For the last few months, her gift hadn't shown a trace of itself.

Gathering her strength, she reached for her...

\* \* \*

"Mag... Mag!" Rachel kept calling desperately, searching for the woman's soul. She didn't want to give up. "Mag, answer me, dammit!"

"Rachel, I'm here."

Rachel moved her spirit to where she heard Mag's voice.

"Thank God." Rachel dropped down next to Mag, her pale eyes staring up at her.

"Don't leave," Rachel begged. She looked up, seeing the bright light approaching, and then held her hand tighter.

"Girl, I wasn't meant to stay here forever. It's time I went home."

The acceptance in her voice had Rachel shaking her head. "Your time is close, but not now. It doesn't feel right," Rachel begged. "Listen to me, Mag. Something is wrong, but it's not anything wrong with you. I would feel the pain. Please stay..." She was unaware of the small cries escaping her as she pleaded with the woman she had come to love.

Rachel felt Mag's acceptance; she wasn't even putting up the least resistance. Life was not given freely; it had to be wanted… she needed to be wanted. The answer came to her.

"I need you, Mag. Who is going to make Cash behave if you leave? Don't you want to stay and see your first great-grandchild born? Isn't that worth living for?"

"I'm going to have a great-grandchild?"

Rachel felt the spark within Mag flicker, the light pausing above her.

"Yes!" Rachel felt no qualms about lying to her if she lived. "Stay, please, stay… for Cash, me, and our child."

Rachel put her last bit of strength into Mag's fluttering heart, holding it steady until she could see the blinding, beautiful light receding away from Mag.

Rachel looked up; the light was moving toward her. She instantly understood the peaceful serenity that Mag hadn't wanted to give up…

\* \* \*

Cash was holding her when she woke. He held his breath as her eyes opened, staring up at him groggily.

"Cash?"

"I want to shake you. Don't you ever fucking do that again. I don't care who it is. Not Ever Again!" His hands tightened on hers, trying to give some of his warmth to her ice-cold flesh.

"Is Mag okay?"

"She's fine. Wants to know what's for dinner."

Relief at his grandmother's rapid recovery had been offset by his fear for Rachel. If he'd had any doubts of his feelings for her, they had been destroyed when he had come so close to losing her.

"What happened? I remember Mag fell and I helped her. I didn't pull back in time, did I?"

"No, you didn't. You almost died. The paramedics had to shock your heart back into rhythm."

"I'll be fine in a couple of days."

Cash couldn't believe the lack of concern she had for her own safety.

"You knew when you helped her what was going to happen, didn't you?" When he saw the guilty look in her eyes, he had to get up. Moving to the window, he stared out.

"I didn't know for sure. After I helped you my gift disappeared, I thought it was gone. My mother and grandmother both warned me that our gift is limited. We can't do what we're doing unless we give away a piece of ourselves. I gave too much."

"It happened when you saved me, didn't it? Lily didn't tell me that part."

"I made her promise."

Rachel's soft explanation raised his fury.

"Stop keeping secrets from me. You didn't tell me that you saved my life, you sure as hell never told me that you're a damn genius, and you didn't tell me you're pregnant."

"What!" She tried to sit up in bed, only to fall back when she couldn't contain the laughter erupting from her chest. "I only told her that to give her the will to live," she tried to excuse the lie she'd told.

Cash wasn't going to let her off that easily. "Mag has told anyone who will listen that she's expecting her first great-grandchild."

"You have to stop her. If my brothers hear that rumor, they'll kill you."

Seeing she was getting upset, he decided to ease her worry. "I'll talk to her," he assured her. "In a couple of days," he clarified. "We don't want to set her recovery back, do we?"

"No, I don't want to do that," she said suspiciously.

"Good. That's settled, then."

"Do they know what happened to Mag? Was it another stroke?"

"No, it wasn't a stroke or her heart. She was poisoned."

"Food poisoning?"

"No, not food poisoning. I wrote down what it was called." Cash took the piece of paper out of his pocket and tried to say the large name. Giving up trying to pronounce it, he instead gave her the paper.

Rachel looked down at the paper, turning deathly white.

"What's wrong?" Cash's hand went to ring for the nurse, but she placed a hand over his.

"Cash, did they tell you what this was?" she asked shakily.

"No. I haven't had time to check it out; I've been with you."

"It means species unknown."

"Well, I knew that much. The closest they could come to was the family it belonged to."

Her voice went low. "This is the plant I've been working with…"

"Could she have been poisoned from touching it?"

"No, it had to be ingested. I don't understand. I only found that plant in one spot on the mountain by a small creek that gets runoff. No one goes there but me. I brought back some of the plants to use on my experiment, but they are all at Mag's house. All five…" Her voice broke off sharply.

"What?"

"A few weeks back, I went into the sunroom and a few plants were missing. There was a broken pot. I thought Mag had broken it and cleaned it up. I didn't check with her. Oh, God, Cash. I should have asked her, but I didn't think to. There aren't any small children around and—"

"When did the plants disappear?"

"I don't remember… Maybe the day you were working on your truck outside, and you came in without your shirt on?"

Cash smiled at what she had remembered about that day. It wasn't all he remembered, though. "That was the day Pastor Patterson and Brooke were there."

"Are you saying Pastor Patterson tried to poison Mag?"

"Not Pastor Patterson, Brooke. I think Brooke tried to poison Lily."

"How would she even know it was poisonous?"

Cash thought a moment, "Does that notebook your always writing in tell that it's poisonous?"

"Yes." Rachel whispered. "I always write down everything in that notebook." She remembered back to that day, Brooke had stayed away from the table for an extended length of time.

"Why would Brooke try to poison Lily? She doesn't like us, but I don't think she would try to kill one of us."

Brooke was a mother, for God's sake. What kind of person would do what Cash was suggesting?

Cash remained quiet.

"I see. I'm not supposed to keep secrets from you, but it's okay to keep them from me." Rachel turned her head on the pillow, hurt.

She heard a loud sigh before Cash answered, "Shade and Brooke knew each other from high school. From what I understand, she has an obsession with him. She hurt Evie in the past because she resented her close relationship with him."

"Brooke hurt Evie?"

"Yes, they're sisters. Evie no longer has a relationship with her because of her sister's destructive behavior."

"That's why she switched churches," Rachel mused.

"Yes. This is confidential, what I'm telling you. Shade is a very private person."

"I won't say anything. Thank you for telling me," she said sincerely, feeling terrible she had made him break a confidence.

Cash squeezed her hand. "The doctor said he'll release you in the morning."

"I have to stay the night?" she complained.

"Yes. Now lie back and get some sleep." She wanted to

argue with him, but she was tired, already closing her eyes.

"Cash?"

"Yeah?"

"Will you stay?"

"I'm not going anywhere, Rachel."

\* \* \*

When Cash opened Rachel's hospital door, Shade was waiting on the other side.

"You got my text," Cash stated.

"Yes. You sure Brooke is the one responsible?"

"We have no concrete proof of the poisoning other than she was there the day the plants disappeared from Mag's house, but I found the motel her and Lewis were using. She was manipulating the stupid bastard."

"She's an expert at that."

Shade's grim visage had Cash questioning him.

"What are you going to do?"

"Nothing for now. I can't take care of personal shit until the mess with Scorpion is cleared up. As soon as it is, I'll deal with Brooke. I'll keep Lily home for now. She's far enough along that she shouldn't put up too much of a fuss."

"Good luck; you're going to need it."

"Lily won't jeopardize our baby; she'll listen."

"I'll ask Rachel if she'll take over the store," Cash offered.

"Thanks, brother."

The men shook hands and parted.

Cash went back inside, staring down at Rachel sleeping. Shade was showing more patience than he would have. That crazy bitch was out to kill Lily, and it was going to take someone just as cold-hearted to stop her.

# CHAPTER THIRTY-THREE

Monday morning she wasn't surprised when Cash asked her if she would manage the church store until after Lily's baby was born.

"Of course." Rachel was just as concerned for Lily's safety as The Last Riders. The store was slow right now anyway.

"Is Knox going to arrest Brooke?"

"No. We have no proof. You didn't see Brooke take the plants, nor did anyone see her put it into the serving she gave Lily. I looked in her kitchen and around the house, but I couldn't find a trace of the plant to get a search warrant."

"She's going to get off scot-free?" Rachel couldn't believe Brooke was going to get away with almost killing Mag.

"I wouldn't say that, only that we can't prove anything in a court of law. If we pressed for a larger investigation, the only tie to the plant is you."

Shocked, Rachel's eyes widened. It was true; she had been the one to uproot the plants and bring them into Mag's home.

"Don't worry, Rachel. Brooke will get exactly what she

287

deserves soon."

"Not soon enough," Rachel complained, furious that the woman had almost killed Mag, and if Lily hadn't had a bout of morning sickness, she would have fallen victim to the crazed woman along with her unborn child.

Cash's arm circled her shoulders. "Want me to give you a ride to work?"

"No, I can drive." Rachel started to move away, only to find herself hauled back into his arms.

"Make sure you play it cool with Brooke."

"I will," Rachel promised. She would be damned if she would let the woman know they were on to her.

"Good. Now give me a kiss," he demanded.

"Did none of your women ever complain that you're bossy?"

"No." His eyes twinkled down into hers. "When I spanked them, they just wanted me to spank them harder."

Rachel shivered at his words, at the picture it planted in her mind.

"I need to get to work," she hurriedly changed the subject.

Cash gave her a brief, hard kiss on her lips. "Hurry home."

She nodded before fleeing.

She was still staying with Mag. Cash had stayed last night with her in her bed, not wanting her gallivanting through the woods after being released from the hospital. Mag would be a few more days in the hospital before they released her.

Rachel had stopped to see her after she had been released. Mag had been beaming with pleasure at the birth of her great-grandchild. Rachel had been unable to break the news that she wasn't pregnant to the happy woman. Looking to Cash for help, he had shrugged, ignoring the silent plea. Rachel promised herself that, as soon as she was feeling better, she would gently break the news to her.

It was anticlimactic that the day passed without

incident. It wasn't until she was about to close the store and Pastor Patterson stopped by that she found out Brooke had gone home to visit her mother. Only Cash's warning had her remaining silent to her pastor of the viciousness his wife was capable of.

She closed the store to find Cash leaning against the side of her car, waiting for her. She looked around to make sure no one was around to hear their conversation.

"Brooke isn't in town. She went to visit her mother."

"She's a smart bitch to get out of town," Cash stated.

"It was everything I could do not to say something to that poor man. He's completely clueless."

"But you didn't?" he asked sharply.

"No."

"Good. Let Shade handle it."

Rachel didn't believe anyone but the police was capable of dealing with Brooke, but if that was the way they wanted to handle it, she would go along with it. For now.

"What are you doing here?" she asked curiously.

"I thought we would have dinner and hang out tonight at the clubhouse."

Rachel knew if she and Cash were going to have a relationship then, sooner or later, she was going to have to deal with being there.

"All right. I'll follow you in my car."

Cash seemed about to argue with her but changed his mind, getting on his bike.

Rachel dreaded the coming evening and had to bolster her courage for the drive to the clubhouse. As she got out of her car, she noticed construction going on at the end of the factory.

"You're expanding the factory?" she questioned.

"Yes. Business is doing well, so we thought we would add some more items to our inventory."

"That's great, right? Will there be more jobs becoming available?"

"One or two. It's still in the planning stage."

"You guys are quick. You already have the walls up," she complimented, going up the steps to the clubhouse.

The kitchen was full as everyone was in line to eat the buffet of food laid out. Rachel relaxed when she saw Lily, Beth, and Winter. She was suddenly hungry.

Filling her plate with fish and a baked potato, she sat down at the table with her friends and their husbands.

"Thanks for waiting for me," Cash said sardonically.

"Sorry." Rachel blushed. She had just been so relieved when she had seen her friends that she had wanted to latch on to the safety of their company.

"It's okay."

Rachel thought he was trying to convey a silent message to her, which she understood, relaxing against the back of her chair instead of being tense at interacting with the women who had shared a sexual relationship with Cash for so many years.

"How was work today?" Lily asked.

"Fine. It was slow. You would have been bored."

"It's better than sitting and watching television all day," Lily complained.

Rachel caught the entreating gaze she cast Shade, which he ignored impassively, continuing to eat his dinner.

Shade was a hard-ass. She had dealt with him several times when he had purchased weed from her brothers for the club. She had to agree with him, though; Lily was safer away from the church after Brooke's attempt on her life.

"How's Mrs. Langley doing?" Rachel asked Beth as she took turns feeding her boys. She hadn't been able to go by as often since she had moved in with Mag.

"Much better. She's finally getting over her gallbladder surgery. She actually got in her car the other day to go to the beauty shop."

"I'm glad."

After dinner, they went into the room next to the kitchen where there was a large television. Rachel sat next to Cash as the others settled around to watch a movie

Train had rented.

She became so engrossed in the movie she barely paid attention as Lily and Beth told her goodnight. Winter and Viper had already gone to bed after they had done the dishes. Rachel liked the way they split up the house duties among them. She was disappointed when the film ended, wanting to watch another.

"It's bedtime," Cash said with a leer down at her.

Self-consciously, Rachel got to her feet, realizing they were alone.

"Go on up to my room. I need to check that the alarms are set for the night and all the doors are locked."

"All right." Rachel left him in the kitchen, going upstairs. She had to pass several bedroom doors on the way to Cash's room, where some doors were open. As she passed the first door, a loud moan had her involuntarily glancing inside.

Train was lying on his back with Bliss on top. Rider was on top of Bliss, both men fucking her. Rachel stopped, stunned. She had heard of two men having sex with one woman, but she had never imagined a woman would actually enjoy it. Bliss was ecstatic, her loud moans and enraptured expression leaving no doubt she was experiencing the height of sexual enjoyment. Rachel found herself watching for several moments before she heard a sound from the end of the hall and fled to Cash's room.

When the door opened a few moments later, she knew Cash had witnessed her moment of voyeurism from his smug grin.

"Don't you dare say a single word, or I'll go home," she threatened.

"My lips are sealed," he assured her with a wicked glint.

He took off his clothes, staring deeply into her eyes, and Rachel licked her bottom lip as his jeans fell to the floor.

Cash unashamedly walked naked to stand in front of her. "Lose the clothes."

291

Rachel swiftly did as she was asked. As soon as she had shed her panties, Cash's hand was between her thighs.

"Get a little excited watching Train and Rider give it to Bliss?"

"I warned you!" Rachel's anger burst out. She bent over to pick up her clothes, only to feel herself lifted and tossed onto the bed.

"You little vixen, you can run back home when I'm done fucking your pussy."

Rachel started to climb off the bed then realized, looking at his sexy body, that she would be denying herself as much as Cash.

When Cash reached out, taking a nipple between his fingers, the tugging sensation on her breast brought a rush of wetness between her thighs.

"Come here."

Rachel moved to the end of the bed on her knees.

"Open your mouth." His hard voice, filled with lust, had her opening her mouth to let his cock slide inside, her tongue licking the drop of liquid off the tip.

Cash's hiss had her opening her mouth wider. She had expected Cash to slide his cock inside gently, but his thrust nearly had her gagging, trying to catch her breath.

"Come on, show me you can take me," he taunted her.

Rachel rose to the challenge, scooting closer as his hand buried in her hair, holding her in place as he began to fuck her mouth. Her hands gripped his thighs as she made herself relax. As soon as she did, an unbelievable pleasure took control, and she began to use her tongue and tightened her mouth on his cock.

"You're going to learn to take every inch of my cock."

Rachel nodded against him, letting him have all the control he needed, while her hands went to his balls, squeezing them gently, discovering every inch of his body.

"Damn, woman, I'm not going to last." He jerked his cock out of her mouth and then lifted her from the bed. "Put your legs around my waist."

Obediently, Rachel twined her legs around him. Cash slammed her down on his cock, burying himself in her pussy.

"You're going to come with me, vixen."

Rachel lifted her hips up and down, trying to take his cock deeper within her. She lost all her senses, scratching and clawing at him as she tried to come. Her cries of need were wrenched from her chest.

"I'm going to give you exactly what you need." His mouth went to the tip of her breast, biting down in a sharp burst of pleasure that had her burying her face in his neck.

Cash gripped her ass hard as he came, holding her until they both managed to move. He then gently laid her down on the bed, tugging the covers over both of them. His mouth traced the tattoo on the back of her shoulder, his hand on her belly, pressing her back against him.

"Cash..." she began.

"Don't worry; you can't get pregnant standing up."

Rachel rolled her eyes. Just how stupid did he think she was? She was going to put a stop to this herself. She would call her gynecologist in the morning and make an appointment. Starting tomorrow, she was going to lay down the law—until she was on birth control, his cock wasn't coming near her again.

His hand on her stomach slid between her thighs. Then she felt his cock hardening against her ass. *Damn*, she thought, already regretting her vow of chastity.

She looked at the bedside clock and saw it wasn't midnight yet.

"Cash, you want to take a shower?"

# CHAPTER THIRTY-FOUR

Cash woke to an empty bed again.

"Dammit." Frustrated, he climbed out of bed to get dressed. He'd had enough of this shit.

Storming from his bedroom, he headed downstairs and went outside to his bike. He ignored Rider's greeting as he drove out of the parking lot, angry at how she had managed to get away from him while he was sleeping. It took him less than five minutes to get to his grandmother's house, where he went inside and headed for Rachel's bedroom.

"Where you going?"

Her voice stopped him in his tracks.

"Woman, what do I have to do to keep you from sneaking out of my bed?"

"I have to get to work, Cash. I didn't want to wake you."

Cash crossed his arms over his chest. "Next time, wake me."

"I think you're being a little ridiculous."

"When people care about each other, they wake up next to each other. They say good morning, give morning-breath kisses. Shit like that. They do not leave without saying goodbye. Ever."

"Oookaayy. Next time, I'll wake you before I leave. Satisfied?"

"Yes," Cash conceded.

She wasn't saying she would spend the night with him, merely that she would tell him she was leaving. He could tell from the defiant expression in her eyes that it was all he was going to get.

Hopefully, he had made his point. If not, then his hand on her ass would make it for him if she pulled that shit again.

"I have to go." She took a step forward, placing her hands on his chest, and raised on her toes to reach his mouth. "Bye." She gave him a brief kiss before starting to move away; however, his hand went to her hair, holding her in place.

"Like this." His mouth covered her parted lips, thrusting his tongue inside and claiming her mouth as his territory before releasing her. He reached out to steady her before giving her a soft push toward the door.

"You don't want to be late," he said, mimicking her words.

"I'll see you later. Mag gets out of the hospital today," she reminded him.

"I'll pick her up and bring her home. I'll even fix dinner." Her shock had him laughing. "Even I can get a bucket of chicken on the way home."

"All right."

Cash stood on the porch, watching until she pulled out of the lot. His phone ringing had him reaching into his pocket.

"Cash." Viper's voice over the phone sent warning signals off. "We have a big problem."

* * *

Cash heard a muffled reply when he knocked on the door. Opening it, he followed behind Viper.

Drake Hall was sitting behind the desk of his realty

company with an ice pack to his badly bruised face. "You could have warned me they would get violent when I refused to sell them the property."

"We didn't know. They've shown no overt physical violence to draw attention to themselves," Viper justified his lack of foresight.

"Well, they sure as shit weren't trying to be inconspicuous when four of them ganged up on me," Drake replied sarcastically.

"When the coach refused to sell to them in Jamestown, they didn't get violent," Cash spoke up for his president.

"They got pretty pissed at me when I told them no. Next time I do your club a favor, I'll pack my Glock." Drake laid down the ice pack, showing his busted lip and two black eyes. His bloody nose didn't look much better.

"We owe you one," Viper conceded.

Drake leaned back in his chair with a self-satisfied smile. "I'm counting on it."

Viper shot him a dark look. "I'll place a couple of the brothers on you for protection."

"Don't bother." Drake opened his desk drawer and pulled out a gun, placing it on his desk. "That's all the protection I need. The next time they come near me, I'll blow their fucking brains out and ask questions later. They threatened Jace if I told anyone. They shouldn't have threatened my son."

"Give us a call. Don't try to take them on by yourself."

"I won't have to. You'll hear the police sirens when they do," Drake promised ruthlessly.

Cash and Viper left Drake, still vowing to whip Scorpion's ass.

They walked to their bikes before talking.

"They didn't touch the coach but beat the hell out of Drake." Viper got on his bike, looking at Cash as he got on his. He paused before starting the motor.

"They're getting ready to make their move," Cash acknowledged what Viper was thinking. Hell was getting ready to break loose, either in Jamestown or Treepoint.

"Send for the brothers in Ohio. Tell them to haul ass. Let Stud know the shit is getting ready to hit the fan," Viper gave his orders.

Cash listened, taking mental notes. "I'll tell everyone to be on alert. They'll be ready to move."

"Everyone but Shade; I want him with the women." Viper started his motor.

Cash started his, also, taking his place beside Viper as they headed home.

* * *

"We going to the clubhouse tonight?" Cash asked, getting ready to go out the door Friday morning.

Rachel hesitated cleaning the breakfast plates in the sink. They had spent the last three nights at his grandmother's house. He had deliberately waited to ask her about tonight, as if it was an afterthought. He was leaving the decision to her.

"I'll meet you there at nine. There's something I need to take care of first." Rachel looked at him over her shoulder, seeing her answer had pleased him.

"See you then."

"Cash?"

Her voice stopped him. "Yeah?"

"Bye."

He walked back to her, bending down to give her a gentle kiss that was unlike any he had given her before. "Bye, vixen."

With a wink, he was gone.

When Rachel sighed, Mag's laughter startled her.

"Girl, you got it bad."

"No, I don't." Rachel began to deny the truth, but Mag was already shaking her head.

"I've already been where you are. Keep the fight up until you have him exactly where you want him."

"And exactly where is that?"

"With your foot right on his balls."

* * *

Rachel sat in the parking lot, staring at the glass window and the customers inside. She wanted to change her mind. She'd almost started her car twice to drive back out of the lot.

"You going to sit there all day, or get your ass out of the car?" Killyama asked, coming to her car window. Rachel had been concentrating on Sex Piston's beauty shop for so long she hadn't noticed Killyama parking behind her.

"Yes." Rachel cleared her throat. "Yes, I am." This time, she sounded more decisive as she got out of her car and went in the shop with Killyama on her heels.

"I was wondering how long you were going to sit out there." Sex Piston came out from behind the counter.

She motioned her to one of the chairs, putting a cape around her. Sex Piston had red hair like Rachel, but hers had more gold. She was wearing a black jumpsuit with a chunky gold belt wrapped around her waist.

She picked up her scissors. "So, you want me to take off a couple of inches?" She held the scissors poised.

"I want it all off," Rachel told her.

"Are you sure?" Sex Piston asked her doubtfully. "Are you going to cry and threaten to sue me if I do?"

"No." Rachel looked Sex Piston directly in the eyes. "When you get done with me, I want to look and feel sexy."

"You think my haircuts are that good?"

"I think you're that good," Rachel agreed.

"You're right about that." Sex Piston pulled Rachel's hair back into a large pony tail then lifted the end into the air. "You sure?"

"I'm sure." Her voice didn't waver.

Sex Piston clipped the pony tail off. Rachel wasn't even tempted to cry when Sex Piston laid it on the counter.

"I brought an envelope to mail it to Locks for Love."

"I'll take care of it." She turned the chair around. "Let's

wash your hair and put some style in what you have left."

Rachel let Sex Piston do her magic. The woman took Rachel's request as a challenge, cutting and snipping her hair after she'd washed it then blown it out. The whole time, Killyama sat watching from a nearby chair. Crazy Bitch waited on three other customers while Sex Piston took her time.

"Beth told me you're seeing Cash."

"Yes."

Sex Piston used the curling iron after she blew it out, going layer by layer.

"Any reason you're wanting to look sexy on a Friday night?" Killyama asked, lowering her magazine.

Rachel didn't say anything.

"She learns fast, doesn't she?" Killyama got up from her chair. "You're going to need more than a sexy haircut to show up those women."

"I don't want to show them up. I just don't want to look like a country bumpkin anymore. The first party I went to, I wore a cream dress and a shrug."

Both women looked at her in pity.

"I don't know why normal women want to tear themselves up over those assholes," Killyama snapped.

"You're just still mad at Train because he didn't come back for seconds," Sex Piston stated matter-of-factly.

"I wouldn't touch that fucker again if he begged me," Killyama snorted.

"He hasn't, and he won't, so get over it," Sex Piston advised.

"What are you going to wear tonight?" Killyama asked, changing the subject.

"I haven't decided. I thought—"

"I'll hook you up. You're my last customer, so when we're done, we can go to my house. You can borrow an outfit of mine. Just make sure you give it back," Sex Piston told her. "Beth tells me that they like to steal the clothes off your back there."

"In more than one way," Killyama said snidely.

"What's your fucking problem?" Sex Piston turned in place on her impossibly high heels.

"I ain't got no problem." She sank back down on her chair, picking the magazine up again.

"Good, then shut the hell up. The girl wants to look good for her man tonight. Leave her be."

Rachel studied Killyama's aggravated expression. Did she have a thing for one of the men? Sex Piston had mentioned Train, but she had seen her nearly run him over with her car after Lily's wedding ceremony. Was she another woman who Cash had been with?

Rachel stared at herself in the mirror. Even in Jamestown, she was faced with Cash's possible exploits.

# CHAPTER THIRTY-FIVE

Cash was sitting at the bar with Nickel when Nickel quit talking, staring toward the doorway. His brother always staked the door out to catch any fresh pussy walking through for the first time.

"Is that Rachel?" Nickel elbowed him, almost knocking him off his stool.

Cash turned to have a look and nearly spilt his drink. "What the fuck!"

Rachel's hair had been cut short, brushing her jawline. The thick mass was tousled, as if she had just been fucked. His little vixen was wearing a short, bouncy, black skirt that barely reached the top of her thighs. His eyes slid down her slim legs, staring at the heels on her feet. Cash's cock thickened behind his jeans. Her top was the piece that he had every intention of playing with as soon as possible. Top? Hell, it was more of a black bra that cupped her tits with a small, thick silver zipper holding the two cups together.

Cash stood up from his stool, unable to take his eyes off her transformation.

"Brother, you sharing tonight?" Nickel's thick voice had him aware he wasn't the only one appreciating how

301

Rachel looked.

"Nickel, touch her and die."

"Just asking." He put his hands up in surrender. "If you change your mind, just yell."

Cash didn't waste any more time talking; too many of the brothers from Ohio were heading in his woman's direction. He strode across the room and an unsure smile met him as he neared her.

His eyes narrowed on her shaking hand as she brushed her hair back. Biting back his first choice of words, he reached out, taking her hand and jerking her to him.

"Cash!"

"Woman, you look fine."

She rewarded him by melting against him.

"Dance with me."

"Okay."

Cash led her to the dance floor, pulling her tightly to him. He carefully thought out what he wanted to say, determined not to screw up.

"Why the haircut?"

Her smile dimmed. "Do you like it? I wanted a change."

Cash's hand went to her ass, pressing her to his hips. "Feel that? Does that tell you how much I like it? As long as you have enough for me to hold onto when I fuck you, I don't care how long it is."

Her eyes darted to the people dancing around them. "Who are these men?"

"The brothers from Ohio came for a visit." Cash didn't see the need to explain why they were visiting. "If a couple of them don't move their eyes away, some of them are going to be heading back tonight," snarled Cash as he stared at Boulder, who hadn't taken his eyes off Rachel's ass since she had come in the door.

"Where did you get the outfit?" He planned to take her shopping for more.

"I borrowed it from Sex Piston."

"Ask her where she bought it."

As a laugh escaped her, his hand clenched on her ass.

"I have a question. Why the change? I don't want you to change yourself for me."

"I didn't change anything for you! I've always wanted to look this way but never had the courage. I don't want to dress like this all the time, but it's fun to know I can look good when I want to."

"Vixen," he lowered his mouth to her ear, "you look more than good. Try sexy as hell."

He felt her tremble in his arms. Unable to resist her fleeting vulnerability, Cash took her mouth to show her exactly how sexy she was to him. As her arms circled his neck and she kissed him back, Cash's desire rocketed. He didn't know what had happened to the woman he had been seeing, but the Rachel returning his kiss was not worried about anyone watching them make out on the dance floor.

Cash broke off the kiss, studying the woman in his arms.

"Okay, where is Rachel, and what have you done with her?" he asked, only half-joking.

Confused, she tilted her head to the side. "I don't know what you're talking about."

He lowered his head to her neck, taking a deep breath of her fragrance, and then raised his head, examining her eyes for dilated pupils.

"What are you doing?" She playfully hit at his shoulder.

"Any of those plants of yours give you a buzz?"

"No."

"Then I don't get the change. Rachel, I love you whether you accept The Last Riders or not. I—"

"Cash, shut up. Everything is fine. To tell you the truth, I guess I just wanted to see what it felt like for once to be more my age before I'm old and it's too late."

Cash understood what she was trying to tell and show him. She had been over-protected by her brothers, and her intelligence hadn't helped, placing a barrier between her and others in her age group. For once, she was trying to act her age and have some fun, and he was stymieing it by trying to overanalyze her behavior.

*Fuck that!*

His conscience appeased, he decided to show her what she had been missing, within reason. He didn't want to give her any ideas on leaving his ass for greener pastures, but he was going to show her why he was worth putting up with.

Cash danced with her, keeping her close as the night progressed. The brothers from Ohio getting rowdy had him looking around the over-filled room.

"Let's go." He stopped dancing, taking her hand.

"Where to?"

"Downstairs. It won't be as crowded." Cash maneuvered them through the large mass of bodies, wisely keeping away from the women who would break the spell Rachel seemed to be in.

Taking her to the kitchen, he turned left, opening the basement door before guiding her down the steps.

"This is nice," Rachel murmured.

Cash left her for a second, turning on the music and going to the mini-fridge to pull them out a couple of beers. Sitting down on one of the chairs, he pulled her down on his lap. The zipper between her breasts drew his eyes.

While Rachel smiled down into his gaze, Cash's hand went to her exposed cleavage, brushing the globes of her breasts. He sighed, lowering his hand, when he heard the door open. Train and Jewell came down the steps with Rider and Stori close behind.

"Did you and Killyama...?"

Her sudden question floored him.

"What?"

"Have you and Killyama had sex?"

"God, no." He shuddered at the thought.

"Good, I like her."

Cash rolled his eyes; he didn't know anyone who could like that bitch. He doubted even Beth and Lily did, both being closer to Sex Piston.

"So, if I've had sex with them, you can't like them?"

"I can like them; I just don't want to be friends with them," she clarified her position.

Casually, he tightened his hands on her hips so she couldn't run away. "Vixen, do you like Evie?"

She stiffened on his lap, her hand going to his hair and tugging it until his head went back. She lowered her face to his. "If you're a smart man, you won't say another word. Evie doesn't count; she's married now and in love with King. That can change if you piss me off."

"My mouth is sealed," he assured her.

As a new song came on, Cash lifted her to her feet. "Let's dance before I get myself in trouble."

"Smart choice."

Cash took her into his arms, dancing in place with her. When he rubbed his cock against her bared belly, her hands slid around his waist, pressing back against him, her fingers holding onto his belt loops. He slowly became aware she was watching something behind him. Skillfully, he turned them as they danced to see what she was staring at.

Train had taken his shirt off and unbuttoned Jewell's top; they were dancing skin to skin. Rider and Stori had deserted the dance floor, going for the couch. His hand was between the woman's splayed thighs, finger-fucking her to the beat of the music.

"They aren't shy, are they?"

"No." He diverted her attention by sliding his hand under the bottom of her skirt. She wrenched his hand away, but not before he noticed something different.

"Are you wearing a thong?" His cock nearly burst his zipper at the thought.

Turning her around sharply, he said, "Come on; I have something cool to show you." He went to a door and opened it. The short hallway seemed to last forever until he finally opened the door at the end. He ushered her inside the room, leaving the door open.

"What's so cool about it? It's just a bedroom."

"I'll show you later." He pivoted on his heel, his hands going to her waist. Not wasting any time, he starting tugging down her skirt.

She wiggled her hips to help his progress and stepped out of the tiny skirt. Cash released an appreciative whistle at the sight before him. The tiny, black-leather panties were a brief patch over her pussy. He could see her fiery curls peeking out the side. The leather bra top was a perfect match for the thong.

"Tell Sex Piston I'll give her cash for the outfit. She's not getting it back," he said hoarsely.

He stalked her as she teasingly backed away from him. When she would have fallen onto the leather couch at the end of the room, Cash caught her, spinning her around.

Not giving her time to react, he used his body to maneuver her to the end of the couch then pressed her over the arm, her ass tilted up to him.

"You're lucky Shade keeps his toys locked up. I'm going tomorrow to buy a paddle. This ass of yours is the best I've ever seen." His palm ran over her ripe bottom. The only thing wrong with it was it needed his palm print, which he was about to rectify.

His first smack on her bottom had her trying to rise up.

"Stay still."

The second, she released a small squeak but didn't move. By the fourth, she was moaning. He plunged a finger into her tight pussy to find her soaking wet.

"My little fox likes her ass whipped, doesn't she?"

When she didn't answer other than to lift her ass higher, he smacked her again, harder.

"Yes." Her answer satisfied him.

Not wanting to disappoint her, he gave her three more while driving his finger deeper inside her. When he couldn't take any more and her ass was a pretty pink, he removed his finger, unzipping his jeans.

He placed his cock at her opening, leaving the thong on. The sexy underwear nearly made him come before he could stroke himself inside her steaming pussy.

His hand went to her hair as the primitive feelings of conquering the woman underneath him had him losing control. His movements became rougher as he drove them toward a climax he tried to contain, but the sexy image of her in the heels and black leather undermined his control. Burying himself as deep as he could go in her pussy, he came when he felt her climax on his dick.

His hand smoothed over her dream catcher tat while using his hand in her hair to lift her limp body from the couch. A feeling of possessiveness came over him.

"Don't think I'll ever let you get away from me again. There isn't an army or brother of yours who can accomplish that. I've let you have your space because I know you fell for me when you were a kid and I hurt you, but that's over." He held her still when she would have skittered away from him.

"Are you still in love with me?" Silence met his question, but Cash hadn't expected anything less from his vixen. "That's okay. You don't have to admit a damn thing."

His hands went to the zipper between her breasts, sliding it down until the cups fell away, revealing her breasts.

"Want to see what's cool now?"

Cautiously, she nodded.

"Take your heels off." Cash hated to see her take the shoes off, promising himself that he would fuck her in them again by morning.

When she removed the shoes, he helped her slide off the thong, tucking it into his jean pocket. He wasn't taking a chance she would give them back. He planned to find out where Sex Piston had bought them and buy her every fucking color.

He shed his own clothes before going to the bathroom door where he motioned for her to come inside. The best part of the night was about to begin.

* * *

Rachel had only seen showers like this in magazines. She went down the steps, staring into the mirrored tiles of one side and seeing Cash come up behind her. His hand reached out, starting the water.

"I may never want to leave."

Cash chuckled. "This shower almost cost Viper a divorce until he put one in just like it for Winter."

The rainfall showerhead was amazing. Rachel lifted her face up to the water, feeling Cash's soapy hands exploring her body. She spread her legs when a soapy washcloth cleaned between them while the side showerheads rinsed her body off. She felt his already hardening cock prodding her ass.

As Cash used the wash cloth to stimulate her clit, Rachel thought she was in Heaven, being surrounded by a luxurious shower while sharing it with the man she had fantasized about for years. *Dreams do come true*, she thought.

The sound of the shower door opening had her squeaking, trying to move behind Cash as Train came inside naked, wetting his hair and grabbing the soap.

"Don't mind me."

Rachel stared at him, having to close her mouth before she choked on all the water blasting at her. Cash hooked her around the waist, her water-slickened body easily dominated by his large one.

"Did I tell you to move?"

Rachel shivered at the tone of command in his voice.

She released an unwitting moan when his fingers returned to her pussy. Her eyes were pinned to Train's as Cash parted her pussy lips to Train's avid interest. Rachel's gaze involuntarily lowered to Train's cock, completely certain his was the size that sent women running. She had trouble taking Cash's large size, so Rachel wasn't sure how a woman would manage with what Train was packing.

"You haven't shaved her yet?" Train's casual question confused her until Cash's fingers moved to play with her curls between her legs.

"Not yet."

"Need some help?"

"All I can get," Cash replied sardonically.

Rachel saw Train pick up the shower gel, pouring some into his hand before moving closer to her. Cash's hand went to her hair, pulling her head back to lie on his shoulder.

"Spread your legs wider. Give the man some room to work with."

Rachel stared into his reassuring eyes as Train's hands rubbed the soap into her fiery curls, his thumb alternating brushing and pressing down on her fleshy clit.

She felt Cash move then saw him hand Train a long-handled razor.

Freezing in place at the sight of the wicked-looking instrument, she let him scrape the razor against her flesh as he shaved her clean. Cash took turns lifting each of her legs as the razor moved dangerously over her delicate area.

As Train took the showerhead off and sprayed directly on her pussy, rinsing her off, the powerful blast nearly gave her an orgasm. Afterward, he hung the showerhead back up then dropped to his knees in front of her.

Rachel had never perceived she could be in a sexual situation like she was in. It went beyond the scope of what she believed herself capable off.

She gazed up trustingly at Cash, feeling Train's finger splay open the fleshy lips of her pussy.

"Let's see how well I did."

While Cash's hand swept down to her breast, the mirrored tiles held her attention as Train's tongue explored her softly, barely making contact with her skin. Being trapped between two highly sexual males raised a carnality which had her pressing against him, asking for a firmer touch.

Cash lifted her slightly off her feet, holding her around her waist while Train lifted one of her thighs, placing it over his shoulder. He then slid his hand to her ass, clutching the fleshy globe.

Rachel gasped at his grip. He was the quietest of The Last Riders, but she had observed him. He always treated the women respectfully, but he never took the bullshit that others took. Crash had carelessly dropped Stori when he was goofing around and Train had flipped out, knocking Crash to the floor as payback. There was something attractive about a man who was so protective over women.

Cash's knuckles teased her nipples while Train's tongue played with her clit, delving into the bundle of nerves before sucking it into his mouth and nipping it with his teeth. Rachel was about to orgasm when Cash turned off the water, breaking the temporary spell she had let herself fall into.

When Train opened the shower door and grabbed a towel, Rachel wanted to wail, thinking she wasn't going to come. The men soon disabused her of that thought.

Cash let Train dry her off before possessively taking her away and carrying her to the bed, laying her down. Then Cash climbed onto the bed next to her, leaning against the headboard.

"Come here."

Tentatively, she inched closer to him, unable to miss his hard cock.

"You know what I like?" he inquired demandingly.

Rachel nodded, opening her mouth and going down on him.

She felt Train climb onto the bed behind her, positioning her ass in the air, facing him.

"Been teaching her a lesson?" Train asked, smoothing a hand over her pink bottom.

"Always," Cash said between gritted teeth.

Rachel let her teeth glide over his cock at his arrogant behavior. Her action resulted in a rough hand in her hair, lifting her from his cock.

"Vixen, the next time you try to threaten me with those sharp teeth when you have my cock in your mouth, your ass will be on fire for a week. Got me?"

"She misbehaving?" Train asked, sliding his cock between her thighs.

Rachel stiffened.

"Yes, she is. And right now, she's pissing me off. Look at me, Rachel. Train and every man in this club knows there is only one dick going in that pussy, and it's mine."

Rachel didn't relax, still nervous, but Train scooted closer to her and began to move. His fingers parted the slick flesh, letting his cock slide across her.

Rachel's hand fluttered against Cash's hips as he slid his cock to the back of her throat as Train's thick cock butted against her clit.

No sound escaped as Cash and Train both rode her hard, neither of them allowing her any leeway, driving her to an orgasm which flung her to the sky as both men stroked themselves to their own release.

Rachel lifted her head, giving Cash a final lick with her tongue, seeing him shudder at the erotic touch.

Train moved away to the bathroom, coming back with a clean cloth. Cash laid a possessive hand on her belly as Train cleaned her. When he was done, he took the cloth to the bathroom while Rachel lay satiated on the bed, refusing to let the full consequences of her behavior hit her yet.

"Going somewhere?" Cash's voice stopped Train from going out the door. "You can stay."

Rachel was hauled closer to his side as Train climbed back on the bed.

She didn't know how she felt about sharing a bed with two men; her mind and body were both exhausted. She lay cuddled against Cash's side with Train's warmth at her back.

"Go to sleep, Rachel." Cash's groggy voice settled her nerves momentarily.

The night she had dreaded had ended differently than she had expected. She had promised herself to experiment with the part of herself she had always fantasized about, but not even her imagination could have taken her as far as she had gone.

She managed to doze off, only to be woken a short while later for another round with the two men. Afterward, Rachel lay on the bed between the two dozing men, running her hand through her new shortened length, still gasping for breath.

She waited until the men were deeply asleep before climbing out from between them, redressing in Sex Piston's clothes. She searched for the underwear, but couldn't find them. The woman was going to be furious with her since it was a matching set; she'd said it was one of Stud's favorites.

Going quietly upstairs, she nearly tripped a dozen times from the floor covered with bikers in sleeping bags before she was able to let herself out the front door. Once outside, she was grateful she had driven her car and didn't have to hike through the woods.

She let herself into Mag's house, sending home her neighbor before going to bed after showering and putting on a fresh gown.

She breathed in the clean scent of the sheets, thinking of her mother and how disappointed she would be in her. After all the years she had stifled the more untamed part of her personality, burying the needs she had felt in her body in books and church, that part of her nature had finally been released. She was deathly afraid she couldn't control it. What if she went too far and had to live with the regret for the rest of her life? She had thought her love of Cash protected her from that part of herself; instead, it had added fuel to the flame.

She needed time to think, to decide if she was going to douse the flame or enjoy the fire until it burnt out, leaving nothing but devastation behind.

# CHAPTER THIRTY-SIX

Jo picked her up at Mag's house. They had to postpone their dinner until Mag had felt better—Rachel had only left her for brief periods of time.

"I'm ready." Rachel had offered to pick her up at her dad's house, but Jo had refused.

"How's it going since you've been back?" Rachel asked as soon as they were both sitting in the tow truck.

"Same as when I left," Jo replied as she drove toward town. "Sorry about the ride. I had to sell my car to help Dad pay a few bills."

"I don't mind. Where do you want to eat?" Rachel asked, turning the subject to something more positive. "We could go to the Diner or the Pink Slipper. There's King's place; it's new, and the food is really good."

"Mick still have hamburgers and fries?"

"I guess. He has bar food, but—"

"Good, I'm hungry," Jo said, bringing the tow truck to a stop in the parking lot of Rosie's.

"Jo, this is a—"

"Biker bar. I know. Is that red Trans Am Curt Demaris's?"

Rachel looked closer at the car in question. Several of

the locals still hit Mick's, leaving before the bikers showed up after dark.

"Yes. It's the same one he's driven since high school."

"I heard he's the coach now."

"Yes." Rachel knew Curt was a sore subject with Jo. He had been the one accused of trying to rape Jo. "Let's go to King's."

"I feel like eating here. It'll bring back old memories," Jo said grimly. "Dad used to bring me here when my mom was at work so that he could get a drink."

"Jo, some memories aren't worth repeating."

"And some are worth confronting," she said ominously, getting out of the truck.

Rachel sighed. She liked Mick, but she was really beginning to dislike his bar.

She went inside after Jo. There wasn't that many customers; Curt and... Rachel swallowed hard when she saw him sitting with Jared. The two were cousins and not only did both believe they were God's gift to women, but both were asses. It wasn't a good combination.

Jo sat down at a table not too far away from the men. She was staring a hole through Curt until Mick came to take their order. Jo's expression softened as she got up from the table to hug the man who twirled her around. Rachel was surprised at the closeness the two shared.

"I heard you were back in town." Mick's misty eyes stared down at Jo.

Jo grinned back. "I told Rachel I needed a good hamburger and fries."

"Coming up. What can I get you, Rachel?"

"I'll take the same."

While Mick went back behind the bar, Rachel felt everyone's eyes on them. Not only Jared and Curt's, but Train was sitting across the room with Crash. She saw him reaching for his phone. She knew he was calling Cash. She wasn't going to feel guilty; she owed no explanations to Cash about what she was doing. From the look on Train's face, however, he didn't agree with her. She blushed bright red remembering Friday night.

"So, I hear you and Cash are an item."

Rachel waited until Mick placed two beers in front of them then left before answering. "I wouldn't say we're an item."

"What would you say, then?"

Rachel cleared her throat. "I don't know."

"I see he hasn't changed since I've been gone. None of the women in town knew, either."

Rachel nodded, knowing Jo wasn't trying to be mean, just trying to help her get her head on straight.

"He's with the biker club that moved into town?"

"Yes."

Jo laughed at her answer. "I never took you for a biker's woman, Rachel. Hell, you and Lily were the only virgins left in our class when I left town."

Rachel winced. Jo hadn't had an easy time being Lyle's daughter. She was still staring a hole in Curt's back.

As they ate the food Mick brought a while later, Rachel was anxious to eat and leave, feeling the tension coming from Jo as the minutes ticked by.

They were finishing their beers when Curt got up from the table, coming to theirs.

"I heard you were back in town, Jo. It's good to see you."

"Why, so you can get me drunk, and then you and your cousin can rape me again?"

Curt's mouth dropped open.

Rachel was shocked. The gossip around town had been vicious about Jo, but none had said that he had actually raped her.

"You were lucky my mom didn't want to drag me through a court hearing, or you and Jared would still be sitting in prison."

Curt leaned down. "I didn't rape you; you begged us for it."

Rachel gasped as Jo picked up her beer bottle and smashed it over Curt's head. Jo then jumped up, going for the knife she had used to cut her burger.

Rachel slowly got up from the table, not seeing Cash, Rider, and Knox come into the bar. She simply stood, not wanting to try to reason with Jo or distract her.

Curt was furious that Jo had a steak knife poised above his throat.

"Lie again, and I'll cut your fuckin' throat," Jo threatened. "I wanted to vomit when I found out you're coaching. You're no role model for high school boys."

Curt was smart enough to remain silent.

"I'm back now, Curt, and I'm not fifteen anymore."

"I can see that."

Rachel thought he was stupid for smarting off while in such a position.

"Um, Jo, I know he's a piece of shit, but he's not worth going to jail over." Rachel tried to reason with the woman who had changed since they had last known each other.

"No, he's not." Jo removed the knife before sitting back down at the table.

Curt moved away; this time smart enough to keep his mouth shut with The Last Riders looking on.

Cash, Rider, Train, and Knox took seats around the table while Rachel introduced the men.

"You going to arrest me?" Jo questioned Knox who was wearing his uniform.

"No, I'm going to buy you a beer." Knox motioned Mick to bring a round. "He always pretended to be a little too nice for my taste."

"It's all an act," Jo confirmed.

Rachel was glad she had never taken Curt up on the numerous invitations he had sent her way.

"What did he do to piss you off? Dump you?" Rider spoke up, reaching for a beer.

As Rachel winced at Rider's words, Jo glared at him before responding. "No, he raped me after a football game." Rider choked on his beer. "To men like you, it probably doesn't matter, but it meant a lot to me."

"What the hell? Fuck...I had no idea. What do you mean, men like me? I've never taken a woman against her will." The usually affable Rider was getting his comeuppance.

Rachel took a drink of her beer to hide her smile.

"No? So you don't just expect every woman to want to have sex with you because you're good-looking?"

"You think I'm good-looking?"

"Jesus." Jo looked toward Rachel. "He a friend of yours?"

Rachel didn't know how to reply, so she went for the truth. "Not really."

Rider looked at Cash. "You know she's not getting my vote, right?"

"You running for something?" Jo cut in.

Rachel blushed bright red, throwing a killing look at Rider, who scowled back unrepentantly. "No."

"Yes." Rachel glowered at Cash as he answered.

At that point, Jo's cell phone rang. Cash shrugged unconcernedly as Jo talked.

"I need to go. There's been a wreck outside of town. I'll drive you home—"

"I'll take care of it. You go on," Cash broke in.

When Jo cast her a quick look, Rachel nodded her head reluctantly, wishing she hadn't when Jo left. Rachel felt uncomfortable sitting alone among the men.

Knox finished his beer. "My deputy is handling the wreck. I'm going home early and waking Diamond up," he said, getting to his feet.

"Later," Cash said, not taking his eyes off Rachel.

She had ignored his calls and texts for the last few days. Instead of laying into her, though, he stood up and took her hand, leading her to the dance floor. They danced silently for several minutes since the music was so loud. It was just her luck that the next song was low and slow.

"You okay?"

"Yes." She didn't avoid his eyes as he stared down into hers.

"Rachel…"

"Cash, I don't want to talk about it. Please?" Cash's hands gripped her waist tighter.

"We'll talk about it later, okay?"

Relieved, Rachel's head fell to his chest, enjoying being held by him.

The bar began to fill. Raci, Stori, and Jewell came in while she was still on the dance floor with Cash. Each of the women grabbed someone to dance with. At their enjoyment, Rachel felt herself relax when the music returned to a fast-paced beat. She didn't worry about her two left feet, only of Cash's body moving against hers.

"Let's go back to the clubhouse."

Rachel didn't protest; all the worries of what she had let happen before evaporating as she felt her body begin to anticipate what was waiting for her at the clubhouse.

When they got there, Cash took her to his room, closing the door behind them. He didn't bother trying to make it to the bed. With her raising her dress up so he could remove her panties, he slid deep inside of her.

Rachel couldn't hold back her scream as he entered her in one hard thrust.

"Fuck, vixen, you're tight."

Her arms slipped around his neck as he fucked her.

A sharp knock on the door next to them had her stiffening. Cash's hand briefly left her long enough to open the door to Train on the other side. Rachel was pinned to the wall by Cash's body.

"Want some company?"

"Take the bed," Cash grunted, not stopping his thrusting inside her.

Rachel's eyes followed Train as he removed his clothes.

"Want him to leave?"

"No," Rachel moaned.

"Good." Cash turned toward the bed where Train lay sprawled, sliding his hand up and down his cock.

"You going to help a brother out?"

"Yes." Cash laid her within Train's reach. As he watched Rachel hand grip Train's dick, he thought his cock would burst.

She was everything he had ever wanted in a woman. Her sexuality demanded satisfaction while trusting him to hold Train back.

He lifted her ass and slid his cock back inside her, giving her what she needed. He reached forward, his hand going to her hair, pulling her hand off Train's cock.

"Whose woman are you?"

"Yours," she whimpered.

"You're only giving what I want you to take. You understand me? No one but me gets this pussy. No one but me is going to make you come. No one is going to take this sweet ass but me. Do you understand?"

"Yes," Rachel whimpered as he smacked her ass while pounding his cock inside of her.

"Cash...?" Train moaned while his hand slid on his cock.

"Ask me."

"Can I have her mouth?" Train groaned.

"You want his dick?"

"Yes." Rachel started shuddering. The erotic commands he was giving her were ratcheting her desire to a place she was trying to reach, her hips thrusting back frantically against his.

"Give it to him, then."

Rachel's mouth covered Train's cock as the man's head fell back against the headboard. She let the men guide her into an explosive climax that had Cash moving to the side so that she could lie down next to Train before lying down on her other side.

Pinned between the two men, she hadn't noticed Rider and Bliss had come in until she heard the noise from the other side of the room. Bliss was riding Rider while they had watched Train and Cash play with her.

She wanted to pull the covers over her, but Train had his chest pressed against her back, lifting her breast to Cash's mouth. Rachel couldn't help herself from watching Rider and Bliss as the men brought her body back to life. Seeing the envy in the other woman's eyes, Rachel knew Bliss wanted to trade places with her.

Rachel looked into Cash's eyes, recognizing the enjoyment he got from watching her with Train. It was the same enjoyment she got from seeing his pleasure.

She had sworn to herself that it wouldn't happen again, that it was a one-time thing. She had come back to the clubhouse tonight, still lying to herself.

Rachel remembered one of her mother's favorite quotes: Hell is paved with good intentions.

# CHAPTER THIRTY-SEVEN

"Damn it to Hell!" He was going to beat her ass when he caught up with her.

Cash sat up in the bed, angry Rachel was gone. She didn't have to work today; therefore, her ass should still have been next to him.

Train came out of the shower, drying his hair. "What's up your ass?"

Cash threw him a furious look. "When did she leave?"

Train shrugged. "I don't know. She was gone when I woke up fifteen minutes ago."

Cash got out of bed, going to take a shower. He had wanted to make sure she was okay when she woke up; he was deathly afraid of what the harsh light of day might have her feeling. She hadn't wanted to talk about last Friday night, had avoided him most of the week. If that had frightened her, last night would have her leaving town.

His stomach was clenched in fear at the thought of losing her. Dammit, he should have thought of that last night before letting Train join in. Train, of all his biker brothers, was the most caring of the women, and he had noticed Rachel's eyes on him when he had been with the other women. Cash thought her gift allowed her to sense the pain hidden inside Train.

He had thought... Hell, he had fucked up. If he lost her now, he didn't know what to do.

The numerous phone calls and pleas he had received from women now came back to haunt him. Rachel's indecision over her feelings and the terror of possibly losing her made him want to call her and settle it. Only the need to see for himself made him wait the few minutes it would take to reach Mag's house.

He was almost to the front door of the clubhouse when the phone rang.

"Yeah?"

"This Cash?"

"Yes. Who's this?" He didn't recognize the feminine voice on the other end of the line.

"Connie. You gave me a hundred to call if I heard anything."

"I remember who you are. Got any news for me?"

"They came in last night. A couple of them hit the bottle pretty hard and started mouthing off that everyone would know who they were after today. Kind of creeped me out, you know?"

"Anything else?" Cash questioned, going back inside the house to find Viper.

"They kept talking about Molly's Valley."

"Molly's Valley?"

"Yes. That's all I heard."

"Thanks. I'll drop some more money off for the info," Cash promised before hanging up.

Why would Scorpion be interested in Molly's Valley? It was on the other side of Jamestown, close to where Lily had gone to college.

Cash called Viper, filling him in during the short time it took Viper to walk to the kitchen.

"Why in the fuck would they be interested in Molly's Valley? From what I remember, it's nothing but farmland," Cash asked Viper.

They quit talking about it when Shade and Lily entered the kitchen. While Lily went for the refrigerator to pour herself some orange juice, Shade drank his coffee, ignoring his wife's baleful glances.

"What has you two looking so serious?" Shade asked.

"We just got some information that Scorpion might have an interest in Molly's Valley. It doesn't make sense to buy property there. There's no…" Cash tried to watch his words so Lily wouldn't become alarmed.

"No one can buy property in Molly's Valley," Lily stated, sitting down at the table. All three pairs of eyes fixated on her. "Well, they can't." She shrugged. "Ask Rachel; she's the one who wrote a huge paper on it in high school. She wanted to do her paper on the effects of mining on the water, but she was too afraid she would be run out of town."

"Why can't anyone buy property in Molly's Valley?" Cash tried to keep her on track.

"Because it's a depository for nuclear waste." The men at the table paled. Lily nodded at their reaction. "I know. It's frightening what happened. From what I remember from Rachel's report, there was ground seepage. They have to monitor it forever."

"Why aren't there any signs? How didn't I know this?" Cash asked, surprised something of that scale had been sitting practically in his front yard and he hadn't had a clue it existed.

"I have no idea." Lily shrugged. "Like I said, ask Rachel. She got an A on her paper. None of us could hardly understand a word of it, but she gave lists of the companies who stored their waste there. She's writing her doctoral dissertation on it. She had to get special permission from the state and federal governments to take soil samples. She's writing about some kind of isotopes."

"Transuranic?" Cash asked sharply, remembering his chemistry.

"That's it!" Lily exclaimed. "I would call her and ask to

make sure, but there's no cell reception there. She went there today to get some samples; her paper is due next week."

"Holy fuck!" he said, getting out of his chair and running after Viper. "Shade, call Lucky. Tell him everything and to notify Homeland Security."

Cash followed Viper's lead as they hauled ass toward Molly's Valley. He prayed, bargained, and pleaded the whole way there, something he hadn't done in a long time and didn't think himself capable of.

They cut their motors as they drew close, seeing the gate standing open. He knew they were too late.

The men climbed off their bikes, motioning for Stud's men, who were coming in, to go quiet, also. They made a line in the long grass, trying to shield themselves as they moved through the land.

His eyes momentarily caught Lucky's when they found the guards dead outside the facility.

The men, many who had served together in the Navy, took the lead while Stud's men came behind as backup.

Once they entered the building, it wasn't hard to find them. Rachel's screams could be heard, leading them in her direction.

Cash's military training went out the door; instead, he became the man he had been born to be. He reached inside his pockets, pulling out his brass knuckles. The men inside thought they wanted a new government, but he was about to give them a whole new world.

* * *

Rachel sat on the dirty concrete floor. "You have to stop. You don't know what you're doing," she screamed.

"Shut her up!" Scorpion yelled.

Vaughn mercilessly smashed his fist into the side of her face.

"You won't have to shut me up. You'll kill us all if you breach that concrete casing," Rachel cried, angry at herself for believing Scorpion was taking her to show her the

325

property he had bought. She had been heading toward Molly's Valley when he said it was in Jamestown. She had stopped by for a quick look, not listening to the warnings about trusting people Tate had drilled into her head for years, and the ones Shade and Cash had given her.

When she had arrived at the property, Scorpion had tied her up and thrown her into a car along with her purse and credentials to get into Molly's Valley. One guard had been killed as soon as he had opened the gate, the other at the facility door. Both guards hadn't stood a chance against the number of men and weapons trained on them.

"Listen to me, Scorpion. Those casings are holding radioactive materials. Anyone near them without protective equipment is going to die."

"I told you to shut her up! I know what I'm fucking doing."

"You didn't tell us this was a suicide mission," Vaughn snarled.

Scorpion raised his gun, firing it at the man standing next to Vaughn.

"If I hear one more word from you, your next." Scorpion raised his gun toward Rachel.

"Go ahead. I'd rather die quick, you dumb-ass."

"Fine."

Rachel closed her eyes, preparing herself, flinching when she heard the gun go off. Surprised she didn't feel the pain, she opened her eyes to see The Last Riders fighting Scorpion and his men.

Rachel sat, watching as the men fought, her eyes glued to Cash until Rider lifted her off the ground, carrying her outside.

Several of Scorpion's men tried to escape, only to be brought down by Stud's men.

Rider untied her, taking her to a car that had pulled in and forcing her inside. "Take her back to Treepoint."

"Wait."

Rider slammed the car door, disappearing back inside

the facility.

Rachel turned frantically in her seat, but the car speeding off knocked her off balance. She worried all the way back to Treepoint about Cash's safety.

The car dropped her off at the police station where Knox was waiting.

"Is he okay?" she asked as soon as she got out of the car.

"Cash is fine. Come on inside; I need to take your statement."

Rachel blinked back tears of relief, going inside the Sheriff's office. All she could do now was wait.

\* \* \*

Cash stood, surveying the carnage around him. They had barely reached Molly's Valley in time. If Viper hadn't called the brothers in from Ohio and Stud's men hadn't arrived in time, ready to battle, they wouldn't have been able to stop them.

As it was, three Last Riders from Ohio were killed and two Blue Horsemen. Rider had been shot in the arm while Cash had received a knife cut on his cheek and was grazed by a bullet on his shoulder.

All of the men looked like they had been through a war by the time Train killed the last of Scorpion's men.

*Willa won't be making that bastard a pie anytime soon,* Cash thought vindictively.

"You all right?" Cash asked, helping Viper to his feet.

"Yeah. You?"

Cash nodded, taking off his brass knuckles and slipping them back into his pocket. Both men watched as Homeland Security secured the facility.

"At least the taxpayers won't be paying to house these dead fuckers," Viper sneered, kicking Scorpion's dead body. "Tell everyone to head home."

Cash spread the word, and the brothers from Ohio headed back there while the rest went back to Treepoint.

He was anxious to see Rachel and make sure she was all

right. The last he had seen of her was when he made sure Rider had followed his orders to get her away as fast as possible.

He made a quick stop in Jamestown to drop off an envelope filled with cash to Connie. The woman deserved it for stopping what could have been a tragedy and saving Rachel's life. He was unlucky enough to find her there. Suffering through her grateful hug, he left hurriedly when her hand went to his crotch. His gratitude didn't include a mercy fuck.

"Call me," she had yelled from the door of the bar.

Cash had to remind himself to be nice, that she had saved hundreds of lives keeping radiation from being released, but it was still difficult when she called him, trying to get him to turn back. He almost threw his phone away, turning her down instead.

He had to stop by Knox's office to file the report he'd promised Homeland Security. Viper and the others had gone on ahead, leaving him to take care of the details. He had to bite back his disappointment at finding Rachel had already left. He was becoming more aggravated by the moment.

It was almost dark before he pulled up in front of Mag's house. He was sore and tired, but he just wanted to make sure Rachel was okay and hold her. Then he would give her fucking hell for leaving him this morning. If she had stay put, she would have been out of harm's way.

He climbed off his bike, coming to a stop when he saw Rachel standing on the porch with a shotgun pointed at him.

"Get on your bike and go on to the clubhouse," Rachel yelled.

"Why in the hell are you pointing your gun at me?" Cash had thought she would be upset after last night, but not to this extent. The day they'd had should have had them spending the night together, lucky to be alive, but did a Porter ever react the way a normal person would? Fuck no.

"Killyama just called me. She said she saw you at a bar in Jamestown, all cozy with a woman there. She had your dick in her freaking hand. Go on back to her and stay away from me."

"I can explain." Cash took a step forward, only to stop when she shot at his feet.

"Dammit, Rachel! I want to talk to you."

"I don't want to talk to you again. Go away!"

"That's my grandmother's house you're living in." His patience was decidedly becoming strained from having his woman shoot at him. Dammit, he had saved her life; he deserved a reward, not having his head blown off.

"She's not your grandmother anymore, she's mine."

"You can't confiscate my grandmother," he told her, admiring her figure in the tight jeans and t-shirt. There was something sexy about a woman who could handle a gun.

"Yes, she can. I told her I would take the trade. I have to watch out for my great-grandbaby," Mag yelled out from the house.

Cash was going to give that old woman hell when he could get close to her again, and he could tell that wasn't going to happen with a vengeful Rachel standing guard on the front porch. He was going to have to leave until he could come up with a plan.

Climbing on his bike, he sat there and debated storming the porch until another shot rang out, going through the helmet he kept for Rachel.

*She is going to pay for that*, he thought, starting the motor.

Putting those two women together was a mistake he was going to have to pay for over several years to come. He was going to personally thank Shade when he got back to the clubhouse. The mean bastard better come up with a way out of this mess.

\* \* \*

Rachel quietly opened the front door. It was still dark outside, and she didn't want to wake Mag. She was

329

terrified, if she did, she wouldn't have the strength to leave. She turned, closing the door behind her, and gave a startled scream when Cash spoke behind her.

"Going somewhere?" He was sitting on Mag's swing, his boot moving the swing back and forth.

"What are you doing here?"

"Keeping you from running off again."

Rachel knew it was useless denying it since she was holding her suitcase in her hand.

"I need to go to the university to finish up the work on my dissertation; it's due this week."

"Lily told me. Funny that you didn't plan on going there until yesterday."

"A lot happened yesterday. I almost got killed."

"The whole state almost died," Cash corrected her.

"Yes. He planned it that way, didn't he?"

"Yep. It would have drawn the attention to the organization he was involved with, to prove how incapable the government was... I don't know... for whatever crazy ass reason they came up with to take innocent lives."

Rachel nodded, moving nearer the steps.

"I prayed today, Rachel." The swing stopped moving. "I honestly don't remember the last time I had. Maybe the day I saw you crying over your parents' grave, or the day I found my grandfather. I didn't pray the whole time I was overseas fighting. I didn't when my parents died. When Mag lay dying in front of me and you tried to save her, I didn't pray. But when Lily told us you were at Molly's Valley, I prayed the whole way there. I made a bunch of promises the good Lord knows I'll never keep, but I made one I will. I love you, Rachel. I told you I was slow, and I've proved that by you. I've made several mistakes I wish never happened."

His foot started the swing moving again. "I didn't touch that woman Killyama saw me with. I was paying her for information, and I took off as fast as I could because I wanted to get back to you, to see how you were, to make sure you were safe. We both know that you're a good enough shot that you're not going to miss what you're aiming at, so I left to give you some time to cool down." His soft laughter filled her heart.

"You see, Rachel. I'm finally figuring you out. You don't sleep in my bed because you're saving that. You don't pull my dirty clothes out of the clothes hamper when you wash clothes because you're saving that. You won't fix dinner for me because you're saving that, too. You might have given me your virginity, but you're saving all your other firsts for another man. It tore out a piece of my heart, when I realized, why you won't tell me you love me out loud. Like ripping off a band aid."

A tear slid down her cheek as his words hit home.

"I knew, sure as shit, you were going to run, just like your mama did when my father screwed up with my mother. I'm asking you to stay and give us a chance."

"Cash, I want a home and children." Her voice broke. "I don't want to wake up in a MC club every morning."

"I can give you what you need, Rachel. I swear I can. Vixen, trust me one more time. I won't let you down. I promise."

She heard the truth in his husky voice.

"You still want to leave?"

Rachel nodded, this time unable to hold back her tears.

Cash's face filled with agony as the sun rose over the mountains.

"I'll drive you, then. Your car won't make it out of town, much less the four hour drive to Lexington." He walked toward her, taking the suitcase.

Rachel climbed into the truck while he placed her suitcase in the back. Climbing in, he started the motor and then backed out with a hard face. At the bottom of the driveway, he flipped on the blinker.

"You're going the wrong way."

When his startled face turned toward her, Rachel reached across the seat, taking his hand in hers. "Let's go home, Cash."

# CHAPTER THIRTY-EIGHT

Cash set the sandwich and cup of tea down in front of the computer. "Eat."

"Let me finish this sentence; I'm almost done," Rachel said wearily.

The university had given her another advisor, since Homeland Security found out Dr. Alden had been a member of Scorpion's anti-government group. He had fed them the information that Rachel would be able to get them into the restricted facility, setting her up to be killed. Rachel wanted a front row seat when he went to court.

"You said that over four hours ago. Taking ten minutes to eat isn't going to set you back. Your paper isn't due until tomorrow at twelve."

"I know, but I want to go to church and—"

"Eat, Rachel, or I'll take the computer away."

Rachel stopped typing long enough to pick up her sandwich while glaring at him. He sat down on the chair next to the desk in his room at The Last Riders' clubhouse.

Cash had been busy fixing up his fishing cabin for them to live in. Monday, the trucks were coming to pave a driveway to the isolated cabin. He'd said that he'd had enough of potholes to last a lifetime. Rachel hadn't argued, too filled with happiness at the thought of living with him at the beautiful spot.

The mountain their parents and Sunshine were buried on looked down on the spot where the cabin was built. Rachel wanted to think all of them would be able to watch her and Cash's lives through the coming years.

Rachel swallowed the bite of sandwich she had taken. "Thank whoever made the sandwich for me."

"You're welcome."

"You made it?" Her shocked gaze met his.

"I did." He grinned, standing up. "Hurry up and finish. When you get done, I'll show you I'm a handy guy to have around." His thumb brushed her nipple. He then let her be after she swatted at his hand.

It was another two hours before she finished, pressing the send button. She didn't bother taking off her clothes, lying tiredly down on the mattress next to Cash.

"Finished?"

"Mmhmm." She had nothing left, letting Cash snuggle her against his side.

"Go to sleep."

Rachel sank into a deep sleep, not waking until Cash shook her awake the next morning.

"Get dressed or you're going to be late for church."

Rachel burrowed under the pillows. "I'll go tonight," she mumbled.

He took the pillows away and pulled the blanket back. "Up." He helped her to sit up. "Get dressed. I thought I would join you today."

Rachel's bleary eyes opened wide.

"But you don't go to church," she reminded him.

"I am today. I need to repent for what we did last Friday and Saturday."

Rachel smacked him in the face with a pillow, jumping out of bed before he could retaliate. "I better go, too, before I break the commandment: thou shall not kill."

She slammed the bathroom door on his laughter.

* * *

"Come on; we should have left ten minutes ago," Lily chastised her as she came down the stairs.

"I'm ready. Let's go." Rachel grabbed her purse. "What's the hurry? Where's Cash; he told me he was coming?"

"He said he would meet us there. Let's go."

"I'm coming. I don't know why you're rushing me. I could crawl and get there faster than you," she teased Lily, whose rounded belly was becoming bigger every time she saw her. The woman looked like she was ready to give birth any minute.

"Very funny. Wait until you begin to show, then you'll see how funny it is for—"

"Wait, what did you say? I'm not—"

"We don't have time." Lily and Beth rushed out the door.

Rachel hurried after them or she would be left behind without a ride.

Razer had already strapped in the twins and was sitting behind the wheel when Rachel got to the car, grinning smugly at Lily when she got in.

Rachel listened as they talked about getting ready for Lily's baby. They had decided not to have a shower with so many hand-me-downs from Beth's boys, and Lily said Shade wasn't up for it.

Rachel looked at Lily's face, glowing with happiness, with a lump in her throat.

At the church, Razer let them out before he parked the car. Beth carried Noah while Rachel carried Chance.

"Rachel, can I talk to you a second?"

Rachel handed Razer Chance as he approached before turning to Cal. "Of course. Lily, you and Beth go ahead. Save me a seat."

"All right, but hurry."

Rachel nodded, aware of the face Brooke made any time someone entered late.

"Is something wrong?" Rachel asked after the sisters had left her alone with Cal, seeing the guilty look on his face.

"I wanted to thank you for asking your cousin to help my dad get a job."

She started to deny it.

"Drake told me."

"Oh. I hope your family is doing better."

"We are. That's why I haven't had to come back for more groceries."

Rachel smiled at him, happy Drake had been able to help.

"There's something I've been wanting to tell you, though. I feel bad since you've helped me out so much."

"What is it?" she asked gently, seeing his remorse.

"I've been sneaking into your brothers' weed patch. I didn't take it for me. My mom's got cancer; it helped her... I'm sorry."

Rachel nodded, unable to speak because she was afraid she would burst into tears. Cal was too young to deal with everything he'd had to for the last year.

"I'll tell Tate. Don't be afraid." Rachel saw his fearful reaction. "He'll keep a small bag for your mother. No charge."

Rachel saw the puppy worship in his eyes. "Thanks, Rach."

"You're welcome. Now, I better go before Lily gives my seat away."

Rachel hurried inside the packed church. The crowd was unusually large. She even saw Mag, who never attended Sunday services, sitting in the front row.

The church choir had already started by the time Rachel saw Lily and Beth sitting in the front with Diamond and Winter. Raci, Stori, Evie, and the other women filled out the row.

"Brooke's not happy," Lily whispered to her after Rachel had managed to squeeze into her seat.

"That's all right," Rachel whispered as Pastor Merrick walked toward the podium.

She scanned the crowded room, looking for Cash, waving back at Mag who had turned in her wheelchair to wave at her. Cash had already promised to get The Last Riders to build an additional room for Mag if she decided to move in with them.

She didn't see Cash until her eyes were caught by his. He was casually leaning against the side of the church, near the pulpit.

Rachel frowned, wondering why he was standing there, facing the crowd instead of sitting in one of the pews.

The Pastor had barely started his sermon when a loud shot rang out. The pastor's voice came to a stop as he stared, open-mouthed toward the door.

Brooke released a scream as her brothers, each carrying a rifle, came to the front of the church, all three aiming their rifles at Cash.

"Cash Adams, we have some talking to do!" Tate yelled.

"What do you want?" Cash didn't seem worried about being cornered by her brothers.

Rachel wanted to warn him that her brothers only picked up their guns when they were ready to shoot.

"I heard you knocked up my sister!" Greer roared.

Rachel paled, getting to her feet.

"What are you going to do about it if I did?" Cash taunted.

The man had lost his mind. Rachel frantically started fighting her way out of the pew.

All three of her brothers pointed their guns at him, but it was Tate, as head of the family, who spoke.

"You're going to marry her and make her your wife. Then, we're going to make her a widow."

As Cash laughed in their faces, Rachel barely managed to step in front of him before her brothers filled him with holes.

"Tate, Greer, Dustin, go home. I'm not pregnant!" Rachel yelled, wanting to hide. The whole church was witnessing her embarrassment. She'd thought Mrs. Langley's party had been humiliating, but that couldn't touch this horror in the making.

"That's not what you told me," Mag hollered from a few feet away. "Told me I needed to live for my great-grandbaby."

Rachel's mouth opened and closed like a landed fish.

"Is that true?" Tate demanded.

"Yes… but I lied. I was trying to save her life," Rachel confessed, sending Mag an apologetic look.

"So, you're not pregnant? You're sure?" Tate asked skeptically.

"Of course I'm sure."

"You've been careful?"

Rachel turned brick red. This was going beyond the realm of what her brothers needed to know.

"No, she's not. We haven't been using any protection," Cash admitted.

"Yes, we have," Rachel snapped. "I went on the pill."

"When? You didn't tell me." Cash lost his casual attitude. He actually seemed angry she had taken steps to prevent getting pregnant.

"Because I don't think that your belief that you can't get pregnant standing up, or in water, or if the weather is too hot is actually considered—"

"You don't actually believe that you can't get pregnant standing up, do you?" Tate inquired while Greer and Dustin looked at her in pity.

"No, I didn't—"

Again, she was cut off. "I told you to let me be the one to give her the girl talk. This is your fault, Tate," Greer accused.

"No, it's not. I know I explained sex well enough that she shouldn't have believed you can't get pregnant if you're in water."

Rachel ground her teeth, losing all patience. "Shut up! Go home!"

"We're not leaving until he marries you," Tate answered with Greer and Dustin's vocal support.

"I won't marry him. I'm not pregnant!" Her voice rose in embarrassment.

"You might as well marry me; they aren't going to believe you." Cash's amusement had her wanting to commit blasphemy in front of the pastor and the entire congregation.

"If you're not pregnant, then you are coming home with us," Tate ordered.

"I'm not coming home with you; I'm moving in with Cash," she refused.

"Hell no, you ain't! My sister ain't living in sin." Greer cocked his rifle.

"Greer, stop it."

"Are we having a wedding or a funeral?" Tate prompted.

"Rachel, I love you." Cash's words drew her attention to him.

Rachel believed him, or she would never have agreed to move in with him.

"I think that's a good start to our courtship." She took a step toward him.

"Courtship's over. We're going to see he marries you before the baby's born," Greer argued.

"I told you, I'm not pregnant." Rachel planted her hands on her hips, practically stomping her foot.

"You will be," Cash promised arrogantly.

"Do you want to die?" Rachel asked him shrilly.

"No, what I'm trying to do is get married."

"Wait, you *want* to get married?" Rachel asked in confusion.

"Will you wash my clothes and fix my dinner?"

"Yes."

"Then let's do it. Dean's here. Why not?" He turned to

look at Pastor Merrick. "No offense."

"None taken," Pastor Merrick replied with a broad smile.

"Will you marry me, Rachel?"

Rachel saw the sincerity in his eyes.

"Yes, but I'm still not going to marry you tonight."

"Is there anyone not here that you want?"

Rachel looked around the huge crowd. "No," she admitted.

"Is a dress important to you?"

"No."

"Then why not?"

Rachel let a smile tug at her lips. He had set this whole fiasco up just to get her to say 'I do.'

"Let's get it done, then. The baby needs his father." Rachel reached out, taking his hand. Then he pulled her closer to the altar.

While her brothers stood by with their guns in hand, Rachel stared down at Mag in the front row. She had tears running down her cheeks.

Cash stood next to her, his expression triumphantly arrogant.

She hid her smile, listening to Dean begin their shotgun wedding. Her hand squeezed Cash's. Her mama hadn't raised an idiot. If Cash wanted to marry her bad enough to do it in front of the whole church, she wasn't going to say no. A wedding dress and a traditional wedding would have been nice, but ultimately, it was the man who was the most important. Besides, there hadn't been anything traditional about their courtship so far. If he wanted to believe he had caught her, she wasn't going to disabuse him of the notion.

Dean's words drew her attention back to the ceremony.

"Rachel, do you take Cash to be your husband?"

"I'll take him," she said out loud, adding to herself, *and never let him go.*

# EPILOGUE

Cash was riding home when he saw Tate's truck. Slowing down, he turned into his homestead property. Cutting his motor, he got off his bike before going up the steep hill that led to the graveyard. He found Tate standing by their parents' graves.

Cash stood silently by his side until Tate broke the silence.

"It was a fucked-up situation."

"Yes, it was."

"I keep thinking that there had to be a reason they didn't end up together," Tate said in rumination.

Cash had lost his faith long ago, thanks to Saul Cornett. The crazy-ass pastor had used the Bible to excuse his sadism. He didn't believe in coincidences, either, but the chain of events that had led to him returning to Treepoint after vowing not to return had him questioning his belief in both.

If he hadn't asked Shade's father to check on Beth and Lily during his travels, then none of The Last Riders would have ended up making Treepoint their home. Four of his brothers and now him had found their women.

Cash stared down at the graves of Tate's mother and

his father side by side in death.

If Lily hadn't been sitting at the table with the information they'd needed, they would have been too late. Hundreds, possibly thousands, of people would have lost their lives. Maybe that was the reason Tate was looking for. He didn't know.

What he did know was he had Rachel, and he was a selfish enough bastard to enjoy his happiness. His father had screwed up cheating on Rachel's mother; he would never be that stupid. Cash knew what he had, and no other woman's pussy was worth losing his hot-tempered vixen.

"You ever going to tell her you and Greer deliberately pissed her off to get her to move out?" Cash questioned with a quirk of his lips.

Tate looked at him sharply.

"Greer was just a little too obnoxious. You're an ass, but you wouldn't have embarrassed Rachel in public like that without reason. Besides," Cash shrugged, "I know you saw me leave that night. You would have confronted her if you hadn't planned to use it to your advantage."

"She still mad?" Tate's voice was hoarse.

"I think it still hurts her. Tell her the truth," Cash told him.

"That I did it to force her to live her own life?" Tate said wryly. "I tried to talk to her when she came home from the university, but she just told me we needed her. She never wanted to admit she was homesick, even when she sold her property to pay for those online classes instead of taking that full, paid scholarship. Rachel turned it down because she would have to leave home. She's a homebody; she doesn't like to be uprooted."

"Tell me something I don't know."

Tate smiled. "She's a handful. When are you going to tell her you bought her property back from Drake?"

"When she tells me she's pregnant," Cash replied, his expression hard.

Tate laughed. "You're doing your best to tie her down."

"I figure, by the third kid, she'll settle down and quit being so skittish."

"Good luck with that. Our mother drove my dad and yours crazy. Neither succeeded in really winning her. Rachel is the very image of her. Has she even told you she loves you?"

"No," Cash admitted. "But I have a plan for that," he retorted smugly. "I know your sister better than you think."

Tate shook his head. "Bullshit. If you had, it wouldn't have taken nearly getting killed to see what you lost."

"I bet you weren't any happier when you and your brothers woke up to find her gone after your performance."

"I underestimated her. I thought she would move into town, not take off without telling me where she was going."

"We both learned a hard lesson where she is concerned. The only thing I don't understand is the night she ran home through the woods. Why didn't you tell me to get away from her? You just left," Cash asked.

While Tate remained silent, Cash sensed his struggle. "I've watched how The Last Riders took care of Lily and Beth. Knox became Sheriff to make Diamond happy. Viper took care of that asshole who hurt Winter. You take care of your women. Rachel will not only be protected by you, but your club. I don't have to worry about her anymore since she'll always have someone at her back if something happens to me and my brothers."

Cash stared at Tate's grim profile. Tate would have been stupid not to realize the danger they were in, dealing the weed they grew.

Tate turned away from their parents' graves. "I told you when you called to tell me Rachel was pregnant I would go along with your plan to marry her on one condition. I expect you to live up to your promise, Cash."

"I'll love her until the day I die," he repeated the

promise he had given Tate without embarrassment.

"See that you do. Because, if I catch you mistreating my sister, I'll whip your ass." Tate turned to leave.

"Tate... thanks," Cash said and meant it, thanking the man who had pushed Rachel in his direction.

Tate turned back, staring him in the eyes. "You're welcome. Want to stop at Rosie's for a beer?"

Cash accepted the peace offering. "Sounds good."

* * *

"You ready?"

"Yes." Rachel smiled teasingly. "How do I look?"

Cash's eyes raked over the black booty shorts with the black bra. "I like it, but I don't know how much I'm going to like the brothers' eyes on you," he warned, already planning on how soon he could lay his hands on that ass of hers.

Rachel walked to their bed, picking up the black lace dress. She pulled it over her outfit. The lace was tightly woven so all you could see was the dark material under the lace. Just like that, she'd gone from sexy to smoldering.

"Let's go. I have a surprise for you."

She caught his arm before they left their bedroom. "Cash, I..." She bit her lip.

"Vixen, nothing's going to happen that you don't want to happen, okay?" His finger smoothed her frown away. "You have a little wild in you, you know that?"

"That's what I'm afraid of," she admitted.

"Don't be. All this is mine." Cash put his hand on her hip, bringing her flush against his dick. "My vixen likes to play, and I like to watch her play, but if you don't, that's fine, too."

After Rachel nodded, they left. They rode in his truck to the clubhouse. They hadn't been back in the last two weeks since they had married; Cash had wanted to wait for his surprise to be finished.

He drove into the parking lot, stopping the truck. Then he took her hand after helping her out. Instead of leading her up the steps toward the clubhouse, he led her to the factory.

"Why are we going inside the factory tonight? I've been begging for the last month to see it."

"I wanted to wait until the new addition was finished." Cash led her toward the back of the factory, opening a door and turning the light on to the new room which had been built.

Her shocked gasp had him searching nervously for her reaction.

"Do you like it?"

"I never expected... this is amazing." She walked around the huge room, touching the different equipment. She lingered in front of the ten different-sized tanks that were set up, ready for her use.

"I'll never want to leave," she whispered in awe.

"You like it?"

She looked at him like he was crazy. "How could I not? The university doesn't have anything this advanced."

"The catch is you now work for The Last Riders."

"I'll get a salary? To do what I was doing for free?"

Cash nodded. "We can help you expand in the areas you want, to offer assistance to countries that need clean water, if that's what you want."

As her expression softened, Cash's breath caught in his chest, his heart beating rapidly.

"I love you."

"It just took ten fish tanks to get you to admit it," he said, bending down to kiss her.

"No, it just took you."

# Also by Jamie Begley

## The Last Riders Series:

Razer's Ride

Viper's Run

Knox's Stand

Shade's Fall

Cash's Fight

## The VIP Room Series:

Teased

Tainted

King

## Biker Bitches Series:

Sex Piston

## The Dark Souls Series:

Soul Of A Man

Soul Of A Woman

# ABOUT THE AUTHOR

"I was born in a small town in Kentucky. My family began poor, but worked their way to owning a restaurant. My mother was one of the best cooks I have ever known, and she instilled in all her children the value of hard work, and education.

Taking after my mother, I've always love to cook, and became pretty good if I do say so myself. I love to experiment and my unfortunate family has suffered through many. They now have learned to steer clear of those dishes. I absolutely love the holidays and my family puts up with my zany decorations.

For now, my days are spent writing, writing, and writing. I have two children who both graduated this year from college. My daughter does my book covers, and my son just tries not to blush when someone asks him about my books.

Currently I am writing four series of books- The Last Riders, The Dark Souls, The VIP Room, and Biker Bitches series.

All my books are written for one purpose- the enjoyment others find in them, and the expectations of my fans that inspire me to give it my best. In the near future I hope to take a weekend break and visit Vegas that will hopefully be this summer. Right now I am typing away on my next story and looking forward to traveling this summer!"

Jamie loves receiving emails from her fans,
JamieBegley@ymail.com

Find Jamie here,
https://www.facebook.com/AuthorJamieBegley

Get the latest scoop at Jamie's official website,
JamieBegley.net

Made in the USA
Lexington, KY
15 December 2014